A PERILOUS

Handsome, hard-driving Elliott Halsey seems the kind of man that Dr. Katherine Crane's dreams are made of. He is not only the dynamic CEO of the world's leading drug firm, he is a superbly trained scientist as well, on the cutting edge of the latest advances in fighting disease. Even more inspiring, he has dedicated his dazzling abilities and his company's vast resources to finding the medical answer to AIDS.

Let radical gay activists protest his methods ... let those under him question his motives ... let a chilling voice on the phone accuse him of mass murder ... Katherine is convinced he is the man to meet the greatest challenge in medicine, and the lover to heal her own emotional wounds.

Now, though, she has to prove it—as the horror spawned in his laboratories spreads across America to kill and kill again. . . .

DEADLY DIAGNOSIS

A NOVEL BY

Martha Stearn

A SIGNET BOOK

SIGNET
Published by the Penguin Group
Penguin Books USA Inc., 375 Hudson Street,
New York, New York 10014, U.S.A.
Penguin Books Ltd, 27 Wrights Lane,
London W8 5TZ, England
Penguin Books Australia Ltd, Ringwood,
Victoria, Australia
Penguin Books Canada Ltd, 10 Alcorn Avenue,
Toronto, Ontario, Canada M4V 3B2
Penguin Books (N.Z.) Ltd, 182–190 Wairau Road,
Auckland 10, New Zealand

Penguin Books Ltd, Registered Offices:
Harmondsworth, Middlesex, England

First published by Signet, an imprint of Dutton Signet,
a division of Penguin Books USA Inc.

First Printing, June, 1995
10 9 8 7 6 5 4 3 2 1

Printed in the United States of America

PUBLISHER'S NOTE
This is a work of fiction. Names, characters, places, and incidents either are
the product of the author's imagination or are used fictitiously, and any resemblance to actual persons, living or dead, events, or locales is entirely
coincidental.

To Ethan, whose magical imagination helped shape this story

ACKNOWLEDGMENTS

Many people contributed to the fruition of this book and to its medical authenticity. I would especially like to thank the following:

My agent, Al Zuckerman, for working with me every step of the way

Dr. Bill Close, for providing support and important contacts

Dr. Joe McCormick and Dr. Susan Fisher-Hawke, formerly with the Centers for Disease Control

Dr. William Fogarty, Department of Pathology, St. John's Hospital, Jackson, Wyoming

Larry Gneiting, for his expertise on corporate matters

Dot Nebel, for some valuable geographical information

Mo O'Leary and Doreen Ward, Department of Medical Education at St. John's Hospital, for their perserverance in searching the medical literature

Kathy McDermott, microbiologist and friend, who contributed ideas and inspiration

Dennis Fill, for his valuable input on the pharmaceutical industry

My father, Jess Stearn, who is always there for me

PROLOGUE

Spring 1994

Trudy Porter, age twenty-eight, punched the time clock before leaving for the day. She was an intensive care nurse at Memorial Hospital in Salt Lake City and loved her work. But today she couldn't wait to get away. Today she felt overwhelmed, even panicky, and she didn't know why, which scared her all the more.

As she headed for her car she decided she was simply exhausted. Not enough sleep. And too much on her mind as she let it wander to the quarrel the evening before with her boyfriend, Mark.

She slid into her Subaru and revved the engine, absently placing a hand to her forehead. It felt hot. Just the flu. Her panicky feeling eased. As she gripped the steering wheel she noticed a spray of bubbly red spots on both arms. She shrugged it off. Flu did all sorts of strange things. She would fix some broth, take the phone off the hook, set the alarm. Be good as new in the morning.

She already felt better as she pulled out of the lot.

When Trudy Porter didn't show up for work, her supervisor, Margaret Ellis, called her home and repeatedly got a busy signal. She was puzzled. Trudy was one of her most reliable nurses.

But Margaret Ellis's immediate concern was to fill the empty spot. The ICU had gotten several new admissions and they were already short-staffed. She meant to check on Trudy later in the day, but it slipped her mind when she herself had to take over Trudy's shift.

It wasn't until shift change at three o'clock that she again thought about Trudy. She questioned the other nurses. One suggested calling Trudy's boyfriend, Mark Adams.

She dialed Trudy's number once more. Still busy. She called Mark at work. In conference. She checked Trudy's address and decided to swing by on her way home. She didn't stop to ask herself why she was going to such lengths.

As she pulled up to Trudy's apartment, she frowned as she recognized the nurse's car. Her uneasiness increased as she climbed the steps and rang the doorbell. No answer. She tried the door. It was unlocked. Curious. She slipped in and called out Trudy's name. She was met with an eerie silence. She tiptoed through the living room and kitchen, then peeked into the bathroom. Nothing.

She came upon a closed door. She guessed it was the bedroom. She felt a churning in her stomach as she heard a buzzing noise from behind the door. It sounded like an unheeded alarm. She knocked, again calling Trudy's name. No answer. The buzzing seemed to intensify. Her mouth was dry. She tried to moisten her lips.

She took a deep breath and reached for the doorknob. She inched the door open. She saw the screaming alarm clock next to the bed. Then her eye was caught by something on the floor. It was a form, bloated and purple, lying crumpled by the bed.

Time froze as her brain finally registered what her eyes already knew. It was Trudy Porter—the nurse who had not shown up. And would never show up again.

Beth Margolis stopped to adjust her backpack. She felt a twinge of irritation as she watched her boyfriend crest the hill ahead. Backpackers were supposed to stick together in the wilderness. She took a deep breath of disgust and scanned the trail behind her for a sign of their friend Danny. Not a trace.

Puzzled, she sat in the patchy shade of an aspen tree to wait. Danny was a veteran outdoorsman, far more fit than she and Tom. His plodding pace didn't make sense. She felt a twinge of concern.

She and Tom had been planning this trip into the Canadian wilderness for nearly a year. As overworked lab technicians at City Hospital in Los Angeles, they could use the change of pace. They had been counting on Danny. It was their first such outing.

Finally, she spotted him ascending the rugged trail. He was straining with every step. They were deep into the wilderness now. They had to keep pushing to get to the cave before dark. And only Danny could find it.

Panting, he drew up to her. He threw off his pack and flopped on the ground. She was alarmed at the way his chest heaved. There was something radically wrong.

"Are you all right, Dan?"

"I think so," he said in a weak voice. "Just the altitude."

She frowned. That wasn't it. "Maybe you have a flu bug. Do you feel feverish?" Her first impulse was to go to him, check his forehead. Something made her hesitate.

"I'm hot. It's gotta be ninety degrees out here!"

She frowned again. It wasn't that hot. She looked at her watch. It would be dark soon. She had to get him moving. "We'd better go on, Dan."

"Yeah." He slowly got to his feet.

They moved out. Within minutes, they came on Tom jogging toward them. "Am I glad to see you guys," he said. "I was getting worried."

Beth rolled her eyes and took Tom aside. Danny stood gazing glassy-eyed into space. She whispered, "Danny's sick."

Tom raised his eyebrows. "He looks all right to me." He turned. "Ready to put the pedal to the metal, Dan?"

Danny nodded. He trudged on behind them. Beth could see he was faltering. His legs were wobbling, and now she noticed a peculiar red rash popping up on his arms.

It was dusk when they got to the cave. Tom took a flashlight and explored while Beth set out to get Danny settled on a shelflike ledge just inside the entrance. She spread his sleeping bag out on the rock and helped him up onto the ledge. It was just a few steps, but Danny had trouble making it.

"Lie down and rest," she said as he sat back against the wall gasping. "As soon as we get a fire, I'll make you a hot chocolate."

"Thanks." He slumped down and started shivering. She laid her jacket over him, then went to unpack the gear.

Tom had returned with a load of dry kindling. He dumped it on the ground and went to building a fire beneath the natural flue he had found. He was whistling cheerfully.

Beth glared. "Don't you care about Danny?"

He kept piling on the wood. "Beth, lay off, will you?" He held the lighter to the kindling and flicked it on. "So he's got a cold. People get over colds." The branches burst into flame and they both moved back.

Just then Beth heard a retching sound. She knew Danny was vomiting. She shuddered and looked at Tom. He was stoking the fire as though nothing had happened. Damn him!

She grabbed a flashlight and tiptoed toward the ledge, craning her neck. "Danny?"

A chill swept up her back. There was no sound.

"Danny?"

She scrambled up onto the ledge. Danny was lying in a pool of blood. She moved the flashlight over him, her hands shaking. She saw his face in the beam of light. His eyes were open and staring. Blood trickled from his gaping mouth. He wasn't breathing.

She threw down the flashlight and screamed.

CHAPTER ONE

Spring 1994

Dr. Katherine Crane stared at the morning paper. Her face clouded as a story caught her eye. Akendo Maury, of the New York Knicks, was dead of "natural causes." What, she wondered, were natural causes in a healthy twenty-five-year-old professional basketball player?

She put down the paper, swiveled her chair and gazed thoughtfully out the window at the blossoming magnolia trees that had played a role in her decision to take the job at the Centers for Disease Control in Atlanta three years earlier. Having been recently divorced, and a Yankee from day one, she'd had reservations about the South. But the magnolia trees had stolen her heart.

She had no regrets—trees or no trees. Her position as investigative epidemiologist was challenging and yes, fun, from the start. Many travels, lots of detective work, amiable colleagues and friends. And an occasional lover.

She thought of Rory McDermott. She knew he was about to pop the marriage question—a question she

wasn't ready to answer. At least the notion of saying
yes made her palms moist. Yet the thought of saying
no didn't make her feel a bit better. A no would probably end a relationship that had been pleasantly comfortable for well over a year. And that would leave a
disquieting void in her life.

A nagging tightness squeezed her throat as she considered her dilemma. She owed Rory an honest answer. She hated it when people hemmed and hawed.
She wasn't about to do that herself.

She looked up as her chief, Dr. Charles Kekich,
filled the doorway with his massive form. A large and
welcome distraction. He must have weighed close to
three hundred pounds. His shadow was like an eclipse.

"Knock, knock," said Kekich jovially.

She smiled. "Good morning, Chuck."

"Mornin', Kate."

She felt an involuntary wince. Kekich was from
Pennsylvania, but he had managed to acquire a sea-
soned Southern drawl after ten years in Georgia. Kate
supposed Kekich's accent bothered her because it
made her wonder if she would one day sound like
him—stringing her words out as if trying to kill time.
Not that she didn't find the Southern way of talking
charming. It just wasn't her.

Kekich ambled in and squeezed himself into a chair
opposite her. "Guess I'm a hopeless male chauvinist,"
he muttered as he eyed the newspaper.

She knew what was coming. Her blue eyes twinkled
as she brushed her long auburn hair back from her
forehead and looked at him over her reading glasses.
"How's that, Chuck?"

"Well, if you were a *guy* reading sports on company
time, I'd be reamin' you out." He stuffed the remain-
der of a glazed donut into his mouth. "Instead, I'm
sitting here with nothin' but awe and admiration."

She laughed. "If it's male chauvinism, it's the painless variety."

"Anything interesting?" Kekich pointed his bearded chin at the paper.

She handed him the page with the item on Maury. "Did you see this?"

He took it with soft chubby fingers, his eyes soaking up the headline. "Heard it last night. A cryin' shame. The boy had a hell of a lot of talent."

"He did have that," she said, tapping her palm with a pencil.

They said nothing for a moment, in silent recognition of the passing of a great athlete. Kate felt her eyes moisten as a wave of melancholy washed over her. Life was so uncertain, the specter of death ever present. Often random and irreverent, as with this young man.

Although she knew nothing of the details, the untimely death gnawed at her. She removed her glasses and looked at Kekich. "Chuck, it's the second death this month of a professional athlete."

Kekich lifted his dark, bushy eyebrows. "You're thinking there's a connection?"

She shrugged, a pensive frown wrinkling her brow.

He handed the paper back. "I figured it was AIDS in Maury's case, couched in the usual euphemisms. You'd think people'd stop tryin' to hide it."

She shook her head. "Maury played in last week's game against Chicago. He scored forty points, Chuck. A man dying of AIDS isn't at the peak of his form a week before his death."

Kekich scratched his balding scalp. He struck Kate as one of the hairiest men she had ever known. Yet he had a shiny bare spot on the crown of his head.

"He could've had a bad case of pneumocystis that wiped him out overnight," he suggested.

"True, but something about it bothers me. Especially after last month's death of the football player."

"You mean Hank Osmond?"

She nodded. "His death followed a 'short illness.'"

Kekich chuckled. "You don't miss a beat, do you?"

Kate grinned. "You trained me well, chief. When I see phrases like 'natural causes' and 'short illness' I can't help myself. I wonder what *really* happened."

Kekich frowned, stroking his salt-and-pepper beard. He had indeed trained Kate Crane well. So well that when she so much as sniffed the air for a potential clue, he stopped everything until she made her judgment. She was that good.

Kekich hadn't thought much about Hank Osmond's death. "It's common knowledge that Osmond was into cocaine. I imagine that either caused or strongly figured in his particular short illness." He pushed himself up out of the cushioned chair with a grunt. "We sure have sugar coatings for a lot of things."

But she wasn't listening. She stared at Akendo Maury's picture, and she could literally feel her heart ache. Maury was soaring through the air—his face seemingly enraptured by his defiance of gravity. His dark skin and sinewy muscles glistened as the ball rolled off his fingertips toward the rim.

Akendo Maury, full of vitality six days ago. Now dead. Natural causes. Sure.

"How're you coming on that staph epidemic?" Kekich suddenly remembered why he had stopped by.

"Hmmm?" She gave him a distracted look.

"Kate, don't go off on a tangent on me now. We've got to find the source or we'll be walking in the stuff."

She shuffled some papers around on her desk until she came up with a thin folder. "Solved," she said with a grin as she waved it at him.

"Solved?!" He approached her with a look of disbelief.

She sat back with a good feeling as he leafed through the report. It wasn't often she got to crack a case right in her own backyard. This one had been tough—a two-month epidemic of staphylococcal gastroenteritis. Fever and diarrhea had swept Atlanta like a storm. She had found the link that would bring the outbreak to a screeching halt.

"It's all in there," she said as she watched Kekich's jaw drop. "A nineteen-year-old college kid turned out to be a staph carrier. He was holding down two jobs. Worked at four different restaurants over the past two months. Mostly bussing tables and working the salad bars."

"The tapioca pudding . . ." Kekich flipped the pages eagerly.

"He handled the puddings and custards at all four salad bars. Those items sit out for hours, and even though they're on ice, just a few staph organisms from his hands could get on the side of a bowl and . . ."

"And wham! Everyone who eats tapioca in Atlanta has got the runs," Kekich finished, the excitement building in his voice. He stuffed the report into the pocket of his white coat. "Poor kid. Must feel guilty as the dickens."

She smiled. "Chuck, he's a teenager. I rather think he enjoys the attention."

Thinking of his own teenage son, Kekich saw her point. In fact, he started to worry. "Uh—you've got him under surveillance?"

"Fear not. We've neutralized the boy with antibiotics. And we'll be culturing his nasopharynx regularly. His food-handling days are over for a while."

He laughed. "Well, you solved that quick enough.

Call me later and we'll go over the caseload together. You can let me know your preferences."

He leaned his outstretched arms on her desk. The wood creaked under his weight. "I could sure use your help on the cholera fiasco in Argentina. An American tour group got hit hard. Washington is on our tail."

Kate suddenly felt very tired. She didn't want to think ahead right now. And she didn't want to look back. Her life seemed to be at some sort of critical juncture. It wasn't just Rory. It seemed that looking inward provided deeper mysteries and challenges than those facing her daily at the world-renowned organization for which she worked.

The image of Rory's smiling face flashed through her mind. She saw his eyes, almost worshipful. Maybe that was the problem. He'd placed her on some sort of pedestal. She didn't feel real around him.

She sighed. Why couldn't life be simple? At least the challenges of her job were tangible. And she got paid for tackling them.

Her eyes wandered back to the picture of the magnificent Akendo Maury. She couldn't get him out of her head. A promising life, so able, so seemingly unfettered by inner conflict. Snuffed out, just like that.

"I don't know, Chuck," she said finally. "Maybe I need to take that vacation you're always riding me about." Maybe she should say the-hell-with-it and run off with Rory. Or without him. Take stock of her life.

Kekich started to say something and checked himself. She hadn't taken a vacation since coming to Atlanta. He realized he didn't know much about her personal life. And he wished he did. He knew she had gone through a sticky divorce. He knew she went out but she never talked about it. He also knew Rory McDermott in Special Pathogens would marry her in a heartbeat.

Kekich had always figured she took refuge in her work. He wondered at times, as he wondered about all workaholics, if she was running away from something. He had steered clear of probing. A good rule.

But now he broke his own rule. "What is it, Kate? Your ex bothering you again?"

She shook her head. "No. He's always popping up, but that's nothing new."

Kekich wasn't so sure. "Where's he living now?"

"New York City. He gave up medicine. He's trying his luck at the stock market. He doesn't last long at anything."

She shot him a glance as she shifted in her seat. "Can't we talk about something else?" Kekich took a kind, paternalistic interest in her, even though, approaching his fifties, he couldn't be more than ten years her senior. Mostly, she appreciated his concern. But at times, like now, his fatherly attitude annoyed her. She didn't want to have to relive the unhappiness of her marriage, and the miscarriage that had so affected her.

He backed off, changing the subject. "You miss your practice?"

She took a sip of tepid coffee. "At times. I miss the patient contact. Knowing that, if only by listening and caring, I made a difference."

Kekich patted the pocket containing her report. "You don't think you make a difference when you stop an epidemic like this in its tracks?"

"Yes, but it's not the same. As an internist, I got to know my patients. Tracking down the roots of an epidemic is very satisfying, but in the end, I feel I'm treating numbers."

She turned to look out at the magnolias. She got up and threw open the window. "What a fragrance!"

As he watched her move gracefully cross the room

he thought how much he admired her. She was beautiful, almost statuesque, as she stood admiring the flowers, now a look of serenity on her face. A magic moment.

Often she seemed restless, searching. He asked the question he was always loathe to ask. "Do you want to go back?"

She returned to her desk, her brow furrowed. "No. Though I have given it some thought. Private practice isn't private anymore. When I think of it, I remind myself how much of my time was spent filling out forms justifying why I did this or that. All for some overzealous bureaucrat."

Kekich decided not to press it. She wasn't thinking of leaving. He would settle for that.

She picked up the paper and studied the picture of Akendo Maury once more. "My ex and I used to go to the Knicks games when we lived in New York. I saw Akendo Maury play at Madison Square Garden, his rookie year. He was astonishing."

"I'll bet he was," said Kekich, still having some difficulty getting used to a woman knowing more about a professional sport than he did.

He turned to leave. "Well, look over that case list and let me know what you'd like to take on next. I'll do my best to get you on it."

"Thanks, Chuck." She picked up the list and looked at it.

"Oh, and Kate . . ."

"Yes?"

"The Hawks are playing the Knicks here next week. You interested? Barb doesn't want to go."

He saw a grin as wide as the Mississippi break through Kate Crane's doldrums. It made his day.

CHAPTER TWO

September 1992

Keith Heinman sat cross-legged on his bed, deep-breathing, his eyes closed. It made him think better. All was in harmony. Mind and desire. Thought and deed.

Right now, he needed to think hard. Thought: I want out of this snake pit. Action: get the idiots to release me.

Tomorrow was the day.

He clutched the Holy Bible in one hand, recalling his first exposure to its wisdom eight years earlier. His Bible-reading had started out as a dispassionate scheme to con his way out of the loony bin with his testimonials of newfound religion. It had turned into an explosive awakening.

Having lived a fragmented and abused childhood in a variety of foster homes, Heinman's only guideposts had been the primeval laws of survival in an indifferent world. Attention was synonymous with a blow to the face or a strap across the back. Before he turned to the Bible, he considered it a copout for the weak in spirit. A mythology designed for people whose lives were dominated by fear. People who needed to spout dumb little aphorisms to keep them going. Not him.

So, no one was more surprised than he when by chance he found himself at home in the pages of this ancient text, particularly the Old Testament. Its words seemed to reach out to some undefined and unnourished need deep within him. From the moment he laid eyes on Genesis to the final passages of Revelation, he had been enraptured with the Bible's vivid references to the violent rendering of the firmament from apocalyptic chaos. To the fall of man, the crucifixion of Christ. The strong survived and the weak followed in their shadow—a world of harsh judgment and no mercy. A world he could understand. Man, the survivor. And the victim.

Heinman's eyes darted around the cheerless room. What a dump. Dull, narrow walls, like the minds of the people who ran this place. Forest Lawn, he called it, for he associated it with death and the stupid sanctimonious ceremonies it engendered, like the ritzy cemetery in California. Death and decay. He sniffed the air, the nostrils of his aquiline nose flaring contemptuously. He could smell the rot. The decay of the minds within the walls of this miserable hellhole.

He looked down at the tattered cover of the Holy Book, and he could envision himself. *His* mind was honed to a sharp and furious edge that sliced its way to the very quick of existence. The essence of the world was at his fingertips, like a drop of the cold, clear liquid form of rarefied air. And he had the Book to thank. It had given him a purpose—something to live for.

He smiled thinly as he thumbed through the dog-eared pages. It seemed that everywhere his eyes lighted, the Bible spoke to him. Like Deuteronomy, one of his favorites: *To me belongeth vengeance, and recompense; their foot shall slide in due time: for the day of their calamity is at hand, and the things that shall come upon them make haste.* (32, 35) And, *I will render vengeance to mine enemies . . .*

Or Ezekiel: *And I will execute great vengeance upon them with furious rebukes; and they shall know that I am the Lord, when I shall lay my vengeance upon them.* (25, 17)

He read a few more passages, absorbing the power of the words. He put his head back and closed his eyes, remembering now the many, many nights he had lain awake plotting his revenge against the Judas responsible for putting him here. And now the time was at hand.

Yet the plan had become much larger than avenging just one man. No, it was more. Much more. He smiled as he thought of all the weak-spined sinners of the world—the queers, the prostitutes, the drug addicts. Then the image of a face—an all too familiar face—flashed through his mind. The face of the man who put him here. His fists clenched. His smile dissipated.

He closed the book and shook away the annoying tremor in his hand. He rested it on top of the Bible, steadying it.

He heard a soft knock at the door. He ignored it. That would be the nurse with his medication. He didn't want their poison. It could take him out of the driver's seat. But he knew he must be agreeable. Tomorrow would soon come. And so he would continue to let them think he was a compliant little vegetable.

What did these retards know or care? Just let them believe you're playing along, and they're stupid enough to think you're under their power. Only he knew the truth.

He heard the knocking again, this time louder.

"Come in," he called. He got up and moved toward the door.

"Keith, it's time for your medicine," a woman's muffled voice came through the crack.

He opened the door and tried on a smile. He put out his hand. "Thank you."

The nurse gave him a vacuous grin and withheld the pills she had in her hand. She was a heavy middle-aged woman. He thought she was crazier than anyone there. Except, perhaps, for Dr. Kraft. Now there was a real nut case. A nut case for whom he had plans. Big plans.

"Keith, you know I have to watch you take these. Otherwise we might hide them, mightn't we?" She giggled, causing the smear of cherry red that was her lips to wriggle like a bleeding caterpillar. Her mascara, applied with a heavy hand, had left little black dots on the perimeter of her eyelids, giving her a macabre clownlike appearance. Looking at her made Heinman want to puke. Instead he laughed with her. Agreeability. Beyond the call of duty.

"You're right, Nurse Ratchett—I mean Nurse Rachel. I've got my chaser right here." He held up a mug half full of tepid morning coffee. "See?"

She giggled again. She was staring at his well-formed biceps muscle as it bulged to bend his arm, like a precision instrument. "Why do you call me that silly name?" she cooed. "I swear. I just don't understand you. Okay, now here we go. Open up."

He tossed his head back and opened his mouth. She placed two blue-green tablets on his tongue, then grasped his hand and guided the cup to his lips. She let one hand slide along his arm to rest on his biceps. He pretended not to notice and made a swallowing motion.

"Now open up again and let's check."

He opened his mouth wide and she peered in with a penlight.

"Good boy," she stated, straightening.

"Now one more thing," she said, her tone serious.

"What's that?" Heinman continued to block the doorway.

"My name is Rachel. Rachel Toohey. You may call me Nurse Toohey or Nurse Rachel, if you prefer to use my first name. But," she gave him an admonishing look. "No more Nurse Ratchett."

He smiled calmly as he thought of tomorrow. "Yes, Nurse."

After she left, he dug between his cheek and upper molars with his forefinger and extracted the pills. He took them into the bathroom and flushed them down the toilet.

He flopped down on his institutional bed with its flimsy gray institutional bedspread. His thoughts turned to the Bible. *Obey, I beseech thee, the voice of the Lord.* (Jer. 38, 20). He laughed quietly. We aren't being very obedient now, are we, Keith?

Well, the Bible didn't have all the answers.

Dr. Ananda Kumar sat at the head of the table. His white coat was so heavily starched that Heinman wondered if the thing was holding Kumar up. The dark skin of Kumar's face formed creases around his mouth as he offered up a dutiful, and, thought Heinman, condescending smile.

"Come in, won't you, Mr. Hen-man." Kumar had a clipped voice and a thick accent of some sort—he was from one of those dipshit Asian countries.

Heinman nodded and stepped into the stuffy room. Pipe and cigarette smoke swirled upward and formed a stagnant milky cloud over the small group of muckety-mucks.

He let the orderly lead him to his seat at the table. His eyes quietly scanned the faces of the committee— five in all, including Kumar. And only one was Caucasian—the demented Dr. Kraft.

Heinman looked each in the eye and put on his amiable smile as he contemplated his odds.

"Well, Mr. Hen-man," began Dr. Kumar. "I do believe everyone is here." Kumar's eyes surveyed the group. "Mr. Hen-man has been with us at Woodlawn ten years already."

Kumar's eyes flicked to Heinman, then back to the group. "Murder, temporary insanity," he said gravely. He cleared his throat. "Mr. Hen-man has requested us, in view of his exemplary performance here, to evaluate him at this time for release."

Kumar sat back, an arrogant tilt to his head. His eyes caught Heinman's and seemed to say, "You may take me to be an interloper in your country, but who is the one running things?"

Heinman stared hard at Kumar. He could feel hatred burning all the way from his gut to his mouth. He wanted to spit at Kumar. Instead, he stared.

"It is our task to assess Mr. Hen-man's sanity, and to determine whether he is fit to return to society." Kumar's eyes broke away from Heinman's.

Heinman looked down at his lap. All his life he had been aware that his gaze made people uneasy. He had learned to use it to his advantage, but at the same time, he knew when to turn it off. This was one of those times. He didn't want anyone in the room to feel intimidated right now. He kept his head down.

"Let us hear firstly from Dr. Kraft," Kumar went on. "Dr. Kraft, you have been Mr. Hen-man's psychiatrist. Tell us your opinion."

Kraft, a short, corpulent man in his sixties, cleared his throat. He had a deranged look to him, Heinman thought, with his bushy, tangled beard, his tinted Coke-bottle glasses, and his gray kinky hair shooting out of his scalp like electrically charged Brillo pads.

Kraft, on the other hand, looked at Heinman and marveled at the finely chiseled features, the ice-blue eyes, the shock of blond hair that had not a streak of gray in it, and the firm biceps muscles—like taut cable wires even at rest. The perfect Aryan, thought Kraft. A man as cool as a cucumber, as calculating as a computer, as cunning as a fox.

In his thick Teutonic accent, Kraft said, "I am quite pleased with the progress of Keith's superego. He has made a monumental contribution to Woodlawn by organizing our first Bible group. And"—Kraft waved his hand with a flourish—"he has furthered his own studies in his field of microbiology."

Or was it molecular genetics? Whatever. No one here would know the difference anyway. Kraft rolled on, oblivious to the bored eyes in the room. "He has even set up his own little research lab and has at times been of assistance to the medical doctors here." He guffawed as though it was all a big joke. "We're probably the only mental institution with a lab capable of culturing viruses. Yes, indeed."

Kraft slapped the table with gusto, his voice cresting. "The question, I think, gentlemen, is not whether Mr. Heinman is ready for society, but whether society is ready for him."

He sat back and chuckled at his own black humor that seemed lost on the others. Of course it would be lost on them. He looked around at the motley group. The dregs of humanity.

Kraft glanced at Heinman and felt a shudder as Heinman looked up and caught his eye. It was, he knew, the reminder he'd been dreading. About the mysterious disappearance of a little Jewish doctor a few years back. A meddlesome troublemaker who was trying to get Kraft fired. Just because Kraft liked to get it on with his patients.

Kraft's eyes darted away, then back to Heinman who now seemed almost supplicant, head bowed, eyes staring down at his hands. What an actor.

Kraft wished he had imagined that moment of eye contact. But he knew he hadn't. For Keith Heinman was a psychopath—pure and simple. The missing doctor was but one case in point. Concepts of conscience or remorse, Kraft knew, had no place in Keith Heinman's world. Sealed away in his confidential file was a list of Heinman's many offenses. Probably only the tip of the iceberg. There was the rape of a teacher in high school who, after showing up with bruises all over her body one day, retracted all charges. Then there was the unsolved grisly murder of a man who had fired Heinman from a summer clerking job for reasons unknown.

Heinman wasn't a man. He was a weapon—a missile of destruction. What troubled Kraft—and only slightly—was that he found himself admiring the man. Maybe that was why he had blabbed just a little too much about his troubles with the good Dr. Goldschmidt. About how he'd wished Goldschmidt would get off his back, out of his life. And then, like magic, Goldschmidt was gone. An unsolved missing persons case.

Kraft's skin crawled as he remembered the session with Heinman following Goldschmidt's disappearance. Heinman had told him in so many ways, without actually saying it, that he had indeed taken care of Dr. Goldschmidt. What, Kraft had wondered, would Heinman want in return?

And Kraft was *still* wondering. He had always known that Heinman would someday come around for his pound of flesh. Now, those cold eyes told him, the day would be soon.

Kraft's mind drifted back to the meeting as he became vaguely aware of Dr. Kumar's impatient twittering. What an odious little man.

"Your opinion of whether Mr. Hen-man should be released, Dr. Kraft?" said Kumar tersely.

Kraft bowed his head dramatically, though he knew it didn't matter what he said or how he said it. The die had been cast. Thanks to federal cutbacks, the bottom line was that Heinman, and many of the other patients, had to go. Either that, or no job for Rutger Kraft. Nor did it matter that in Kraft's opinion the government was diverting those funds to worthless causes. Like putting more dirtballs on the welfare rolls, or funding AIDS research. Kraft was all for letting AIDS run its course—Nature's solution to the pervert problem. Heinman, he knew, would agree with him on that point.

Kraft looked up to see his colleagues staring at him. He must have been daydreaming again. He scratched at his beard. "We have nothing more to offer Mr. Heinman," he stated. "He is an intelligent man with good scientific training—not very often do we get a crack scientist passing through our doors." Kraft smiled at the humorless group, his grin wide enough to show a scattering of crooked, yellow teeth. And good riddance, he thought. He cleared his throat and sat back.

Kumar paged through Heinman's records. "You do not consider Mr. Heinman a danger to himself or others?"

Kraft's heavy brows formed a V shape above his bulbous nose. "Certainly not." His eyes flicked to Heinman but nothing registered in Heinman's face.

Supporting Heinman's release, he knew, was not the payback. He felt a lump congeal in his throat.

Kumar, without looking up, said, "Thank you, Dr. Kraft."

Kumar's gaze landed on Lemuel Duarte, Heinman's social worker. "Mr. Duarte," Kumar began. "You have been preparing Mr. Heinman for reentry into society. Your thoughts, please?"

Heinman felt his hand begin to tremble. He shoved it in his pocket and fixed his ice-blue eyes on Duarte, whose eyes and skin were as dark as molasses.

Heinman was pleased to see those black eyes flit away from his. Duarte had been the only one he was unsure of. Charm and machination hadn't been effective. The man seemed to be lacking a cog somewhere. What could you expect from a damn jungle-bunny with a French accent?

Duarte had a blunt naïveté about him. Under different circumstances, Heinman might have found it amusing—even challenging. But, all things considered, he had felt obligated to make a last-minute move to assure Duarte's cooperation.

He thought Duarte had gotten the message on that rainy night in the parking lot. Duarte had driven Heinman to town to get his driver's license. They had just gotten out of Duarte's car when Heinman told Duarte how attractive he found the social worker's teenage daughter. He had seen her from a distance, of course. But, he intimated, he could move closer. You know, get a better look.

He had said it with just the right smile. Not quite a leer. Subtle enough so that if it came up later, Duarte would wonder if he hadn't just imagined it all.

Now Lemuel Duarte looked tense. He hesitated before he answered Kumar, frozen by Heinman's cold stare. "I believe ... Mr. Heinman is a ... dangerous man," he stammered. He looked around, as though waiting for the aftershock, but everyone just sat there. Even Heinman hadn't moved.

Kumar looked at his watch. "Why do you say that?"

Heinman could tell it had taken every bit of Duarate's courage to say that much. He caught the social worker's eye and winked. Duarte looked away. "I really can't say, Doctor. It ... it's just a feeling I have."

Kraft burst out laughing. Whispers wafted back and forth. Kumar tapped his water glass with a ballpoint pen. "We are professionals here. We do not hold a man's destiny in the balance by our feelings. I think, Mr. Duarte, you have said as much as we have time to hear. Let us move on."

Heinman felt a moment of amusement as he watched Duarte squirm in his seat. Then a more intense feeling of hatred seized him. Duarte had willfully disregarded his threat. He stared at Duarte until he saw him turn away.

The meeting seemed to be over as quickly as it began, and Heinman found himself shaking hands as people got up and filed out. He looked for Duarte, but Duarte was gone. People were congratulating him on his freedom. But suddenly it meant nothing. All he could think of was Duarte. Duarte. Lemuel Duarte—the man who had disobeyed him.

"Congratulations, Keith." Kraft came up and clapped him on the back. Heinman, still confused, almost turned and swung at the crazy psychiatrist. He couldn't remember what had happened in that room from the moment Duarte challenged his freedom.

He collected himself and smiled at Kraft. "Thank you," he said softly. "I am looking forward to returning to the real world."

Keith Heinman entered Dr. Rutger Kraft's office at the Woodlawn State Psychiatric Hospital for the last time. Officially, at least. He stood for a moment, just looking around. He had never been quite so aware of the room's shoddiness. And how many times had he been here? Over a hundred? Amazing.

The room reflected the nature of its occupant, Heinman decided. The walls were painted a dull green, somewhere between the color of bread mold and pea soup. Where the paint was peeling, Heinman could tell the previous color had been a garish pink. The walls held a few dust-covered degrees stenciled in German. Cobwebs trailed down from the ceiling and the overhead light fixture.

Kraft was sitting at a painted steel desk with his feet propped up. He was probing his yellow teeth with a toothpick. Heinman dropped into a coffee-stained upholstered chair across from Kraft. He casually slung one leg over the arm.

"So, my dear Keith, our last visit," said Kraft with a cheerfulness he did not feel. "Much water has flowed beneath the bridge, eh?"

Kraft chuckled as he brought his feet down and stretched to reach a file cabinet. "I'd better get your record, to give our last visit an official ring to it."

"This is not our last visit."

Kraft felt a stab of fear. Squelching it, he broke into a gale of laughter. "What mischief are you up to now?"

Heinman extracted from his pocket a slip of paper with something scribbled on it and tossed it toward the desk. It fell short and fluttered onto the threadbare carpet. He left it there. "You're going to get me a job."

"Oh, I am, am I?" Kraft snapped the toothpick and dropped it into an ashtray. He watched his hand tremble with a strange feeling of detachment. This was it. The pound of flesh.

Heinman said nothing and let his head rest on the back of the chair, his eyes closed.

Kraft looked at him, waiting for a response. The only sound came from a fly buzzing at the window-pane behind him. Kraft became increasingly uncomfortable, and finally broke the silence. "We have occupational counselors for these matters. I will be happy to make suggestions to them. With your wonderful science background, I think you would do well to look at the local hospitals ..."

"You know damn well you're going to do this," Heinman interrupted. "And why. Don't feed me your holier-than-thou crap." Heinman's eyes remained closed. He clasped his hands behind his head.

Kraft ran tobacco-stained fingers through his beard. He smiled as a thought came to him. "I see. Now that you think you're guaranteed your freedom, you're getting a bit cocky." His voice rose. "Well, don't be too sure of yourself. Rub me the wrong way and I could change my mind about turning you loose."

He distractedly rummaged through his drawers. "Yes, indeed," he muttered.

Heinman opened his eyes and gave Kraft a withering look. "Nobody gives a damn about your opinion."

Kraft found a cigar and shoved it in his mouth. He snapped on his paperweight lighter and puffed vehemently until a cloud of foul-smelling smoke rose over both men. "The hell they don't!"

Heinman rolled his head back. "The government needs me to go. They don't have the money to keep this place full. You're just a cog in the flat tire of progress."

"Nonsense!"

Ignoring him, Heinman lazily stretched his arms. "I want the job by next month."

Kraft rose and paced. He brushed past Heinman and stooped to pick up the piece of paper. He stared at it. "Alatron Laboratories. The pharmaceutical company?"

"Right."

"I have no influence with them. What makes you think I can help you—even if I want to, that is?"

"You'll figure it out."

"I don't like your attitude."

"You'll like even less what I have to say about your requesting me to kill a colleague."

Kraft felt his heart stop. So that was how it was going to be. He snatched up a magazine, rolled it up, and slammed the buzzing fly against the pane of glass. The glass shattered. He spun around to face Heinman, his eyes bulging.

"Are you threatening to blackmail me, you lying, miserable . . ."

"I don't have to blackmail you."

Kraft sat back down at his desk, venting a loud sigh as though the air had been knocked out of him. He could feel his temples throbbing with the rush of blood to his head. No one should be able to do this to him. No one. Especially a patient. He tamped out his cigar and took some deep breaths.

"Suppose I do decide to help you? How about a job someplace else? I have some connections."

Heinman shook his head. "No."

"Why not?"

"I have a score to settle."

"A score to settle?" Suddenly he understood. "Of course. Alatron's the company you sued." He smiled. "And lost."

Heinman yawned. "Congratulations. You go to the head of the class."

Kraft rubbed his hands together. "They made you

kill, you said. A silly little sleeping pill drove you over the edge." He chuckled. "But we both know you don't need a pill to turn you into a killer, do you, Herr Heinman?"

Heinman stood up. Kraft could see his muscles ripple under his T-shirt. He wondered if Heinman had used those muscles to kill Goldschmidt.

"Just what are you planning?"

"You'll find out soon enough." Heinman removed his wallet from a back pocket and took out an index card. He handed it to Kraft. "Here's the name I'll be going by, as well as a list of the documents I'll be needing."

Kraft took the card and squinted at Heinman's scrawled penmanship. "Kenneth Butler. Driver's license, social security number, passport . . ."

Kraft's voice trailed off. "Anything else, Mein Herr?" He bowed his head mockingly.

He felt the cold eyes fix on him as Heinman said, "The sooner you take this seriously, the better. For you."

Kraft threw back his head, still trying to make it all very amusing. "You seem to think I'm some sort of black market gangster. Really, it's hardly my style."

He started to hand back the card, but Heinman made no move to take it. Kraft shrugged and dropped it on the desktop.

Heinman's eyes were like a serpent's, unblinking. "A week should be about right for the documents, but you can hold them until you land me the job."

Kraft shifted in his chair. "You know, in the case of the unfortunate Dr. Goldschmidt, it is your word against mine. I'm afraid you'll need something more persuasive."

"I'll kill you," Heinman said quietly. He gave Kraft a lopsided smile. "Persuasive enough?"

Kraft felt a chill creep along the back of his neck. He stared at the card on his desk and felt an unremitting hollowness as he considered his limited alternatives.

Heinman turned to leave. "I'll be around until the job comes through."

Kraft made his decision. "Wait. How do I contact you? What about a résumé?"

"You'll know my whereabouts when I want you to. All I want is a custodial position. Make something up."

Kraft sighed as Heinman closed the door behind him. He went to his private bathroom. Nerves.

He knew he had no choice. Those hard eyes told him that. The sooner the better. Heinman would be Alatron's problem then. The thought of it made him smile. The poor suckers.

CHAPTER THREE

Winter 1992

Heinman squeezed the mop with his bare hands. He liked to do it that way. Watch the muscles of his arms glide and swell with the twisting motion. Everyone else used the foot pedal. Company rule. Protect the peons from the deadly germs produced by the Patrician research scientists. That was Alatron's way—make everybody believe he's part of some big happy family.

He took a moment to look around. Here he was, at long last: Alatron, one of the fastest-growing pharmaceutical companies since Elliot Halsey—Elliot the Great—took over. But that was all going to change.

Heinman watched the filthy mop water drip into the bucket at his feet. He squeezed the mop again, this time one-handed. The last little bit of gray water trickled out.

"Hey, Ken! You trying to strangle that thing?" Willie Akers, a veteran custodian at Alatron, and black as a Goodyear tire, came up behind him and clapped him on the back.

Heinman looked up and gave Akers a thin smile.

"Yeah, that's right." He returned the mop to the bucket and rolled the sleeves of his gray uniform back down.

Something about Heinman's expression seemed to give the usually ebullient Akers pause. Akers leaned against the wall and stuck a cigarette in his mouth. "You know, Ken, you take this job too serious. Maybe it's 'cause you new here. But man, you just a damn janitor."

Heinman checked his watch and leaned over to pick up the bucket. He needed Akers the hell out of there. Albert Buell, the little wimp from purchasing, was due to meet him any minute. "Yeah, well, the Lord gives us all a time and place to show who we are. I try to please Him."

Akers rolled his eyes. "Jeez, man. What you need is get a little drunk, loosen up. Night out with the guys. Know what I'm sayin'?"

Heinman looked past Akers and spotted Buell coming down the stairs. He gave Buell a stony-faced signal to stay put. Then he turned back to Akers. He knew how to get rid of the bumbling man. "All right, Willie. I'll go out with you guys after work. Tonight. Okay?"

Akers pushed off the wall. "Hey, man, good deal. Ain't nothin' in that Bible of yours say you can't have a good time, now is there? Catch ya' by the lockers." He danced off.

Heinman motioned to Buell, who was waiting beneath the stairs. "In here," he said, pointing to a closed set of double doors.

Buell followed him into what looked like a laundry room. Huge dryers buzzed away. Heinman pulled up a chair for Buell while he remained standing, his arms folded across his chest.

"What have you got?" He stared at the scrawny weasel of a man. Buell was one of those eggheads who had to be hand-led through life. He could understand anything if it was in a book, but he couldn't find his way to the grocery store without a map. That, plus Buell's position, plus the burden of guilt he carried around for God knew what reason, made him the perfect man.

It had taken Heinman less than a month to find his mark. He'd gotten his little Bible group up and running within two weeks and already had four members, Buell being among the first to join up. It took another few weeks of getting to know Buell well enough to figure out how to hook him. It had been easy. The guy had been yearning to be lured out of his little stream of lonely misdirection. His sense of reality was so knotted up inside him that he would believe just about anything. And with Buell's position in purchasing it had been a breeze to doctor the books and gradually procure the expensive and sophisticated equipment Heinman needed to assemble his own home laboratory. Scot-free.

Buell, wide-eyed, looked up through horn-rimmed glasses at Heinman. He pulled a notepad from his pocket. "They're growing the AIDS virus on the fourth floor. You need top clearance to get in. I only know one guy who works there, Tony Imperata. He keeps to himself, doesn't talk about what he's doing."

"What about the other viruses?"

Buell consulted his notepad. "They've got one of the recently discovered African viruses on the floor above. Maximum containment." Buell looked up. "Same story. CIA-like security. The viruses are deadly, like you said." A proud smile crept over the sallow face. "And you were right. Alatron is the only pharmaceutical company in the country with a maximum containment lab. Pretty strange, huh?"

Heinman ignored the question. "What do they claim they're doing with the African virus?"

"Working toward a vaccine. They have a giant lab up there with guinea pigs, mice, rats, the like. I guess they're running trials on them."

Heinman slammed his fist down on the table. "I told you, Buell, you don't waste time guessing. God gave you a mind. Use it."

Buell flinched. "I'm sorry, Ken, it was just a figure of speech. I'm not guessing. I know. You're right. I know." He looked at Heinman expectantly. "You think the bit about the vaccine is just a cover?"

Heinman fixed Buell with a cold stare. "Of course. You know what they're doing."

"Yeah, but it's just so hard to believe. Germ warfare . . . wow. You think we can stop them?"

"That depends on you, doesn't it? You keep getting me the equipment, we'll stop them."

Buell's eyes widened. "Jeez, it's like a movie. Wait'll it gets out . . ."

Heinman's hands moved like lightning to Buell's collar. He all but lifted the man out of the chair. "You're never to speak of it. Do you understand me?" He let go and Buell fell back into the chair like a rag doll.

"I'm sorry, Ken."

Heinman paced a small circle around Buell whose eyes rolled after him. "I want you to find out who the head of the cleanup crew is on those floors," said Heinman. "That's where I need to be."

"What about me?" Buell whimpered.

"I have nothing for you right now."

Buell looked down at the floor. "What about our Bible group?"

Heinman let an extra tick of time pass while Buell's

eyes hounded him. Then he gave Buell a cool smile. "Of course."

Buell stood up. "When do we meet again?"

Heinman stared at him until Buell giggled nervously.

"I will send word," he said softly.

CHAPTER FOUR

Spring 1994

At the same time,
And she had given him for one day to refrain
from the effects of depression which she had been...

Kate Crane found herself sifting aimlessly through a stack of reports on her desk. It was one of those days she couldn't concentrate. She dialed Rory McDermott's number, thankful he was not at his desk. She left a vague message with his secretary.

She picked up the morning paper with a feeling of apprehension. There was a follow-up article on Akendo Maury. His death was a deepening mystery, this time commanding the front page. Her eye stopped at a familiar name. Dr. Allen Cosgrove. The beloved Harpo of medical school days! A bit of a clown with an irrepressible smile and a mop of curly blond hair.

She paused as her mind reached back across fifteen years. She and Harpo had been close. They had gone through so much together. She remembered that heady sensuality that comes after long hours of body closeness and trigger-sharp minds working back and forth at three in the morning as they crammed for exams. They had made love, laughed together, even wept together over the endless rewards and tragedies of becoming a doctor, torn by the unremitting procession of the sick and dying.

She had loved Harpo for his lightness and spirit of adventure. She remembered how he had entertained them all with his clowning and magic tricks as they studied for exams. He had been best at card tricks and juggling. Then, to relax, he would have everyone amused yet mesmerized as he stood on his head in the corner of the study room, his incredibly limber body allowing him to fold his legs into a lotus position at the same time.

And she had loved him for his ability to rebound from the depths of depression over life lost before its time. She had, in truth, loved him deeply. But it hadn't been enough. And so she had said no when he asked her to marry him what seemed a lifetime ago.

She sighed. She supposed he was married now. And he was with the Medical Examiner's office in New York, a pathologist. She felt a surge of the old warmth, the old connection. And she picked up the phone.

She got through to the Medical Examiner's office with amazing quickness. All she had to do was mention her CDC affiliation.

Harpo promptly came on. "Kate Crane! I'll be damned! To what do I owe this honor?" His voice had the old ring.

She smiled into the phone. "How are you, Harpo? It's been a long time."

"Missing you, Kate. Always missing you."

She felt a glow. "Thank you, Harpo. You sound the same."

"I feel the same. But the hair—it's giving out. Haven't heard the old nickname since med school. So, how the hell are you?"

"Pretty good."

"You like being a CDC honcho?"

"Hardly a honcho. It's fine. I have no complaints. I suppose you're married. With a dozen kids."

"Three. All girls. And a wife. I'm surrounded by women."

"And what's wrong with that?"

He laughed. "I feel outnumbered at times. Go to ball games by myself, that sort of thing." He paused, as though suddenly realizing she hadn't called to make small talk after fifteen years. "Forgive me for carrying on. What can I do for you, Kate? CDC business?"

"In a way, but not completely. I saw your name in the paper, and I had to call. I have a request."

"Well, let's hear it—anything for an old friend."

"You know what a Knicks fan I've always been, Harpo. What's the scoop on Akendo Maury?"

There was an awkward silence. Then she heard a sigh. "Kate, I have to eat my words. Anything but that."

Her voice dropped. "What's wrong?"

"We're keeping a lid on things. Too many unanswered questions. Quite frankly, the autopsy was botched by a small-town bozo. We got the body after that. Nothing's been resolved."

She was disappointed. And yet didn't want to press him. She understood.

Harpo seemed to sense her disappointment. "I'll tell you this much, Kate. Akendo Maury died of something I've never seen before."

She felt her heart pick up a few beats. "I knew there was something."

She could almost hear him thinking. "Kate, I have an idea. How about giving us a consult? If you're officially involved, we can talk. I'd like to crack this one myself, but I'm in over my head. It's a perfect case for the CDC."

"Harpo, I could kiss you. You always could bend

my arm." She paused. "I have a funny feeling about this case."

"How soon can you be here?"

She felt her spirits lift. "Let me make a few calls. I just finished a project and I'm due for some time off. I'll try for the first morning flight."

"Great! I'll meet you."

"It will be wonderful to see you, Harpo."

"Kate, I want you to remember one thing."

"Yes?"

His voice dropped into a mock growl. "This is my turf."

She laughed. As students, they had joked about the turf battles waged by doctors who thought they owned their patients.

"Of course, Dr. Cosgrove."

Kate had no difficulty spotting him. Hair or no hair, he still had the sassy wiry look she remembered. They hugged each other as hurrying throngs brushed past. Harpo stepped back and gave a nod of approval. "You're lovelier than the day you graduated."

She felt herself blush. "Thanks, Harpo. You look wiser. More distinguished."

He laughed. "Amazing what a bald spot can do for image."

She playfully patted his thinning hair and slung her overnight bag over her shoulder. They moved past the baggage area to a waiting taxi.

They drove through a dull gray Queens into a bustling Manhattan. Kate marveled once again at the New York skyline. New York had always been her city of enchantment. She had her roots there. Her father had practiced medicine on Park Avenue, and the seeds of her future were sown there.

As she looked up at the towering buildings silhouetted against the sky, she felt a warm glow. It was still her city. A city of exciting contradictions with its gleaming avenues and dirty byways. A city of strife and of life. The city that never slept.

She could feel Harpo watching her. He was strangely silent, with an odd grim look on his face. Tense about something.

Their eyes met and for a moment his face softened. "I've thought of you a lot, Kate. I've never lost touch, even if you don't get the proverbial Christmas card." He stared out the window. "I heard you got married."

"And divorced."

"I'm sorry." He gave her an impish look. "Sort of."

She laughed and squeezed his hand. "He wasn't my type. It took me five years to figure it out."

He gave her a questioning look. "What is your type?"

It was her turn to watch the traffic stream by. "I don't know, Harpo. I honestly don't know."

"You'll know when you find him."

"Perhaps." She felt an inexplicable sadness as she looked at him.

He placed a hand on her shoulder and quickly changed the subject. "Hey, how's Mary Quaid, champion of causes? There was a time you two were inseparable."

She smiled. Good old Harpo. Ever cheerful. And a little shy when it came to making serious talk. She decided to go along. "You wouldn't believe it, Harp, she's got five kids!"

His eyes registered genuine surprise. "Mary? The girl who was never going to get hitched because it was family or career?"

"The very one. She didn't give up her dream, though. She's director of a women's clinic in San Francisco."

"Sounds like Mary." He looked at her. "What about you, Kate? Any kids?"

She shook her head and fought back unexpected tears. "I had a miscarriage. Before that I never thought I wanted kids."

He put a comforting arm around her. "I'm sorry."

They rode the rest of the way in reflective silence. The cab pulled up in front of Metropolitan Hospital, an ancient-looking ivy-clad brick structure. Harpo paid the cabby and hopped out. As he reached to help her out, she was struck again by the grim look on his face.

He whisked her through the dank musty halls of the old hospital. They bypassed the morning clusters of white-coated doctors and their students, as well as the usual array of technicians and orderlies. And bewildered-looking visitors mired in an endless maze of dark corridors.

Finally, they arrived at his office. He escorted her into a large room cluttered with microscopes, papers, books, journals, and shelves of human organs floating in gigantic jars of clear fluid.

The desk looked like he had been building forts out of stacks of paper. The unpleasant scent of formaldehyde permeated the air. Kate wrinkled her nose and wondered for the millionth time how anyone could be a pathologist.

"Excuse the mess," he said as he pointed her toward an incongruently elegant leather chair.

She sat down and surveyed the room. "You never were one for neatness."

He plopped down behind his desk, where he looked at home. Maybe it was indeed a fort of sorts, Kate mused. He suddenly seemed inordinately formal, which puzzled her. She decided to watch, wait, and proceed with caution. This was, after all, his turf.

He pulled a manila folder out of his desk drawer

and leafed through it. "This is the file to date on Maury."

The folder was unusually thick for someone who had died only days before. She said nothing, but raised her eyebrows and looked at him.

Harpo's poise suddenly deserted him. "Kate, I've got to level with you. I'm no good at games." His voice was strained. "I can't use you as a CDC consultant."

"Oh?" She was startled for a moment.

"I want your help. You, as an infectious disease specialist. Not the CDC."

She took a deep breath. "Harpo, just tell me what's going on. I've come a long way."

He handed her the folder. "Maury was HIV positive."

She nodded. Kekich had been right. She felt a surge of disappointment. She opened the folder and scanned the first page of the autopsy report.

"Then he had AIDS?"

"There's the catch. He didn't. I've spoken with his physician. Maury wanted it kept quiet. He didn't want to be another Magic Johnson. He was at the peak of a brilliant career. He didn't want to deal with what going public would bring. He had no sign of AIDS or even AIDS-related complex. His lymphocyte count was normal a week before his death."

The week he scored forty points, she thought. "How was the autopsy botched?" The original report was signed off in a name she didn't recognize.

"Maury and his girlfriend stayed over a few days in Arizona after the Knicks whomped the Suns in Phoenix. He got sick one morning and died that night. Clearly a coroner's case. The post was done at the nearest hospital—only thirty beds. The pathologist is an old codger who does maybe four autopsies a year. Need I say more?"

She shook her head. "Viral studies?"

"That's where we're really messed up. Maury almost certainly had a viral illness, but the pathologist made it impossible for us to identify anything. He did take tissue for viral studies. But stored it at the wrong temperature. Nothing viable. His slides were useless."

"Were you able to get your own tissue?"

Harpo threw up his hands. "He injected the body with formalin before he shipped Maury back here. I could strangle the guy."

"Any E-M studies?"

"We can see evidence of cellular damage everywhere on electron microscopy, but there again, viral identification is impossible."

She was leafing through the folder when she came to a photograph that stopped her. She closed her eyes and sat back, resting her hands on the arms of the chair. Her palms were damp. She took a deep breath and looked again at the picture in her lap, not touching it.

"My God, what happened to him, Harpo?"

"I don't know, Kate. If it's an AIDS-related infection, it's one that no one's seen before." He shrugged. "But he didn't have AIDS."

She made herself reach for the picture and held it up in horror. It showed a body with its face chewed away by the ravages of ... something. It may have been a virus, though at this point she wasn't prepared to rule out foul play. She shuddered at the thought and turned back to the picture. She saw lots of blood and some sloughing of skin that revealed a hideous expanse of underlying mushy-looking muscle.

The next picture was a close-up of the face—or what had once been a face. Chunks of dried blood caked the nostrils and rimmed the eyes and mouth, obliterating the features. The skin was puffy, and in places reminded her of odd-looking, multisized red bubbles. The largest one, on the forehead, was the size of a tennis ball.

Kate closed her eyes again. She knew she was hyperventilating, but she couldn't help it. She could feel her fingers and toes begin to tingle. She put the pictures aside and stood up, walking over to the window for air. Harpo was beside her in an instant. He rested a hand on her shoulder.

"Pretty grim, isn't it?" he said softly.

She nodded, staring through a soot-covered glass pane at the grimy walls of the hospital. A far cry from magnolias, though the view somehow suited the occasion.

She called on her professional self, forcing her mind to push through the network of conflicting emotions. Harpo had asked her for help. She would give it, but she needed more details.

"He bled to death?" she asked, still staring out the window. Her throat felt tight, her voice small, as though the words had to squeeze their way out.

"Yes. Every organ in his body showed signs of hemorrhage. The awful thing is the rapidity with which it happened. He and his girlfriend had taken a hike in the mountains the day before. The next morning he thought he had the flu. That night . . ."

Kate's mind seized on the new information. The Southwestern desert. Hemorrhage. "The plague?" she said simply. She knew Harpo must have thought of bubonic plague, which in this modern age no longer spread in epidemic proportions, but could still be deadly, and cause hemorrhage.

"We're still working him up for that, but initial antibodies were negative. And there have been no fatalities in Arizona for years."

"You've checked antibodies to the African hemorrhagic viruses?" She was very familiar with this group of viruses, which were highly contagious and just as lethal because of the way they assaulted the coagulation system of the body.

"You bet. Marburg, Ebola, Lassa, a couple others. Negative. Plus he's never been to Africa. No cases acquired yet in this country, except by lab techs working with the virus."

"What about Congo?"

He gave her a puzzled look. "Congo?"

"A new African virus. Hasn't been written up much yet. Like the others, it's deadly."

He broke into a grin and slammed his fist on the desktop. "I knew you were the right person! You can check antibodies at the CDC?"

"Sure. I'll take back a tube of Maury's serum." She was glad to see Harpo smiling, but she was skeptical that Maury had Congo. Outside the CDC and perhaps one or two research facilities, the virus was nonexistent in the Western hemisphere. Maury didn't die from Congo.

She moved back to the leather chair and picked up the folder, stuffing the pictures back in without looking at them. "Give me time to assimilate this, Harpo."

"Take all the time you need. Why don't we meet after lunch and brainstorm? I'll take you to the physicians' lounge. The library is next door if you want it."

"Actually, a nice coffee shop teeming with life may be just the ticket right now." She took a deep breath as she brushed her hair back.

Harpo laughed. "I see your point. We have a great one just a block away." He paused. "Kate, I have another confession."

"Yes?"

"I didn't really want to request an official CDC consult because I can't stand that jerk who heads up the AIDS division."

"You mean Roger Peck?"

"Yeah. His arrogance is matched only by his ignorance."

"I've got good news for you. Roger's at Fort Thacker now. He didn't fit in at the CDC. For one thing, I think Roger still believes that AIDS is a disease confined only to certain groups of social deviants."

Harpo laughed. "Meaning Dr. Lily-White-Perfection doesn't have a whole lot of motivation to eradicate it?"

"Exactly."

He gave a groan of disgust. "You know something, Kate? If the AIDS virus does succeed in wiping out the human race—which, by the way, I consider a very real possibility—it'll be thanks to ignoramuses like Peck."

"Harpo, you have a way with words. I couldn't have summarized more eloquently myself."

He smiled. "But now you're here ... Why bring in the whole CDC and make a big to-do when I've got their best investigator all to myself?"

"Absolutely, my dear classmate."

Kate spread her things out in a booth toward the back of the coffee shop. The place was just as she'd imagined—people everywhere, coming, going, smiling, grumbling, eating, slurping coffee. She loved it. She even loved the din of voices accented by the clinking of plates, cups, and silverware. The brisk ambience helped her shake the sickening feeling she had been left with after seeing the photographs of Akendo

Maury. She was even able to forget for a moment that she had just plunked Maury's folder on the table in front of her.

The waitress, a chunky woman with a brusque manner and a nasal accent, almost beat Kate to the table. "What'll it be, hon?" She leaned over to pour a cup of coffee while she simultaneously extracted a pad from the pocket of her white apron and whipped a pencil from behind her ear. Her name tag said to call her Sal.

"I'll have a cheese Danish, please," said Kate, ignoring the menu. New York had the best Danishes in the world.

She opened the folder on Maury after her Danish arrived, careful to keep the pictures face down in the back of the chart. She leafed through the pathologist's gross and microscopic autopsy report and found nothing she hadn't already learned from Harpo. She was relieved to note that the possibility of violence had been addressed and dismissed. No gunshot or stab wounds, no evidence of blunt trauma.

As she completed the Arizona doctor's report, she realized he hadn't examined the brain. Not that unusual, probably per the family's request. People had a hard enough time allowing the bodies of their loved ones to be violated by a knife after death, much less the brain. For many, the idea of taking a saw to the skull and slicing into the brain was more than they could endure. Nevertheless, Kate made a notation on a separate sheet of paper to talk to Harpo about considering opening the skull. If the source of infection had been the brain or meninges, the diagnostic approach would be different.

She moved on to the tests Harpo had ordered since receiving the body. With the exception of Congo, there were studies on every virus she could think of that would cause the body's coagulation system to go haywire. They were all negative, as she would have expected. None of the hemorrhagic viruses were endemic to the United States. Most originated in Africa, and, thank God, had not spread beyond there.

On the other hand, she was well aware that almost any virus or bacteria could break down normal coagulation if it got enough of a hold in the body. She looked over Harpo's list of positive antibody results. They represented antibodies that just about everyone had at Maury's age: mumps, measles, and chicken pox.

The trouble with most antibody levels was that they only told whether the patient had been exposed in the past and had no direct bearing on the present. For that, they really needed another sample of blood a few weeks down the line for comparison. If the titers went up, that was more suggestive of recent infection. Of course, in Maury's case, this would not be possible.

She jotted down the positive antibody findings, including one she came across for herpes simplex. Again, she knew many people were positive for herpes type I, yet may never have known they'd been infected. At most, they had an occasional canker sore. But there was always the rare unfortunate individual whose immune system would somehow allow these relatively innocuous viruses through the ranks, whereupon all hell would break loose. And with an HIV positive patient, such a dilemma was not unusual.

As she finished reading, she jotted down a few suggestions for Harpo, and a reminder to herself to take a look at the tissue cultures. Unfortunately, she knew these would be pretty useless for the reasons Harpo had enumerated. She wondered if she ought to look at the body, though Harpo had told her the pictures were probably as helpful.

The waitress came back with more coffee and refilled her cup. She eyed the folder. "You a lawyer, hon?" she asked with what Kate took to be terse New York friendliness. The "hon" part grated on her, but she had learned years ago not to overreact once she saw that the gray-haired chief of medicine, a male, was often given the same endearing nickname by his patients.

She smiled. "I'm a doctor."

Sal gave a hearty chuckle. "Nice to see a gal who knows how to hold her own." She pulled her pad out. "Anything else, hon?"

"How about another Danish for the road? That was one of the best I've ever had."

"Be right back."

She pulled out her compact and deftly reapplied her lipstick. She snapped it closed, stuffed it back into her handbag, and took a deep breath. She needed to look once more at those pictures of Maury. To see them again after the initial shock, give them a more objective perusal. She looked around to make sure no one was watching, then turned the two photos face up. She studied them with a clinical detachment that she hadn't been able to muster earlier. Yet she wasn't seeing anything that hadn't already been dramatically imprinted in her memory. Except maybe . . . She bent down for a closer look, wishing she'd brought a magnifying glass.

"Oh my gawd!" Sal had suddenly appeared with the check and was peering over Kate's shoulder.

Kate's hand reflexively covered the photos as her head shot up.

"What happened to him?" Sal's tough exterior looked as though it had suffered a deep gash.

"I wish I knew," Kate said, closing the folder. She felt her annoyance ebb as she noticed a spray of goose bumps on Sal's fleshy arms. "I'm sorry you had to see it."

Sal didn't take long to recover. "I've seen a lot in my day, hon. That poor soul. Looks like someone dipped him in a vat of scalding water." She shook her head as she parked her pencil behind her ear.

Scalding water. The phrase poked at something in Kate's brain. Of course! The scalded skin syndrome. Why hadn't she thought of it? She had never seen a case, but it was a well-documented, albeit rare, complication of staphylococcal bacterial infections.

She guessed Harpo hadn't thought of it, either. No staph was growing from the cultures, but that didn't matter. It wasn't too late. They could still check the blood for the culprit, staphylococcal exotoxin. Kate felt like cheering. Thanks to serendipity and one nosy waitress, she might be able to put the several manifestations of Maury's terrible misfortune under one roof with the diagnosis of staph sepsis.

"Thank you," she said to Sal, as she picked up the check and took out her wallet. "You've been a big help." She slipped a ten-dollar bill under her coffee cup and slid out of the booth.

Sal swept up the ten and ran after her. "Don't forget your Danish, hon!"

CHAPTER FIVE

"Okay, Steve, thanks for calling.

Elliot Halsey, chief executive officer of Alatron Pharmaceuticals outside Denville, New Jersey, stared at the phone. His hand felt like it belonged to someone else as he watched it slowly return the receiver to its cradle.

He felt like screaming, the pain was that strong. His son, Barry, was in the hospital. Again. This time with diarrhea and dehydration.

His eyes stung. When would it end? Then came the familiar tightness in his throat, the dam holding back the tears. For he knew the answer. Never. It would never end. Not until Barry was dead.

Because his son Barry, twenty-three years old, had AIDS.

Halsey rose heavily and moved his tall frame to the window. Even his limbs felt heavy, as though gravity were his adversary. He looked out over the vast Alatron complex. As he took in the brightness of the early summer day, the colorful splashes of flowers and the magnificent fountain below, he could only feel his anguish build. Such beauty seemed to stand in defiance of a perennial lament: Why? The question never left him. It haunted him, threaded its way into every facet of his life.

Why did Barry, so full of life's magic, have to taste life's tragedy so soon? He tried not to agonize about it, tried to accept it. The way Barry did. There was so much he could learn from his son. There always had been.

Halsey turned back to his desk, knowing he had to move on. Push through personal hardship and get back to the cold reality of running a company. Besides, he told himself with a bitterness he was still learning to swallow, he knew why Barry had AIDS. Barry was gay. He belonged to one of those risk groups that people were so fond of citing. It was a way to reassure themselves that *they* couldn't get AIDS.

Like hell they couldn't.

It was this realization that made him so determined to steer his company with a heavy hand. He could see the writing on the wall, even if the rest of the board couldn't. AIDS was a disease that was evolving, changing form, like a living organism. In a way, it *was* a living organism, thriving on the ignorance of the life forms upon which it fed.

For Elliot Halsey knew there was really only one risk for acquiring AIDS. And that was simply being alive.

He reached for the phone to call Susan, his ex-wife, in Indiana. He wanted to call Barry, but Steve, Barry's lover, had suggested waiting until tomorrow. Barry was resting peacefully now for the first time in days.

Susan and Halsey weren't that close, but where Barry was concerned their tie was strong. They were parents, and they would always have that connection. Even after Barry was long gone, the memories would give them a special bond. The joys and heartaches of raising a son, and the wrenching tragedy of losing him. It would all be there, locked in their minds as long as they lived. He could feel the lump in his throat swell.

As he dialed Susan's number, he saw the button for his private line light up. He stopped and punched the button to switch lines, his heart thrumming in his chest. It had to be about Barry.

"Hello?"

He heard an impersonal hum on the line. "Hello, hello?"

Then he had a sinking feeling as he heard the voice. And the same low nasty snicker he had heard before. " 'The time is come, the day of trouble is near.' " The voice was soft, menacing.

"Who is this?" he demanded.

" 'Thou shalt remember thy ways, and be ashamed,' " the voice went on, undaunted.

"Who the hell are you?" Halsey felt the bile rush to his throat. A surge of feeling, an amalgam of anger, frustration, and fear, made his head reel. He kept seeing Barry, but the voice kept drawing him into the phone.

A laugh. "It's Ezekiel, Elliot."

Halsey felt a jolt. It took him a moment to realize why. "How do you know my name?"

"Read the Bible, Elliot," the voice went on, ignoring the query. "You'll understand in due time." A caustic laugh. A click. A dial tone. It was over.

Halsey hung up and sat back, running his hands through his dark graying hair. His world was spinning out of control. He could feel his breath catch as he tried to make sense of it all. This was the second threatening call he had received in the last month, the fourth in the past six months. He hadn't been counting—till now.

The first few he had passed off as flukes. He was prepared to shrug this one off as well, but he knew he wouldn't succeed. Not when he had been addressed by name. Not when the call had come through on his private line. He couldn't remember how the others had come. But he was sure this was the first time the caller had actually used his name. Now he would have to consider the possibility that none of the calls had been from some innocuous prankster.

Halsey was used to cranks. There were any number of people unhappy with a large corporation, and the CEO was among those most likely to take the brunt of abuse. But usually the calls were quite specific in their demands. Not some biblical mumbo jumbo.

As Halsey reflected on the past few months he let his mind ramble, pushing open doors previously sealed shut. For there had been other strange and disconcerting events, not just the calls. He had experienced more than the usual turns of bad luck, even for a chief executive. But actually, as he thought about it, most of the adversity had involved his personal life.

There had been the nontrip to Indiana last Christmas to visit his seventeen-year-old daughter Mara, and Barry, who requested they all spend Christmas together. Barry's plea had touched his heart. They all knew, though nobody was saying it, that Barry would not have many Christmases left. Even Susan had been enthusiastic about Halsey's coming.

He could feel his throat tighten again as he recalled what happened. When he arrived at the airport he learned his reservation had been canceled. By someone. Or perhaps a computer fluke.

What with the holiday traffic, he couldn't book another flight, and he missed the reunion. He tried to shrug it all off but an odd superstition stayed with him, a gnawing fear that maybe he had missed the last chance for them all to be together.

He saw Barry several times after that, since Barry lived and worked in Manhattan as an assistant editor in a publishing house. Barry had seemed a little cool after the Christmas fiasco, as though Halsey had deliberately canceled out. That had hurt. And he saw Mara when she came to New York over spring break. But it just wasn't the same.

As for the flight mix-up, he knew people got bumped all the time, especially during the holidays. He left it at that.

But when he added that to some of the other messups, he had to wonder. There had been the trip to the Caribbean with Liz, the woman he had been dating for over a year. Their relationship had been strained for months and he suggested the trip as a way to revitalize it. He took little cash, relying on plastic. But when he went to use his MasterCard, he learned it had been reported missing. He even found himself accused of stealing his own card. To make matters worse, his other credit cards *were* missing.

Then, as though some pagan god of the islands had placed a curse on him, the hotel had no record of his reservation. After much fuming and fighting he and Liz ended up in the Caribbean equivalent of a Motel Six with no money and only Liz's American Express card.

Hardly a vacation. They had to cut it short. And that's exactly how he was left feeling—short. It wasn't long after that he and Liz drifted apart. The trip had been the last straw.

He knew he could remember other such incidents, if he put his mind to it. He chose not to. But he looked back on his behavior over the past six months and realized he was gradually withdrawing from social obligations and pleasures, like a child who had been burned too many times. Increasingly he immersed himself in his work, sitting through dull meetings, hovering over the researchers until he made a nuisance of himself. Immersed, yet distracted in an odd sort of way. He had even converted the office adjacent to his into a studio apartment of sorts and often slept over.

He felt a stab of fear. Had someone been doing this to him? Shaping his life without his knowing it?

Ridiculous. Maybe he needed more sleep. Or exercise. Though he considered himself fit for a man of forty-five. He worked out at the gym three days a week and ran on alternate days. Played some racquetball at times, but not for months now. Another sign of his changing lifestyle.

If someone was toying with him, it had to be someone familiar with his every move. Someone who seemed to know him better than he knew himself. He could think of no one in his life who would even qualify.

He thought of Gil Stryker and his pack of AIDS FIRST demonstrators. They were hostile enough. But even so, it was Alatron they were after, not him. And their attacks were overt, straightforward—not fraught with twisted malice. The calls were not their style.

He shook his head. He was letting his imagination run away with him. Because of that phone call. And because of the news about Barry.

He took a deep breath and got up from his desk to pour a cup of coffee. As he sat down again, he wondered if he was going to pull through. And if Alatron was going to pull through. It seemed as though his life had become synonymous with the life of the company. And they were both faltering.

Alatron had had its ups and downs over the past few years. Before Halsey took the helm, they had put all their eggs in one basket, banking on a new clot-busting drug for treating heart attacks. The drug, Tendol, looked promising. It worked better than any drug out there. The whole medical profession had been waiting for it. But when Tendol finally hit the market, it soon became apparent that the incidence of brain hemorrhage was alarmingly high. Alatron quickly withdrew the drug and their stock took a nosedive. An eighty-million-dollar tax credit.

During the difficult times that ensued the company managed to avoid merging with more economically robust companies and resisted buyout offers. Under Halsey's guidance they turned their attention to AIDS drugs and a promising new drug for Alzheimer's disease. They were settling back into a healthy growth curve. But would it last?

No drug company these days escaped harsh public scrutiny. And nobody was more aware of this than Halsey. Pharmaceutical companies were painted as ogres out to make a buck without giving a damn about the "victims" of the drugs they produced. If a company like Alatron had the courage and social-mindedness to turn its efforts to AIDS, as he had persuaded his board of directors to do, the public became even more demanding: Why wasn't Alatron moving faster? Why was the company charging astronomical prices for its two new AIDS-fighting drugs? Why weren't they handing the drugs out for nothing?

It was a double bind of the worst kind. The company could do nothing right. If they set up a program for compassionate use, the question came back at them—why hadn't they done it sooner? If they dropped their price on Virostat, their best drug against AIDS, it was "See? We knew you were taking us to the cleaners!" That, amid a clamor for more government controls on profit-hungry drug companies.

The battles Halsey found himself fighting seemed futile and unnecessary. He knew now he had made a big mistake in accepting the CEO position. He had taken it in a moment of exalted vision—what his ex-wife called his white knight syndrome. He was convinced that by stepping out of the role of scientist and putting on the hat of chief executive, he could lift Alatron out of its doldrums. Turn the company into a leader—a trailblazer in the fight against AIDS.

He sighed, staring out the window. He should have stayed on the scientific end of things. He had the background in microbiology. True, Alatron's successes since he took over could to some extent be attributed to him as he pointed the company to the future. But most of his contributions had come earlier in his research role. His dogged pursuit in using the live AIDS virus, and working on ways to modify it to make it safe for use in vaccine development, had given Alatron its edge in the race toward a successful AIDS vaccine.

He knew now he should have been suspicious when the board took so readily to his suggestion that he be chief operating officer. It just so happened, they said all too eagerly, that they were in the process of restructuring. Would he like to be chief executive officer as well? What could he say but yes?

He soon learned about restructuring. The CEO's authority was being gradually restructured out of existence. Lowell Bekin, the board member holding the most shares in the company, was doing his best to take over.

Halsey realized he should have seen it coming. Having him on the board allowed Bekin to keep him in tow. Bekin and the rest seemed to take a perverse pleasure in denying him the resources he requested. When he wanted the final word in hiring the head of the AIDS vaccine project, they had listened politely enough, then brought in their own pick, Dave Parsons, a pharmacist by training, with a stellar background in sales. Halsey considered Parsons completely wrong for the job.

He finished his coffee and turned to Parsons's report, glaring proof that he was right. He grimaced as he leafed through Parsons's shabbily prepared account of the first phase of the AIDS vaccine pilot project. It showed no understanding of the scientific method. Where the project was to have been a double-blind study, meaning some people got the vaccine and others got a placebo, Parsons had eliminated the placebo. Halsey cursed to himself.

As he read on, he knew what he had to do. It didn't matter what the board thought. He had checked the company bylaws. In emergency situations, summary suspension of any employee was within jurisdiction of the CEO. And this could become an emergency, if it wasn't already.

CHAPTER SIX

Dave Parsons sat across from the glowering CEO. Parsons was a short, squat man with thinning hair and a bland pudgy face. He made up for his lack of stature by wearing expensive tailored suits and cultivating an engaging manner that had years earlier shot him to the top of the heap in sales. He was good, damn good. A foot-in-the-door man if there ever was one.

So what he was hearing now was incomprehensible. And therefore couldn't be true. Halsey couldn't fire him. The board would reverse it in a flash. He would call Lowell Bekin as soon as Halsey finished reaming him out. Meanwhile, he tried to decide how to play it.

Once he looked at it that way—as a game—he could feel the knot in his gut ease up. He knew Halsey was a no-nonsense type of guy. So he would play it cool yet concerned.

He looked down at his well-manicured nails. "I don't understand," he said. "I'm dedicated to this [   ] t's my life." He looked up with a puzzled [   ] n't the dismissal of an executive a board [   ] Yeah, way to go, Dave. Play dumb.

He watched the Alatron CEO tap his fingers impatiently on the desk, his face a picture of disgust. Halsey wasn't buying it. He could feel the dark eyes pierce his smooth facade. He shifted in his seat and smiled nervously.

Halsey held up Parson's report. "This is one of the worst pieces of work I've ever seen. The AIDS vaccine is our most important project. I can and will take full responsibility for dismissing you."

Parsons stared at the neat creases in his trousers—Italian made and carefully fitted. He had a closet full.

He considered storming out. Why should he have to put up with this bull? After all, he was a company man. It was Halsey who was the maverick, the peg that didn't fit.

He crossed his legs and wiggled his foot, the leather of his sleek Italian shoe creaking. He liked the sound. Simmer down, he told himself. The board will come through. He smiled to himself as he imagined the look on Halsey's face if he were to learn what was *really* going on.

"Well," he said with a shrug. "You're the boss. Uh, you don't mind if I discuss this with the board. They *are* the ones who hired me."

"Discuss it with whomever you wish. You have a month to finish up, find yourself another position."

Parsons suddenly felt his heart race, his stomach churn. Halsey didn't seem the least bit put off by his reference to the board. What if the man really could fire him? His world would fall apart. Everything he'd been working toward gone—money, prestige, women, a European villa—the list was endless.

He had a month to follow through on the coup that would change his life. A month. He shot his cuffs and studied his fourteen-karat-gold cufflinks. They glittered at him. He felt his confidence return. He could do it.

He stood up, full of apologies and no explanations. Not that Halsey expected any. Halsey clearly considered him inept. Well, let him. He offered a few platitudes about how he would try harder.

As he arrived back in his own office, he let his mind ramble, grasping for the straws that would restore his confidence. He remembered well how he had brought it off—the coup. It had started with Gil Stryker, the AIDS FIRST leader. He met Stryker in the hovel they called headquarters, which was nothing more than a battered old van. Stryker gave him a suspicious look as he climbed in.

"I've got a deal for you," Parsons said after introducing himself. He looked Stryker over closely with an accomplished salesman's eye and made a quick assessment. The wary activist was young and muscular, early thirties. He had fiery red hair and an equally brilliant beard. A perfect male specimen. You'd never guess he was a fag.

Stryker stared at him with narrowed green eyes, not bothering to invite him to sit down. "We don't make deals," he growled.

Parsons chuckled and took a seat anyway. "Of course you don't. But what if I told you I've got something so big you might want to make an exception?"

Stryker continued to watch him with a deepening scowl, yet made no move to throw him out. Parsons smiled to himself. Haven't lost your touch, Dave. Even with this militant queer you get your foot in the door before he knows what hit him.

"You want to hear it or not?" asked Parsons, enjoying Stryker's undivided attention.

Stryker sat back and propped his feet on the flimsy metal table that served as a desk. He laced his hands behind his head. Parsons noted the activist was wearing what looked like a pair of combat boots. How appropriate. But what he really noticed was that he had Stryker hooked. A guy doesn't go out of his way to look nonchalant unless he's feeling just the opposite. Only the yawn was missing.

"All right," Parsons said, leaning forward, elbows on knees. "Here's the deal. You want this vaccine project to go forward at a rate somewhat faster than a snail's pace—am I right?"

Stryker gave a snort of disgust. "We've spent the good part of a year putting our freedom on the line to make that point."

Parsons grinned, undaunted. "Do I detect a note of sarcasm?" He sat back and propped a foot across his knee. "Okay, I see you're a no-nonsense kind of guy. My kind of person. So let's cut to the chase. The FDA is the stumbling block here. You know it, I know it. We gotta jump through so many hoops for those pencil pushers we don't know whether we got us a circus or a drug company."

He paused, deliciously enjoying the fact that Stryker was no longer bothering to appear bored or even hostile. "I've got a plan for sidestepping the FDA that'll knock your socks off. We've got the vaccine ready to go, all packaged in neat little vials. What if we, me and you, conduct our own little study? Recruit our own volunteers—HIV negative—administer the vaccine ourselves, keep our own records. I say 'we' because I need you guys to pull it off. I can't use Alatron people for obvious reasons."

Stryker eyed him warily. "What's in it for you?"

Parsons stared at the activist. What was wrong with this guy? "What do you care? You want to see the vaccine thrown away on a bunch of rats and monkeys just because the FDA doesn't have the guts to let us try it on humans?"

"You haven't answered my question."

Parsons emitted a short laugh. "I have my own motives, it's true. But let me ask you something. What do you care what I get out of it as long as you get what you want?"

Stryker gave him a scathing look. "You're just a shyster, like all the rest."

Parsons lurched forward and grabbed Stryker by the shoulders. "Don't you get it? Phase Three trials for the live vaccine in humans are *years* off. Thanks to all the bureaucrats who could care less what happens to guys like you. I'm offering you the chance of a lifetime."

Stryker flung his arms out and shot to his feet. "Take your hands off me!" He towered over Parsons. "Don't think for a minute I believe a corporate creep like you gives a damn about AIDS or what happens to—quote—guys like me."

Parsons fell back in the chair, startled by Stryker's vehemence but not dissuaded. He was used to having the door slammed in his face. "Sure there's something in it for me," he admitted. "We get results, we take 'em to the media. With the help of media hype we won't need that much. Maybe fifty to a hundred subjects. We vaccinate 'em, turn in our initial results after a year. We get a good statistician, we can make the figures look just like we want 'em to. The FDA will be too embarrassed to come down on us. You'll have your vaccine. Me, I'll be the guy who made it happen. I can write my own ticket."

He could see it in his mind's eye. The phone ringing off the hook. Interviews galore. The *New York Times, USA Today,* the *Washington Post. Larry King Live.* You name it.

He looked up at Stryker who was still standing over him, his arms folded across his chest. "Suppose something goes wrong?" said Stryker.

He gave Stryker a look of befuddlement. "Like what?"

"Side effects, for one."

He threw up his hands. "Side effects, schmide effects. Hell, the vaccine is harmless." He pointed a finger at Stryker. "Why am I sitting here having to convince you? You're the ones handcuffing yourselves to flagpoles, risking your freedom, as you so aptly put it."

Stryker moved to sit down, putting his feet back up on the desk. "What do you want from us?"

"Like I said, I'll need your help rounding up volunteers. On the QT of course. But I can't bring any of this off until I'm head of the project. *That's* where you boys come in. Let's face it. You guys are a pain in the neck. So here's the pitch I make to the board—tit for tat. They give me the job as vaccine project director. I get AIDS FIRST off their backs. You guys lay low, tone down the demonstrations and bad P.R."

Stryker stared at the ceiling, forming a steeple with his fingers. He laughed softly. "What makes you think the board will go for it?"

"*Go* for it? Hell, they'll think it's Christmas. You guys are the bane of their existence."

Stryker dropped his feet to the floor. "Meet me and my partner Paul Resnick here, tonight."

The deal went through. Parsons got the position. His clandestine project was underway. Not everything had run smoothly. Resnick hadn't gone for it. Stryker and Resnick even split up over it. And there was the little matter of the AIDS FIRSTers not keeping their word, if you could believe the racket going on outside.

He sat down and turned on his computer with a renewed sense of urgency. A month. He had work to do. He knew he was right. It made no sense to test a vaccine that was supposed to *prevent* a disease in people who already *had* the disease. It was the people who *didn't* have AIDS who needed the drug.

So his volunteers were HIV negative. He took a few people from each of the cities used for the legitimate pilot project. No problem finding volunteers—just hit the risk groups—hospital workers, gays, the sexually promiscuous. He and Stryker agreed to steer clear of the drug addicts. Too many problems.

Once the word seeped out—AIDS FIRST had all kinds of connections—people were pounding at his door. They accepted the stipulation of complete secrecy without hesitation.

Parsons maintained secrecy by keeping his own records on the project and storing them in a locked file. He contacted the volunteers himself to mark their progress and forbade them to call him at work. He had, in a few months, accumulated a respectable number of volunteers, about twenty in all. Not all had gotten the live virus, though—only this last round. Even he was cautious. He tried first using the earlier version of the vaccine. The one made up of DNA fragments from the viral shell—the same vaccine other companies were using. Not risky. And no problems yet.

He examined the computer printout before him. The results were dull, dull, dull. The guys with AIDS who had gotten the vaccine were continuing on with AIDS. The vaccine didn't seem to be slowing the course of the disease.

He reached into his briefcase, which was stashed in the bottom drawer of his desk, and came out with his unofficial list of volunteers. It was time to make his second round of calls this week. This time it was a very special group. The first HIV negatives to get the live virus. The initial round of calls had gone well.

He was feeling a glow of confidence and a tingle of excitement as he punched out the number of the first name on the list. The hell with Halsey.

The call was to Terry Alderfer, a mortician. He remembered Alderfer well. A real weirdo, complaining about how nobody thought of morticians as a high-risk group for AIDS. We're always messing with dead people's blood, the guy had said with a leer. Parsons shuddered. Takes all kinds.

"Heaven's Haven, how may I help you?"

Parsons felt a moment of relief as he recognized Alderfer's voice. Though he wasn't about to admit it, he was worried that something could go wrong. Whose law was that? Whatever can go wrong will go wrong? Couldn't remember. Murphy's, maybe. Oh well, Alderfer sounded healthy enough.

"Mr. Alderfer? Dave Parsons."

"Oh, yes, Mr. Parsons. How may I help you?"

Surely Alderfer remembered him? He had just talked to him a week ago, the day after receiving the vaccine. "How's your arm?"

"My arm?"

"The vaccine?"

"Oh, yes. Yes. Why, it's just fine, just fine."

"Any temperature?"

"Oh, I forgot to check, but I feel just fine."

Parsons went on down his protocol, largely taken from the one devised by the research department at Alatron. His confidence grew as he shot questions at Alderfer, who answered them as quickly as Parsons could ask them. A piece of cake. Alderfer was in good shape. No reactions. No questions.

After he hung up with Alderfer, Parsons dialed the

next name on the list, Ramon Fernandez. No answer. Probably out on the streets. Ramon was a cross-dresser, and also went by Ramona. Parsons snorted and shook his head. A colorful guy, Ramon. Amazing he was still HIV negative. He made a note to call Ramon tomorrow.

He moved on to number three, Lorna Mankevich, and was told by her boyfriend she was out of town. Parsons put a check mark next to "no reaction." Obviously doing okay if she could travel. He smiled, his confidence building. An image of a chagrined Elliot Halsey flitted through his mind. He was on a roll.

He had one more person to call in the Los Angeles area, Danny Townsend, a lab tech. Townsend had confided that he was gay, but HIV negative on four separate occasions over the previous six months. He had been almost desperate to try the vaccine. Townsend seemed sure he was going to get AIDS—like it was his karma, somehow. He had even used that word—karma. Jesus. What could you expect from those California fruits?

Parsons was about to hang up when a low, barely audible voice said, "Hello?"

"Danny Townsend, please."

There was a long, disquieting pause. "Hello? Hello? Someone there?" Parsons said impatiently.

"Who is this, please?" the voice said, almost whined.

"An acquaintance. Tell him it's Parsons, long distance. He'll know."

"I'm sorry," the voice said. "Danny has ... passed away."

"What!!?" Parsons jerked bolt upright and stared at the list before him, forcing his eyes to zero in on the biographical sketch he had compiled on Danny Townsend. Townsend was a healthy thirty-year-old male. He had received 0.5cc of Alatron's AIDS vaccine into the deltoid muscle of the right arm one week earlier. He had reported a slight reddening of the arm a few hours after the injection, and a mild feverish feeling a day later. Otherwise, he was doing fine.

"What happened?" He stood and began pacing in a tight little circle, the phone in his hand. He rummaged through his desk for something to quell the tempest brewing in his stomach. He swigged down half a bottle of chalky white antacid.

"I don't know. Nobody knows. He went for a hike and . . ."

"You've got to know something, dammit!" Parsons could feel himself on the verge of panic. Relax, he told himself. You're overreacting, that's all. Coincidence, got nothing to do with you. Take it easy. He wiped his brow.

"Just who is this?" The whiny voice had acquired a hint of authority, as though its owner sensed the desperation on the other end.

Parsons knew he wasn't getting anywhere. "Never mind," he snapped and slammed the phone down. He looked at the list—he had a few more calls to make. He couldn't do anything right now. He had to get out. Get a drink. Something, anything.

His hand moved toward the phone again as he thought of Stryker. Maybe his guys had messed up. They had administered the vaccine. He drew his hand back. No, he didn't think he'd better tell Stryker yet.

He grabbed his jacket and shoved the list into his briefcase. He threw the briefcase into his desk drawer and exploded through the door into the corridor, pushing past a janitor sweeping up. He was in too much of a hurry to see the strange twisted smile on the janitor's lips. Not that it would have meant anything to him.

*   *   *

Keith Heinman watched Dave Parsons's back disappear down the hall. He felt a wave of disgust. Parsons had the fat cushy rear end of a man who sat around all day emitting orders. He pushed his broom around a few more times, shot a glance down the empty corridor, and pulled out the keys. He let himself into Parsons's office and locked the door behind him.

He couldn't believe his luck. To have a numbskull like Parsons paving the way was almost an embarrassment. It was too easy. This was not how he had planned it. He had been watching Parsons for weeks now, and decided that using the fat Alatron executive for this part would work better than the plan he had already worked out. But Parsons would need Heinman riding him every minute, which could get tiresome fast. Parsons was ambitious, but like most ordinary types shooting for the top of the heap, he was weak-kneed when the going got rough. And the involvement of AIDS FIRST added a big unpredictability factor.

Heinman sat at Parsons's desk and rummaged through the drawers, at first finding only personal items like bottles of aspirin and antacids. Then he came on the briefcase. He pulled out Parsons's list. His eyes ran down the checklist that Parsons had filled out, and when he came to Danny Townsend, like Parsons, he stopped. A shaky-looking check mark had been made in the "expired" column. And he knew why. He felt a bolt of excitement shoot through him like electricity.

Townsend's death had to be what freaked Parsons out. Parsons hadn't gone on to the next name on the list. He felt another thrill, almost orgasmic in its intensity. He studied the list a bit longer, savoring the feeling.

Finally, he got up and inspected the file cabinets.

He rifled through the file folders. Mundane stuff. Protocols, rules, forms. Then he noted a drawer marked Miscellaneous. It was locked. He smiled. It looked promising. He had no difficulty picking the lock.

After examining the file marked PARTICIPANTS, he went back to Parsons's checklist. Same names. He sat back and considered his next move. Things were going better than planned at this point, thanks to the greed of one David S. Parsons. "S" for stupid. Parsons had already set it up, even doing the footwork for him.

But he wanted more participants, bigger numbers. No one was going to notice a death here, a death there. It was time to expand. And good old Dave was going to help him.

He stood up, stretched, and returned the file to its proper place. He consulted his watch and decided to make a call on his newfound friend and colleague. He knew exactly what he needed. And he knew which bar Parsons frequented after a hard day of plugging quarters into the Coke machine.

Heinman worked his way through the crowd of Happy Hour enthusiasts. He had changed into a white T-shirt and jeans. Cigarette smoke hung in the air like a stagnant cloud but he was able to spot Dave Parsons easily. He was seated on a barstool smiling like a hyena at a tall blond woman with a beehive hairdo and fingernails like red stilettos. Parsons's thin head of hair was mussed and his face was slack. He looked like he was on his fourth or fifth drink.

Heinman agilely slipped between Parsons and the blonde and gave Parsons a clap on the shoulder. "Dave, buddy, I knew I'd find you here."

Parsons looked at him blankly, then a scowl formed on his face. "Hey . . ." he muttered, trying to catch the blonde's eye over Heinman's shoulder.

Heinman turned to the blonde and smiled. "You'll have to excuse my buddy. He promised me the next dance." He put his arm around Parsons and the woman slipped away with a scornful look.

"Hey . . ." said Parsons.

"It's okay, Dave. You and I have important business to discuss."

Parsons gave Heinman a feeble push. "What're you doing? I don't even know you!"

Heinman smiled and hailed the bartender, ordering himself a club soda and Parsons a coffee. "You're going to know me, Dave. We're going to be partners, you and me."

Parsons's eyes focused on Heinman's face and a hint of recognition spread over his features. "You're the janitor. What the hell . . ."

Suddenly Heinman had Parsons's full attention as he leveled him with his eyes and said in a low but distinct voice, "Dave, I know about your little vaccine project. You're in over your head. But don't worry. I'm going to help you."

Parsons felt a cold claw of fear tearing at his stomach. He looked around, as though trying to spot a vat of antacid. He looked at Heinman and closed his eyes. Someone tell me this isn't happening, he thought. Something else told the cocksure salesman to say nothing. Some instinct for survival that was set off the moment he let himself see those ice-cold blue eyes.

Heinman sipped his drink and pushed the coffee at Parsons. They were both oblivious to the din of the crowd and the random pokes of elbows. "You need to expand your list, Dave."

"What?" said Parsons with a start.

"You heard me. I want another fifty volunteers, from all over the country."

Parsons's mind felt like a nuclear blast had gone off

and it was fallout time. Everything kept dumping on him. He had given up trying to figure out why a god-damn janitor was sitting in a bar bossing him around. Much less, how the goddamn janitor knew all about his project. Then he couldn't get rid of that other enigma—the image of Danny Townsend.

"Piece-a cake," slurred Parsons with a twinge of sarcasm.

"You're due to make site visits to five cities next week. See if you can move it up to this week."

"Sure," said Parsons. He knew he must be sounding agreeable. He didn't feel that way. He wasn't quite sure how he felt. He was too stunned.

"Contact me at Alatron the day before you're ready to leave. Here's my name and beeper number." Hein-man slipped him a small piece of paper.

Parsons took the paper and shoved it in his pocket without looking. He felt numb.

Heinman gave Parsons a clap on the back. "I'm sure you'll think of some questions. I'm available any time." He rose and was gone.

Parsons looked around the bar. No one gave him a glance. He suddenly felt small and invisible. He tried to feel indignant. What made this janitor character think he, Dave Parsons, would do his bidding? What made him think Parsons wouldn't report him—get him fired? Somehow, the answer didn't matter, because he knew it was irrelevant.

He tossed a wad of bills on the bar and pushed his way through the crowd into the quiet street.

He dreaded tonight. He dreaded tomorrow. Dave Parsons, the man with the foot in the door, had just gotten it stomped. He doubted he would ever recover.

CHAPTER SEVEN

Kate Crane was back in her cramped Atlanta office after a few harrowing days with Harpo and the Maury case. She stared at the green print on the screen before her. She tapped the search button and typed in "AIDS," then cross-referenced it with "skin disorders." She sat back and folded her arms as the computer digested her commands. The screen went dark except for a polite message—green—that told her to wait.

She heard a knock at the door and spotted an all too familiar shadow through the frosted glass. "Come in, Roger," she called, a hint of annoyance in her voice.

A tall, white-coated man in his fifties entered. She looked up briefly and gave him a curt nod. As she took in his tortoise-shell bifocals, receding hairline, and unctuous smile, she wondered how she had ever found him attractive. Yet she had. Along with a string of other women. There was something about a womanizer that made him appealing to his prey. She guessed it reflected some primordial instinct between the sexes—a magnetism that had probably kept the human race going all these millennia.

As she saw Peck giving her the once-over, she shuddered. One thing about instinct—it could be overridden by judgment. And in her judgment, Roger Peck was a loser. Scientist turned bureaucrat—the worst kind of turncoat. She wondered how he managed to find time for playing up to the media. His name was always popping up.

"How'd you know it was me?" said Peck casually as he dropped into a chair.

She shrugged without taking her eyes off the screen. The computer was starting to spew forth the information she wanted. Her eyebrow shot up. "I think it was the forked tongue."

He gave an artificial laugh. "Be nice, Kate."

She jotted down a reference, removed her glasses and leveled her eyes at him. "What do you want, Roger? A few secrets to take back to Fort Thacker? Having a little chat with the *National Enquirer* later?"

"You know, you're much prettier when you smile," he said as he rummaged through his pockets for his pipe.

"Please get to the point. I don't have time for this."

He smiled again, revealing a splendid set of even white teeth. Fangs, she thought.

"The point is this, Kate." He jammed the pipe into his mouth and held up a hand as he saw she was about to object. "Don't worry, I'm not going to light it." He tapped the bowl with a well-manicured finger. "I hear you're on the Akendo Maury case."

As Peck's words met with silence, he shifted in his chair and cleared his throat. "I don't have to tell you that you're obliged to keep Fort Thacker apprised of anything AIDS-related. Government orders."

She turned off the computer monitor and swiveled

her chair toward him. "I'm doing a favor for an old friend, and it is none of your business, Roger. Let's leave it at that."

"AIDS is my business, Kate. It doesn't matter how you got involved. You have to keep me updated."

She'd been expecting this. She took a deep breath. "What I have on the Maury case at this point is preliminary, and strictly between Harpo and me."

He gave a rude laugh. "Harpo? Harp-o?"

She reached for the phone.

"Going to call Chuckie?" His voice dropped. "Don't bother, Kate. Kekich and I see eye to eye on this."

She held the receiver to her ear and gave Peck a searing look. "Maureen? It's Kate Crane. Can you run off a copy of an *Annals* article, pages twenty-five through thirty, volume ninety, number eight, and get it to me by five?" A pause. "Great, thanks."

She put the receiver back and stood up. "Is there anything else, Roger? I have work to do."

He rose, dropping his pipe back into a pocket of his white coat. "Just be ready to hand over whatever you've got on Maury." He sighed as he turned to leave. "I certainly wish you would learn to work with us. Fort Thacker does its best to cooperate with you guys. We don't hoard our data."

"No, you broadcast it."

He smiled the unruffled smile of amused tolerance. "The public has a right to know, Kate."

"Roger, let's not get into this again. It's counterproductive." She disapproved of his style in general, but it was a particular incident—the one that had gotten him "resigned" from the CDC—that still grated. The time he publicly announced evidence of the transmission of the AIDS virus from HIV positive surgeons to their patients.

Peck's announcement created a huge brouhaha and was milked to the hilt by the media. As it turned out only one surgeon was involved and there was evidence he had intentionally infected his patients. By the time the connection was noted the surgeon had died of AIDS. Meanwhile a ripple of fear kept people from having the surgery they needed.

Peck's amused smile infuriated her. "Fort Thacker is a joke, Roger. The government thinks the answer to this epidemic is to create yet another bureau. All you people do is eat up tax dollars and get in our way. You don't know the meaning of research."

His smile faded. "I don't need this. Just get the reports on that case to me," he snapped, turning on his heel. He slammed the door on his way out.

Kate took a shaky breath, angry at herself for letting Peck get to her. She picked up the Maury folder and immersed herself in her notes.

She and Harpo had gotten nowhere. The scalded-skin syndrome had been a false alarm. No further positive antibodies. The gruesome swaths of dead skin had been cultured and nothing was growing. The formaldehyde had made the body sterile, unyielding to analysis. The only thing they had going was that Maury was HIV positive. Was this a new manifestation of AIDS?

As she pondered, the skirmish with Peck all but forgotten, her secretary buzzed. Kekich wanted to see her the moment she was free. She gathered up her notes and walked down the hall two doors to Kekich's office, her anger resurfacing as she decided to give Chuck a piece of her mind about Peck.

Kekich was at his desk, the phone plastered to his ear. As she walked in he frowned and hung up. "Damn. Why are doctors so rude to each other? Bullard always does that—has his secretary get me on the line, then makes me wait forever."

Kate jumped right in. "Chuck, did you tell Roger Peck about the Maury case?"

Kekich straightened his massive body and tugged at his tie. "Listen, Kate, when you go off on your own, you put me in an awkward position. I have no authority."

She pointed a finger at him. "Chuck, you know better. The authority is there if you want it. And if you're not in charge, how can you give Roger the go-ahead?"

He looked genuinely surprised. "I did nothing of the kind."

She gave him a piercing look, but she knew he was telling the truth. Peck was a master at twisting people's words to suit his needs. She sat down.

"I'm sorry, Chuck. I should have known you wouldn't do a thing like that." She stared at her hands. "How do people like Roger get to such a position of responsibility when they're so irresponsible?"

He ran his sausagelike fingers through his beard. "Don't you want to know why I asked to see you?"

"Of course. I'm sorry."

He picked up a folder and handed it to her. "Take a look at this."

She opened it, fully expecting to see a data sheet regarding her next assignment. Instead, she found herself leafing through a hodgepodge of reports about an autopsy done on a nurse in Salt Lake City.

It was the pictures that stopped her. There were four-color photos of a bloody corpse with the face obliterated by caked blood and giant blisters of skin. The photos reminded her so much of the Maury case that she found herself blinking hard and rereading the name of the unfortunate victim.

She looked up to see Kekich watching her. "How did you come by this?"

"The son of a friend of mine is a pathology resident in Salt Lake. Name of Koji Kobayashi. He sent it on the QT. No diagnosis. Wants any help he can get. Says there's too much political infighting. The infectious disease people are battling with the pathologists about what tests to do. One guy resigned because he wasn't gonna let another department boss him around. Koji's worried the case might fall through the cracks while the honchos duke it out."

Kate's thoughts raced with questions and possibilities. Her stunned mind sought automatically for similarities. "Was the nurse HIV positive?"

"Yes."

Now she found her heart racing, in tandem with her thoughts. "Did she have AIDS?"

He shook his head. "Koji says she was HIV negative just a month earlier. She worked in the ICU, which put her at some risk, but no reports of needle sticks or other accidents."

Kate wasn't too put off by the negative test a month earlier. People with the AIDS virus may not show evidence in their blood for as much as a year after exposure. Still, it added one more jag to the puzzle.

She took up the folder again and looked over the antibody tests and electron microscopic analysis of the victim's cells.

She was careful to note they had checked for African hemorrhagic viruses, with the exception of Congo, the one Harpo had also missed. Negative.

Electron microscopy studies showed a nonspecific pattern of cellular damage. Translated, she knew that meant the study wasn't normal, but neither did it point to any answers.

"The similarities to the Maury case are astonishing." She looked up at Kekich. "I'd like to pursue this."

He gave a satisfied smile. "I thought you might. Take the reports with you and let me know your thoughts."

"I will." She stuffed the folder under her arm with Maury's folder.

"I foresee one problem," Kekich said.

"Roger?"

"Roger. We've got two diagnostic dilemmas here, and the only thing they have in common is HIV. He's gonna want to get involved, Kate. And I can't stop him. You know we have orders from Washington to cooperate with Fort Thacker."

She grimaced. "It seems we have the same problem as your friend Koji—politics."

He shrugged. "You know anyplace that doesn't?"

She laughed, recalling the turf battles she and Harpo had joked about in med school. Some things never changed. She gave him a grateful look. "I appreciate your efforts to keep the peace."

He sighed. "It's becoming too much a part of my job these days. My other problem is that I need you here. I can't have you going off on a wild-goose chase while our caseload keeps piling up. This cholera epidemic in Argentina is driving me up a wall. We're under the gun to solve it, and fast."

She looked at him. Poor Chuck. Always acting as though the top brass were breathing fire down his neck. He lacked the drive to move up in the government hierarchy—which she considered to his credit—yet he couldn't stomach working for others.

"The American tour group?"

"Yeah. Over half the folks got stricken—some fifty or so people. We haven't been able to track down the source. A couple of lawyers in the group are trying to

initiate a class-action suit against the tour company."
He shrugged. "Can't find anyone else to blame."

"Lawyers will be lawyers." She thought a moment.
"You've checked out all water sources?"

Kekich nodded. "Got a crack team down there.
Don Luccia's heading it up. They're just not finding
the bug."

"Any layovers outside the U.S.?"

"They might've stopped over in Mexico or Central
America. But it would've been a class hotel. Bottled
water. No other reports coming through."

"It's still worth checking out. And check out all
seafood exposure. Remember Kekich dictum number
one hundred and forty: Never assume anything."

He chuckled. "You got me there. I'll make sure
Don runs it down."

"You want me to go down there?"

"Maybe. Let's see what Don's team comes up with
over the weekend."

Kekich's phone rang. He snatched it up. "Yes?
She's here, I'll put her on." He held out the receiver.
"For you."

Kate stretched for the phone. "Dr. Crane."

"Dr. Crane, thank God I found you. It's Dennis
Jamison in virology. The serum you gave me? It's positive for the Congo virus."

Congo! She let the word roll around in her head
for a moment, unable to integrate it into her thoughts.
"You're sure, Dennis?" Maury died of Congo? How
on earth had he gotten it? Her mind couldn't grapple
with the flood of questions.

"Two hundred percent. I rechecked it three times.
And I checked it against the other African viruses to
be sure there wasn't cross-reactivity. It's for real."

She felt an odd churning in her stomach. "Thanks,
Dennis. You did a good job." She paused a moment

as she considered the more immediate dangers. "Were you double-gloved?"

"You bet. Working under the hood, too. I don't believe in taking chances."

"Be sure to warn the other techs. And go to maximum containment immediately."

He laughed nervously. "Don't worry, we've notified the BSC Four lab already. Most of us have been here long enough to remember Al Rivera."

She felt a jolt and the churning crescendoed. She knew the story all too well, even though Rivera's tragic death was before her time. A nicked glove while handling a test tube full of viruses. Dead a week later.

"That was the Marburg virus, wasn't it?" She could see Kekich out of the corner of her eye. He looked like he was holding his breath as he stared at her.

"Yeah, and Congo's ten times more potent."

"All right, Dennis," she said, uncomfortably aware of her own breathing. The air came in short jerks as she felt a tight band around her chest. If her mind hadn't fully acknowledged the potential dangers facing them all, her body had. "I'll stop by in a while."

As she slowly handed the phone back to Kekich, she knew her face must be registering the horror she felt. She saw worry in Kekich's eyes. He said nothing.

She stood up, feeling a bit unsteady. "Chuck, I have to call New York. That was about Akendo Maury. It wasn't AIDS that killed him. You can call Fort Thacker and tell Roger to back off."

"You'd better fill me in, Kate," said Kekich quietly. His hands were clasped neatly on top of his desk. Stoical, bracing himself.

"Congo," was all she said, the word seeming to fall off her tongue.

"The African virus?" He tugged at his beard. "Good God, Kate. How?"

"I don't know. I think we're going to be in on this one whether we want to or not."

Kekich pointed toward the folder under her arm. "We better be sure and check that Salt Lake gal for Congo."

"Absolutely."

He nodded gravely. "We better notify Special Pathogens."

She hesitated. The Special Pathogens branch of the Epidemic Intelligence Service meant working with Rory McDermott. Even through her mounting horror she could feel herself digging her heels in, resisting a situation where she and Rory would be thrown together. "It may be premature, Chuck. We don't have an epidemic."

"Not yet." He tapped his fingers on the desk top. "Kate?"

"Yes?"

"That the only reason you don't want Special Pathogens?"

She made herself look at him. She saw only a desire to understand.

"I'm not sure."

He nodded sagely. "Want me to hold off a little?"

"Only if you think it wise, Chuck. I'm not so objective these days."

"Who is?"

When she got back to her office, Kate saw a note on her desk to call Dr. Cosgrove. She got through to him with no difficulty. Before she could tell him a thing, he had some shocking news of his own.

"Kate, we've got a break on the Maury case. Maury volunteered for an AIDS vaccine trial under an assumed name."

She felt dizzy, as though she'd been punched between the eyes. Her mind couldn't seem to process the information.

"Kate? You there?"

Finally, she reacted. "My God," she cried. "What next? And I've got a shocker for you, Harpo. Maury's serum is positive for the Congo virus."

There was a pause and all she could hear was the hum of their long-distance connection. "Kate," said Harpo solemnly, "what the hell's going on?"

"I'm not sure. You know I've had a strange feeling about this case from the beginning."

He managed a strained laugh. "Woman's intuition. Where do we go from here? How the hell would Maury get Congo?"

"I have no idea. There's never been a case reported in the Western hemisphere."

She stared at her hands. She was getting nervous. Was the red spot on the back of her left wrist there this morning? She felt a cold fear whip through her. She had enrolled in the AIDS vaccine project in Atlanta, at the university medical center. They had needed a few more subjects before they could wrap up their preliminary studies and move on to the next phase. She had volunteered in the spirit of doing her part to speed up vital research, receiving the vaccine only a week ago. There had been no problems.

"We better find out where he's been, and pronto," said Harpo.

She rolled up the sleeve of her blouse and inspected her left arm. No other red spots. Still, she felt rattled, her heart racing. Get a grip, she told herself.

To Harpo, she said, "We'd better call the New York and Arizona health departments. Track down his contacts."

"Think we ought to initiate quarantines?"

She pondered a moment as she rolled up her right

sleeve. "Perhaps. But only intimate contacts." She was relieved to see no spots. She could feel her heartbeat slowing slightly.

Harpo gave an ironic laugh. "Kate, the guy was a celebrity. There could've been a hell of a lot of intimate contacts."

"Let's hope not. Why don't you call the New York health department, have them contact Arizona? And maybe you can do some more sleuthing about this vaccine thing, though I doubt a connection."

She pulled out her compact and checked her face. Nothing. "I'll get the ball rolling on tracking down the Congo virus."

"Kate, are you okay?"

"I'm fine," she said, perhaps a little too quickly. She wasn't about to burden Harpo with her fears. It was the old med school paranoia syndrome all over again. When you were sure you had every disease you read about. She thought she had outgrown it.

"Good," said Harpo. "You sound a little edgy. Listen, we've got another problem."

She could feel a headache coming on. She'd better check her temperature. "What's that?"

"We don't know what name Maury used when he enrolled. So we don't know which vaccine he got. It could have been the live virus, Kate. Phase Three trials are just getting underway in humans."

Kate knew what he was thinking. A backfire phenomenon. AIDS vaccine studies had been going on for years now, but until recently human studies had been restricted to use of the protein fragments in the HIV protein shell. That was what she had received. She knew there was little if any danger of causing the disease you were trying to prevent. Nevertheless, the thought was chilling.

She also knew that moving into the field of live

viral testing was a different ball game. There could be trouble, albeit rare. It had happened before—the smallpox vaccine causing smallpox, the early polio vaccine causing polio.

Still, the widespread use of vaccinations in the twentieth century to prevent disease had revolutionized medicine. The benefits far outweighed the small risks involved.

"How did you find out about the vaccine?" she asked, calming down as she reminded herself she had only received a protein fragment. Nothing could go wrong.

"Maury mentioned it to his girlfriend. She didn't call us until this morning. Said she was beginning to wonder if it might have some bearing."

"Smart girl."

"Scared girl." Harpo paused. "I've got a line on which companies are most active in the vaccine programs—Alatron and Dalmouth-Keller. Both in New Jersey. But, Christ, Kate, I don't know what to do with this new grenade you just tossed in my lap."

"Neither do I. Nothing seems to be adding up." She suddenly remembered the Salt Lake case. Another grenade? "Harpo, there's something else. I just learned of a case with striking similarities to Maury. A woman. We're going to run her serum for Congo. She's HIV positive as well but I have no information on whether she was a vaccine volunteer."

After a moment of static she heard Harpo laugh. It was not a pleasant sound. "God almighty, Kate."

CHAPTER EIGHT

Dave Parsons shifted in his seat and gave a sidelong glance to the man sitting beside him. He was experiencing a strange sense of unreality that made him want to pinch himself. Here he was, riding first class in a jet to Los Angeles, a cocktail in one hand, plenty of leg room, just the right cabin temperature, and the cutest little stewardess he'd ever laid eyes on. So why wasn't he happy?

No trouble answering that one. It's the guy next to you. Some psycho janitor, a chameleon, now masquerading in a three-piece suit, leading you by the nose in the project you once reigned over like a king, exempt even from the chief of the company. Parsons gave a bitter snort. What's wrong with this picture?

He shot another furtive look at the man he knew as Ken Butler. Heinman was staring ahead, as though completely unaware of Parsons's existence. A real weird dude. On some secret mission of his own. Or perhaps a mission between him and God. Parsons hadn't missed an occasional quote from the Bible that the guy seemed to pull out of a hat, his tone soft-spoken, eyes distant.

You looked at a guy like Heinman and you thought of a statue. A soldier, maybe. Or even a world leader. But a loner. And not one of the good guys. Definitely not one of the good guys.

Heinman leaned forward and pulled a briefcase from under his seat. It was Parsons's briefcase. He handed it to Parsons and said, "Get rid of the drink."

Parsons gave him a weak smile, gulped down his gin and tonic, and snapped open the briefcase. He still wasn't quite sure what Heinman wanted of him. There hadn't been time for questions. Or maybe it was just something about Heinman that made you think twice, even three times, before asking too many questions.

Parsons sifted through his papers, including his own private files that Heinman seemed to know all about. He looked up once to see Heinman watching him. In an odd sort of way, he felt a twist of relief. At least the guy was acknowledging him. Before now, from the time Heinman came by in a cab to pick him up for the airport, he had felt . . . invisible. That was it. Invisible. And yet, too visible.

Parsons gave his head a shake, as though trying to break loose the webs that bound his mind. He felt like a flying robot, circling, circling but never landing. Heinman had taken over the controls.

"What are we working on?" Parsons finally had to ask. He hated silence, never had been able to tolerate it. Part of the sales persona was to draw people out, get a reaction. Good or bad, made no difference. You knew where you stood. You couldn't move unless you knew where you were moving from.

But Heinman fell outside the rules as Parsons knew them. It was like the guy knew exactly what bugged

Parsons the most, and he kept doing that one thing. In this case, the cold, silent shoulder.

Heinman reached into the briefcase and extracted the questionnaire Parsons had used for the AIDS vaccine volunteers. The one Parsons had redesigned for his own use.

"Get rid of this," Heinman snapped as he handed the form to Parsons.

Parsons gave him an uncertain look.

The ice-blue eyes grazed his face like a bullet, making him wince. "Tear it up. You'll use the one with the Alatron letterhead."

"But if we're going for more HIV negative volunteers . . ."

"You have a problem?"

"Ten volunteers in L.A. alone, that's a hell of a lot. Especially when we're not sure if maybe there's some difficulty with . . ."

"Shut up, Dave," Heinman said, his lips barely moving. Parsons knew, as he watched Heinman's face, what cold fury meant. He felt his stomach do a somersault and he wished to hell he had brought his antacids along.

He looked out the window, at the earth thirty thousand feet below. It looked like they were flying over the Midwest. A flat, boring quiltwork of green and brown. Right now, boring looked good. He wished he was there. Without his malevolent sidekick.

The plane suddenly dropped into an air pocket as it entered a giant cloud bank. Parsons felt his stomach bounce off the ceiling. He shot a look at Heinman who sat like a rock, unmindful of the realities that plagued the normal human. He felt a strange mixture of nagging impatience and fear. He wanted to blame the tumult inside him on the plane's bumpiness, but he knew better. He loosened his tie and mopped his brow.

Then he did a dumb thing. Maybe it was the alcohol, maybe he had a death wish, but suddenly he blurted out the question that kept plaguing him. "What exactly do you want from me?"

Heinman didn't seem to hear. Which was just fine, because as soon as he asked, he knew it was a mistake.

Then Heinman slowly turned his head and riveted Parsons with those stark eyes. "I will tell you what I want when I want it."

Parsons nodded. His people skills were useless with a man like this. He said nothing.

As Heinman occupied himself with studying the papers, Parsons took the time to assess where he was. He was in over his head, that was abundantly clear. One of his volunteers had died and two were untraceable. He hadn't told Stryker or anyone else with AIDS FIRST, but he figured when they heard, they'd come after him.

And of course there was the matter of having been fired. Now he found himself actually welcoming the dismissal. It would provide an opportunity to get out before all hell broke loose. But then, speaking of hell, Heinman had appeared.

The irony of it all did not escape him. Heinman was forcing him to follow through on his own blatantly ambitious idea of recruiting HIV negative volunteers—for some mysterious purpose of his own.

Which brought up another question. Why was he, Dave Parsons, doing this? What power did this creep have over him? Why didn't he just take his walking papers and disappear? Or be a hero and let it out that some psycho was trying to sabotage the company?

As he felt the pain when he tried to swallow, he was reminded that he already knew the answer. On a gut level. He touched his fingers tentatively to his throat, where Heinman had pressed a thumb hard against his windpipe until he'd almost blacked out. Heinman had made it all too clear what could happen if he didn't cooperate.

He sat back and wondered again what this flint-eyed man wanted. Maybe he was out to destroy society's deviants. The biblical quotes had certainly smacked of a self-righteous vindictiveness. Or maybe he was just out to get Alatron. or both. One look at those eyes, that face, and you knew Weirdo had enough hate in him for all of the above.

So many questions and no one to ask. Parsons felt a sudden drowsiness come over him—maybe it was the alcohol. Weirdo didn't look like he had any use for him right now. So he levered his seat into the reclining position and dozed off. Maybe when he woke up he would find it had all been a bad dream.

"Bonita Gridley?" Parsons stood outside a cubbyhole of an office at St. Anthony's Hospital in West Los Angeles. It was a private hospital, unaffiliated with any medical training program. Bonita was the first volunteer on his list, which had been compiled by a couple of AIDS FIRSTers who had scouted ahead.

By now the scouts were probably in Salt Lake, Parsons's next stop. Gay Scouts, he thought. Under different circumstances he might have laughed at his little play on words. But he didn't feel like laughing. He felt like running.

A heavily made-up woman got up and walked toward him with an arid smile. He could smell her sickeningly sweet perfume a mile away. She looked like a prostitute. She wore a short, tight-fitting skirt, a plunging neckline, and earrings that clanged and glittered. Her hips swayed sensually.

He escorted her into a small office, went through a list of questions and explained the vaccination procedure and follow-up. He was vaguely aware that he must sound something like a tape recording. It was pretty much the same routine he had used before. There was only one difference. These volunteers were now part of Alatron's official program, at least ostensibly. A sheet that Heinman had given him proclaimed that this study was by order of company president Elliot Halsey. Halsey's signature, looking quite authentic, decorated the proclamation. Parsons shuddered as he imagined how Halsey would react when he found out.

Parsons tried to envision his future and saw nothing but a bleak dead end. He felt like he had a hissing rattlesnake around his neck, its head moving for his jugular.

The presence of Bonita Gridley brought him back to the present. Though Bonita had a tough facade, she seemed oddly nervous and vulnerable. He watched her a moment as she filled out the form, then said, "Ms. Gridley, if you'll follow me down the hall, our technician will administer the vaccine."

She followed Parsons without a word into a small room where a man in a blue smock awaited her.

Parsons said, "This is Mr. Butler. He will take care of you from here."

Heinman nodded at the woman and picked up a syringe as he said, "Have a seat, please, and roll up your sleeve." He drew up an aliquot of the vaccine from a small vial.

As Heinman approached the woman, Parsons turned to leave. He had been standing nervously in the doorway, watching. Everything Heinman did seemed fascinating, although when he thought about it, it was all rather mundane.

He turned his head away. He couldn't bring himself to watch Heinman inject that stuff into the woman's arm. Something in the back of his mind kept trying to break through. It had to do with being an accomplice to a crime. He didn't know what the crime was, and he had no evidence. So it was easy enough to cope with it. As long as he didn't watch.

He backed out of the room with a smile. "I'll leave you with Mr. Butler now. We'll be in touch within twenty-four hours. You have our emergency number." Another of Heinman's directives. Not in a million years would Parsons have given out Alatron's number.

He returned to the room where nine other volunteers were waiting anxiously. Parsons was not a man who normally felt compassion. But as his eyes surveyed the group—most of them clearly gays or prostitutes—his heart went out to each of them. He wouldn't give a plug nickel for their future.

Keith Heinman slipped off his blue smock, rolled it up neatly, and stuffed it into his overnight bag. He entered the hospital's employee lounge. It was empty. He stood before the full-length mirror. He flexed his muscles, did a few stretches, took a few deep breaths. He felt good.

He took his three-piece suit out of the closet, but before changing he sat down in one of the cheap vinyl chairs and reviewed his list. Ten volunteers. Five had received the vaccine, five the placebo.

He had planned it the way he knew Halsey would. He reintroduced the placebo and the double-blind aspect that Parsons so stupidly excluded. The study had to appear scientifically flawless. It had to be Halsey's study.

Five people received the vaccine today, five the placebo. He didn't know who received what, but the five who got the vaccine would die. It didn't matter who they were. They were all scum—prostitutes, gays, the sexually promiscuous. Sinners, all of them. It didn't matter that there was an occasional health-care worker. They all deserved it, the perverts. He smiled as he recalled Isaiah: "He shall destroy the sinners."

He in this case being Elliot Halsey. With the help of Keith Heinman.

Heinman stood up before the mirror and flexed his biceps again. He felt like working out. But he was on a tight schedule. He and Parsons had a plane to catch for Salt Lake City. It was only the first leg of the trip that marked the end for Mr. Halsey.

As Heinman imagined Halsey's face when he learned of the deadliness of his vaccine—his pet project—he burst into a harsh, throaty laugh. Then, as he watched himself in the mirror, an uncontrollable rage overtook him. He saw Halsey's face staring back at him. A hypocrite of a man who had so self-righteously made the case against him. A case that took ten years off his life.

With the quickness of an untamed animal, he picked up an ashtray and hurled it at the mirror. Glass shattered with a noise that brought a couple of nurses running. As they burst into the lounge, Heinman gathered his suit and bag and calmly pushed past them.

CHAPTER NINE

The Horace J. Albright Conference Room was a well-appointed affair, with a forest-green deep pile carpet, tall narrow windows framed by lush green draperies, and a cherrywood conference table with a half-inch-thick glass top. A glittering crystal chandelier hung overhead. A fully stocked bar with silver and crystal serving sets lined the back wall.

Elliot Halsey sat at one end of the long table with a solemn face. He looked at his watch. The "emergency" board meeting with its quorum of directors had already dragged on for close to an hour. And board chairman Stanford Robbins still hadn't gotten around to the reason for calling the meeting. But Halsey knew what was coming. The reason was listed innocuously enough as agenda Item Three—financial philosophy.

As he heard Robbins clear his throat, Halsey concluded Item Three was close at hand. The rest of the directors—nine men—seemed attuned to the nuances of Robbins's throat noises as well. They leaned forward in their black leather chairs.

Robbins tapped his water glass with a spoon, oblivious of already having the attention of the room. He smiled benignly and looked briefly at Halsey who nodded acknowledgment. The gaunt gray-haired man seemed harmless enough. With his trim mustache and rimless spectacles he looked every bit the Casper Milquetoast. He had an annoying habit of twitching his cheek whenever he smiled, requiring him to constantly readjust his glasses.

"Let's go on to the next item, gentlemen. Item Three." He turned to Halsey with a smile. "We may as well get right to it, Elliot. We're concerned about the direction the company is taking. You see in front of you a financial summary I've had prepared for the purpose of this meeting: income is down thirteen percent from last quarter, forty percent from your projections. And as you are well aware the last quarter showed disturbing trends you claimed were only brief anomalies. One glaring cost example is R and D, which you assured us had peaked at our last meeting. It is up another twelve percent."

Robbins paused and gave Halsey a sober look. "Unfortunately, our overall profit decline parallels the problems associated with your pursuit of the AIDS vaccine."

There it was, thought Halsey. About as much to the point as Robbins was ever likely to get. He could feel his hands clenching into fists. He could feel his influence, his blueprint for innovation, slipping away. To these tradition-bound men, the cutting edge never moved from the bottom line. And too often pertained to such weighty issues as whether to package a drug in a box or a blisterpack.

They were too concerned with revenue, markup, and FDA approval. And they were shortsighted or surely they would see that if Alatron came up with a workable AIDS vaccine it would rake in profits. They had no feel or appreciation for the rigors of science or the future.

He did not respond, but looked around the room at the ten men in their pinstripe blue power suits. They lined the giant table as though posing for a portrait. They represented an assembled quorum of the old guard, handpicked by Robbins from the twenty-odd full board.

Halsey himself had never felt comfortable in a suit and was the only senior executive to wear casual clothes. Today he wore black canvas pants and a blue cotton shirt, an outfit more suited to the mountain climber he was than a climber of the corporate ladder. The board had accepted this as one of his quirks.

Robbins shrugged and went on in the placid friendly voice of an older man talking down to a younger. "Elliot, I know you believe in this project. And I'm sure you're right when you say biogenetics is the future. But we also have to deal with the present. Quite frankly, based on these figures, we're no longer reassured by your estimates. It's time, I'm afraid, to decide whether to go on with your project or to surer options."

Halsey bit his lips. Surer options meant putting out the umpty-umpth version of a well-established drug line—like a new ACE inhibitor for high blood pressure, or a new penicillin derivative for sinus infections. A "me-too" drug. It was a philosophy that might provide short-term profits, but at the price of the company's future. Because when the time came for "me-tooing" the biogenetically engineered drugs pouring out over the next decade, Alatron's stand-pat technology could easily be obsolete.

His glance moved around the table until it rested on the chairman. He saw no give anywhere. "Stan," he said, "you know my position on sure bets. They're the status quo. They represent the excellence of the past, but they'll never launch us to a new level of excellence or prosperity for our future. We have to constantly explore new technologies if we want to sustain profits."

He saw no reaction, not even the blink of an eye. He pressed on. "The AIDs vaccine is not 'my project'. I stood here before all of you three years ago and first presented the proposal." Before he knew Barry had AIDS. Before he knew his son was gay. They couldn't accuse him then of what he knew they silently accused him of now—lack of objectivity because he had a son dying of AIDS.

He fought back the bitterness roiling in his throat, took a deep breath, and went on. "Moving ahead on the vaccine was endorsed by every man here. It was understood then that the financial payback would not be immediate. I further proposed we pursue two new AIDS drugs that had come out of our research department—Virostat and Genovir. Both showed great promise in slowing disease progression—so much so they were fast-tracked by the FDA."

A cherub-faced Lowell Bekin poked a hand in the air and interrupted. Halsey knew him to be the leader of the board in all but name. And at sixty-three, the youngest member present, excluding Halsey. "But only Virostat has paid off, Elliot. Genovir's side-effect profile is far too high, a fact you may have realized at the time . . ."

Halsey felt a wave of indignation. He pointed a finger at Bekin. "I knew nothing of the kind, Lowell." His voice rose. "Why would I push a drug I knew would fail?" He fixed his dark eyes on Bekin and leaned his arms on the table. "Tell me that, Lowell."

Bekin's eyes broke away from Halsey's as he took

a sip of his martini. "Perhaps you ignored the obvious for reasons of your own. Perhaps . . ."

Halsey straightened to his full height. "Lowell, I did not know then that my sons had AIDS. I have said it once." His eyes swept the table. "That should be enough."

He watched, with a strange sense of detachment, as Bekin winced and looked down at his lap.

Robbins held up a hand. "Gentlemen, let's not get personal. Elliot, your intentions were good. We don't question that. What we need to address today is the future. The near future." He looked at Bekin, smiling, his cheek twitching. "Let me explain what I consider, after a careful review, the sure bets." He consulted the pages before him. "We're about to launch a major sales campaign for Technol, our new calcium blocker for high blood pressure. The side-effect profile is lower than any in its class."

"The second prospect is Calmbium, a new benzodiazepine tranquilizer with impressive antidepressant properties." Robbins looked up, his eyes surveying the group and resting on Halsey. "Both drugs look promising. But we need to consolidate our resources toward marketing them. Right now, most of our budgeted revenues are being routed to the AIDS vaccine. And all of our cost overruns can be attributed to that project alone."

Halsey said nothing. He felt a chaotic mixture of emotions, from disappointment and frustration to smoldering anger.

Lowell Bekin summarized. "I think what Stan is saying here, Elliot, is we need to decide what we want for Alatron over the next two to three years. Biogenetics is too new and uncertain. And potentially dangerous. Vaccines are dangerous. We're talking the live virus here—you can't tell me the risks aren't huge.

Look what happened to Littleton Labs after the disaster with the polio vaccine in the sixties—the virus in the vaccine mutated to a more virulent form. They went bankrupt. Or how about the swine flu vaccine a decade ago? Rotterdam Labs is still trying to extricate itself from the lawsuits. Our investors will not support a dangerous product."

Another director, Emmett Calloway, piped up. "That's right, Lowell. I received a call just yesterday from one of our biggest stockholders who spoke of pulling out because of the vaccine."

Bekin gave a knowing smile. "My point exactly. Save the cutting edge for new companies jockeying for position among themselves. They have little to lose. Look where keeping pace with the AIDS market has gotten us," he went on. "Bus loads of activists tying us up, putting us on the front pages with serial killers and rapists." He threw up his hands. "Who needs it?"

Halsey stared out the window, using the moment to get a handle on his anger. He noticed a ladder drawn to the window but made nothing of it. The workmen were probably on break. As he thought about it he realized the problem wasn't just with Alatron. The Japanese recognized forty years earlier that short-term profit was the deadly flaw in American business. And they profited by it.

He fought to control his voice. "Lowell," he said evenly, "you're taking the issue out of context. Vaccines, overall, do not kill or maim. They save lives. They are not dangerous. And using an example from the sixties, when we've come so far since then, is hitting below the belt."

He let his eyes wander over the group, ignoring Bekin's scornful look. He knew he wasn't getting through to these men, set in their ways, relics of an age past. But a part of him drove him on, the resolve that said one man can make a difference.

Again his eyes circled the table, looking each of the patriarchal faces in the eye. He could see they were waiting for him to finish, some with scornful smiles. "We can't live in the past," he said. "We should be spearheading the cry for change, not simply reacting to it. And certainly not resisting it."

His voice rose ever so slightly. "We're at war against a disease bent on destroying humanity. And we, the pharmaceutical companies, are the makers of the weapons. We can't abandon the people in the front lines—the health professionals who are helpless without us."

His eyes met Bekin's, the man he knew he must convince. Bekin's eyes were narrow slits, unreadable. Robbins's face was an empty mask. Halsey played a last card.

"Sure, the AIDS vaccine is a gamble. I'll grant you that. Success is likely years off. The virus, we know, changes its face constantly. Ongoing mutations make effective vaccines obsolete by the time we come up with them. And that's where the live vaccine comes in. We have a better chance of fooling the virus and neutralizing it if we use the live AIDS virus in the vaccine. The venture is worth the risk.

"If you're concerned about bottom-line performance—a proper concern—the vaccine will give it to us. We've already incurred the expenses, including the maximum containment lab. We're the safest and best prepared to market the vaccine. Our research department has produced what we've asked and has outperformed our competitors. We'll get FDA approval after the tests bear out what I know to be true. We have a fine product. And we need to put our full support behind it."

His voice stopped, the words choked in his throat. He saw the exchange of glances between Robbins and Bekin. His head throbbed as he sat down.

Robbins, remaining seated, cleared his throat and gave him a paternal look. "You speak well, Elliot, and we credit your sincerity. But we are a business, and a business must look to its financial security first. The AIDS vaccine is a noble endeavor, to be sure. But nobility doesn't pay bills. I know we've come far. But there are many problems to overcome—you just said that yourself. The AIDS virus is a chameleon—a master of disguises—mutating constantly. It's playing games with us—expensive games. It's all so uncertain. A company does not prosper in an atmosphere of uncertainty."

Bekin nodded and added, "Stan's right, Elliot. Uncertainty and safety are the issues here." A smile flitted across his face. "Are you prepared to guarantee the vaccine's safety?"

"No guarantees," said Halsey wearily. "And you know, Lowell, there are never guarantees in this business. We are, after all, dealing with a highly unpredictable entity—life." He no longer made an effort to bite back his sarcasm. He knew, with the looks of exasperation, the grimaces and rolling eyes, that his time was up. He made his last plea—one that came straight from the heart, as it ached for his ailing son.

"You people sit here thinking you're immune. You're not a drug user, you're not gay, it can't happen to you or your family. Well, you're dead wrong. As many as forty million people will be infected with the AIDS virus by the turn of the century. And that's a modest estimate. Can you be sure that no one you love or care about will be included?" He turned a fiery eye on Bekin. "Any guarantees there, Lowell?"

He looked back at the board. "What about your

children? And their children? Look what's happening in Africa—AIDS is sweeping its way into the general population, mocking the definition of risk groups. The trends in this country are only a step behind Africa—it's just a matter of time. Heterosexuals are the fastest-growing group of victims. Heterosexuals. People like you and me. The virus is not only killing off more and more of us, it is attacking us in the only way we can stay alive as a species: the act of reproduction. And what about all the other diseases acquired by AIDS victims, like TB, which can be transmitted to any of us by a simple sneeze?"

Halsey saw that suddenly all eyes were on him. Frowns were pulling at faces. He leaned his arms on the huge table. "Whether we like it or not, we are all part of this plight. We owe it to ourselves and our public to pursue the vaccine project. We can't save the people who are already infected. God knows, we can help them, but we haven't been able to save a single one of them. Even drugs like Virostat only buy time. Prevention is the answer. And that means the vaccine."

He saw a hand go up, a mouth begin to form angry words. Emmett Calloway always had to get a word in. Halsey shook his head. "Please, Emmett, let me finish. We've spent as a nation over ten billion dollars in the past year on HIV and AIDS. And these are just the direct costs. Indirect costs are another fifty to sixty billion—refurbishing dental offices to handle AIDS patients, equipping and training police departments to deal with HIV-infected protestors and criminals, screening the nation's blood supply—the list goes on. If you want to talk saving money, talk prevention. Look at TB. Studies have shown that every dollar spent on TB prevention and control in this country results in a minimal savings of three to four times that."

He crossed to the window, his back to the group. He had heard a scraping noise. Likely someone coming up the ladder outside. Inside, no one said a word. You could hear a pin drop. He felt a mixture of hopelessness and anger. He thought of Barry, who would never reach the age of any man here. He closed his eyes and summoned his strength, fighting back the tremor inside him.

He turned and leveled a finger at the group as he moved to the table. His voice rose. "How can you sit there and complain that it's too uncertain? The future of the human race is uncertain. And no amount of burying your heads in the sand will change that."

He had abandoned all hope of reaching them. "Gentlemen, you will one day recognize the truth. That is if you live long enough." He sat down and crossed his arms. It was clear he couldn't care less what they thought.

The board members began whispering and clearing their throats. A few of them looked to Stan Robbins, the rest to Lowell Bekin. Surely someone would know precisely how to deal with this assault on their communal self-respect.

Just then the crash of shattering glass caught their attention as a rock came hurtling through the window. The rock landed on the conference table, splintering the thick glass top into an intricate web of cracks. Drinking glasses spilled, papers got soaked. Everyone sat stock-still. Before they could comprehend what was happening, a form—a human form—hurled itself through the broken window and landed with a thud on the floor.

The room suddenly became bedlam with a babble of confusion and fright. Board members stood and huddled together in a corner. "Call security!" someone yelled, while another hurried to a wall phone.

Halsey rushed over to the body. "Are you all right?" he cried. He couldn't make sense of what was happening. Maybe one of the workmen had fallen.

The figure shrank from Halsey's touch. It was a man, maybe forty, dressed only in shorts. He sat up and pushed himself back against the wall. His arms were bloodied from the broken glass. As his head came up, Halsey thought he looked vaguely familiar.

Before Halsey could say anything further, the man shouted in a raspy voice, "Goddamn murderers—killers! I have AIDS—do you hear me? The life ebbs out of my body while you count your money!"

He then rose, clenching in his fist a triangular shard of glass. With his eyes aflame, he drew the glass across his chest, bringing a streak of blood. Cries of horror arose from the corner of the room. He then held the piece of glass up and beckoned with a finger. "I dare you to dip your hands in my blood." He let out a caustic laugh. "Blood—for you, the fountain of life. For me, the curse of death. Over fifteen years and there's still no cure for AIDS. Thanks to the greed of men like you." He made a step forward.

No one moved, seemingly frozen by the audacity of the intruder's invitation. He seemed to feed on their fear. Waving the shard of glass, he yelled, "Pigs! You care nothing about us!"

The board members edged deeper into the protective corner of the room. Only Halsey, who now recognized the wild man as Paul Resnick, one of the AIDS FIRST activists, dared to approach the man. He knew Resnick to be Gil Stryker's lover, and one of the AIDS FIRST leaders. Resnick was not crazy. It was his act.

Figuring there was a method to Resnick's madness,

Halsey moved over to the broken window and cast a glance at the courtyard four stories below. Sure enough, two news trucks had pulled up.

"You might want to hold off, Resnick," he said dryly. "The press boys don't have their cameras ready."

Resnick scowled and pointed to his face and chest, disfigured by clusters of purplish-gray bumps. "See this? Kaposi's sarcoma. There are going to be millions more like me because you pigs are dragging your feet, holding out. And for what? The almighty dollar!"

Halsey was aware of the board members summoning courage as they realized they were dealing with only one man—blood or no blood. A few snickered nervously and filed out of the room. He heard Bekin whisper, "These people are a disgrace. I thought we were rid of them."

An Alatron security guard burst through the door, his hand on his holstered gun. A heavy-set fireplug of a man with a handlebar mustache, he stood at the doorway, his feet planted wide, surveying the room. "What's going on here?" he growled.

Halsey held up a hand. He could see no point in pressing charges. That's what Resnick wanted, no doubt. The martyred AIDS victim. "I think we have things under control, but you may want to stay around just in case."

He moved toward Resnick. "Do you really believe what you're saying, Resnick?"

Just then a stream of reporters and cameramen pushed past the security guard. They quickly assessed the situation and surrounded Halsey and Resnick. Cameras flashed, mikes were shoved in faces. The remaining board members tried to slip out. A reporter caught up and returned with Stanford Robbins, whose exit was hampered by an arthritic knee.

"Who's in charge, here?" shouted another reporter.

Halsey looked at Robbins who gave him a plaintive look. He then turned toward Resnick. "He is," he said.

Resnick sneered. "If that were true, the AIDS vaccine would be available by now. Virostat would be half the price. And I wouldn't look like this." He pointed to his skin.

A dark Hispanic man in his thirties moved in. He shoved a mike at Halsey. "Your name, sir?"

Halsey's eyes were riveted on Resnick. "I'm Elliot Halsey, president of this company. But Mr. Resnick here seems to have taken over."

Resnick snatched the microphone from the reporter and pushed himself between Halsey and the camera. He thrust his face within inches of the lens, clearly comfortable in the limelight. The reporter, his eyes fixed on Resnick's bloody arms and chest, backed off a step.

"Make no mistake, people of America," Resnick said, his eyes glowing. "Before these pigs get around to lifting a finger, AIDS will be in *your* home. It will attack *your* loved ones. It will attack *you.*"

Resnick pointed to Halsey. "Remember this man's face. Remember his name. When you get AIDS, this is the man to thank. Mr. Elliot Halsey, president of Alatron Laboratories, a bunch of corporate pigs with no conscience."

Halsey stood by and took the abuse. He sensed whatever he did would only aggravate the situation. In time sanity would prevail. And in a way, it did.

The reporter, angry at losing control of the interview, attempted to snatch the microphone from Resnick. But Resnick hurled the mike across the room and disappeared out the broken window. Halsey stepped through the slivers of glass and watched Resnick climb down the ladder. He didn't see the usual melange of demonstrators below, but didn't think much of it. Not then.

The reporter retrieved the mike and approached Halsey. "We'll hear now from the president of Alatron. May I have a statement, sir? Is there any truth to the AIDS FIRST accusations? Is Alatron holding out for more money before proceeding with the AIDS vaccine? Is the pilot program showing promise? Is . . ."

Halsey gave a short laugh and held up his hand. "Hold on a minute. One question at a time."

He took the microphone with a calmness he did not feel. His voice was steady considering the mileage he had given it. "There is no truth to the accusations you just heard. If we appear to be dragging our feet, it is because of obstructive government regulations. Money is not an issue. Not in the sense Mr. Resnick implies. It is too early to comment on our new pilot project. However, we are moving as fast as we can. I want to point out that ours is the first AIDS vaccine project to use a modified live virus for human testing."

Halsey picked up on the reporter's interest and decided to go on. Maybe something good would come of the board meeting after all. "Earlier, we and other research interests, including the CDC and National Institutes of Health, had been working with protein fragments of the viral shell. Scientists hoped that using these stimuli alone would activate a sufficient immune response. But that was not the case. The viral shell mutates too quickly. With the new project we envision a vaccine that will eventually prevent the contracting of AIDS as well as boosting immunity in those who already have the disease. People like Mr. Resnick," he said. People like my son, he thought.

The reporter gingerly took back the microphone. "Thank you, Mr. Halsey." He faced the camera squarely, keeping Halsey in the frame. "And so, the efforts to contain a deadly epidemic grind on, though not quickly enough for AIDS FIRST, the nation's most vocal and militant AIDS activist group.

"The multibillion-dollar question has yet to be answered: Will history's most devastating epidemic consume us? Or will dedicated institutions like Alatron Laboratories come to our rescue? This is Raphael Ortega. Eyewitness News."

As the television crews packed up and saw themselves out, Halsey stood by the shattered window and stared out at the Alatron campus. It was a beautiful place, with a courtyard of landscaped flowers, shrubs, and trees, surrounded by sleek glass multistoried buildings. The cobblestone drive encircled a giant fountain, some visionary's idea of elegance. To Halsey, it was an extravagance, a prime example of conspicuous consumption. He often wondered how many man hours of research could have been funded with the tens of thousands of dollars that had been sunk into that fountain.

He watched the activity below. The TV crews were packing their equipment into large vans. Raphael Ortega stopped briefly to converse with Resnick, who was slipping into a T-shirt. Halsey could see the familiar AIDS FIRST logo imprinted on the blood-red shirt that was their uniform. He wondered where the rest of the group was, and as he thought about it, he realized he hadn't seen many for several weeks now.

He wondered something else. Had Resnick been making the cryptic phone calls? He tried to imagine the abrasive voice toned down to a malevolent whisper. Maybe.

As he recalled the most recent of the threatening calls, he felt a twinge in his stomach. He had to find out who it was. Trying to shut it out was not going to work.

Maybe it was Resnick. He hoped so. At least then he would have someone he could confront and deal with.

As he turned to leave the board room, Halsey dismissed the security guard and made a note to have his secretary call housekeeping. He stopped abruptly when he saw Stanford Robbins seated at the other end of the room. Robbins's elbows were propped on the table and his head was buried in his hands. Halsey thought he saw the frail body shake. He approached the older man with concern and rested a hand on the board chairman's shoulder.

"Stan? Are you all right?"

Robbins looked up at him, and Halsey could see he'd been holding back tears. His eyes were red and moist, his face pinched with pain. "I'll be fine, Elliot. Thank you."

The old man sat back, bringing his chin up in a feeble gesture of pride. Halsey sat down next to him.

"I don't know what to do anymore, Elliot," Robbins said. "It was once an honor to be on the board of a pharmaceutical company. Particularly this one. We were the foot soldiers who fought disease and won." He smiled sadly. "I remember the early days of the polio vaccine. We were part of bringing it to millions of people. Money wasn't an issue. No one called us greedy pigs. No one threw rocks at us. The government didn't make us lockstep behind their silly regulations. Our hands were unbound. We did good deeds and good people appreciated us."

Robbins tapped a thin finger on the table and gave a weak smile. "Of course, we did make a bundle of money, but those were the days of the work ethic. Do good, work hard, reap the rewards. Things don't work that way anymore."

He looked up at Halsey, a single tear trickling down his cheek. "It's time, I think, for me to step down. I can't even keep up with the vision of my own president. I do believe in you, Elliot. I would like to see your project succeed. But I can no longer bear to watch people like that hideous demonstrator try to destroy us."

Halsey was surprised at how deeply touched he was. Perhaps it was the verbalization of a support he had long dreamed about. Perhaps the pain of an old man nearing the end of the road. He was ashamed of the animosity he held against this fragile shell of a man.

He groped for the right words. "Stan, I don't know what to say. You've lived through a lot of changes. I see how hard it must be for you. I'm sorry."

Robbins shook his head, a stoical smile stretching his dry lips. "No, Elliot, don't feel sorry for me. I would be the first to say that change is what keeps a company vital. Change is our lifeblood. Perhaps it's the fight that inevitably accompanies change that keeps us on our toes. I don't know. I do know we must have change, despite the impulse to stick with the sure bets."

Halsey was confused. There was an unexpected bitterness in the old man's voice. Halsey's face must have reflected his puzzlement, for Robbins chuckled softly. "Why do I challenge you every inch of the way if change is my recipe for success?"

Halsey laughed. "I guess that's a fair summation."

"I don't have a good answer, Elliot. I could say that I believe the fight is what makes us strong. So I force you to draw your sword. There may be some truth in that. But I don't believe I'm quite that clever. Nor that strong."

Robbins slowly shook his head. His body was bent over, as if shouldering the burden of the world. He shivered as a cool morning breeze came through the broken window. Halsey thought he should get Robbins back to his office, but the chairman had more to say.

"I'm just a crotchety old man who finds it hard to believe anymore that anything of use can be accomplished in this mean-spirited world. I don't know. I often think I've become that way myself."

Halsey felt a jolt of surprise as he realized how much Robbins sounded like himself at times—the times when he was most frustrated. You find your friends in the oddest places at the oddest times, he thought.

"It's all right, Stan," he said. "We'll manage." He rose, gently gripping Robbins's arm. "Right now you're tired and I'm going to get you back to your office. How about a cup of coffee?"

Robbins stood stiffly and smiled at Halsey. Somehow he seemed different, but Halsey couldn't quite put a finger on it. "Thank you, my boy," said Robbins.

He led Robbins into the corridor, where a lone custodian was pushing the vacuum. "Just a minute, Stan." He approached the custodian, whose head was down. "Say, fella," he said, putting a hand on the custodian's shoulder. "I'd appreciate it if you'd call one of your buddies and clean up the broken glass in there. Be careful of the blood. It's HIV positive."

The custodian seemed not to hear him at first, then slowly looked up at him with a strange smile. "Sure thing . . . Sir."

Halsey nodded and returned to Robbins. There was something unsettling about the custodian, but he let it pass. He had too much on his mind.

He took Robbins by the arm. And as the two men

walked slowly and silently toward the elevators, Halsey suddenly realized what was different about Robbins. His cheek hadn't twitched.

After Halsey left Robbins with his attentive secretary, he decided to head over to the research building. The board would be resuming its meeting later in the week, and he needed to gather whatever ammunition he could find.

He walked across the courtyard, which was uncannily quiet after all the commotion. Except for the fountain, of course, which hissed and sputtered. He saw one last cameraman packing up to leave. As he approached the fountain, he heard a muffled shout, then a splash of color caught his eye. He turned toward the fountain and blinked in disbelief. Through all the water, he thought he could make out a figure.

Like a giant gusher, the water spouted from an invisible source, reaching eerie heights, then spiraled downward like a circular waterfall. And through the cascading wall of water he saw something that didn't belong there. Something alien and incongruous.

It was a man! Standing, waving his arms. He seemed to be shouting. Halsey squinted hard. It was Resnick! Before the question even formed in his head, the answer became obvious as Halsey heard the camera truck's motor start up behind him. More publicity for AIDS FIRST. The more bizarre the circumstances, the better TV. Resnick was scoring big today. He shuddered as he thought of the fountain cleansing the HIV-positive blood from Resnick's skin and taking it ... where?

Halsey concentrated on shutting out the noise of the crashing water, but he still couldn't make out Resnick's words. The tone, however, was unmistakably Resnick—tauntingly obnoxious.

He felt like bashing the man's head in. He leaned over the cement wall at the edge of the cascading water. The fountain's cold spray drenched his face. "Resnick, get the hell out of there."

Resnick shook his head.

"Come out of there, or I'll come in after you, by God!"

Resnick laughed. "Come and get me, Prez," he bellowed.

Halsey stood there a moment, staring. Finally, something inside him snapped. He didn't stop to think about it. He tore off his shirt, kicked off his shoes, and sprang over the concrete wall that separated him from the crashing water. He plunged through the water, stunned by its force. It knocked him over once, and he gasped for air.

He saw Resnick easily now. He was standing inside the arc made by the falling water, now within a few feet of Halsey. Resnick's mouth was gaping as he stared.

"Come on, Resnick, dammit. I want to talk to you!"

Resnick stood transfixed. Speechless.

With a tremendous surge, Halsey slogged through the water and grabbed Resnick's arm. Resnick tried to pull back but he was no match for the stronger man. Halsey kept hold of him and dragged him back through the waterfall and over the outer cement wall.

The two men flopped down on the ground. Water ran off them and trickled over the cobblestones. It was approaching noon, and the courtyard was beginning to bustle with lunchtime activity. Heads turned toward them as people hurried by. Some stopped but carefully kept their distance.

Halsey and Resnick sat up and glared at each other, still breathing hard. "What in the hell were you doing in there?" Halsey gasped.

Resnick was still taking huge gulps of air, his strength sapped by an illness that each day brought him closer to the grave. Halsey felt a fleeting moment of pity.

Resnick seemed to catch his breath. "Taking a shower."

Halsey stared at him. He felt like laughing. Resnick, taking a shower. Washing the AIDS virus off his bloodied, infected body. Alatron's sewage system sucking it up. It made more sense than Halsey cared to admit. He said nothing. Then he remembered why he wanted to talk to Resnick. "Have you been the one calling me?"

He saw a look of genuine surprise on Resnick's face. "I don't know what you're talking about."

Halsey's eyes narrowed. He could feel the heaviness of the water on his lashes. "I don't believe you."

Resnick looked up. He was a pitiful sight. His skin had turned the same purplish shade as the malignant lesions that fed upon it. His teeth were chattering. "I don't make anonymous phone calls. I'd cut your damn phone line and make sure you were watching. That's how anonymous I am."

Halsey's anger left him as he looked at the man shivering beside him. Is this what Barry would look like in another year? Six months?

He picked up his shirt and held it out to Resnick. "Here, you must be freezing."

Resnick glared at him, his arms wrapped across his chest. He made no move to take the shirt.

"Come on," said Halsey with a wry grin, waving the shirt in front of Resnick, "I'm already responsible for your dying. Don't add a cold to it."

Resnick's eyes met Halsey's for a moment. He took the shirt and quickly looked away. He peeled off his wet shirt and slipped into Halsey's. "Thanks," he muttered to the ground.

Halsey watched Resnick with growing fascination. He felt compelled to know something—to understand. "What is it you really want? What are you after?"

Resnick sat huddled up, his arms encircling his knees. His teeth had stopped chattering and his color was improving. He seemed to be thinking. Halsey waited. It was a tenuous moment, as though Resnick was deciding whether to end it there, or to reveal something of himself.

"I don't know." Resnick stared into space, his voice softening.

Halsey felt a pang. It wasn't the Resnick he knew. There was a person there. A person who was hurting. It wouldn't be AIDS that killed this man, thought Halsey. It would be something else. Something even more deadly.

"That's too bad," was all he said.

Resnick's head whipped around. "What's that supposed to mean?" The hard edge had snapped back into his voice.

Halsey shrugged. "All that bitterness and destruction. And you don't know why. What a waste."

"What would you know about it?"

The words stabbed into Halsey like so many knives. What indeed? My son is dying, you jerk, he wanted to scream. But he said nothing. His heart ached. He was assaulted by colleagues who accused him of caring only about AIDS and a public claiming he was concerned only about profits. It would have been laughable if it wasn't Barry's languid face he saw when he looked at Resnick.

"I'm not the one wasting time," Resnick said at last.

Halsey wearily got to his feet. "Keep the shirt." He

turned to leave. Then thought of something. "Where's your friend Stryker?"

"You have a short memory."

"What are you talking about?"

Resnick must have read the perplexed look on Halsey's face. "Stryker sold out."

"Sold out! To whom?" Halsey was standing directly over Resnick now.

"To you. Alatron."

Something clicked in Halsey's mind. "You mean he agreed to lay off the demonstrations?" He saw Resnick nodding and went on. "In exchange for what?"

"I don't really know. I don't negotiate."

"Who were the negotiations with?" Halsey felt like he was tumbling around in a nightmare.

Resnick shrugged. "I assumed they were with you and the board. If not you, some other company man."

"For how much?"

"Not money. It had to do with the vaccine. A way to push it ahead faster. That's all I know."

Halsey shook his head. He felt betrayed. His self-righteous board was dealing behind his back. Who else could it be?"

He stared at the man at his feet. "You're wrong about me, Resnick. It seems we have something in common. We're both in the dark."

CHAPTER TEN

"I'm sorry, Rory." Kate reached across the table and took his hand. They were finishing breakfast at a small restaurant near the CDC.

He stared at her with soft brown eyes, full of warmth and understanding—and confusion. She felt a twinge of guilt. They were compatible, true, but there was something missing.

The naked truth seemed to stare back at her as she felt herself looking through Rory. As though the answer were scrawled on the wall behind him. Compatibility wasn't enough. Not without that certain chemistry that said it all.

"I'm just not ready for marriage again," she said.

He squeezed her hand. "I understand, Kate. You need more time."

She dabbed at her eyes with a tissue she fished out of her purse. She needed more than time.

"Hey," he said. "Cheer up. You can't get rid of me that easy. Besides, you might be needing me on this case you're nosing around in."

She raised an eyebrow. "Where did you get that?"

"Everybody knows about it, Kate. We're hovering over the Salt Lake case. If that nurse is positive for Congo, Special Pathogens is set to go."

Her eyes widened. "Why didn't you tell me?"

"I didn't want to make you mad." He winked and gulped down his coffee. "Time to get back."

Rory had a certain resilience that allowed Kate to dismiss her ruminations about their relationship. She let herself think he was indeed as untouched by her refusal as he seemed.

As they left the restaurant, Rory picked up a newspaper. He put a hand on Kate's shoulder. "Hey, check this out." He pointed to the front page.

She moved closer and read, her eyes widening. AIDS VACCINE BACKFIRES, KILLS TWO. "What on earth . . . ?"

They stood over the paper. Kate read aloud. " 'Dr. Roger Peck, head of the AIDS division at Atlanta's Fort Thacker, links two recent deaths to a possible defect in the AIDS vaccine produced by Alatron Laboratories in New Jersey. The company has been a leader in AIDS research and treatment.' "

"That bastard," she said.

Rory gave her a bewildered look. "Where do you suppose he got this?"

"It's no secret the Salt Lake nurse was a volunteer for Alatron's AIDS vaccine project. I don't know where he got the information about Maury. We're still tracking that down." She threw her head back. "Knowing Roger, it wouldn't surprise me if he improvised a bit."

"C'mon, Kate, he's not that bad. He likes his name in print, that's all."

They began walking, Kate's pace picking up with her anger. "The AIDS vaccine is up in the air. People are afraid to hope, afraid of side effects. A story like this could really set things back. I have a mind to call Roger ..."

Rory shook his head. "You'd better let me handle this, Kate. I'm afraid you might kill the guy."

She smiled. "Not a bad idea."

Kate felt a jolt as she entered her office. There, sitting at her desk, was an apparition bearing a strong resemblance to Harpo Cosgrove. The apparition was reading the same edition of the newspaper Rory had just picked up.

As she stood in the doorway, Harpo jumped up and crossed the room to give her a big hug. She was afraid for a moment he had cracked her rib. Hardly an apparition.

"Harpo!" she cried. "What a wonderful surprise!"

He put his arm around her and led her to the leather chair behind her desk. He handed her the paper. "I need your help again, Kate. It's my turn to come to you. So here I am."

He shrugged, a sheepish grin on his face. "Besides, Molly and the kids are visiting her mother upstate."

She laughed. "Harpo, you're like an angel from heaven. I was just wondering what to do next." She sat down and looked at the paper. "Roger Peck has lit a fuse. God knows when it will ignite. And where."

Harpo dropped into a chair. "It's already beginning—another reason I had to get out. I couldn't get a damn thing done. Everyone wants a statement. I decided to leave that to the politicos. Meanwhile, you and I might try to solve this thing before we have an epidemic on our hands."

She suddenly felt right. A mystery. A partner. And a long overdue vacation. This time, more than a couple of days.

She pulled out the Maury file, to which she had

added the file of the Salt Lake nurse, Trudy Porter.
And with it a list of questionable cases trickling into
the CDC, brought to her by a contact in the public
health department. She hadn't had time to get to the
names on the list. But she would. Now that Harpo
had appeared.

"Where," she said, "shall we start?"

"Way to go!" Harpo cheered. "What a pleasure not
to have to submit a slew of forms, then wait and wait.
Only to learn there's no money in the budget."

"You haven't answered my question."

"I think we've got to clear up this vaccine thing. I
suggest we go to Alatron first. Talk to the CEO and
the head of the vaccine project." He reached into his
khaki slacks and pulled out his wallet, then extracted
a card. "Elliot Halsey is the CEO. The other goes by
the name of Dave Parsons. Doesn't return calls."

"All right. We'll need to look over their protocols,
possibly interview everyone in the vaccine trials. We'll
miss our staff people."

Kate swiveled her chair toward the window, the
sight of the magnolia trees giving her a moment's
pause. She liked it here, overall. It was a good institution, dedicated to solving the mysteries of nature as
they adversely affected humanity.

She thought of Kekich. She hated to leave him high
and dry, but she'd make it up to him. Somehow.

She saw that Harpo was staring at her. She smiled.
"We'd better line up some appointments."

Harpo examined the card again, then stuck it back
in his wallet. "We're set. Tomorrow morning with
Halsey, nine o'clock. We can nail Parsons after that."

"You've thought of everything, haven't you? But
you should have stayed in New York. The Alatron
plant must be just minutes from the city."

"It is, but I thought I might have to twist your arm."

She laughed. "I'll bet you already made plane reservations."

"Delta's first morning flight to Newark."

"Awfully sure of yourself, aren't you?"

"Just sure of you, kiddo."

Her phone rang. She picked it up. "Yes?"

"Dr. Crane?"

She recognized the virology tech's voice immediately. "Hi, Dennis. Anything yet on the Salt Lake case?"

"Yes."

She could tell by his solemn tone it wasn't good. She shot a glance at Harpo who was leafing through the paper. Her grip tightened on the receiver.

"Congo?"

"No question. Blood antibodies are off the scale."

She saw Harpo's head shoot up. His eyes could have been a pair of question marks. She gave him a grim look and nodded.

"Thanks, Dennis. Hold tight. I'll be over. Meanwhile, don't talk to anyone."

She hung up. She and Harpo stared at each other wordlessly. Congo. Her mind raced, in tandem with her heartbeat. She thought of Rory and the crew in Special Pathogens, waiting to pounce. She wanted to get a head start. She and Harpo could handle it. She could tell by the steadfast set of Harpo's face that they were thinking the same thing. They were in it together, to the end.

Keith Heinman sat reading the paper in the barren living room of the old single-story house. There were no rugs on the worn pinewood floor, and no furniture in the room except for the second-hand couch on which he sat, and the coffee table.

The premises were isolated, surrounded by woods,

which suited his purpose just fine. The only people who happened by were hunters, and most of them could read the No Trespassing signs.

He had no worries. All was well under control. He hadn't expected the papers to break the story of a death possibly linked to the vaccine just yet. But once again, he found an unexpected ally, some media-worshiping idiot at Fort Thacker—Roger Peck, a self-aggrandizing jerk who hadn't the slightest clue.

Now all hell would break loose. He liked that. Make Halsey squirm a little, then really slam him when the victims of the expanded pilot project Heinman had engineered started dropping off like flies. Another week or two and Halsey would be begging Heinman to take him out of his misery.

He heard a sound from the basement. Parsons. He'd almost forgotten. The poor slob must be famished. He'd concluded Parsons needed to stay with him after they got back from their little business trip. Too much of a blabbermouth. And besides, he liked the company. Somebody to talk to.

He decided to take his guest a little breakfast and the morning papers. He went into the kitchen, got some juice out of the fridge, threw some whole wheat bread into the toaster, and poured a glass of nonfat milk. He put the dry toast and drinks on a cookie sheet with the papers and headed down the rickety wooden stairs.

He kicked open the door to his right and flicked on the overhead light. Parsons was huddled in a corner, arms and legs tightly bound, his mouth gagged. Parsons looked at him bug-eyed, blinking as he adjusted to the light. The small windows were so filthy that almost no light filtered through.

Heinman set the tray down and stood off, his hands on his hips. "Brought you some breakfast, Dave-boy."

Parsons's eyes fixed hungrily on the food.

Heinman regarded his captive. Even though the room was cool and dank, Parsons's round, pudgy face was beaded with sweat. His undershirt was damp and grimy from having slept on the dirty cement floor.

"You don't look so good without your expensive threads, Dave," he said as he looked at Parsons's fat paunch. Soft and pink, it gaped between Parsons's undershirt and the painter pants Heinman had given him.

Heinman felt a sudden urge to rub him out. Just like that. The man was a blight—human pollution.

With his foot he pushed the cookie sheet along the floor toward Parsons. He moved behind Parsons to untie the gag and arm ropes. "See the papers, Dave? All about your fine vaccine project. A couple people biting the dust. A little too ambitious, going off on your own like that."

He pulled the gag off and finished untying Parsons's arms, Parsons gasped for air and grabbed for the toast, wolfing it down. He was reaching for the juice when Heinman, who had been watching with growing disdain, kicked at the cup with such force that the contents swirled through the air as the cup flew across the room.

Parsons's eyes, big as saucers, followed the trajectory of the cup, then turned to Heinman. He buried his face in his hands and sobbed. "What're you doing? If you let me go I promise I won't tell a soul. I'll do anything you say."

Parsons's mind raced, searching desperately. Surely someone would look for him. But he kept running up against the same sorry fact: not a soul would miss him. His wife had kicked him out and he'd been living out of a suitcase. He'd been fired. No one would be surprised if he just stopped showing up. Especially when it came out about the vaccine. The board would be singing in the streets when they learned he was gone. A convenient scapegoat.

Heinman squatted down before him, drawing him away from his fretful speculating. "You already did 'anything' Dave, remember? That's why you're in this predicament. But since you brought it up, let's have a chat." Heinman straddled a wooden chair in the middle of the room and rewarded Parsons with a cruel smile.

Parsons collected himself and sat up straight. He had stopped sobbing and now all he felt was a cold pit in his stomach. He kept trying to push it away, like he had yesterday and the day before, but it kept coming back. Now he had no control over the feeling. "What are you planning for me?" he asked. He could hear the tremor in his voice.

"I don't know if I'll be needing you, Dave. We'll just have to wait and see how things go for Mr. Halsey."

Parsons saw Heinman's eyes change. They stared off into space for a flicker of a second, but in that moment the eyes seemed . . . disembodied. There was a boundlessness, a hatred without end, a madness that made Parsons's heart feel like it had just sputtered to a stop.

But my heart must be working, he thought inanely. I'm still alive.

"Let Mr. Halsey see his company fall apart. With his vaccine about to bring on an epidemic. That should stretch him out, don't you think? But he may need more. He's a stubborn son of a bitch. We'll be ready for him, though. Right, Dave?"

We'll be ready. The words rattled around in Parsons's head. He was no saint—he'd had his own selfish motives for pushing the vaccine through. But the thought of innocent people dying because of Heinman, and because of him, made his blood run cold.

Where do I come in? he wanted to ask. But he didn't. He was too afraid. The cold pit in his stomach got colder.

Heinman had long since made it clear that Halsey was the target of his scheme, but Parsons still didn't know why. And right now he didn't care. All he could think of was his own survival. He didn't understand why Heinman had brought him here, why he was being treated like this. He didn't know how to get the answers, so he said nothing. Heinman was in a mood to talk. He would listen.

"Where you come in," said Heinman, as through reading Parsons's mind, "is, you can help me learn a few more ropes at Alatron. Plus, we can't have you spilling the beans. We want to make Halsey stretch his memory. Why would anyone want to do this to him? You see, he hasn't realized yet that I've been planning this for ten years. And you know what?" Heinman looked thoughtfully at the ceiling, "I think he needs to be punished for having such a bad memory. He doesn't seem to remember me, Dave, and that annoys me. Know what I mean?"

Parsons was beginning to get the picture. He nodded and for a moment he actually felt lucky. As he considered what was about to befall Elliot Halsey, he decided he wouldn't trade places with the man for anything.

CHAPTER ELEVEN

Halsey shut off the alarm, rolled on his back, and stared at the ceiling. A bluish dawn light filtered through the partially closed Venetian blinds. His bedside clock said six A.M. but it felt more like the middle of the night. He was exhausted after yet another emergency board meeting—this one going into the wee hours of the morning. And now he had to face another day and the news media. He grimaced at the thought and tried to find the energy to get up.

He'd been dumbfounded twenty-four hours earlier at the word that Roger Peck was linking recent deaths to Alatron's vaccine. It hadn't taken Lowell Bekin long to rattle off a string of "I-told-you-so's." The live vaccine—hadn't he warned of its dangers?

"But, Lowell," Halsey had said, "the doses we're using are minuscule." The company's live virus AIDS vaccine trials weren't fully underway, he emphasized. At this point, in accordance with FDA guidelines, they were giving no more than test doses to a small number of volunteers in five urban areas. True, Salt Lake and New York were among those cities. Yes, it turned out the Salt Lake nurse might have been one of the volunteers, and he was concerned about that. He had shot Liam Kennedy from R and D out to Salt Lake as soon as the story broke. But the other cases Peck alluded to were not enrolled in the program.

He pondered over the nurse. How could the small dose she would have received do any harm? The inoculum was far less than anyone would get from a contaminated needle stick. And you could practically count the number of needlestick-acquired AIDS cases on one hand.

Moreover, the vaccine did not include the "wild" strain of the virus. It had been "attenuated," by repeated passages through cell cultures. A standard and safe technique, used for other proven vaccines such as polio and influenza.

He had tried to reach Peck, but the man wasn't returning calls. He questioned Peck's reputation enough to wonder if Peck had a quiet deal going with one of Alatron's competitors. Possibly Dalmouth-Keller, the only other company even close to coming out with a live virus AIDS vaccine.

While Halsey respected the integrity of most pharmaceutical houses, he had seen Dalmouth-Keller's tactics become increasingly cutthroat since their mega-flu vaccine failed and their stock cratered a few years earlier. He also recalled a recent scandal involving a Dalmouth-Keller spy caught snooping around the molecular genetics lab at Rockford Pharmaceuticals.

There were plenty of ways to delegate blame. But they didn't prevent him from taking a hard look at his own backyard. He called a meeting of the research department, and they pored over the computerized reports from the test sites. There had been gaps in the data. Follow-up on volunteers was haphazard at best.

As he got into it he was dismayed. Project director

Dave Parsons was more inept than he'd realized. He should have stepped in far sooner, fired Parsons long ago. He should have bit the bullet, dealt with the board's protests and personally overseen the details of the project himself. But there had been so many distractions.

The bizarre phone calls—they had gnawed away at him, leaving gaping holes in his judgment. He could see that now and it rattled him. Perhaps that had been the intention.

To make matters worse, Parsons was nowhere to be found. He should still be around, collecting his paycheck. But Parsons's secretary reported he hadn't been in for three days. His wife hadn't seen him, either, but said they were separated.

He sat on the edge of the bed and shook the cobwebs out of his head. Three days! The most important project in the company—maybe the country—and the man in charge had disappeared.

He thought about the board meeting. Overall, he demonstrated he was on top of matters, moving speedily and with a sureness he did not feel. His openmindedness and willingness to look for answers had made a dent on Stan Robbins and a few of the other board members. They had backed off somewhat, much to the chagrin of Bekin.

But it didn't look good. The Salt Lake nurse worried him more than he cared to admit. He knew if he let himself believe for one moment his company was responsible for her death he might just fall apart.

He got up and headed for the shower, wondering what lay ahead. Another day of grueling self-examination. And another media circus once the stories came out. The press would set up camp outside his office. And AIDS FIRST, God knew what they'd be up to.

It was then that he thought about Barry. Barry, who

was gay and had AIDS, but who would have no part of AIDS FIRST. Halsey wanted to believe it was out of some sort of loyalty to him that his son refrained from joining ranks with the activists, but he knew the real reason. Barry was a fatalist—too skeptical to try to change a society that turned its back on him.

He returned to the bed and reached for the phone. Steve had said to call this morning. Barry was doing better. And it wasn't really too early. He knew the nurses would have waked the poor kid up already with their morning rituals. He dialed the number direct to Barry's room.

He heard a weak voice. "Hello?" He closed his eyes, tried not to see his son, the body that went with the voice, wasting away.

"Hi, Barry." The words pushed through the lump in his throat.

"Hi, Elliot."

Halsey felt his hold tighten on the receiver. His son had stopped calling him Dad in high school. He had never gotten used to it and he never would. Though Barry denied it, the change represented a growing rift between them. Susan was still Mom.

Halsey took it as a statement. But unlike Barry's long hair and ragged clothes, it had been more than teenage rebellion. It was a commentary by his son— eloquently executed by the omission of one word— that Halsey had failed as a father. He was not a role model, not someone to look up to, not a buddy.

To hear his own name in this context was like being lashed with a whip. It stung all the more because he knew there was truth in it. He had been too busy carving out a future, working long hours in the name of supporting a family he rarely saw. His single-mindedness had destroyed his marriage, made him a stranger to his children.

He felt his eyes sting. He hadn't been there for Barry and now Barry was gay. And dying of AIDS. Somehow, had he been a better parent, he was sure things would be different.

"Steve says you're doing pretty well," he said, pushing aside his pain.

"Yeah, I'll live. Going home tomorrow." An awkward pause. "Guess you're having problems with the company. I saw the paper."

Halsey could hear the strain in his son's voice, the effort to make courteous conversation. Why couldn't they break through the polite patter and really talk to each other? In that sense they were too much alike, both clamming up too easily, both too ready to keep things to themselves.

He managed a laugh. "Things are a mess all right." He looked up at the ceiling. "Barry . . ."

"Yeah?"

"Steve seems nice. I'd like to meet him."

"Okay."

"I'm going to try to get into Manhattan this week sometime."

The line hummed. "That's nice."

He took a deep breath. This wasn't working. But he felt a modicum of relief. Barry sounded like he was going to be all right. "Well, listen. I've got a day packed with meetings . . ."

"Yeah. Thanks for calling."

"How about dinner later this week? I'll come in, take you and Steve out."

"Steve's gone on a business trip."

"Then just you and me. I'd like that."

"Sure. Give me a call."

"You'd better take this week off, rest up," Halsey suggested.

"I'll be okay. They want me back as soon as possible."

"You want me to talk to them? You need your rest."

He could almost see Barry impatiently roll his eyes. "No, thanks. I can take care of myself."

He sighed. There had always been too much of that in him when it came to his kids—a meddling overprotectiveness. Perhaps a way of making up for lost time. Would he ever learn to keep his mouth shut?

"I'm sorry, Barry. I know you can handle things."

"It's okay."

"Well . . . goodbye. And take care."

"Goodbye, Elliot."

As soon as Halsey hung up, the phone rang. As if things weren't bad enough, his secretary informed him he had an appointment first thing with doctors from the CDC and the New York Medical Examiner's office. Great. Friends of Peck's, no doubt—vultures circling overhead, waiting to strike.

When he finally got into the shower he made the water hot as he could stand it. He wasn't looking forward to the day.

Harpo hailed a cab at Newark airport. After chatting idly with the driver for a while, he and Kate rode on in reflective silence.

Kate looked out the window and glanced at her watch, suddenly struck by the fact that they were barely moving. The morning traffic was bumper to bumper. "We're going to be late," she said. "We're starting off on the wrong foot."

Harpo shrugged. "Our CEO's got the company image to protect. It won't be easy in any case."

She nodded. She didn't like corporate types. Too

slick and self-involved. The world revolved around them. As she watched her marriage fall apart three years earlier, she realized how she and her ex were so different in perception and character. He was attracted to the glitz and power of the corporate world. She hated it. The difference became symbolic of all that was wrong with their marriage.

She had a fair idea of what to expect from the up-coming meeting, having been involved with pharma-ceutical companies before. She had found the boards and CEOs to be tricky and misleading, invariably dis-tracting her and her crew from getting at the crux of the problem.

"Halsey will probably try to lead us astray," she remarked.

Harpo glanced at her. "You know him?"

"No, I just know the type."

"How's that?"

"Remember the epidemic of paralysis after Dal-mouth-Keller's mega-flu vaccine a couple years ago?"

"Sure. They had some great notion that people would only need to be vaccinated every five years. Were you involved in that?"

She nodded. "Peripherally. The FDA was running the show. But I got sent out as the CDC rep. It was an open-and-shut case. A whopping thirty percent of the people involved in the initial trials got neurological side effects. And ten percent of those had the most severe complication—paralysis due to an ascending myelitis."

Harpo frowned. "I remember that. Terrible. Did the company deny responsibility?"

"Not the hard-core researchers. But it was like pull-ing teeth to get to them. It seemed that everywhere we turned, the CEO and his board of conspirators were there. So willing to provide pat answers, so eager to wine and dine us. It was offensive."

"What finally happened?"

"The company admitted its culpability, settled a bunch of suits out of court, and got its corporate hand slapped by the FDA."

"So you figure Halsey will pull a Dalmouth-Keller?"

"No question," said Kate. "They all dance to the same tune."

"Yeah, the almighty dollar."

At nine-fifteen their cab pulled up to the gate of the Alatron complex. Traffic was at a standstill. There were press vans, television camera crews, and mobs of demonstrators and police pushing and shoving at one another.

A group of protesters in red shirts that said AIDS FIRST were effectively blocking traffic. Horns honked, people shouted, and above the chaotic din rang out the rhythmic chant, "AIDS first! AIDS first!"

The AIDS FIRSTers strung themselves across the road, hand in hand. Blue-coated police carrying shields and batons were scuffling with the protesters, dragging them off the street. As each protester was taken away, another would replace him in the blockade.

Harpo leaned forward and muttered to the cabby, "Looks like we'll be here all day. Any idea how far the main buildings are?"

The cabby was a jaundiced type—swarthy-skinned with a knit cap and a black beard. He shrugged. "Quarter mile or so. They gotta impress ya with the flowers and shrubs. Make ya feel like you're in a rain forest. Instead of on top of a ghetto. You could walk it. Get there a lot sooner." He snorted. "Unless these queers stop ya."

As though on cue, a tall, spindly man in a red shirt hurled an egg at the cab. It splattered against the rear window. Harpo and Kate looked at each other. The cabby swore. "Friendly bunch, ain't they?" He rolled down his window. "Get lost, you goddamn fags!" No one seemed to notice.

Kate shook her head in amazement. "Is it like this every day?"

"Them red-shirts hang out here, but not that many. And the cops and TV crews—they came in earlier. Something's comin' down, looks like."

Kate nodded. They were all here for the same reason. Roger Peck and his big mouth. She could almost feel her blood pressure shoot up at the thought. She watched a group of AIDS FIRSTers lie down in the street as the police tried to shoo them off. Another egg thwacked against the cab, this time smearing the windshield. The cabby shot his head out the window with his middle finger skyward.

Kate was outraged. "For all they know, we're on their side."

The cabby hooted. "Lady, nobody's on their side. Even if you *think* you're on their side, believe me, you ain't. They don't wanna hear about it. They *wanna* lay down in the street. They *like* dirt."

She smiled. He was a typical street-wise cabby, overflowing with unsolicited opinions. She watched two AIDS FIRSTers handcuff themselves to the bumper of an Alatron delivery truck inching in their direction. "You may be right," she said.

"You bet I'm right."

Harpo pulled out his wallet, a frown on his face. He looked at Kate's sensible shoes. "Shall we walk?"

She glanced at her watch and nodded. A demonstrator pressed his face up against the glass on her side and stared at her. The cabby turned and shook his fist. The demonstrator disappeared, swallowed up by the crush of bodies.

Harpo paid the driver and they slid out of the cab into the crowd.

Halsey sneaked in the back door with little difficulty. He took the stairs to his office on the fifth floor of the Administration Building and gave the reporters yet another slip as he walked through the back door to his inner office. He tossed his briefcase down and buzzed his secretary.

"Mr. Halsey?" she whispered into the phone. "You're here?"

"Unfortunately," he said. "How about a quick update, Rose."

He could sense her hesitation. There were probably reporters hanging all over her.

"Why don't you come in here, Rose," he said.

"Right away."

Within moments she was in his office, looking a bit ruffled. She gave him a strained smile and glanced nervously over her shoulder. "I've never seen anything like this, Mr. Halsey. They're camping out in the front office, waiting for a statement from you."

His lips tightened. "I have a mind to give them a statement all right."

She shook her head. "I don't think you want to tangle with these people. They seem quite distraught."

He smiled at her. Rose was a gem. An overly correct, somewhat severe-looking woman in her forties, she had followed him up from R and D and had stuck by him. Loyal to the core. She would shudder when a subordinate called him by his first name. Proper employees simply did not do such things.

"I'm sorry you have to go through this, Rose," he said. "The world is turning into a crazy place." He sighed. "And so is this company."

He looked at the schedule she gave him, then checked his watch. Nine-forty. "Are the flunkies from the CDC here?"

"They just arrived. Only one, Dr. Crane, is CDC," she corrected. "The other, Dr. Cosgrove, is with the New York Medical Examiner's office."

"Well, let's get on with it." He had an idea he might do better with the cannibal press. These two were probably here to close him down. Thanks to good old Dr. Peck.

Neither of them was what he'd expected. She looked like a dream. She must have been in her late thirties, but appeared younger. Her midlength auburn hair blended with a clear peaches-and-cream complexion. The intent blue eyes held a quiet look of amusement. She was dressed professionally. A tailored white linen jacket and a deep maroon skirt cut just below the knee. Enough to show the turn of a shapely leg.

He wondered if she was as cool about everything. The man looked interesting. Oddly, his dress was as casual as hers was formal. No tie. No jacket. Khaki slacks, Madras shirt, loafers without socks. His eyes were bright and probing. They were a good match, surely the best of what the bureaucrats had been getting of late.

"I'm Allen Cosgrove," he heard the man say with aplomb and an outstretched hand. "New York Medical Examiner's office. This is my colleague from the CDC. Dr. Katherine Crane."

Halsey's eye fell on the ring on Cosgrove's left hand. The marriage finger. Then turned casually to the woman. Her fingers were long and tapering. Devoid of rings. And beautiful.

"Please sit down," he said. They sat down. There was an awkward pause as they took stock of one another.

Turning from one to the other with a smile that lingered on her, he said, "What can I do for you?"

Harpo glanced at Kate. They had decided to let her open the discussion.

She had been studying their host. The strong hawk-like face with the dark hair combed back and a touch of gray at the temples. Distinguished. The eyes a deep brown, almost black. Their gaze made her disquietingly aware of herself. And him.

She straightened in her seat. "We have questions about the safety of your AIDS vaccine." She was startled by her abruptness. Her voice sounded harsh to her own ears. She saw Harpo's head whip around toward her. She knew he had picked up on it. They had decided they wouldn't put Halsey on the defensive. And here she was, all but pointing a finger at him.

Halsey felt a wave of disappointment. So much for intuition. She had interested him. And it hadn't just been her beauty. He had sensed a warmth, an integrity. An individuality not evident in bureaucrats—people who were always sniffing around, looking to criticize. Unable to contribute anything on their own.

"Some people think so," he said finally. "We're handling it."

"Oh," said Kate, squaring her jaw. "So you're handling it? What does that mean?"

Harpo jumped in. "We want to help any way we can. That's why we're here."

Halsey gave them an icy nod. "Thank you. We don't need your help." His eyes shifted to Kate. "I don't believe that's why you're here. Not for a minute."

"Now just a moment," said Harpo. "We're on your side. Make no mistake. Your company is close to bringing out the AIDS vaccine, probably the most important medical endeavor of the century. You have our support."

"I see nothing of that in Dr. Crane's posture. I have an idea who sent you. The good Dr. Peck. The bureaucratic hit man."

Kate felt the hackles rising on her neck. She could see the alarm in Harpo's eyes. But it was not enough to shackle an anger that had come out of nowhere. "Your priority is to protect the corporate image, is that it, Mr. Halsey?"

Halsey got to his feet. "I see no point in continuing this conversation."

Harpo gave Kate an incredulous look. "Please, Mr. Halsey. I would like a moment alone with Dr. Crane."

Halsey gave a perfunctory nod and went back to his papers.

Harpo seized Kate by the arm. "Come with me, Dr. Crane.

"Have you lost your mind?" he exclaimed as they stepped into the corridor. "What the hell has come over you, Kate?"

She leaned against the wall, brushing a hand over her eyes. "I don't know, Harpo. I can't seem to do anything right. Not when it comes to men." She blushed and lowered her head.

Harpo slapped his forehead. A lightbulb flashed in his head. "Not when it comes to men ... He knocked you over, didn't he? That's it, isn't it? Goddamn!"

She looked at him with a misty eye. "I'm afraid I've ruined everything, Harpo. I'm sorry. Let's go back in and I'll apologize."

He gave her another look and held back a smile. She must have been hit hard. He was touched by her vulnerability, once he saw it that way. He threw an arm around her, embracing her. "Okay, lady. Let's try again. I understand. I really do."

He knew, by the lift of her chin, that whatever it was had passed. He looked up, suddenly diverted. He pulled Kate toward him as the janitor brushed by them with his mop.

They found Halsey sifting through the papers on his desk. He looked up with apparent disinterest, still wondering how she could have affected him as she did, and then not been what he thought she was. A woman apart. A *rare avis*.

He motioned to a chair and they sat down.

"We would like to start over," said Harpo, who looked first at Halsey then Kate. "Our intention in coming here is to offer our services in an unofficial capacity. Avoid the media. Possibly head off an epidemic. Nobody, not Roger Peck, not the CDC, sent us. We feel there is nothing more important than the fight against AIDS. You and your people are among the leaders in that fight. You've taken the big step in using the live virus. It's a courageous step, one that could bring you considerable loss if you fail."

Halsey settled back in his chair. He didn't know what to believe. Cosgrove suddenly sounded like a walking advertisement for Alatron, yet he seemed sincere—a straight shooter. But Dr. Crane. He didn't know about her. He was befuddled, no longer trusting his instincts. On the other hand, he was curious. And he found himself fascinated by her. It was still all he could do to keep from staring.

She looked at him. "I'm sorry for what I said." Their eyes locked. "I had no right to pigeonhole you. I hope we can start with a clean slate."

As Kate and Halsey stared at each other, there

seemed to be a meeting of minds. He felt a thrill as if an electric current had coursed down his spine.

Harpo snapped open his briefcase and pulled out the records on Maury and Porter. He handed them to Kate.

She smiled at him. She opened the folder and leafed through it. "We think that Trudy Porter, a recipient of your company's AIDS vaccine, died from Congo fever, caused by the lethal African hemorrhagic virus. Akendo Maury, the basketball player, apparently did also, though we're not sure whether he received the vaccine. If he did, we don't know if it was Alatron's."

She leaned forward and handed the records to Halsey. "We'll be glad to explain those . . ."

Halsey experienced a ringing in his ears and for a moment he saw his visitor's lips moving, but the ringing filled his head. Congo fever! The words resonated in his mind, as though a loudspeaker had gone wild. Surely there was some mistake. His mind raced as he reached for the reports. "Thank you," he said in a subdued voice. "I think I'll understand them."

He leafed through the pages, forcing himself to look at the pictures, note the similarities, fully absorb the fact that the nurse was indeed the one who had received his company's vaccine. "Our company is the only private institution working with the Congo virus," he announced in the manner of a confession as he looked up. He could hear the dismay in his voice as the ringing receded. "It's part of a comprehensive vaccine program we initiated a few years back."

Kate nodded. She seemed concerned.

He turned back to the reports. "How can this be?" he exclaimed, moving through the papers more rapidly, as though trying to find the answer, or verification that it was all a tasteless hoax.

"Maybe the vaccine was contaminated," suggested Kate.

"Impossible," snapped Halsey. The moment the word escaped his lips, he regretted it. "At least, I hope it's impossible," he said in a softer tone. He went back to examining the virology reports.

Kate and Harpo watched in silence, giving him time to digest the information. Kate welcomed the opportunity to quietly observe him and analyze her reaction. Harpo was right. She found Halsey attractive, and she was frightened by the impact of her own feelings. Was he another man like her ex-husband? A man who sublimated his own humanness to corporate and social image? She couldn't take another man like that. Not in this life.

Finally, Halsey looked up. He appeared tired. "I wish I could offer you an explanation, but I can't. I was planning to go over to our research facility this morning. Perhaps the two of you would like to join me."

"We would love to," they said in unison.

Halsey stood up, arranging the papers in a neat stack, wishing the thoughts pounding at him could be filed away in such a tidy fashion. Instead, he felt as though a dam had just burst. What was his world coming to? Nothing was what it seemed. Had he, in his zeal to bring a cure to the world, unleashed a deadly epidemic? He couldn't let himself think that, even for a moment. He would prove to these people, to himself, that all was in order. There was some mistake, an explanation at least, that he could swallow without choking.

"Well, then," he said, "follow me."

CHAPTER TWELVE

Keith Heinman watched Halsey's two visitors with interest. He smiled at his cleverness in choosing a custodial position as his cover. While everyone else had to slink around to avoid the press, he could sweep the floors right under their noses. No one asked him for a statement nor pestered him in any way. Yet, he knew when the time came he could bend their collective ear at will. And he had a key to every room in the plant. No one gave him a second thought. Just another blue-collar worker humbly putting in his hours.

He was pleased to see Halsey's guests. He had witnessed the entire conversation between the woman and the man in the hall as he scrubbed around them. The fireworks were just beginning. As he shoved his mop around on the linoleum floor at the back entrance to Halsey's office, Heinman planned his next move. Halsey and the two doctors would be going over to R and D soon. They would surely take samples of the HIV cultures used to produce the vaccine. And they would analyze the bottles of vaccine and find a

little surprise. Halsey would have to announce to the
world that Alatron's negligence had caused innocent
people to die.

There would be panic as they found that even more
people were marked for death. Halsey would proclaim
his innocence, but no one would believe him. He
would be looking at the end of his career, deploring
the horrible accident and damning Dave Parsons for
illegally extending the vaccine project behind his back.

Then, just as Halsey was concluding matters
couldn't get much worse, and when it suited Heinman's purpose, Halsey would discover the unimagin-
able—the chilling fact that *none* of it had been an
accident.

His life would become a nightmare, his fate the
mercy of one man. Only death would give him peace.
Death, which Heinman intended to make Halsey wish
for before he, Heinman, accommodated that wish.
Heinman relished the thought. Yes, Mr. Halsey, the
chickens are coming home to roost. You don't make
a man spend a decade in a loony bin without paying
a price. A very expensive price. After all, ten years of
interest had accrued.

A member of the press scurried by, apparently looking for the action. He gave Heinman an indifferent
glance. Heinman felt a swell of anger. If the scumbag
only knew who he was ... what he was doing. He
would know, in due time.

Heinman dropped the mop into the bucket and
headed over to the research building.

Harpo and Kate accompanied Halsey across the
cobblestone courtyard to the research building. It
housed virtually all the research scientists and projects
for Alatron, including the AIDS vaccine project. As
he led the way, Halsey felt a touch of embarrassment

at the opulence of the grounds, especially the fountain. He noticed a knot of media types and red-shirted demonstrators across the way, apparently preoccupied with the police and a couple of delivery trucks.

"We need to hurry," he said in a low voice, his head down as he kept a step ahead of Kate and Harpo.

Kate was amused at his cloak-and-dagger manner. She felt a mixture of excitement and apprehension as she trotted to keep up with his long stride. And there was something else. Something to do with her reaction to Halsey the man. Something she still wasn't ready to deal with.

He was acutely aware of her presence. She had a softness about her, and a subtle perfumed scent that had him envisioning her sitting across from him at a candlelight table. He felt his breath catch in his throat. You must be crazy, he told himself. You don't even know her.

He suddenly picked up the pace. A group of reporters was bearing down on them.

The three of them ducked into the back entrance of R and D and stood for a moment inside the door to catch their breath. Kate laughed and brushed her hair back. "Whew! I feel like a fugitive."

Halsey looked at her, then laughed, too. It was crazy. She could make him laugh when only a moment earlier his throat had been tight with apprehension. He tried to shrug it off.

There was a sudden clamor of excited voices as reporters surged into the lobby at the other end of the corridor. Halsey placed the flat of his hand on Kate's back and gave her a gentle push. "Second floor and turn right."

They ran up the stairs, the sounds of their feet echoing in the narrow stairwell. Halsey had his key ring out, deftly turned the lock, and led them through a

door marked BIOHAZARD. They entered a vestibule
with benches, clothing hooks, and a row of sinks and
lockers along one wall. They could see through large
glass windows into the laboratory.

"No one will follow us here," he said.

Kate peered into the laboratory beyond the vestibule. It was lined with sterile white counters on one
side and biosafety cabinets with hoods on the other.
She knew the cabinets were ventilated with negative
pressure systems and laminar airflow. HEPA filters
would screen out the smallest particles, including
viruses.

You couldn't be too careful, she knew. A couple of
air droplets could carry enough inoculum of deadly
airborne viruses to kill a roomful of people. There
appeared to be a high-level containment—most likely
biosafety three.

Adjacent to the hoods were tall refrigerator-looking
structures she recognized as incubators. Two white-
coated figures were seated on stools just outside the
hoods. Their arms disappeared into the cabinets
through holes. Heavy rubber gloves covered their
hands, which were handling test tubes and glass pipettes. The two technicians appeared to be absorbed
in their work. You had to be, she thought. If you
wanted to live to collect your paycheck.

Warning signs were posted all over, including BIO-
HAZARD and SPECIAL HANDLING, but Kate suspected
these people didn't need reminders. They lived on the
edge, day in, day out. One slip was all it took. She
could feel herself tense up inside, just watching them.
She remembered when she worked in the high-con-
tainment facilities at CDC. She could never get
through a day without a splitting headache.

There had been some narrow calls. Once a building
inspector had walked blithely through the lab while

she was working under the hood with a TB culture. She had panicked and screamed at him to get the hell out as he moved too close to the hood. She had felt the breeze created by his body as he brushed past. A breeze that she knew had to be sucking contaminated air from inside the cabinet out into the room. Terrified, she had pulled her hands out of the hood and with lightning speed donned a surgical mask.

She had known of many lab disasters from just such instances—some idiot carelessly reversing the direction of airflow was all it took. She tested positive for TB not long after, but fortunately never developed an active infection. Nor, miraculously, did the building inspector.

Her eyes roved around the room. A few white-coats were milling around. There were several empty work sites. Even though there were not a lot of techs working, the place exuded a kind of intense energy that was palpable. She shot a look at Harpo and thought he was sensing the same thing.

Halsey opened a closet and extracted three folded, starched white coats. "We'll need to wear these," he said as he handed them out. "Normally this place is pretty busy, but people are running late because of the mobs outside."

As Kate put on her lab coat, she pointed to the safety cabinets. "Is this where you keep the HIV cell cultures?"

"Yes. The African viruses are on a different floor. Level four containment. We're working with both Congo and Marburg, another Filovirus," he went on. He was beginning to feel better. Surely there was nothing wrong here. "We're banking on the possibility that a vaccine for one will be effective for the other. We'll soon be ready to initiate testing in humans."

He put his hand on the doorknob. "Let's go in. You'll want to see our setup, I'm sure."

As they entered, a few heads turned in their direction, then turned back to their work. True scientists, thought Kate. Not interested in entertaining visitors.

"They don't seem to mind our being here," she observed.

Halsey laughed. "They're used to visitors. The FDA is always springing surprise inspections on us. If we didn't proceed with business-as-usual, we'd never get anything done."

Kate tried to figure out how the Congo virus could have gotten tangled up with the AIDS vaccine. The two projects would be in completely different areas. She could understand Halsey's reluctance to consider contamination.

Still, the Congo virus was in the same building, making contamination an attractive hypothesis. There were plenty of cases, albeit rare, of strange and inexplicable viral spread, as in the case of a British photographer years earlier who contracted and died of smallpox due to faulty ventilation of a containment facility one flight below.

Harpo had been poking along, not saying much, but craning his neck and turning to Halsey now and then. "Where are you making the vaccine?"

"Across the hall. We can go there next."

"Do any of the people on this floor work upstairs with the Congo virus?" Kate asked.

Halsey shook his head. "No. That's why I think you're barking up the wrong tree. If those two people died from Congo fever, it's practically impossible that it came from our lab. We have rigorous standards, far and above those required by the government. We've never had a laboratory-acquired infection in the twelve years I've been with the company."

Kate glanced at Harpo. He looked frustrated. Then she looked at Halsey. She saw no guilt, no deception in the dark intense eyes.

"It's still a possibility," said Harpo. "Accidents happen. Sterilization procedures break down. Spills, broken pipettes, any number of things. Techs don't always go by the rules. You can't control for the human element."

Halsey stared at him thoughtfully, saying nothing.

"We'll know soon enough," said Kate. "We'll need samples of your HIV and Congo cultures, as well as the vaccine itself."

"Of course," said Halsey with a touch of formality. He led them deeper into the room, talking of the setup as they moved. How they passed the AIDS virus through multiple cell cultures, how they controlled for adventitious agents, how they preserved and stabilized the vaccine. And why he felt so strongly in favor of pursuing the live virus vaccine—because it was the best chance to provide prolonged and complete immunity. It was the best way to mobilize the body's T-cells, so essential to fighting off the virus.

As Kate listened, she thought Halsey's knowledge impressive, his methodology impeccable. This man was a scientist. A visionary. And a corporate executive. He didn't fit any stereotype she could think of.

"Who's running the pilot project?" put in Harpo.

Halsey had been dreading the question. He took a deep breath as they headed out of the room. "A fellow by the name of Parsons, Dave Parsons." In truth, Parsons was still head of the project despite the fact that he had been fired. So why, Halsey wondered, did he feel as though he hadn't completely leveled with his guests?

"Perhaps we could meet with him."

Halsey pushed the door open into the vestibule and

waited for Kate and Harpo to exit. As he followed them into the vestibule, he was already slipping out of his lab coat. "He's not here right now," he said.

Kate looked at Halsey with a frown, sensing reservation in his voice for the first time. "Will he be around later?"

"I don't think you'll find him very helpful."

"Oh? Why is that?" Kate's ears perked up. A quick glance in Harpo's direction told her he, too, sensed the subtle but unmistakable change in Halsey's tone.

"Actually, he isn't with us anymore. He apparently decided not to stay around after he was given a month's notice. That's about all I can tell you."

Harpo and Kate removed their lab coats in silence, processing the information that had just been dropped in their laps. Kate had a sinking feeling as she sensed that Halsey was holding something back. She was going to have to revise her opinion of him after all.

"He was fired, then?" said Harpo.

Halsey nodded.

Kate and Harpo exchanged glances. "Why is that?" she asked, her eyes shifting to Halsey.

Halsey shrugged. "I'm not in a position to divulge the reasons." He watched them uneasily, knowing his answer was as unsatisfactory to them as it was to him. But, he told himself, it really wasn't any of their business. "I'll try to answer any questions you may have for Parsons," he offered.

They nodded, again giving each other knowing looks. "We'll need to get moving on collecting the specimens," said Kate. "Hopefully we can get them to Atlanta first thing in the morning."

"You're welcome to use our facilities if you'd like. Transporting these materials, as you know, is complicated and hazardous."

Harpo glanced at Kate. "What do you think, Kate? It could save running back and forth."

She frowned, turning the possibilities over in her head. She didn't like the idea of obligating themselves by using Alatron's facilities. Especially when she sensed that Halsey was not completely open with them. On the other hand, if the vaccine turned out to be contaminated, she would need to be here.

"Let's think it over," she said. "I'd have to make a list of what we would need. Including a couple of our technicians."

Halsey nodded. "I can provide you with techs also. Excellent ones, who already know the ropes."

"Let's work on it," she said, knowing all along what she would do. There was no way she was leaving here now. She wasn't even going to try to sort out all her reasons.

There was an awkward silence as Halsey's and Kate's eyes met. "All right," said Halsey. "Let me show you where we're working on the vaccine. Then we'll go to the upstairs lab. Where we keep the African viruses."

Halsey sneaked through the back door into his office. He had been able to dodge the media all morning. Probably because he had been in the maximum-containment lab where no reporters were allowed or dared tread. One thing about the press, they had a healthy respect for bugs—at least the kind that could kill you.

He looked at his agenda for the rest of the morning. The board was not going to try to have a formal meeting. Not with the media on their backs.

But they had evolved an alternative plan for "damage control." Halsey would meet with board members Robbins and Bekin in one of the basement employee lounges, then contact the rest privately as to their plan. Most board members, Halsey knew, were of the opinion that if Bekin, Halsey, and Robbins could come to an agreement on anything, the others would go along.

He had half an hour before meeting with the two board members. As he sat down for a breather, he went over in his mind the earlier meeting with the two doctors. Despite the ill tidings they brought, he was actually relieved to have them here. They could help take over the responsibility for internal monitoring that would normally fall on his shoulders. They appeared to be fair, to the point. No hidden agendas.

He tried not to think too much about Kate Crane. He began shuffling through a stack of reports on his desk, but he could not erase her from his mind. The way she walked. The way she moved her hands. Her profile, her hair, those amused blue eyes that seemed to see all.

He hopelessly tossed the reports aside and turned to look out the window at the courtyard below. Still, he saw her face. He shook his head with frustration. He didn't want this. Just when he was simplifying his life by immersing himself in his work, she had to come along. He hoped she was married or involved.

He laughed aloud at how transparent he was. No, he hoped nothing of the kind. He hoped she was free. He ran his fingers through his hair. He felt an urge to look in the mirror, to see himself as she might see him.

He reached for the phone in an impulse to call her. He let his hand rest on the receiver, studying it as he hesitated. Then, his heart leapt as the phone rang. Was it her? No, she didn't have his private number. Or did she? He picked it up. "Hello?"

All he heard was a humming noise. "Hello, hello?" he barked impatiently.

He listened a few moments and heard only the incessant hum of an empty phone line. He was about to hang up when he heard a bone-chilling laugh. It was not a loud or raucous laugh. It was calm and quiet. He had heard it before. He felt his heart begin to race. It was The Caller.

"Who's there?" he demanded angrily. "Speak up, dammit."

"Hi, Elliot," the voice, a male voice, drawled.

"Who are you?"

"You haven't figured that out yet, have you, Elliot?" The caller seemed to be whispering, but it was very easy, too easy, to hear him.

"Tell me what you want or get off the line."

"You're not ready to hear what I want, Elliot. Take a look around you. You'll figure it out." Another laugh, malicious.

"You're crazy. When I find out who you are, I'll . . ."

"Temper, temper, Elliot." Now raucous laughter. In waves.

"Shut up!" Halsey shouted, loud enough for his secretary to hear. She stuck her head in the door, a worried look on her face. She started to say something but when she saw the look on Halsey's face and the way he was gripping the phone—so hard his knuckles were white—she popped back into the sanctuary of her own office.

Halsey slammed the phone down as the laughing rolled on and on, like some goofy joke.

He stood at his desk staring at the phone, leaning his arms on the desktop. He was shaking, and he could feel his heart pounding. He resisted an impulse to pick up the phone and heave it through the window. All images of the lovely Dr. Crane were rudely obliterated from his mind. He dropped into his chair. What in the hell was happening to him? And what was happening to his company?

CHAPTER THIRTEEN

Young Rachel Dixon made it to the rest room in the nick of time. She rushed to an empty stall and vomited into the toilet. A mixture of stomach acid and a partially digested hot dog filled the bowl.

She stood up, wiped her brow with the sleeve of her white coat, and took a few tremulous breaths before moving to the sink. She rinsed out her mouth and splashed cold water on her face. It felt good. For a moment she was able to forget what she had just seen. But only for a moment.

As she envisioned once again the patient she had admitted to the intensive care unit, she felt a wave of nausea. And the smell. She couldn't erase the smell. She let out a sob and hung over the sink, bracing herself with her arms. She couldn't go back there.

But she had to. She was a doctor, with one of the most prestigious medical centers west of the Mississippi: Salt Lake Memorial. It was the first and toughest day of internship. A med student one day, a doctor the next. She told herself nobody was expected to move easily from one to the other. Somehow the thought didn't help.

She summoned up her courage and marched back to the ICU to present her case to Bill Mitchell, the pimply faced, tough-acting resident who was her immediate superior.

Rachel and Mitchell stood at the bedside of the critically ill patient. An ICU nurse stood quietly in the corner, fiddling with one of the monitors.

The patient, a thirtyish woman named Sunny Smith, was clearly terminal. Her face was bloated and blistered, with a strange purplish hue. Her eyes were swollen shut. Clots of caked blood crusted her eyelids, nostrils, and mouth. Curds of thick putrescent green pus seemed to erupt from every orifice and every break in the skin.

She was hooked up to a ventilator. The tape wrapped around the endotracheal tube was crimson with blood leaking from her mouth and nose. Another tube came out her nose. It was draining stomach contents—pure blood, dark brown in color. She had an intravenous line in each edematous arm with two units of blood running into her veins. Another line went into a neck vein and on into her heart to measure pressures. Yet another line was taped into her wrist artery, where it provided continuous measurements of her falling blood pressure. A blood-filled catheter draining her bladder snaked out from between her puffy bruised thighs.

Rachel glanced at Mitchell. He suddenly didn't seem at all tough as he stared solemnly at the patient. She began her presentation in a controlled voice. "Sunny Smith is a thirty-four-year-old prostitute. Her roommate brought her to the ER three hours ago. The only history available is from the roommate. The patient was able to talk when she first arrived, but was confabulatory. Initially, I felt her confusion was due to her high fever, which was 104 degrees on admission and shot up to 106. Then her right pupil enlarged and she became unresponsive. Judging by her coagulation abnormalities and her profuse bleeding, I suspect she had a massive bleed into her brain."

Mitchell interrupted. "First tell us the history, Dr. Dixon. Save your impressions for when you sum up."

"I'm sorry," she said, swallowing hard. Her throat felt like sandpaper. "Her roommate, also a prostitute, says Ms. Smith was well until two days ago, when she complained of a headache and a flulike feeling. This morning she had a bad nosebleed and wouldn't eat. She was delirious and kept covering her eyes. She started carrying on about being shot, or shot up. I checked her arms for needle tracks and it doesn't look like she's an IV drug user. There is a red area on her upper arm that looks like a bite of some sort . . ."

Mitchell gave her an exasperated look. "Present your physical findings *after* your history, Dr. Dixon."

Rachel looked at him. He seemed unusually irritable, even for a tired, overworked resident. She decided it was his way of coping.

"Okay," she said. "The patient's roommate brought her to the hospital after she started vomiting blood."

Rachel went into the physical findings in painstaking detail. As she summed up, Mitchell said, "Try to be briefer next time. What's your differential diagnosis?"

"I'm not sure," said Rachel, trying to ignore the dig. "An infectious disease of some sort. Maybe Rocky Mountain spotted fever?"

"Ironically," said Mitchell with a superior smile, "Rocky Mountain spotted fever is not endemic to the Rocky Mountains. But her symptoms would certainly be consistent with that." He paused, studying the patient.

Rachel was acutely aware that he was avoiding

touching Sunny Smith, not even placing his stethoscope on her chest. A resident would typically proceed with a brief exam while the intern discussed the case. Mitchell's wariness made her uneasy.

Mitchell looked at her, his arms hugging his chest. "Did you send off an HIV?"

She nodded.

"How about bubonic plague titers?"

She shook her head, her eyes widening at the thought of such a rare and devastating disease. She had never seen a case.

"Call the lab and have them draw a redtop tube for acute titers."

"Okay."

Mitchell turned to leave. "Let's put her in isolation, and don't anybody come in here without a mask. We don't know what the hell this woman has, but it could be contagious. Let's get an infectious disease consult."

As they left the room, Rachel saw a tall, handsome Asian man in a white coat parked in the doorway. She brushed by him, but gave him a tentative smile as she eyed the name tag on his front pocket.

He followed her to the nurse's station. "Excuse me," he said. "My name is Kobayashi. I'm a path resident. I heard about this case."

"Yes?" said Rachel, her curiosity piqued. Pathologists were not known to frequent sanctuaries of the living.

"I was involved in the post of an ICU nurse who died here a short while ago. I thought there might be a connection."

Rachel had heard about Trudy Porter. The nurse had died before Rachel's arrival in Salt Lake. She hadn't thought much about it, what with so many other things on her mind. But now she felt a queasiness in the pit of her stomach. "What did she end up having?"

Kobayashi squirmed ever so slightly. "I'm ... I'm not sure, but I'd appreciate it if I could draw a couple tubes of blood."

Rachel studied him a moment. She liked his sincerity. "I don't see why not," she said.

He nodded his appreciation and extracted a syringe and two glass tubes from his pocket before heading into Sunny Smith's room. He was glad to be *doing* something. He had been moving amid the shadows too long.

The Trudy Porter case had escalated into a hot political issue. Koji didn't want to get into more trouble. He had already been read the riot act for going to the CDC behind the department head's back. Then, when he came up with an answer, reactions had been mixed. Either way, the department was sitting on the fact that Trudy Porter had antibodies to the Congo virus. The powers that be were still trying to decide how to handle it. The last thing they wanted was to deal with the media, a bunch of vicious ignoramuses according to the head of the medical center.

Meanwhile, Koji knew the critical factor in controlling epidemics was timing. Sitting on information was like sitting on a time bomb. So each day he reviewed the emergency room logs as well as the medical ward admissions and infectious disease consults. Sunny Smith was the first case to fall into his net. Now all he needed was a sample of the woman's blood.

He felt his body tense up as he looked at the pathetic creature that was Sunny Smith. He donned a surgical mask and gown, and double-gloved before approaching the patient.

Like Rachel Dixon, he, too, noticed the swollen red area on the patient's upper arm. Unlike Rachel, however, he had a pretty good notion how it got there. His heart pumped with growing excitement. He was on to something.

He drew the blood, took it to the nurse's station, labeled the tubes, nodded his thanks to Rachel, and was off to the lab to Fed Ex the specimens to Chuck Kekich at the CDC.

And then he would wait.

Dayton Trask, M.D., was the prototypic burned-out doctor. He was in his early fifties, wishing he was ten years older so he could cash in his retirement plan and escape this stinking town. The City of Angels. Somebody had a sorry vision of heaven when they named this place, he thought morosely.

Trask drank. He had a "drinking problem," according to his wife and what few friends he had. He was not unaware of his nickname among the hospital staff, especially the flip young residents. Trask the Flask, they called him. But he knew he could stop any time he wanted. That meant it wasn't a problem, merely a choice. Furthermore, no one could provide him a good reason to quit. At least, they couldn't provide him with anything he considered that good. They railed at him about his health. So what if fulminant liver disease whisked him away? It would be a blessing.

No, Trask had plenty of reasons to keep right on drinking. Like hiding the stench of this godforsaken pathology department in this second-rate medical center smack-dab in the heart of the Los Angeles slums. Like going home at night and downing his nightly dose of selective forgetfulness. For a few moments he could pretend that he hadn't stooped to this kind of life—slicing up corpses and extemporizing diagnoses. Because autopsies, for all their repute, were not all that conclusive.

He was tired of having doctors throw the burden of why their patients died on him. And that had gotten him in trouble more than once. All too often his answer was a smiling, "I don't know, maybe you killed him."

And his other tasks? Looking at PAP smears day in, day out. About as stimulating as counting your toes after five or six drinks.

This was Dayton Trask's state of mind when the two DOAs rolled into the morgue at City of Angels Hospital on that hot July afternoon. Too many things were wrong. The timing stank. He was getting ready to leave for the day, looking forward to a quiet night with his bottle.

At five o'clock the first DOA arrived, a drug addict from the barrio. Before Trask even had a chance to look at the body, the second one rolled in—a prostitute from the Hollywood area. Jesus H. Christ! What was he supposed to do now?

He decided to take a quick look at the corpses to satisfy the residents and other busybodies poking around. Those damn residents were always looking for an opportunity to do in Trask the Flask. He supposed it earned them brownie points.

He glanced around the dank morgue, a styrofoam cup of tepid coffee in his hand. Everyone seemed to be transfixed, their eyes darting between Trask and the two gurneys. There was the obsequious little Korean girl, a first-year path resident who was terrified of him for no discernible reason. And Ralph Gallagher, the assistant who had worked with him for years. Then there was the team of EMTs who had brought in the prostitute. They stood around waiting for him to pat them on the back for bringing the victim in only thirty minutes dead instead of three hours dead. Big fat deal. He cast a dark look in their direction and one of them slinked out of the room.

Trask ran on to himself. What was wrong with these people? Didn't they understand that the requirements of the walking dead outweighed those of the ... *dead* dead? Oh, well. He would take a look at the bodies, just so these people wouldn't cause any trouble. Troublemakers. That's all they were.

He put down his coffee and moved over to the gurney bearing the prostitute. After all these years he still felt a nervous pang before throwing back the sheet. With a quick motion, he lifted it up. His eyes widened at the bloated and disfigured form. The stench almost knocked him over. There was blood exuding from every orifice. Purulent green sticky material had oozed out of the nose and mouth. Flaps of skin were torn away by the ravages of something he couldn't begin to imagine, exposing pulpy corroded muscle beneath. The skin over the breasts had sloughed off, revealing rotting mounds of decomposing flesh.

He felt light-headed, and realized he had been holding his breath. He grabbed the side rail of the gurney to keep from keeling over. Then he experienced rage. He threw down the sheet and glared at two of the EMTs who had inched forward, their faces rapt with morbid fascination.

"Is this some kind of joke?" he demanded. "The report said this woman was alive less than an hour ago!"

One of the EMTs, a young man with a subdued look said, "That is correct, Doctor. She was still breathing when we arrived at her apartment."

"That's impossible. This woman's been dead for days! Nobody who's just died looks—or smells—like that."

He moved over to the other gurney and yanked off the sheet. Someone behind him gasped. Trask could feel his pulse pounding. For a moment everything was a blur as though his brain had short-circuited. He made himself stare at the body. There could be no doubt. The two bodies were similarly ravaged in a way too horrible to describe. The drug addict and the prostitute had obviously died from the same cause.

For a long time now, Dayton Trask thought he had seen just about everything. Until today.

He slowly turned and left the room with the others, uncertain what to do. He had no idea what he was dealing with, but through all the years of calculated indifference and the dulling effects of alcohol, a feeling surfaced that he hadn't experienced before. Terror.

After tossing and turning a good part of the night, Trask succeeded only in banishing his wife to the guest bedroom. At the break of dawn he stepped out on the balcony and stared at the smog-filled city of Los Angeles below his hillside home. What horrible disease was lurking there? What had killed those two people? A prostitute and a drug addict. What did they have in common? He puzzled over it for a while, then his mind grabbed at a solution to his dilemma. Of course! AIDS. Both were high risk. He would check for HIV before doing anything else.

He moved back into the house with a frown. But if they had AIDS, it was a bizarre presentation. He didn't like it. Suddenly, a light went on in his head, bright as a flash of sunshine. That news story on the radio this morning. The interview with Roger Peck. He remembered Peck well from their days in med school. Peck was always a self-styled expert on something. Now it was AIDS.

He would give Peck a call. Turn the cases over to Fort Thacker. Ship the bodies the hell out of LA— out of his life.

His decision made, he went back to bed and was asleep within minutes.

CHAPTER FOURTEEN

Kate and Harpo sat over coffee in the Alatron cafeteria. The place was elaborate for an employee eatery with its thick carpet, soft lighting, and gleaming tables. The lunch crowd had peaked and the conversational din was gradually subsiding.

Harpo took a sip and raised his eyebrows. "Not bad," he said. He craned his neck and looked toward the cafeteria line, then got up and wandered over to the pastry case.

Kate stirred cream into her coffee, staring idly at the swirling liquid. She didn't have much of an appetite. The tour of the maximum-containment facility, having to wear the clumsy spacesuits, was unsettling.

She had been impressed with the company's safety and security measures. Yet she couldn't dismiss the possibility of deadly contamination of the vaccine.

How could it happen? A defect in the vent system, the filters, the culture tubes, waste disposal? And why weren't the Alatron employees getting sick, too? She had asked these questions of herself and Harpo. And Halsey. He knew of no problems, though he was clearly concerned. She had the feeling her questions were equally disturbing to him.

She considered how it might happen. Handling of the AIDS vaccine was not assigned Biosafety Level 4 containment (BSC 4) because airborne transmission of the virus was not a factor. With Congo, on the other hand, the air around the virus could be swarming with the tiny protein packets. Weird stuff, viruses. Neither dead nor alive. Just deadly, as viruses like Congo or HIV incorporated their own genetic material into the gene coding mechanism of living cells.

While techs handling the AIDS vaccine wouldn't need to wear masks, those dealing with Congo wore not only masks, but their own air supply. They couldn't afford to breathe the ambient air. If the vaccine were contaminated, every breath could mean death.

Yet there was nothing—none of the techs was sick. She thought she should feel relief, but what she felt was deepening bewilderment.

On the other hand, where was project director Dave Parsons? Unlike many executives, he had been involved at a hands-on level. He had personally supervised administration of the vaccine at the urban trial sites. Why had he been fired? And what had happened to him? The possibilities gave her the shivers as she imagined a man she had never met looking like the picture of Maury or Trudy Porter.

"A penny for your thoughts?" Harpo plunked down a tray with two Danishes, fruit salad, an assortment of crackers, and a bowl of soup. He sat down and rubbed his hands.

Kate laughed. "You pathologists are all alike. Even an autopsy doesn't dent your appetite."

He smiled happily. "It's all a matter of perspective, my dear." He tore the cellophane wrapper off the saltines and crumbled them into his soup. "Help your-self to a Danish."

He slurped down the soup and sat back, studying her. "Something's eating at you."

She looked over the rim of her cup. "Who asked you?" she said with mock grumpiness. Then pursed her lips thoughtfully. "I don't like it, Harpo. I have a bad feeling about this place."

He smiled. "More woman's intuition?"

"I hope I'm wrong."

"Listen, Kate," he said in a serious vein, "I don't have that gut feeling, but let's face it. We've got the AIDS and Congo viruses in the same building. And we've got two people receiving the AIDS vaccine who are now dead, probably from Congo fever. You don't need to be a rocket scientist to figure a connection."

He dabbed his lips with a napkin and tossed it back on the tray. "What does that intuition of yours tell you about our Mr. Halsey?"

She shrugged. "I just don't know."

Harpo attacked the fruit salad. "The big question facing us is what to do if the vaccine *is* contaminated. Evacuate the premises? Shut down the company? Set up quarantines?"

She felt a stab of fear at the pandemonium that might ensue. None of it seemed real to her. Could they—she and Harpo, and now Elliot Halsey—be standing at the edge of a massive outbreak?

"Now we know," she said, "how our colleagues who first recognized AIDS must have felt as they watched the disease unfold under their noses. Strange, rare ill-nesses, showing up only in gay men. Kaposi's sarcoma. Pneumocystis pneumonia. A case here, a case there, cropping up all over the country. The thrill of discov-ery, quickly overshadowed by the horror of a deadly new disease. Incurable."

Harpo nodded solemnly. He was about to respond when his attention was drawn to a woman hurrying into the cafeteria. A worried expression distorted her face. her eyes scanned the room. At that moment he recognized her—Halsey's secretary, Rose.

Kate followed his gaze and felt her heart skip a beat as she saw Rose's eyes home in on her. Rose hastened over to the table. "Dr. Crane," she gushed as she unfolded a piece of paper. "I have a message for you to call a Dr. Kek ... this man, at the CDC." She pointed to the name—Dr. Charles Kekich. "They said it's urgent."

Kate smiled politely. "Thank you," she said. She stared at Chuck's name and felt a nameless dread.

"There's a phone over there you can use," said Rose, pointing across the room. "Or the one in our office."

Kate stood up and saw some people in white coats grouped near the phone. "I'll use yours, thanks."

She followed Rose to the elevator, leaving Harpo to finish his snack. Rose ushered her into Halsey's vacant office, explaining he was at a meeting.

Kekich was on the line in a matter of seconds. "Kate," he said, his voice taut. "Something big is going on, something damn big. We've got the state health departments of Utah and New York, the Cook County Health Department in Illinois, and New York City's Medical Examiner's office beatin' down our doors. What's more, word's out that Peck got a call from a pathologist in L.A. who's shipping two bodies to Fort Thacker. They've all got the same story. Strange deaths. Looks like the victims may have received Alatron's AIDS vaccine."

Kate felt weak. There it was—her worst scenario. The vaccine. Strange deaths. She knew what Kekich's answer would be, but she had to ask. "Strange in what way, Chuck?"

"Sudden flulike illness one day. Dead the next. Skin like hot grease spilled over it. Blood and pus from every orifice. Koji Kobayashi, the fella in Salt Lake, Fed Ex'd me the blood of one of the cases. And a picture. The poor woman is still alive. Carbon copy of Maury and the Porter gal."

"Oh my God," was all she could say. She held the receiver back from her ear, as though it might soften the impact of Kekich's words.

"That's not all. And here's why I thought you oughta know while you're still up there ..."

"I'm listening."

"Koji said this woman definitely received Alatron's AIDS vaccine."

"Oh my God," she said again. She looked around Halsey's office with horror.

"Seems you were onto somethin' all along, Kate. I'm turning all this over to Abe Feldman in Special Pathogens. I wanted to talk to you first."

"Yes."

Silence.

"Kate, you all right?"

"Yes."

"Kate?"

"I'm having a hard time accepting it, Chuck. I've been working with the Alatron president." Her heart ached. She had tried hard not to let her growing feelings for Halsey interfere. Now this. "I thought he was leveling with us."

"Well, he may be. Some things are simply beyond our control, Kate. We humans are just egotistical enough to think we can control our world. There's nothing more humbling than helplessly watching a host of microscopic organisms consume one life after another." He sighed heavily. "Let's not be too hard on 'em up there. They're gonna need all the help they can get."

She felt anger wash over fear and disappointment. "Why didn't they stop the trials when Maury and Porter died, Chuck? This is terrible. People dying needlessly while Alatron is busy covering its tracks."

"Let's not jump to conclusions, Kate. We don't have their side of it. The bottom line is all AIDS vaccine projects using the live virus will have to go on hold. And that's a damn shame."

She agreed. "I'd better stay on here. Tell Abe I'm working on it."

"You bet." Kekich paused. "The cholera outbreak in Argentina pales next to this."

"At least they know what they're dealing with."

"Yeah. That's all I have for now, Kate. Be careful and stay in touch. I'll let you know what the blood on this latest Salt Lake case shows."

She slowly replaced the receiver, looking up to see Elliot Halsey standing at the door, his face ashen. He appeared devastated.

"When did you find out?" she asked quietly.

"This morning. Calls are flooding the switchboard." He dropped into a leather chair opposite her. "Nothing's making sense."

"It makes sense once you acknowledge the vaccine's been contaminated." She heard the coldness in her voice. She guessed he did, too.

"That's not what I'm talking about."

She sat back, her arms across her chest. "Perhaps you could fill me in?" She had no patience for a man who, once the writing was on the wall, was not willing to read it.

Halsey stood up. His face was still drained, but he moved with an erectness that spoke of an unbowed

will. She felt a grudging admiration, which irritated
her.

"Yes, Dr. Crane," said Halsey. "I would very much
like to fill you in. Where is Dr. Cosgrove?"

"The cafeteria."

"Let's pick him up. There's something I want to
show you both."

They entered a roomful of computers. A few people
were seated at word processors, gazing intently at their
monitors. They barely noticed Halsey and his two
guests.

Halsey sat down to one of the computers. He
switched it on and his fingers moved nimbly over the
keyboard. As the screen lit up, he sat back. "This is
a list of the participants in the Phase Three AIDS
vaccine trials, categorized by city. You'll see that
Trudy Porter and Akendo Maury are not here."

Harpo shrugged. "We know that Maury used an
alias. Maybe the Porter woman did, too."

Kate studied the list with a frown.

Halsey turned to Kate. "I thought the Porter
woman was one of ours because that's what I was told.
But when I double-checked it last week I couldn't find
her in the computer. Why do you think she received
the vaccine?"

Kate sat down at a table next to the computer and
laid open her file. She scanned the forensic report
from Salt Lake. "It says here she told her boyfriend
she received the vaccine."

"She's not in the official trials."

"At least not under her real name," repeated
Harpo.

"What about all these cases coming in now?" demanded Kate. "Where's your list on them?"

"I don't know how their names got hooked up with

the company. They're not ours, either." Halsey moved back to the keyboard and punched a few keys. "I'll show you. I'll have the computer search for all Phase Three human trials."

The computer hummed and softly churned as it responded to Halsey's command. "Please Wait," it said.

All three sat captivated by the screen as they did what they were told—waited. Kate glanced at Halsey. His eyes narrowed as he studied the screen. His body became rigid. She knew the computer was finding something.

Finally, a screenful of green words popped up. At the top of the screen it said, AIDS VACCINE PHASE III, PART B. Beneath the head was a long list. Kate and Harpo looked at each other, then moved in closer to read along with Halsey.

There were urban subheads—New York, Los Angeles, San Francisco, Salt Lake City, and Chicago. About ten names were listed under each city.

Halsey moved the cursor down the screen. More names appeared. He said nothing. Kate glanced at him again. His face was white as a sheet, his jaw clenched. The names meant nothing to her, but she had an idea, judging by Halsey's reaction, that he had stumbled on a bombshell.

"What are we looking at?" asked Harpo.

Halsey's mind was racing. Nothing made sense. Part B trials should be nonexistent at this point. Part A data were only now being collected and submitted to the FDA for approval to extend the trials. It would be months, probably longer, thanks to Parsons's sloppy reporting, before the FDA would give the go-ahead for Part B.

Yet there it was, displayed on the monitor in no uncertain terms: someone had gone ahead to Part B without his knowledge or approval. Surely it couldn't

have been Parsons. He wouldn't have done something
this blatant. Too risky. And stupid.

He had an idea whoever did this wanted him to find
it. The Caller's voice shot through his head. *You
haven't figured it out yet, have you, Elliot?*

No, but he was beginning to. He felt a murderous
rage wash over him. His hands froze on the keyboard.

He felt the two visitors' eyes on him and he knew
he had some explaining to do. Right now he was short
on explanations. "We're looking at something that
doesn't exist," was all he said, not caring that he made
no sense at all.

"What is it?" Kate asked.

He turned on the printer and as it whirred to life,
he entered the commands that would transpose the
horror on the screen into indelible black and white.
Then he sat back and looked at Kate. "Something is
terribly wrong. I don't yet know what these names
mean, or whether they have anything to do with the
reports coming in from all over the country. At the
very least, someone has been tampering with our computer program."

"But you suspect it's more than that."

"Yes." He thought again of the phone calls. The
evil laugh that made his skin crawl. He tore the pages
off the printer and folded them.

"It's time," he said, "to face the music."

CHAPTER FIFTEEN

Kate and Harpo pored over manuals, stacks of forms and regulations, even blueprints, as they sat at a small conference table in the makeshift office at Alatron's R and D building. Papers were strewn all over the table. Computer printouts spilled onto the floor. A fax machine sat by the phone. A basket of writing implements, scissors, staplers, rulers, and tape, sat in the middle of the table. Empty coffee cups and trays cluttered with dirty dishes were stacked in a corner. Computers were set up at either end of the table. A chandelier provided barely adequate light.

Kate was studying the vent systems of Alatron's third- and fourth-floor research labs. It was tedious work, and she wondered why she was bothering. As she stumbled through the technical terminology, it was evident she didn't have the right background. At this point she was only speculating about the theory behind backflow devices, directional airflow, pressure differentials.

Yet she persevered. Was there a design problem that allowed the escape of deadly pathogens from one floor to another? If contamination of the vaccine had occurred, it was apparently limited to the fourth-floor biosafety cabinets. This would explain the lack of spread to the lab techs.

Harpo was bent over one of the safety manuals. "I have to hand it to these people," he said, rubbing his temples. "Not only do they follow all federal regulations, they go above and beyond the call of duty."

She looked up, glad for a chance to rest her eyes. "Such as?"

"Such as," Harpo repeated, his finger finding the place in the manual. "Their procedure for decontamination of all specimens leaving maximum containment involves not only a dunk tank, but a fumigation chamber *and* an airlock."

He shook his head wearily. "Meticulous, I'll say that for them. Makes contamination unlikely." His eyes moved down the page. "And materials brought into maximum containment come through a double-doored autoclave."

Kate nodded. "It *sounds* good."

"Meaning?"

"Are they actually following all these rigorous procedures, or is it only on paper?"

Harpo peered up at her, pushing his reading glasses on top of his head. "Do I detect a note of skepticism?"

She laughed. "Realism. With a touch of exhaustion."

He stretched and leaned back stiffly in his chair. "Exhaustion? I knew there was a word for how I'm feeling." He worked the kinks out of his neck, wagging his head from shoulder to shoulder. He checked his watch. "It's getting late. What do you say we call it quits?"

Kate frowned at the drawing before her. "I'm not

quite ready. Why don't you go on to the hotel, Harpo? I'd like to finish up before Abe Feldman and the crew get here tomorrow."

He got to his feet and yawned. "Okay. I wish I didn't have to go back to New York in the morning."

Slipping his glasses back on, he piled papers, manuals, and notes into neat stacks. "I'll leave these here. Call me at my office late morning after you've had a chance to look over my notes."

He glanced around the cluttered conference room. "Looks like a tornado hit. Sure you'll be okay here? The place is deserted."

"I'll be fine. Besides, our friend Halsey is still around somewhere. I might go over things with him."

"Uh-oh. First you spark and sputter at this guy, now you're talking late-night trysts." He shook his head in mock disapproval. "I dunno, Kate. You never acted that way with me."

She laughed and shooed him away. "I'll talk to you in the morning, Harpo."

"Good night, Kate." He gave her shoulder a squeeze. "Want me to leave the door open?"

"Thanks. It's stuffy in here."

She bent over the drawings again. For a moment she thought she had something. How air might escape from the third-floor biosafety hoods into the vents that fed the fourth floor. But then she ruled it out. She leaned back and closed her eyes, rolling her shoulders to release the tension of hunching over for hours.

When she opened her eyes, she practically jumped out of her seat. A man was standing over her. She made an involuntary gasp. He was close—too close. How had he appeared without her knowing it?

"Hi there," she said as she realized it was just the janitor. He wore a khaki uniform with a laminated name tag hanging from his front pocket. She couldn't make out the name.

He handed her some papers. "Found these on the floor," he said with an odd smile. His gaze swept the room and his eyes narrowed. "You aren't making my job any easier, you know."

She thought she should laugh, but there was something about him that stopped her. It was his eyes that gave her pause. They were ice blue, with black pinpoint pupils that seemed to leap out at her like antennae. They seemed intimately probing, yet devoid of warmth.

He was tall and lean, strong looking. He had a narrow stony face, not unattractive. The way he smiled at her made her flesh crawl though she couldn't have said why. She shook her head, puzzled by her own reaction.

He leaned over and picked up another sheaf of papers. "What're you doing? Looks pretty important."

"Oh, nothing really."

He smiled that smile again. "Working pretty late for nothing important."

"I was finishing up," she said, gathering the drawings. "I imagine you'd like me out of your way."

He stared at her. "Maybe."

She waved a hand toward the pile of trays and dishes, feeling increasingly uneasy. "Perhaps you would return those to the cafeteria for me."

"Of course." He pulled up a chair and sat across from her, his arms folded across his chest. "What's your name?"

She realized as she fumbled with the papers that she ought to be angry. Who was he to be questioning her? But she found herself answering. "I'm Dr. Crane. I'm doing some consulting work here. This is my temporary office."

As she recognized how intimidated she felt, she stopped what she was doing and looked at him more closely. The years of doctoring and quick assessments clicked into place without a second thought. Her experienced eyes examined his hands. They were capable-looking, but not calloused—not the hands of a manual laborer. She went back to his eyes. His pupils remained pinpoint, leading her to speculate about drug use. Yet she saw no uncertainty or wariness. And his movements seemed fluid and purposeful, without a hint of tremor.

For an uncomfortable moment their eyes locked, and she resisted an urge to look away. She felt something was at stake, though she had no idea what. Finally, she let her eyes drop to the papers in her lap. This is ridiculous, she thought. He's only the janitor. I've been working too hard. I should have gone with Harpo.

She rose and stuffed the papers into her briefcase. She took one last look at the room.

"I'd appreciate it if you would lock up when you're done cleaning. You do have a key?"

The janitor stood up. She couldn't read his expression. "Yes," he said softly. "I have what I need."

"That's good," she said inanely, glad to be getting out of there. At the same time, she felt strangely drawn to stay. She turned at the door, briefcase in hand, and looked at him. "What's your name?"

"Ken," he said.

"Just Ken?"

"Ken the Janitor."

Elliot Halsey sat within the peaceful confines of his office library, staring at the television. It was late, and barely anyone else was around. Even the press was gone for the night, which gave him a sense of freedom he hadn't felt all day.

The library was his own creation, and he was proud of it. He also made good use of it. Shortly after he took over as Alatron's president, he changed the office adjoining his into a study of sorts. Actually, it was more like a studio apartment, with a refrigerator, bath, and walk-in closet as well as a homey couch for sleeping. There were also a couple of comfortable leather chairs and a coffee table to accommodate the occasional visitor.

Mostly, there were books. Many dealt with AIDS research, though most of those were downstairs in the employee library, or over in the R and D building. He kept several shelves of entertainment reading that ranged from mystery novels and medical thrillers to biographies and history books. He also had a large science collection that included anthropology and books on wildlife.

But his most cherished and exhaustive collection was devoted to Western Americana, especially those books dealing with the long-lost era of fur trappers and Indian traders. He and Barry still shared that interest, though they rarely spoke of it anymore. He remembered fondly the fishing and hiking trips they had made to Jackson Hole in Wyoming when Barry was eleven or twelve. Those had been good years— when Barry still called him Dad. He shook his head, his eyes misting over. What had happened? Where had things gone wrong?

He rose and crossed to the Western Americana section and pulled from the shelf one of his favorites. It was a tattered signed copy of *Give Your Heart to the Hawks*, by Winfred Blevins, a book that had inspired Halsey's love for the mountain West. He remembered how he and Barry had read from its pages to each other by the campfire before they crawled into their sleeping bags. They would imagine what it might have been like to be one of the first men to spot the massive Tetons tilting on the horizon or to see the steam of the earth's core hiss and billow out of invisible scars in the ground.

He leafed through the pages with a growing sense of yearning. How he would enjoy a vacation right now in a mountain cabin high in the heart of the country that Blevins so vividly described. He and Barry, like the old days. Away from all the turmoil of the corporate competitive world. Away from the world where people scrutinized your every move, just waiting for you to make a mistake.

The fantasy lost some of its appeal as he silently acknowledged the gulf between him and his son. The thought of Kate Crane flitted through his mind and he dismissed it just as quickly without examining why. He knew only that whenever he thought of her he experienced an inexplicable restlessness. It was at once a heady yet maddening feeling.

He took the book by Blevins and crossed the plush gray carpet to the sofa, where he had spent many a night when he hadn't the time or energy to commute home. The room had become a home away from home. He felt less alone here. It suited him fine to have his meals in the Alatron cafeteria, a newspaper for company.

His decision to stay over this night had been almost superstitiously founded. It seemed that each time he left the grounds, some new disaster cropped up. Maybe if he hung around he could watch over things better. He knew that Kate Crane was putting in long hours over in the research building and he felt a strange disinclination to be away from her.

His thoughts were interrupted by the familiar fanfare introducing the late night news. He put the book down and looked at the TV screen. He had learned not to underestimate the press. He was always interested in what they had to say. In the past he had picked up useful information from newsbreaks, such as the recent exploits of Meridan, Stone, and Roth, one of Alatron's most aggressive competitors.

He remembered the incident well. MS&R Laboratories had been racing against Alatron to get rebutarol, a highly touted new asthma drug, on the market. MS&R's attorneys had discovered a loophole in the FDA's rigid New Drug Application regulations. Subsequently MS&R was about to beat Alatron to the punch until Halsey received a tip from a financial reporter with the *Newark Post-Ledger*. After a few quick calls and emergency meetings, Alatron was still able to get its drug out first.

He directed his attention to the TV. He turned up the volume as Roland Pettigrew, the anchorman for a New York station, launched the story he had been waiting for.

"On the medical front, there is concern that a new AIDS vaccine formulated and administered by New Jersey's Alatron Pharmaceutical Laboratories may be causing serious side effects, including several deaths," said Pettigrew gravely. "Opinions vary widely as to how the vaccine—a drug meant to save lives—may be doing the opposite. Eyewitness News has learned from sources outside the company that the vaccine may actually be causing and accelerating the course of AIDS. Spokespersons for Alatron declined to comment, but Dr. Roger Peck, an expert on AIDS with the government's Fort Thacker, had this to say:"

Peck's smug face filled the screen. "There have been a series of strange deaths in the past few weeks," said Peck. "Some of the victims were recipients of Alatron

Laboratory's AIDS vaccine. At this point we can only speculate, but the most likely cause of death would appear to be a new and virulent manifestation of AIDS, perhaps set off by the vaccine itself."

Halsey gritted his teeth. Peck would say anything to maneuver himself into the limelight. He knew Peck was aware of the possibility of Congo virus contamination, but it didn't suit the man's purpose to mention it.

Pettigrew's square-jawed face reappeared on the screen. "Meanwhile, Alatron Laboratories has stopped all vaccine production. Persons having received the vaccine who have questions or concerns are advised to contact Mr. Elliot Halsey, the company's president."

Halsey sat back, fuming. He flicked off the television with the remote control. Well, at least they got the last part right. He had established a consumer hotline when he took over.

The hotline program was a success. He had a handpicked team manning the phones day and night. They passed more difficult calls on to him and he either answered them himself or instructed his staff. With the current publicity about Alatron's vaccine, the phone lines were jammed.

A knock at the door startled him. Most people knew if he was in his study he was not to be disturbed. He felt a flicker of annoyance. He opened the door a crack and saw Kate Crane standing there.

"Hello," he said with a grin, his annoyance evaporating. "How did you know where I was hiding out?"

"One of the custodians."

"A custodian?" He laughed. "My secret has been blown. Come on in." He headed over to the refrigerator, which was set back into a recess. "Care for something cold to drink?"

"Sounds great. Any juice?"

"How about orange?"

"Fine."

"Make yourself comfortable and I'll be right with you." He poured them each a glass of orange juice and tossed in a few ice cubes. He set hers down on the table beside her chair and took a seat opposite her.

Kate sat back and crossed her legs. She was wearing an Alatron lab coat a few sizes too big. It seemed to swallow her, giving her, thought Halsey, a charming childlike quality.

She seemed preoccupied, unmindful of his assessment. "I thought I'd give you a summary of what we've learned today." She extracted a notepad from the pocket of the oversized coat. Strands of auburn hair fell onto her forehead as she slipped on her reading glasses and consulted her notes. Halsey resisted an impulse to reach out and touch her hair.

"I'd like to hear your conclusions."

"All right," she said. "The HEPA filters in your maximum-security lab check out fine. Your people have been inspecting the vents in the third- and fourth-floor laboratories and Harpo and I have been studying the blueprints. No problems. You have a highly competent crew here, I might add. Of course, you'll want to let Abe Feldman from Special Pathogens have his people look your setup over as well." She peered at him over her glasses. "They'll be here in the morning."

He nodded. He fought an inclination to smile every time she said something.

She looked back at her notes. "The preliminary report on the vaccine cultures we forwarded to CDC shows no growth of the Congo virus . . ."

"That's good," he said cautiously.

"Yes," agreed Kate in an equally careful tone, "but

keep in mind that viruses can grow slowly. Cultures may not turn positive for days, even weeks."

"Right. We wouldn't want to get too pleased, would we?"

She sat back and seemed to be inspecting him. He saw a hint of amusement in her eyes.

"Are we feeling sorry for ourselves, Mr. Halsey?" She had an odd smile on her face.

"Why, yes, Dr. Crane."

She removed her glasses. "Since we'll be working together quite a bit, I suggest we address each other by our first names."

"I think that's a very sound idea . . . Kate." He took a sip of juice, watching her. He thought his eyes must be twinkling. Would she see it?

"Now," she said with the hint of a smile, "where were we?"

"Feeling sorry for ourselves."

She laughed. He realized how hard he had been trying to elicit that response, and now he knew why. It made him want to laugh, too.

He smiled, then swiveled in his chair, his lips pursed as he got down to business. "So, what do you think is going on?"

"I don't know. I could speculate but that's all it would be. Maybe Abe Feldman and the crew will come up with something more substantial."

"Roger Peck seems to think the vaccine has somehow caused the AIDS virus to mutate into a virulent form."

"Roger is a fool."

"Even fools can stumble onto the truth."

Kate's eyebrows arched in surprise. "You're more generous than I. Personally, I think if Roger stumbled over the truth, he would damn it for tripping him."

They both laughed, their eyes linked by a common feeling that neither was prepared to name.

The phone broke their connection. Halsey looked at his watch. It was ten-thirty, too late for any reasonable person. And it was his private line. He knew what that meant, remembering only too well the last call he had received on that line. He felt his throat constrict, his hands turn cold. He looked at the phone, and watched it jangle. He had the feeling that if it was The Caller, the sound would somehow be different—insistent, loud, abrasive. But it was none of those things. It just rang. He didn't move. It kept ringing. He saw Kate watching him with a puzzled expression.

"Would you like me to leave?" she said.

"No, please stay." He lifted the receiver and slowly put it to his ear. "Hello," he said.

There was silence at the other end, as he knew there would be. He could feel the dread growing inside him. "Hello," he repeated. "Is someone there?"

"Elliot," the voice finally said. "You were expecting me this time, weren't you?"

"Yes," said Halsey. The anger he had felt before was eclipsed by fear.

The caller assumed a mocking tone. "That's good, Elliot. Your memory is improving. I like that."

"Yes," said Halsey, conscious of Kate's eyes. "What do you want?"

"It's more like what I don't want, Elliot. I don't want you getting too complacent. If you think things are bad now, just wait."

"All right."

"What's the matter, Elliot? Losing your fight? I'm disappointed."

"Sorry." Halsey moved to hang up. He felt numb.

"Elliot!" the voice snapped, as though the caller knew his intention. "One more thing."

He put the receiver back to his ear.

"If you have any notion of enlisting help, keep this in mind: you'll be dragging others into a fate planned for you alone. That's all, Elliot. You may hang up now."

There was a soft menacing laugh, then a click. He hung up and stared at his hand as it rested on the receiver. He could feel a pall of doom moving over him. And he could feel Kate Crane watching him.

He lifted his head and met her gaze. The amused twinkle had been erased by a look of concern. How could he tell her a madman was possibly plotting his death and didn't care how many others he might take? He felt his life catapulting toward an abyss. The deadly plunge would come soon.

Kate was shocked by the change. The color had drained from Halsey's face. She saw his eyes lose the perceptive glint that had caught her off guard the day she met him. Now all she saw was an unreadable glaze. As he replaced the receiver his movements seemed slow and cumbersome.

Her eyes followed him as he pushed his chair back and shuffled over to the refrigerator.

"More juice?" he said.

"No, thank you." Her eyes bored into his back. "What was that all about, Elliot?"

He poured himself more juice, not looking at her. "Nothing."

She stood up, gathering the papers she had brought with her, preparing to leave. "Tell me to mind my own business, but don't lie to me."

He spun on his heel and gripped her arm. "Please, don't go."

She sensed the desperation in his voice. Flat and metallic. The voice of a man without hope.

He led her back to a chair, then sat cross-legged at her feet.

Her anger left as quickly as it had come. She sensed he was about to unburden himself and it wouldn't be easy.

She stared at him. His face was etched with pain. "Who was it on the phone, Elliot?"

He leaned against the couch and took a deep breath. "A crazy demented man. Who's threatening my life."

She felt a chill down her spine. "He's called before?"

"Several times. He seems to know all about me. I sometimes wonder . . ."

"What?"

"A lot of strange things have happened in the last several months."

She studied him for a moment. She could see his pallor return. "You need to talk about this. You haven't told a soul, have you?"

"I've been trying to ignore it."

"Denial." She had a doctor's impatience with it. How many people had died of heart attacks, cancer, rampant infections, because they thought ignoring their problem would make it go away? "I call it the Big D."

"The Big D." He smiled. "I like that. Maybe some-day we'll make a drug to dissolve it."

"An appealing thought," she said with a laugh.

Halsey stood and stretched. "It's late and you're tired," he said. "You don't need all this tonight. It'll keep. I'll take you to your hotel."

She didn't move. "I think it's kept long enough."

He looked at her and in that moment he wanted to scoop her up in his arms and embrace her.

CHAPTER SIXTEEN

He took her arm as they entered the dimly lit bar adjacent to the hotel lobby. They sat at a corner table, away from the piano where a man in a tux was bent over the keyboard playing a saccharinè version of "Moon River."

A waiter appeared and took their orders. Kate had an Irish Cream and Halsey a brandy. When the drinks arrived, Kate held up her glass. "To Truth," she said with a smile, "May the Big D bow beneath its weight."

Halsey laughed as they clinked glasses. "To Truth," he echoed, suddenly solemn.

"So," she said after taking a sip, "tell me about the caller." She studied his face. In the candlelight his dark eyes looked soft and vulnerable. In no way did he fit her image of a corporate executive. Or of someone hiding something.

She resisted an urge to reach out to him, at the same time suppressing an uneasiness about their evolving relationship. Something was happening to her—to them. Something that could affect the professional objectivity she had brought to this project.

"There's a lot to tell," he said, looking away. In that moment she wondered if he was feeling what she was feeling. She watched him toy with his glass, swirling the golden liquid.

"I think the caller has sabotaged the vaccine," he went on, his gaze coming back to hers.

They locked eyes. A double shock. Sabotage and a saboteur. She looked for a smile, a wink, a sign he was joking. His face was gravely serious.

"Sabotage! Why?"

"Hatred."

Her eyebrows arched. "That simple? How can you be so sure when you don't even know who he is?"

"His voice. It's full of hatred. He's been peeling away at the outer layers of my life. Now he's striking at the core—my work, the vaccine." He stared at the pianist, who was now pounding out a song from "The Phantom."

She couldn't, wouldn't believe him. It made no sense. Then she remembered their toast and she took a deep breath. "Tell me about it."

He seemed lost in thought. "I keep thinking of one man," he said softly. "It was so long ago."

She could almost see his mind reaching, not only back, but through—through a fear she guessed he had spent too much time denying.

He looked up at her. "This man—I'm blanking on his name—claimed our sleeping pill, Somnolot, made him crazy, made him kill his wife." He smiled without humor, his eyes narrowing as they moved back to the brandy. "Can you believe that? He blames a murder on a goddamn *pill*?"

"What does it have to do with you?"

"I had recently joined the company, in the research department. I had a degree in both microbiology and biochemistry—an unusual background suiting the needs of a pharmaceutical company. I jumped right in—even had a part in developing Somnolot. We were excited about it—the first effective nonaddictive hypnotic." He paused. "Then this madman comes along, tries to blame the medication for his own deranged violence."

"And what happened?"

He looked at her with a glint in his eyes that she couldn't quite read. "I took one look at this man and I knew he didn't need a pill to make him violent. I decided to probe into his background, talked the company into hiring a private investigator. Sure enough. He had a shady past. Had beaten a girlfriend within inches of her life. Arson in high school. A teacher who had been raped but wouldn't press charges. In fact, he always managed to beat the charges. Probably through intimidation.

"Even so, there was enough that Alatron's attorneys were able to get some of it admissible as evidence. Not only was Somnolot absolved, this guy . . ." Halsey's face suddenly brightened. "Heinman! Now I remember—Keith Heinman. He ended up in a hospital for the criminally insane."

Kate sat back and put a hand to her mouth. "What a story. And you think he may be out now?"

"Possibly. He made some threats as they dragged him out of the courtroom that day. I was nervous about it at the time, but nothing ever came of it. He was sentenced to a good long term. As the years went by, I forgot about him—even his name." He gave her a wry smile. "More denial."

She frowned. "How could he suddenly turn up?"

"I don't know. He may have been released early."

"Have you checked it out?"

"No, I didn't want to think about it." He reached

for her hand and gave it a gentle squeeze. "But your coming along got me thinking about him again."

She laughed, glad for a break in the tension. "Thanks a lot."

He smiled. "I feel . . . protective of you. The thought of a man like that on the loose . . ."

She could feel a churning in her stomach. "Let's consider it," she said, trying to shake the feeling with a dose of logic. "Imagine a crazy killer out there, plotting his revenge. How could he concoct such a scheme? If indeed the vaccine is contaminated, he would have had to somehow gain access to the virus, sneak into the vaccine lab, past all your automatized security precautions, past your guards, and manage to get hold of the correct lot . . ."

He shook his head. "This man is brilliant. He has a background in molecular biology."

"Oh," she said with a frown. She sipped the last of her juice and set it down. "I think we're obliged to find this man."

"We?"

"And why not? You don't feel we could make a team?" As she said it she felt her breath catch. She felt a stirring she hadn't felt in a long time. A team, yes. The possibilities knocked her over. She felt her objectivity slipping. And she didn't care. She would let Special Pathogens take over, as well they should. Abe Feldman and Rory. She grimaced at the irony of it—turning the case over to the man who wanted to marry her so she could help the man who was sweeping her off her feet.

"It would be an honor to be on your team," he said, his eyes picking up the glow of the candlelight.

"Where do we start?" She felt excited, energized.

"Maybe we should wait until we find out for sure whether the vaccine is contaminated."

She shook her head. "The sooner we start, the better. You've already seen where waiting around gets you."

He nodded.

"Why don't we check the hospital," she said. "If he's there, that writes him off in a way. He can call but he can't visit."

He stared at her. She saw the pain in his face, the strain. It was clear the burden he'd been carrying. "It's past midnight," he said, glancing at his watch. "I'm going to let you get some sleep. Let's see what the morning brings."

She stood and stretched her arms. "I'll walk out with you. I could use some fresh air."

They crossed the lobby and stood outside the hotel's glass doors. Kate felt a cool breeze and took a deep breath. It was starting to sprinkle. She looked down the street. A crowd was emptying out of a movie theater down the block. Couples leaned against each other, laughing as they passed by. Traffic jammed the streets, cabs weaving in and out, horns honking. She smiled as she felt the rain on her face.

She saw Halsey watching her and realized he had something to do with her feeling of well-being. He seemed to understand something basic about her that she herself didn't understand. She looked back at him and smiled. Rory never made her feel like this. Her ex had never made her feel like this. Not even Harpo. It was something new for her. And very exciting.

"I've enjoyed our evening," he said, brushing her cheek gently. "Good night, Kate. I'm glad you're here."

She liked his touch. She wasn't ready for good night. "I'll walk you to your car."

"Okay," he said. "And I'll drive you to your door."

*   *   *

His car was in a lot a block away. They walked quietly hand in hand, the rain just enough to freshen the air. He felt a kind of peacefulness around her. The sense of loneliness that had been creeping its way into every aspect of his life suddenly seemed impotent. Life's problems seemed nothing more than just that— problems. Problems that could be dealt with, one by one. Challenges. Life itself was what mattered. Being alive.

He looked at her holding her face to the rain and he knew she had taught him something important without even knowing or trying. He allowed himself to think about Barry and for the first time in a long time the distance between him and his son didn't feel insurmountable.

He was in this serene state of mind as they turned into the lot. He looked up and spotted his car. He froze. Then instinctively drew Kate to him, stepping between her and the car.

"Oh my God!" she gasped, peering around his shoulder.

The two of them stood there, clinging to each other, staring. Bonded by a common nemesis, unknown, and pervasive.

The car sat on its hubcaps, all four tires deflated. Across the windshield, scrawled in giant red letters was painted the word MURDERER.

Keith Heinman unfolded the red shirt he had picked up at AIDS FIRST headquarters—a giant van parked near Alatron. He removed the khaki custodian's shirt and tossed it on the bed. The bedroom was as barren as the rest of the house with the exception of a full-length mirror and a neatly made-up full-size bed without a headboard. There was no spread, just a thin blue thermal blanket, white sheets, and two pillows. The simple wooden nightstand held a reading lamp, an old-fashioned windup alarm clock, and a stack of books and scientific journals.

He stood before the mirror and regarded himself with a self-satisfied smile as he recalled the night before. It had gone well. Too bad for Elliot—such a nice car. He had seen the briefest flicker of fear on Halsey's face as he watched from the shadows. He had been the least bit unsettled by the way Halsey and the woman seemed to be drawn closer by the incident. But after he thought about it, he made a connection that he could use. The woman clearly had come to mean something to Halsey. She would be another route of access. Just like Halsey's son was going to be. He smiled at the thought.

He leaned over to pick up a set of barbells. He hefted them up and down, one in each hand, watching his chest and arm muscles ripple. He exhaled forcefully with each repetition. When he had done several reps and felt the burn in his upper arms, he set the weights down and put on the shirt, tucking it neatly into his pants. He stared at the AIDS FIRST lettering with a combination of fascination and disgust. He turned around and craned his neck to look at the back of the shirt. He liked the fit. It showed off his nicely tapered torso.

He had a niggling desire to share the secret of his new image before attending the AIDS FIRST meeting that evening. He recalled his handy audience in the basement and smiled. He needed to visit Parsons anyway. Poor guy hadn't eaten all day.

He strode into the kitchen and opened a can of tomato soup. He mixed it with water and heated it up in the microwave, threw a spoon into the plastic bowl and carried it down the stairs. He kicked open the door and slid through, flicking on the overhead light.

Parsons was bound up in the corner, his face coated with a film of grime and sweat. His eyes fixed on the plastic bowl in Heinman's hand, then on the shirt. Heinman set the soup down in front of him, then went through the routine of untying the arm ropes and gag.

"Pee-you, Dave. You need a shower."

Parsons grunted, lifted the bowl to his mouth, and drank hungrily. His hands were so shaky that a portion of the soup slopped over the sides.

Heinman crumpled up a paper towel and threw it at him. "Clean up, Dave. You're turning into a regular pig."

Parsons obediently wiped his hands and mouth, then looked at Heinman. He felt a wave of nausea as he saw those hard eyes boring into him. The soup seemed to gurgle in his throat, causing him to gag. "What are you going to do?" he stammered.

"I'm joining AIDS FIRST, Dave, what's it look like?"

"But why?" He could feel the soup swirling around in his esophagus. He swallowed hard.

Heinman shook his head. "Dave, you can be so dense. Remember that little deal you made with the AIDS FIRST boys, the one where they agreed to back off if you pushed through the vaccine?"

Parsons felt himself flinch. It all seemed so long ago, and so foolish. He kept his regrets to himself and nodded. He felt as though he was losing his ability to form words. Rotting away in the corner, he had a lot of time to think. His thoughts had made a subtle transition from words to images. He was thinking now mostly in images, often vividly frightening, as in a nightmare. Words seemed hard to come by. He had decided it was best to say as little as possible to Heinman, who mostly seemed amused by their conversations.

"So, Dave-boy, what do you think? Like my new outfit?" Heinman raised his arms and turned to show off the bright red shirt.

Parsons nodded. "Why?" Every time he spoke the soup gurgled some more. The nausea came back.

"Why, Davey? You want to know why? You look worried." Heinman leaned toward him. "Afraid maybe I'm a faggot?" He poked a finger at his chest. "No, Dave-boy, just business. You see, I believe the AIDS FIRST boys can be of help to the cause. Just like you were. But they have a little rift among the ranks. I need to make sure the right guy is in the right place at the right time. Know what I mean?"

Just like you were. That was the only phrase that stuck. The soup roiled and splashed. The significance of the past tense did not escape Dave Parsons. He had a feeling his usefulness to Heinman was approaching an end. He always listened carefully to Heinman's use of words, straining to read a hidden meaning,

He once thought he knew every one of the games people played—until he met Heinman. Heinman did not play by anyone's rules. He marched to his own beat.

Parsons didn't know what to say. So he grunted.

"There you go again, Dave. So loquacious. What're we going to do with you?"

Parsons eyes shot to Heinman's face, desperately searching for the answer to that question. One thing he *had* figured out about Heinman—he never asked a question he didn't already know the answer to.

Heinman's face held no answers, just a look of cold disdain, and a thin cruel smile. He tied Parsons's arms up and slipped the gag back in place without a word. He suddenly seemed angry about something and Parsons wished he had a clue. Something about the shirt.

Heinman had shown him the shirt and Parsons hadn't reacted like he was supposed to. He would think about it while Heinman was off at his meeting. He would do better next time.

If there was a next time.

CHAPTER SEVENTEEN

The morning traffic was sluggish due to the continuing downpour. The rhythm of the cab's wipers had a hypnotic effect. Halsey could barely keep his eyes open. He'd gotten no sleep after he and Kate had discovered his car. He thought he should be worrying about the car, but instead his worries revolved around her. Would she be next?

As the cab turned a corner, approaching the Tremayne Hotel, he could feel a layer of gloom lift. Somehow, facing the day seemed less formidable if he could face it with her.

The cab pulled up to the hotel and Kate suddenly appeared, sliding in beside him. She wore a navy trench coat and a scarf over her hair. "Good morning," she said, setting her briefcase on the floor.

"Hi." He smiled. "I didn't mean for you to wait outside."

"I enjoy being out in weather like this. I think better after a stroll in the rain."

She removed the scarf and shook her hair free as the cab pulled back into traffic. Her auburn locks looked remarkably dry but he noticed the shoulders of her trench coat were wet. "And did you get some thinking done?"

"Mostly fretting, I'm afraid."

"Me, too." He took her hand. "I hope you're not regretting your time here."

She looked at him. "No regrets."

He saw the strain lines around her mouth. "You look worried."

"Abe Feldman called early this morning from Atlanta, just before boarding his plane. They've cultured the Congo virus from one of the vaccine lots we sent."

Halsey felt his jaw clench. He had been hoping against hope the vaccine would be clean. Even so there would be problems. Violating FDA regulations. Misrepresenting the vaccine. People dying. None of it his doing. All of which he could have prevented—somehow. He wondered about Parsons's role and whether Parsons was part of the sabotage or as much a victim. Either way, Halsey would be seen as the culprit who, out of arrogance and greed, flew in the face of government regulations.

Kate looked at him, concerned by his silence. She was amazed at how attuned she was to the nuances of his demeanor. She saw the constriction in his throat. His search for inner strength as his hands opened and closed. The tightening of his jaw muscles as he gritted his teeth. He said nothing. He didn't have to.

"I'm sorry," she said.

He took a deep breath. "Christ," was all he could manage to say. His mind couldn't comprehend what was happening. It was too vast and too terrible. He felt his chest tighten, his breathing now coming in quick shallow pants. He tried to focus on the sound of the rain, which sometimes relaxed him. Not this time.

Kate said, "Special Pathogens will take over from here, though Abe asked me to stay on."

"I hope you will." His voice sounded flat to him. He was afraid to let her know how much she had come to mean to him. And he was afraid to let anyone else know—especially whoever it was out there, trying to destroy him.

The cabby accelerated to run a yellow light. The light turned red and the driver slammed on the brakes, skidding into the intersection. Horns honked and arms shot out of windows. Pedestrians scowled as they scurried across the street. None of these events had any impact on the cab's two passengers, still trying to gauge the impact of Abe Feldman's news.

"What's Feldman like?" said Halsey as the cab backed up.

"Abe's a very reasonable man. He's been with the CDC for years. He knows what he's doing."

"Then I'll look forward to meeting him," he said.

"Abe's good at dealing with the media." She laughed. "He knows how to make them think they've got a story without giving them one."

He gave her an appreciative grin. "I like that. If you don't give the media something, they'll jump on any wacko rumor."

He looked out and saw they were a few blocks from Alatron. He could already spot the throngs of demonstrators down the street. He leaned forward and said to the cabby, "Turn right where it says service road. There's a locked gate about a hundred yards down. You can drop us there."

He turned to Kate. "It's the best way if you're up to walking. We'll miss the demonstrators and media."

"Excellent idea," she said. She tied the scarf over her head, preparing for the elements and whatever else might come.

*   *   *

Abe Feldman was sitting in the anteroom when Halsey and Kate arrived. One look at the man told Halsey that Kate's description was right on. He guessed Feldman to be in his sixties. He had broad stooped shoulders and a large leonine head. His white hair was swept back from a domed forehead. Beneath his sharp nose was a thick white mustache. He had dark brown eyes set deep under a shelf of heavy eyebrows. He looked like the personification of wisdom, a bit on the pontifical side.

Feldman rose as they walked in. He grasped Kate's hand in his large paw. His grip was warm and certain. "Hello, Kate," he said in a resonant voice. "And congratulations. From what Kekich tells me, you've had a line on this matter from the start."

His eyes briefly shifted to Halsey, then back to Kate. His gruff features broke into a grin. "Sure you don't want to come over to my division?"

She smiled. "Maybe someday, Abe. For now, it's your show." She placed a hand on Halsey's shoulder. "Meet Elliot Halsey, Alatron's CEO. He's been more than accommodating."

Feldman gave her a sidelong glance. He nodded his head slightly and extended a hand. "A pleasure, Mr. Halsey. Abe Feldman. Dr. Crane told you, I'm sure, that we have indeed isolated the Congo virus in your AIDS vaccine." He shook his head. "A bad situation."

"It's a terrible situation, Dr. Feldman. I'll do whatever I can to help." He motioned them into his office.

They sat in leather chairs around a glass table. Halsey poured them coffee. Kate said, "Who did you bring with you, Abe?"

Feldman leaned back, resting his arms on the chair.

He was wearing a navy blue suit, overdressed for the job at hand. Proper and old-fashioned.

"Two of our top field officers," he said. "Rory McDermott and Mort Cohen. As you know, McDermott's got an engineering background. He'll supervise inspection of the vent systems and containment facilities. Cohen's specialty is virology. He'll be culturing the vaccine and sampling the Congo strain here to make sure we have a match."

Kate nodded. She'd been afraid Rory would come. She looked at Halsey. He seemed drawn into himself, yet she could see him watching her. She sensed an energy between them, almost palpable. Suddenly, Rory's whereabouts seemed irrelevant. She was, amid the unfolding drama of an epidemic, developing a sense of what she wanted to round out her life.

Feldman, oblivious of the dynamics between Kate and Halsey, leaned forward and sipped his coffee. "A few more of our people are on standby in Atlanta, but several of our best officers have already fanned out to the five urban areas where the vaccine was administered. There's surprisingly little evidence of spread considering what we know about this virus's level of contagion."

"Highly contagious," observed Halsey, his eyes still fixed on Kate.

Feldman gave a single nod of his head. "Highly," he agreed, his eyes appraising Halsey.

Kate watched the two men with a degree of apprehension. She could almost see Halsey bristling at what he might take to be Feldman's innuendoes: something like "We see a danger in the tendency of large corporations to relax their vigilance in the name of profit."

"Elliot isn't like that," she wanted to blurt out. Instead, she said, "Alatron is the only company working on a vaccine for the African hemorrhagic viruses, Abe.

The others won't even touch it. Too much financial risk."

Feldman's head slowly turned to the Alatron CEO. "A vaccine for the African viruses may have suddenly become profitable, Mr. Halsey—quite profitable. You would do well to put your crew on it full tilt."

Halsey said nothing. Kate could see the anger in his face. She knew what he was responding to. She, too, had heard the irony in Abe's voice. She made an effort to veer the conversation to a more constructive vein. She gestured toward her briefcase. "A pathologist colleague of mine and I have already looked over the vent systems on paper. We saw no structural problems. And the manuals show impeccable safety standards."

Feldman smiled. "That's of course helpful, Kate, but we'll need to eyeball those vents inch by inch. Cracks won't show up on blueprints. We'll have to examine all safety precautions for compliance. If they say they're using two HEPA filters in their exhaust system, that's fine. But we'll have to check not only the number, but the placement of the filters and when they were last changed."

He looked at Halsey. "We could use some of your people to help us. McDermott will supervise. We'll need to look at the drain traps and analyze the chemical disinfectants. Check the seals on all penetrations. Make sure your directional airflow manometers are working. That sort of thing."

Halsey nodded. "Whatever you need."

Kate could tell that Halsey was not going to bring up sabotage. She understood why. She made a decision to do so herself. "Abe, before you get too far in your plans, there's something you should know."

A bushy white eyebrow shot up. Kate looked at Halsey and caught an admonishing look. She chose to ignore it. She knew Abe Feldman better than Halsey did. With Abe you said what was on your mind or he might say it for you. And you might not care for the way he put it.

"Mr. Halsey has reason to suspect sabotage," she said.

Without turning a hair Feldman said, "Of course sabotage is always a consideration in situations like this. Statistically, however, human or structural error is far more likely."

Kate and Halsey exchanged looks. Kate pushed a few strands of hair off her forehead. "If you look for the statistically likely causes first, Abe, you could lose a big chunk of time if you're wrong. Time that could be critical."

"Perhaps. But we have to start somewhere, don't we? You know the old saw. When you hear hoofbeats, think horses, not zebras." He gave a deep chuckle. "Unless, of course, you're in Africa."

Kate, like everyone else who had gone to medical school, readily recalled the saying. It had proved helpful many times. Especially as a student, when you were eagerly diagnosing all the exotic diseases you'd read about and considered the routine rather humdrum.

But right now, she wasn't so fond of the old rule. "Even when the horse has stripes?" she said, chagrined at the hint of belligerence she heard in her voice.

Feldman's brow wrinkled into a frown. He sat back with a thoughtful look. "Mr. Halsey," he said finally. "May I have a moment alone with Dr. Crane?"

Halsey stood up. "Of course. Please stay here. I can work next door."

"Thank you," said Feldman with a slight bow of his head.

As Halsey quietly slipped out, Feldman leaned forward and fixed Kate with a solemn look. "We need to be unified on this matter, Kate, or the media will make us look like a bunch of bumbling bureaucrats." He stared off for a moment, lost in thought. "You're too young to remember—probably a tenderfoot in medical school—but I remember all too well how merciless the media were during the outbreak of Legionnaire's disease in the summer of '76."

Kate watched him and waited. She had an idea of what was coming. She'd heard the story before, but only in fragments, and never from Abe Feldman's lips.

"I was part of the CDC's investigatory team back then," he continued with a sigh. "What an exciting time it was, tracking down a deadly new epidemic. At the time, we thought it was a once-in-a-lifetime opportunity. Epidemics, thank God, have not been all that common." He frowned. "Little did we know then that AIDS was lurking just around the corner.

"All in all, we did a damn good job," Feldman went on, "although it was months before we had an answer. But to the public, the time it took to solve the case might just as well have been an eternity. You know how people are—especially lay people. They want an answer yesterday."

Kate nodded to acknowledge she was listening. While wondering why he was going into such detail about the past when they had their hands full with the present.

He seemed to read her mind. "We had plenty of opportunity later on to pinpoint just why things had taken so long. In fact, opportunity turned to necessity as Congress questioned the delays. We took a good look at ourselves, and you know what, Kate? It paid off. We learned there were two recurring themes that explained most of our tie-ups." He paused, gazing at her with a reflective smile. "Care to take a guess?"

"Lack of a unified case-reporting system for one," she said quickly, having herself been part of a team helping to correct the problem years later.

He nodded with vigorous approval. "And the other," he said, with a dramatic pause, "was what I call the sabotage myth. He wasted vast amounts of time on reports of suspected sabotage." He held up his hands. "There were so many theories, we had to assign them names: The Truck Theory, the Contaminated Soda Theory, the Poisoned Onion Theory, the False Teeth Theory, and so forth."

Feldman laced his large weathered hands behind his head and appeared to be studying the ceiling. Kate could see he was thoroughly enjoying himself now—and so was she. He could be fascinating.

"My favorite Legionnaire theory," he said almost dreamily as his mind reached back nearly twenty years, "was that the chemical-biological warfare boys over at Fort Detrick had deliberately contaminated Philadelphia's Bellvue Hotel with a new toxic substance they were testing." He frowned, fingering his mustache. "Unfortunately, that particular theory was so plausible we ended up spending valuable time running it down. Even though chemical-biological warfare research was banned by then, the belief prevailed that Fort Detrick was still fooling around with it. The media enjoyed keeping the myth alive. My colleague Bill Oldham and I fell for the theory ourselves after we interviewed the top brass at Detrick. They were so damn evasive and uncooperative we were convinced there was something to it."

Kate was beginning to feel impatient as she surmised what he was driving at. "Are you leading up to something, Abe?"

He gave her a wounded look. "My point is that sabotage theories are as unlikely as they are popular." He shifted in his chair, plucking a piece of lint off his trousers. "Let's face it, Kate. Sabotage is a tempting explanation, especially for someone feeling the walls closing in on him, like your Mr. Halsey." He wagged a finger at her. "Don't get caught in the web of a mysterious conspiracy theory, my dear lady, or you will be of little use to the team. Take it from me, it has happened to the best of us. I often wonder how many lives all that agonizing about Fort Detrick cost us."

Feldman got up and poured himself another cup of coffee and filled her cup. "Thank you, Abe," she said, taking a sip. She sat back, crossing her legs. "I have a comment, a piece of advice, and a question."

He laughed. "Yes?"

"Comment: It seems to me you're bringing a bunch of useless old baggage to our present dilemma. Advice: beware of letting the pendulum swing too far in the opposite direction. Question: What if you're wrong and what we're looking for is in fact a zebra?"

Feldman met her challenging gaze, then looked away. "Then we will indeed be in a very embarrassing situation." He slowly got to his feet, and Kate thought for the first time that he was showing his years. He walked toward the window, his hands clasped behind his back. "You know, Kate, I may be old-fashioned but I'm not blind. I believe there's more between you and Mr. Halsey than meets the eye." His voice lowered as he turned and leveled his eyes at her. "I'm concerned about your objectivity on this project."

She felt surprisingly liberated, even touched, as he verbalized what she had begun to see herself. She held his gaze. "So am I," she said, setting her cup down. "And now you know the whole reason I'm glad you're

here. I have no right to make sweeping generaliza-
tions. But I'm here to help if you want me."

He approached her and patted her hand. "It's all
right, Kate. I'd like you on the team."

She smiled as she studied his creased face. She saw
no disapproval there. "I appreciate your confidence in
me, Abe. You'll tell me if you think I'm overstepping
my bounds."

His large head made a nodding motion. "Of
course." He turned toward the door. "Now," he said,
tugging at his collar, "where is that Mr. Halsey?"

Halsey dialed Information and obtained the number
for Woodlawn State Hospital for the Criminally Insane. As a recording slowly announced the number,
he wrote it down. He felt the fine tremor in his hand
with a sense of dismay. After he hung up, he stared
at what he had written. Ten digits and the word
Woodlawn jumped off the page at him. The act of
seeking out the number had served to open emotional
floodgates, tapping memories in a way that retelling
the tale to Kate Crane had not touched.

He remembered everything like it was yesterday.
Not as a chronology of events, but as one giant emotional meteorite, barreling through the protective atmosphere he had built around himself. As the memory
loomed larger in his mind, its intensity made him realize why he had worked to keep it out. It was hard to
accept the presence of that kind of evil in the world.
He had never had to deal with a Keith Heinman before, and hoped he never would again. He had felt
the magnitude of Heinman's evil then. And now he
realized by ignoring it all these years he had made its
influence stronger. Heinman had sunk a hook into him
ten years ago. And was still hanging on. Even if the
man had nothing to do with the calls, nothing to do

with the vaccine, Halsey's evasive attitude had served to grant Heinman even greater power over him.

He took a deep breath and wiped away the perspiration that had gathered on his forehead. All that agony, just from getting a damn phone number. No, he told himself. No more self-deception. It's not the number. It's that you've finally admitted to yourself he's still in your life. Never left. You never dealt with it.

Funny, he thought. Acknowledging evil was like learning to grieve. You had to take it in stages. If you stopped at any one stage, you stagnated emotionally, and you could never let the feelings go. They would continue to haunt you.

Halsey felt a bitter anger stir inside him as he punched out the Woodlawn number on his Touch-Tone phone. He could feel his heart pounding. After the fifth ring he felt himself calming down. He could hang up. Put it off a little longer. The very realization made him grip the receiver all the tighter, refusing to allow himself the luxury of procrastination.

Finally, a woman's voice announced in a bleak monotone, "Woodlawn Psychiatric and Correctional Institute, how may I direct your call?"

Halsey took a moment to react. They had changed the name, gotten rid of the criminally insane bit. Correctional Institute. He laughed to himself. How are you going to "correct" a guy like Keith Heinman?

"Hello?" insisted the voice with a touch of impatience. "May I help you?"

"Yes," replied Halsey. "I'm trying to locate one of your inmates, by the name of Keith Heinman."

"Sir, we have no inmates. They're clients."

He fought the impulse to make a stinging rebuke. "I'm sorry," he said in a controlled tone. "One of your clients. By the name of Heinman—Keith Heinman."

"Just a moment, please."

Halsey's heart did a flip. Was Heinman there after all? He didn't know whether to be relieved or concerned. While he considered the possibilities, a new, equally robotlike voice came on the line, this time male. "Client information. May I help you?"

Halsey switched the receiver to his other hand and wiped his moist palm on his thigh. "I'm trying to locate Keith Heinman, a ... client. It's important."

"Just a moment, please."

Halsey took a deep breath. The wheels of bureaucracy turned ever so slowly. He heard the man tapping away at a computer. At least he wasn't sorting through a file cabinet in a musty backroom. Finally he came back on. "I'm sorry, we have no one here by that name."

"Listen to me," said Halsey, feeling his control slipping. "I know he's there. If you can't locate him, get me someone who can."

"I'm sorry, sir, he is not in our active client file."

"Well then what about your inactive file," he snapped. "Surely you people could be a little more helpful."

"Would you like to speak with my manager?" The man's voice now had a threatening intonation, as though daring Halsey to consider going over his head.

"Yes."

After a few more contacts, Halsey ended up with the information that Keith Heinman had been discharged a year ago. No forwarding address. When he pressed for more information, he was given the name of Dr. Rutger Kraft, the psychiatrist who had written the discharge order. Dr. Kraft still worked there, but only part-time. And he happened to be out of town.

Halsey slammed down the receiver. He pushed back his chair and stalked over to the refrigerator for a cold drink. He wasn't really thirsty, but he was restless. Doing something purposeful, after all that purposeless runaround, at least gave him a sense of control. And it gave him an opportunity to reflect on what little information he had gleaned.

It was no surprise Keith Heinman was gone. As Halsey rummaged through the refrigerator, he stretched his mind back to try to date just when odd things had started happening to him. He'd thought it was six months or so, but it could have been more like nine. And if he really thought about it, he might even be able to stretch it to a year.

He found a small can of tomato juice, snapped it open, and crossed back to the sofa. He took a sheet of paper and placed it on the glass table near him, and pulled a pen out of his pocket. He made himself write Keith Heinman's name at the top of the sheet. He wasn't sure where he was going from there, but he knew he would have to sort out in his mind just what he thought Heinman was up to, if in fact Heinman was The Caller. And if in fact Heinman had sabotaged the vaccine.

He thought about how to locate Heinman and decided to look into putting a tracing device on his phone. He knew nothing about such matters, but guessed it would mean involving the police. The idea made him nervous. Was he overreacting? He wasn't sure he wanted police swarming around. Not until he had more.

But how would he get more? After tapping the pen idly on his hand, he began setting down his thoughts. Motives. Means. Anonymity—pros and cons. The more he wrote the more convinced he became it was Heinman. Heinman, on the loose. Heinman, out to destroy him.

For a moment, as he felt the full impact of the realization, a bolt of raw terror shot through him. Every nerve in his body seemed to quiver. His heart raced, his face flushed, the lump in his throat swelled from the size of a walnut to a grapefruit.

In that moment he wanted, more than anything, to run. But he knew he would stay. As he thought of Kate Crane, as he thought of his company, as he thought of his son and all the other AIDS victims, he knew he would see it to the bitter end.

CHAPTER EIGHTEEN

Kate scanned the headlines as she waited for Halsey in the hotel coffee shop. She nibbled absently at her morning Danish. Stories about Halsey and the vaccine scandal were all over the front pages. Like something out of a medical thriller. Even staid papers like the *Times* exuded a tabloid jauntiness with banner headlines like the one that popped out at her. AIDS VACCINE BACKFIRES, CDC FIRES BACK. A subhead read, "Mystery at Alatron." There was a picture of Abe Feldman looking up at Rory McDermott who was on a stepladder, peering into a hole in the ceiling.

She had to laugh at the expression on Feldman's face. He looked as though he would like to clobber McDermott, the camera having caught them at an awkward moment.

She had felt like clobbering Rory herself when he approached her with a hangdog expression the day he arrived. As though asking forgiveness for pressuring her into a marriage decision. After a tense conversation they agreed not to discuss it further while preoccupied with the Alatron project. That was the last she'd seen of him other than a brief passing in the hall.

She felt a hand on her shoulder and looked up to see Halsey smiling at her. "Good morning," he said with a smile.

"Good morning, yourself," she said, gesturing toward the seat next to her.

"What's the latest from the media circus?" He sat down and craned his neck to see the paper.

"The usual. Your company is unspeakable." She laughed and pointed to the photo. "And Abe looks like he's ready to wring Rory's neck."

She watched him scan the headlines. She enjoyed looking at him. His face was lean and weathered from the sun. He was an outdoors type, strong and capable looking. She liked that. There was an intensity in his eyes, the clear look of a vibrant man—one of those irresistible men who became even more attractive with time.

"Everybody's edgy these days," he said, looking up from the paper. "Including the board. The company's foundering. We'll be having a brainstorming session later this morning." He took a deep breath. "But first I want to take you away from all this."

"I'm ready," she said. Our first date, she thought, feeling absurdly young and foolish.

He took the paper from her. "You won't be needing this."

"Where to?" she asked with a smile. "Or is it still a secret?"

"Water," he murmured cryptically.

She frowned. "Water . . ."

"You know, the stuff that floats under canoes."

"Canoeing? I have to be back by noon."

"We'll be back before Abe Feldman finishes his morning coffee, I promise. It's only a short drive."

Kate shot him a sidelong glance. She had visions of floating in a New Jersey swamp behind some drab factory, clouds of black smoke wafting overhead, mutated frogs croaking under oil-soaked lily pads.

He gave her a roguish smile and took her hand. "Trust me."

She had a feeling of peace as she looked at the lake that came suddenly into view. The water was so clear and still that the thickly wooded shoreline was reflected in perfect detail. She glanced at Halsey. He had one hand draped over the steering wheel as he watched her.

"Like it?"

"It's . . . magical."

He pointed toward a small log cabin partially obscured by the tall pines. "That cabin has been in my family for generations." He paused. "I'm the only one who comes here anymore."

She detected a sadness in his voice. "Thank you for bringing me here," she said quietly.

He took her hand and gave it a gentle squeeze, his eyes meeting hers. "Shall we walk down to the water?"

They scrambled down a small embankment, hand in hand. Kate laughed. "A short little breather, you told me. You knew I'd love it, didn't you?"

His eyes sparkled. "You're on to me."

He led her onto a wooden dock that wobbled under their feet. The sound of the creaking wood and the water gently lapping at the pylons flooded her with a powerful nostalgia for the summers of her youth. He did that to her, made her feel like a girl again—expectant, breathless, and a little sad.

Tears welled up in her eyes as she watched him untie a battered old aluminum canoe. She turned away, hoping he wouldn't notice.

He looked up at her. "Are you okay?"

She sniffled slightly and nodded. What was wrong with her, anyway? A man she barely knows is nice to her and she bursts into tears.

He stood up and offered her a hand. "Canoes are temperamental things."

His grip was firm as he guided her into the canoe, then eased in behind her. He handed her a paddle. "Know how to use one of these?"

"Yes, from summers on the Finger Lakes. A lake almost like this." She paused. "It brings back lots of memories."

He dipped his paddle in the water and brought the boat forward with surprising swiftness. "For me, too," he said softly. Something about his voice seemed to make room for her. "This place was one of my child-hood haunts. I'd like to show you a special spot."

"I want to see it." She felt a bond that thrilled her. She knew it wasn't just the lakes and canoes they had in common. It was the intimacy of their memories.

They paddled in perfect synchrony toward the cen-ter of the lake, the water darkening as the lake deep-ened. For a while, they said nothing, absorbed in their own thoughts and the tranquility of the surroundings. The only sound was the gentle ripple of the water as the canoe left a narrow wake.

Halsey stopped paddling and shipped his oar. Kate did the same and they sat in the water, the quiet of the morning broken only by an occasional bird's song and the rocking of the boat.

"Tell me about yourself, Kate Crane." His voice was inviting.

She thought a moment, staring at the water, the shimmering sunlight causing her to squint. "Nothing too exciting. I'm a kid from Queens. My parents were divorced when I was in grade school. My mother, sis-ter, and I moved to a farm in upstate New York where

I became a fanatic horsewoman. My father was a Manhattan internist and I dreamed of being just like him. I married the wrong man. I love my work."

She looked over her shoulder at him and laughed. "How am I doing?"

He studied her with an intensity that made her feel completely visible. "Better than you know."

"Okay, it's your turn." She moved to face him, swinging her legs over the seat.

He laughed. "All right, I'm game. I'm a kid from Arkansas. I grew up on a farm and dreamed of living in the big city, doing big things. I've always loved science and baseball. I'm an outdoors nut. My father was a salesman. He died of emphysema before I finished college. I wanted to go to medical school but quit to help my mother and kid sister. I turned to research later and found I was damn good at it. I married the wrong woman. I have two children." He smiled self-consciously. "How am I doing?"

"Terrific. What happened to your Southern accent?"

"Radio."

"Radio?".

"I'd listen to it for hours on end. I wanted to talk like those guys—the newscasters, the sportscasters. I never felt like a Southerner. More Western."

She nodded, imagining a young Elliot Halsey glued to the radio. "You forgot the part," she said with a smile, "about wanting to change the world."

His eyes jumped up to her face. "Modesty forbids."

They laughed together. It was a good sound. Then she saw his face grow sober. He had plenty of reason to be sober, but she sensed it was due to something he hadn't alluded to yet.

Without knowing why, she said, "Tell me about your children."

She could see an immediate change in his face. It ran the gamut of feelings, from pride to anguish. She knew she had hit on something.

"My daughter's a senior in high school. My son works in publishing in the city."

She continued to look at him expectantly. He was too reticent. It was the son, she was pretty sure. "Tell me about your son," she said softly.

He responded immediately, as though the question were perfectly natural and expected. "He's gay. He has AIDS." His voice was heavy with feeling.

Her heart went out to him. For a moment she regretted having pushed him. Then she realized she hadn't pushed, only invited. It was something he needed to talk about. "That must be hard, on both of you. Are you close?"

He looked away. "We used to be."

"What happened?"

He shook his head. "No single incident. I blame myself for his being gay. I wasn't there when he needed me. I might have tipped the scales."

A hawk swooped overhead, then veered off toward the trees. Kate's eyes followed its flight, then came to rest on Halsey. The pain she saw in his eyes was heart-wrenching. "Is anyone to *blame* for another's sexual orientation?"

He gave her an uncomprehending look.

"What I mean is, do you think he's immoral, for being gay?"

He frowned. "No, of course not."

"Then why would a word like blame even come up?"

She saw a look on his face that moved her. She had given him a new way of looking at it and she could see a layer of anguish melt away.

"Well," he said, "I'm not sure."

She leaned toward him. She was on to something. Something important. She had given homosexuality a lot of thought. When you were in the infectious disease field you had to. She knew what was plaguing him. "Do you think he's unhappy because he's gay?"

By now his eyes were glued to her. It was as though he couldn't believe anyone would understand or care the way she was understanding and caring. "I think he had a hard time with it at first. Peer pressure, ridicule, that sort of thing. But after he found his own peer group ... I guess I'd have to say no, he's not unhappy he's gay."

"If you put aside your own standard for happiness, it works, doesn't it?"

He nodded thoughtfully. "He has a ... friend, named Steve. They really seem to care about each other."

"But he has AIDS," she said. "You blame yourself for that."

"I think I do, yes."

"And you wonder about your motives for pursuing AIDS drugs and the vaccine. Are you a humanitarian, or just working off your guilt. Something like that."

He continued to stare at her. "You're unbelievable."

She laughed and shook her head. "No. I just have a lot of maternal intuitiveness that I've never had an opportunity to use. Tell me more about him."

And he did, as he paddled the canoe toward the special place. He poured his heart out. She listened. When he was done, she had only one thing to say. "He sounds like a courageous young man—like his father. I'd like to meet him."

"I'll see that you do," he said with a smile that made her feel happier than she had in a long time.

* * *

They glided into a small cove. He jumped ashore and drew the bow up onto the pebbly embankment. He helped her out and led her through the woods along a narrow path. They came upon a clearing surrounded by fallen trees that made perfect benches. He pointed overhead.

"There it is. My tree house, a child's dream place."

She looked up to see a hodgepodge of boards nailed into the shape of a small shack nestled in a giant oak. A thick frayed rope hung down, swaying gently in the breeze.

She imagined a young Elliot sitting up there reading and staring out at the lake, planning his mission to save mankind. Not knowing how important his mission would become and how much trouble it would be.

"It's wonderful," she said softly.

"As a kid I used to sit up there in the dark and read Thoreau's *Walden* by candlelight. That book was my bible, got me interested in the environment."

She sat down on a log. He joined her. "So how did a budding environmentalist end up as CEO of a pharmaceutical company?"

He looked at her for a long moment, and she could almost see his mind working. "I've been studying ecology for a long time, mostly on my own. It became evident to me that as we impact the environment, it comes back at us in strange and terrible ways. Infectious diseases, epidemics, floods, holes in the ozone, more infectious diseases. I wanted to be in a place where I could do something about it."

She couldn't believe her ears. He was on the verge of voicing some of the newest thinking in the infectious disease world—emerging infections. How did he know what she was barely versed in herself? Concepts that were at once fascinating and frightening. "Are you familiar with emergent-strain theory?"

He looked at her sharply. "A little. You know what I'm getting at?"

"I think so. Most of the so-called 'new' pathogens, like HIV and the hantavirus, are not new at all. They have been well entrenched for decades, even centuries, without harming their hosts. Why do they suddenly emerge as human killers?"

His eyes glowed. "That's the very question that's been gnawing at me. We know the first case of AIDS occurred as early as 1959. So what made it explode twenty years later? It has to have something to do with changes in people. A different morality. Maybe the way we're polluting the environment, sucking it dry. If the atmosphere, the climate, the forests are affected, how can people be exempt?"

She nodded, sharing his excitement. They were among a new breed of pioneers. "It's probably a combination of factors," she said. "Revved-up international travel, changes in lifestyle like the free-love generation of the sixties. More cardiac surgeries and organ transplants, calling for more blood transfusions. And a whole new spectrum of carriers."

"It's like a mathematical equation," he chimed in. "Cause and effect. Look at Rift Valley Fever. Once only a disease of sheep and cattle. Then some two hundred thousand people in Egypt affected. All because of man's affront to nature."

She was amazed at his knowledge and insight. He had to be referring to the Aswan Dam, built in 1970. It had flooded hundreds of thousands of acres of arid land, creating a new breeding ground for mosquitoes, which in turn brought the Rift Valley virus to northern Africa with its previously unexposed "virgin" population.

"Are you sure you never went to med school?" she quipped.

He laughed. "I'll bet you don't learn this stuff in med school."

"You're right about that. I learned most of it after coming to CDC." Which made his knowing it all the more impressive, she thought. Her eyes lighted on her watch and she felt a jolt of disappointment. "I can't believe how the time had flown." She stood up and brushed the dirt off her slacks. "We should head back."

He rose and wrapped an arm around her shoulder. "I wish we could spend the entire day here." He laughed. "You seem so easy to get to know, yet it's so hard to get to know you."

"I promise to make it easier," she said, reaching up for his hand as they walked back to the lake. It felt right, their being together. There was much more to be said about the important matter of emerging infections. But she knew it wasn't their like-mindedness on such topics that made for their closeness. She and Chuck Kekich had many of the same conversations, yet never had this bond.

No, it was something else—an energy, a chemistry, a force. Whatever it was called, it was there, and it was precious. She knew he felt it, too, in the way he touched her, the way he looked at her.

They said little as he guided the canoe back to the shore with deep powerful strokes. Suddenly he stopped paddling and she sensed something was wrong. She looked back to see his body tense. She followed his gaze to the shoreline, which they had been rapidly approaching.

She didn't see it at first. "Elliot, what's wrong?"

He didn't answer right away, but began paddling hard. "I can't see the car," he said, his voice even and controlled. Too controlled.

She tried to remember where they had parked.

Should they be able to see the car from here? "Isn't it behind some trees?" She knew the moment she said it that the car had been in a clearing.

He didn't answer. He was paddling faster now, making the canoe surge forward. The canoe made a loud grating sound as he landed it. He jumped out, his face grim, and quickly helped her out. They ran up the bank and stood gaping at the flat graveled area where the car had been.

There were skid marks where the tires had peeled out. The only other sign that someone had been there was a copy of the newspaper Kate had been reading that morning, laid out neatly on the ground, each corner held down by a rock.

The headline, MYSTERY AT ALATRON was circled with a blood-red marker.

It was past noon when they arrived at Alatron. Kate's feet were sore from trudging the three miles to the highway, where Rose came and got them. Halsey's anger smoldered, but Kate appeared to be his primary concern. As they rode in the backseat of the sedate silver Oldsmobile, he never let go of her hand.

At Alatron, they pushed their way through the ever-present throngs and sneaked through the back corridors to Halsey's office.

Halsey gave Rose a peck on the cheek and sent her home. He sat Kate down in the seat opposite his desk. He then snatched up the phone and buzzed Alice Rampel, the veteran Alatron secretary who was covering for Rose.

"Alice, I'm back. I sent Rose home. Dr. Crane is with me. Who's out there?"

Alice, usually a model of poise, sounded flustered. "The same old reporters," she whispered. "We ought to start charging them rent." Her voice changed. "Dr.

Feldman called. He wanted to speak with you the moment you came in. He sounded upset. There's a man here from Fort Thacker—insists on waiting for you." She paused, and when she spoke again, Halsey detected a trace of amusement in her voice. "He's wearing a white coat and has two young men with him, also in white coats. They look like they just walked off the set of *General Hospital.*"

"Did you get a name?"

He could hear Alice's voice fade. When she came back on the line she said, "I'd better go now," and hung up.

Halsey returned the receiver to its cradle and took a deep breath, running his fingers through his hair. He looked at Kate and couldn't believe what he saw. She was smiling. It wasn't a smile of amusement. He wasn't sure what it was, but it made him want to smile, too.

"Why are you smiling?"

"I was thinking of our morning together."

"It seems like a long time ago, doesn't it?"

"Oh, not that long."

He looked at her. Her auburn hair was tangled and windblown. Her blue eyes radiated a warmth that he could almost feel. She was beautiful. And she was smiling. Suddenly the missing car and all the people wanting a piece of him seemed unimportant.

He rose and came around the desk. He pulled up a chair next to her. "Thank you for setting my priorities straight."

She was remembering their conversation beneath the tree house. She could see the twelve-year-old boy reading *Walden* by candlelight and spinning fantasies of a heroic odyssey out of the mist that rose over the lake. He had touched her heart.

"Your priorities are just fine."

He leaned forward and brushed her cheek with a kiss. She raised a hand to his temple and gently stroked the side of his face, sensing the fine bone structure beneath the skin. He closed his eyes and his lips found hers. He put his arms around her, drawing her to him.

And then in the midst of this bliss there was a commotion at the door.

They looked up, still embracing, to see a tall man in a white coat burst through the door, Alice wringing her hands behind him. He moved with a swagger that Kate recognized immediately with a sinking feeling.

"Well, isn't this cozy," drawled Roger Peck, his lips drawn in a smug smile. He stood with his arms folded across his chest, his head cocked to one side as though appraising a used car for flaws.

Kate was on her feet. "What in God's name are you doing here?" She stormed toward him with her fists clenched. Peck flinched.

Peck's eyes moved over her. "I might ask you the same thing, Dr. Crane. Official business?" He gave her a sly wink.

Halsey approached them, his manner calm and controlled. "I'm Elliot Halsey, Dr. Peck. This is my office. If you have business with me, make an appointment with my secretary. If you wish to speak with Dr. Crane, you may do so, but not here."

Halsey had moved close to Peck, causing Peck to take a step backward. Kate noticed they were about the same height, yet Halsey seemed to tower over the other man.

"Before you leave," Halsey said coldly, "you will apologize to Dr. Crane."

Peck seemed to regain his composure but was no longer smiling. "I don't think you're in a position to tell me what to do, Mr. Halsey."

"Does Abe know you're here?" Kate demanded.

Peck shrugged. "Abe Feldman has his job, I have mine, Kate. And you have yours. Waiting for you back in Atlanta."

Halsey moved to the door and took a quick look at his outer office. It was teeming with reporters. The apology could wait. "Look, it's a jungle out there. Why don't the three of us sit down and talk?"

Peck sat down and whipped out a folder from his white coat, now all business. He addressed Kate, ignoring Halsey. "I have two reports from a Los Angeles pathologist. Two DOAs he believes died of an AIDS-related illness. Their blood is HIV positive." He paused, flipping open the folder. "I have the morgue photos here. They look exactly like the victims you've been chasing down, Kate."

She reached out a hand and Peck passed her the photos. Although she was inured to the horror of it all, her breath caught in her throat as her eyes skimmed over the disfigured bodies. She swallowed hard and handed the pictures to Halsey.

"Has their blood been checked for the Congo virus?"

"Yes." Peck flashed a superior smile.

The smile was all the answer she needed. "It may be too early for the antibodies to show up," she said.

"Unlikely." Peck took the pictures back and returned the folder to his pocket, continuing to ignore Halsey. "To answer your question, Kate, I'm here because we think you and your CDC cronies are way off base. You're assuming the vaccine is contaminated. We have a more objective viewpoint. I think, Mr. Halsey," he said, finally acknowledging Halsey, "that your vaccine is dangerous. It is irresponsibly premature to be working with the live virus. These people are dying of a new and virulent form of AIDS, probably due to a mutation evolving from the vaccine."

Kate bristled but she saw Halsey had himself well in hand.

Halsey looked Peck in the eye. "You must know, Dr. Peck, that if you persist in publicizing your views and you turn out to be wrong, you will have set back the vaccine for years and cost untold human lives. Are you prepared to live with that?"

Peck leveled his eyes at Halsey. "And if I'm right, Mr. Halsey. Are you prepared to live with that?"

Kate saw Halsey's jaw harden. "I'm prepared for whatever happens."

Peck stood up. "We shall see, Mr. Halsey. We shall see."

CHAPTER NINETEEN

Halsey was making notes for the morning meeting with the top board members. It was late, and he was tired and frustrated. The police, already overworked, hadn't been at all amused when the car he reported stolen turned up in its usual parking spot in the Alatron lot. They were quick to suggest he had a rather ingenious prankster on his hands.

He knew better. He had a dangerous maniac on his hands, and he wasn't making any headway in locating him. Kate wanted to help but he tried to keep her from getting involved. He knew it was Heinman and he knew how Heinman worked. Heinman would make good use of Halsey's growing attachment to Kate. For her sake, he had to draw back, pull away from her. But he couldn't. He couldn't get enough of her. He felt like a starving man who had stumbled onto a feast. She had become as important to him as life itself.

He pulled open his desk drawer and stared at the pistol—a gleaming steel-blue thirty-eight automatic. He didn't like guns, but his father had been a collector. It was the one memento he allowed himself from his father's collection. He normally kept the thirty-eight at home. But one day—it was after he had met Kate—he had slipped the gun into his briefcase and brought it to the office. He told himself it was because the gun would be less susceptible to theft.

But he knew the real reason—The Caller. None of the calls had been to his home number. If he ever met up with The Caller face to face, it would be here, at Alatron. He was certain of that. And he would be prepared.

As he closed the drawer, the phone rang. His heart leapt into his throat. It was his private line. It might be Kate, but he knew it wasn't. He snatched it up. "Hello," he snapped.

"Well, well, what are you all worked up about Elliot?"

"What do you want this time, you son of a bitch?" Halsey could feel a murderous rage tearing away at his insides. He was sure now the caller was Heinman, but there was an advantage in playing dumb. He sensed that his obtuseness truly annoyed the man. So much the better. He wished he'd talked to the police about putting a tracer on his phone, but he had felt like such a fool after the car incident.

"Well, I'm glad you asked that, El. Because I want to tell you."

Halsey made no reply.

"It's about your son, what's his name? Barry? Barry the faggot, right?"

Halsey felt cold dread twist his gut. "I'll kill you, you goddamn . . ."

A nasty laugh. "I don't think so, Elliot. I hate to make you fret about your son, just when your company's falling apart and all. But that's life. Or death, as the case may be."

Halsey's mind raced. He tore open the drawer and

stared at the gun. He heard Heinman laughing at the other end of the line. He knew, had there ever been doubt in his mind, that he was capable of killing a man. This man laughing at him. The man thriving on his pain, and now threatening his son.

His voice trembled as he held the phone in a death grip. "You'd better hope we never meet, you piece of scum . . ."

"Oh, I wish you could see me, I'm trembling in my stocking feet." Laughter. Then, "Now hang on a minute. Let me grab a pencil, make sure I've got Barry's address right . . ."

Panic rose in Halsey like hot acid. He slammed down the phone, then picked it back up and frantically dialed Barry's number.

"Answer, goddamn it," he muttered, looking at his watch. It was after eleven. Barry should be in bed by now. Steve was out of town. Why wasn't he answering? Was Heinman already there?

Finally he heard the sleepy voice of his son. "Hello?"

He felt giddy. "Barry," he said, laughing. "You're all right?"

"Elliot? Yeah, I'm all right. What time is it? Are you drunk or something?"

Halsey could hear the annoyance in his son's voice but he didn't give a damn. He plowed on. "Barry, there's a guy, a crazy man, who's threatening to kill you. You need to get out of there. Now. Take a cab to my office, don't worry about the money, I'll pay for it."

"What? You *are* drunk. I didn't think you drank."

"I'm not drunk and I'm not crazy. Barry, you've got to listen to me."

"Look, you're not making any sense. Maybe you

should have a drink, and calm down. I have to get some sleep . . ."

"Barry, if you don't promise me you'll get the hell out of there right now, I'm coming to get you. You decide."

There was a long pause while he could almost hear Barry processing the information, weighing his choices. "Okay, I'll come."

Halsey felt like a load had been lifted. He didn't think beyond the moment, how he would protect Barry down the line. But at least tonight, Barry would be safe. "I'll see you about midnight, then."

"Okay."

Halsey hung up and took the gun out of the drawer. He always kept it unloaded. Now he swept his hand deep inside the drawer and found the cartridge clip. He slammed it into the grip and worked the action, dropping a shell into the chamber. It was ready. He was ready. He put the gun back in the drawer and wiped his damp palms on his slacks.

Keith Heinman awakened to a noise in the basement. It took a moment to orient himself, then he remembered his prisoner. The animals are restless, he thought with a smile as he sat on the edge of his bed and stretched.

He stood up, yawned, and crossed to the window to flip up the shade. He looked out on a dreary rainy morning, but his spirits were not dampened in the least. He had a big day planned. He had Halsey on the run now. Making his son come stay with him. As though Halsey could protect him. What a laugh.

As he slipped into his standard outfit of jeans and T-shirt, he tried to recall how many days Parsons had been his guest. More than three, he decided, laughing as he recalled the old joke about fish and guests stinking after three days.

As he stood before the mirror watching himself do a few knee bends, he cracked up at his little joke. Poor Dave. Maybe he would take pity on the slob and let him take a shower. Or maybe he would just hose the fatso down. That thought cracked him up even more. He stood in the middle of the room, his body buckling over with gales of laughter.

Finally, he took a deep breath and decided to get to work. It was a Saturday, so he wouldn't be going into Alatron unless it suited his purpose. He wolfed down a bowl of multigrain cereal with skim milk, then headed for the phone beside the couch. Time to get a few more balls rolling.

He heard the scuffling noise again and decided to check on Parsons. He picked up two slices of stale bread before bounding down the steps.

He kicked open the door to Parsons's den. "Morning, Davey-boy. Hungry?"

Parsons wasn't in his usual corner, but Heinman wasn't concerned. He spotted his guest right away. Parsons had edged his way toward the door. Must've taken him all night, considering his arms and legs were bound.

"Going someplace, Dave?" Heinman held the bread up and shook his head. "I don't know, Dave. I was going to give you a little breakfast, but I don't think I should reward your sneaky behavior. If I didn't know better I'd think you were trying to escape."

He made a tsking noise with his tongue and leaned down to catch Parsons's eyes. "Dave, you're just not being the model guest."

He straightened back up. "For starters, you stink," and with this he wrinkled his nose. "And you're a gluttonous drooler. And now this." He wagged his head mockingly as he planted himself in front of Parsons.

He decided to spice up his guest's day and provide himself with a little entertainment as well. He tossed the bread into the corner Parsons had occupied before struggling toward the door. "See there, Dave? Let that be a lesson to you. If you had stayed put, you'd be enjoying breakfast right now. Instead, you've annoyed me. What's more, you're ungrateful. You know how that makes me feel? Unappreciated, Dave-o. And I don't like that."

He gave Parsons's shoulder a shove, catching an expression in Parsons's eyes that pleased him. "Calm down, Dave. I'm going to untie your legs and give you a change of scenery. Maybe we'll even get you cleaned up today."

He squatted and began untying Parsons's legs. "It's all up to you." He chuckled. "You're the master of your destiny."

He jerked the rope off and gave Parsons a brisk kick. "On your feet, fatso," he barked, suddenly dropping his taunting singsong style. "Upstairs."

Parsons struggled, but his legs were so numb from lack of movement that he was unable to rise on his own. Heinman grabbed him by the arm and jerked him upright, causing him to reel against the doorjamb. Parsons was sliding to the floor when Heinman again hauled him to his feet. "Come on, Bozo, on your feet and up the stairs."

Parsons felt the uncertainty he always felt with Heinman. The man was always acting, always on a razor's edge. At times almost helpful—then mocking, with a rush of anger to where he seemed out of control.

He struggled up the steps, Heinman giving him a push now and then. At the top of the stairs Heinman guided him toward the living room, then shoved him onto the couch.

"Sit down, Dave. Take a load off your feet. I have some phone work to do. You might like to listen. After all, you got things going. It's always rewarding to see how one's life impacts others, don't you think? Oh, and I *know* you'd like to hear how my AIDS FIRST meeting went. I'm just so busy I don't get to chat with you like I should."

Parsons shrugged helplessly, then nodded. He thought it best to just sit and look attentive. He was aware that Heinman could read a lot from the eyes— the windows to the soul. Right now, looking at Heinman's cold blue eyes, he wasn't sure the human soul existed.

He felt a wave of relief as Heinman picked up the phone. Someone else was about to become Heinman's target. Parsons actually felt a cry of laughter rise in his throat. He was smart and quick enough, even in his debilitated state, to turn it into a cough before it escaped his lips. He didn't dare think of what Heinman might do if he thought Parsons was laughing at him.

Heinman stopped dialing long enough to study Parsons. Then, apparently satisfied with what he saw, resumed dialing.

There was a pause as Heinman held the receiver to his ear. Parsons thought he could hear a voice at the other end. He then saw Heinman go into action, his voice taking on a bubbly, almost innocent quality that Parsons hadn't heard before. He stared in amazement as he listened to Heinman's end of the conversation.

"Hello?" said Heinman. "I'm an employee at Alatron Pharmaceuticals. I have information I think the public should know . . ." There was a pause, and Parsons saw a bland look cross Heinman's face as he said,

"Of course, I'd be glad to talk to the reporter covering the story. But I can't give my name, you understand."

Another long pause. This time Heinman looked over at Parsons and winked, the hint of a cruel smile flitting across his face. Heinman sat back as he launched into his story. "You're the reporter covering the Alatron vaccine story? Right . . . Well, if I tell you my name, you'll promise to keep it a secret? . . . Yes, you see, I'm afraid for my life . . . No, I can't meet you. It's either now, on the phone, or not at all . . . Okay, good."

Heinman, looking calm and relaxed, gave Parsons another wink. Parsons looked away, frightened, not sure what was coming. He decided to listen. And he could look around, even out the window, maybe get some idea of where he was and how he might escape should he somehow free himself.

His rambling thoughts were interrupted by Heinman's voice—something Heinman said. His mouth gaped open in disbelief.

"That's right—Dave Parsons," drawled Heinman. "Yes, I know everyone's looking for me. But until the president of Alatron, Elliot Halsey, is brought to justice, I have to stay low. He made me break FDA rules, you know. Made me push up the numbers of volunteers getting the AIDS vaccine . . . That's right, it was to stay ahead of the competition. He's a ruthless man. And dangerous. He has a gun, you know . . . Everybody knows it. He keeps it in his office . . . Yeah.

"Now that his plan has backfired, he's acting like he knew nothing about it—pretending it was all my idea. It wasn't. . . . I did it because he told me he'd have my job if I didn't. He had me believing the vaccine was safe."

Parsons wanted to scream. Suddenly the gag across his mouth felt like it was going to choke him. His throat was parched yet the gag was soaking wet. He could feel his chest tighten and his breathing become shallow and irregular. Black dots, like crawly spiders, swarmed before his vision. He thought he was going to pass out as the ringing in his ears crescendoed.

As he watched Heinman jabber on, he suddenly couldn't hear a sound. It was as though he was locked inside his head. Sensory overload, maybe. He tried to take a deep breath to calm down. Okay, he told himself, closing his eyes. What's the problem? So this maniac is impersonating you—big deal. What did you expect? The guy is crazy.

Parsons's internal monologue did nothing to ease the growing constriction in his chest. Nor did it slow the rivulets of sweat streaming down his face. What was he so afraid of?

Then it came to him. He knew why his body was reacting so violently. And with that realization, everything relaxed. Too much—like a wildly swinging pendulum. He felt his rectal sphincter release. He felt his trousers, as brittle as cardboard from days of sweat and dirt, become warm and moist as his bladder relaxed. The constriction in his chest gave way to a feeling that his lungs could soak up air, but he couldn't empty them again. They felt like bottomless pits—craving oxygen that didn't exist.

His body had the answer before his mind could spell it out. But finally he saw it with resounding clarity: Keith Heinman was going to kill him.

"Hey, Dave. What's your trouble now?" Heinman was shaking Parsons by the shoulder.

Parsons blinked and shook his head, feeling for a moment that he didn't know where he was. Then, as he felt the dampness in his crotch, he remembered.

"You passed out, Dave." Heinman laughed. "How

are we going to get you into the shower if you pass out on me?"

Heinman seemed unusually cheerful, even manic. Something more must have transpired on the phone while Parsons was unconscious. Heinman leaned over and untied the gag, tossing it on the floor. "Come on, Dave. I think you ought to eat something. Tell you what, I'll untie your hands and you can even eat at the kitchen table."

Heinman seemed to flutter around him like a cheerful bird. Parsons knew the pattern well enough by now not to get too excited by this surge of generosity. But maybe it would last long enough for him to at least get some food. Maybe even a real shower and a change of clothes.

Heinman grabbed him by the arm and led him into the kitchen. He filled a cereal bowl and poured milk into it, then set it in front of Parsons. He pulled up a wooden stool and straddled it, staring at Parsons with a satanic grin.

"Yeah, Dave. Things are starting to line up just right. The papers will have the story about how Elliot Halsey strong-armed you into administering the vaccine. The AIDS FIRST boys are going to feel really betrayed. They thought they were just dealing with you when all the while it was Halsey. And it wasn't for them that he did it. It was for the money."

Heinman's eyes had a gleam that made Parsons suddenly unable to finish his cereal.

As Parsons felt the constriction in his chest once again, he ignored all warning signs and blurted out the question that knocked at every door in his mind. "What are you going to do with me?"

Heinman, who had been quietly enjoying some joke of his own, shifted his eyes to Parsons. Parsons could see them change from cool blue to ice blue as he watched. "Why do you ask a question like that, Dave?"

Parsons shrugged, regretting that he had spoken at all. He said nothing.

Suddenly Heinman was on his feet, his face inches from Parsons's. Parsons could see the veins in Heinman's neck bulge. "You'd better level with me, Dave."

"I'm just worried," said Parsons. Now the vein in Heinman's forehead popped up and Parsons searched frantically for some way to appease his captor. "That's all."

Heinman snatched the cereal bowl and threw it into the sink, where it smashed to pieces with a loud clatter. His eyes never left Parsons. "Level with me, Dave." His voice rising, echoing inside Parsons's head.

Parsons knew he had no choice now. "Are you going to kill me?"

"Kill you!" Heinman paced around him. "Kill you?" he screamed. He leaned into Parsons's face again, poking his own chest with a finger. "Do I look like a killer, Dave?"

He had never seen Heinman so angry. Should he respond? If he told the truth, Heinman might snuff him out in a fit of rage. His fear solved the problem. When he tried to speak, nothing emerged but a meager croak.

"I am not a killer, Dave," screamed Heinman, now pacing in large circles around the room, occasionally throwing a dish or salt shaker against the wall. "Elliot Halsey is the killer."

He grabbed Parsons by the shoulders and shook him until Parsons felt his neck might snap. "Understand, Dave?"

Parsons tried to swallow and couldn't. He nodded, his eyes glued to Heinman.

"Good," snapped Heinman. He straddled the stool again, watching Parsons.

Parsons felt a shiver up his spine as he saw the cruel smile again cross Heinman's face.

"If you should come to an unfortunate end, Dave, my boy," said Heinman, his face now the picture of passivity, "you will have Elliot Halsey to thank."

CHAPTER TWENTY

Lowell Bekin and Stan Robbins wouldn't look directly at him. If he didn't already have an idea what was on their minds, their eyes would have clinched it.

He had a perverse urge to stare them down, but he restrained himself. He knew they weren't any happier about this than he was. And they were, after all, the only ones brave enough to show up.

They were sitting in the "press-proof" hideout—a windowless room in the basement that normally served as a lounge for the few employees who smoked. The place reeked of stale cigarettes, and Halsey noticed that the white ceiling plaster actually had a gray tinge to it. The only sound was the gurgle of a coffee urn in the corner.

Robbins sat a few inches behind Bekin, who had pulled his chair up to the small glass table and was absently toying with one of the green plastic ashtrays. Halsey sat at the opposite end of the room, an elbow propped on the table, his chin resting in his hand. He knew what was coming, and he was prepared.

They had all prolonged the ritual of getting a cup of

coffee, making small talk near the urn as they opened packets of sugar and nondairy creamer and stirred their coffee more than it needed. Now there was an awkward silence as neither board member seemed able to take the initiative.

Glancing at his watch and considering all the things he had to do, Halsey decided to break the ice. "Shall we get started?"

Robbins cleared his throat and smiled. Bekin's pudgy face looked pastier than usual. Halsey guessed Bekin had been losing sleep lately.

"Elliot," said Bekin in a grave tone, "the board has asked me to represent them in this matter. Be assured that I have had the input of each and every one of them."

He turned toward Robbins. "Stan will verify that." Robbins nodded, his cheek twitching.

Bekin sipped his coffee. "With all that's happened in the past few days, this company has become hostage to public opinion, the media, and demonstration groups. I could barely get my car through the gate this morning . . ." His face brightened as he smiled nervously, having found yet another way to veer away from the job before him.

Halsey decided to make it easier for all of them. "Let's stop beating around the bush," he said. "Does the board want me to resign?"

Bekin assumed a more confident tone now that Halsey had said it for him. He straightened in his chair and looked at Halsey directly for the first time, nodding. "We think it would be in the best interest of the company. The negative publicity seems to be focusing on you. We all know you have the best interest of the company at heart, and that your sidestepping the FDA on the vaccine, while unfortunate, is understandable. . . ."

Halsey's hand shot up like a stop sign. "Lowell, didn't you get my memo?"

Bekin looked briefly at Robbins, whose face was blank. A pink flush came to Bekin's cheeks. "Yes, I saw the memo, but . . ."

"No 'buts', Lowell. What I said holds. I had nothing to do with sidestepping the FDA."

"All right, I know that's your position, but . . ."

Halsey slammed his fist on the table. It was all he could do to keep from lunging at Bekin. "Dammit, Lowell. That is not my *position*—it's the *truth*."

Bekin nodded. "All right, Elliot. Let's not quibble over words. The point is, you're too controversial. If you resign now, without fighting us on it, we think it will serve to defuse the attack on the company."

Listening to Bekin's careful choice of words, Halsey knew there was no point in trying to persuade him. Nevertheless, he felt compelled to set the record straight. "Lowell, *I* was not the one who hired Dave Parsons. You know I was against him from the start. Nor was I the one to make deals with AIDS FIRST. You may recall that against the wishes of the board, I was the one who fired Parsons."

There was a pained look on Robbins's face. "Please, gentlemen. Let's not turn this into a session of finger-pointing." He held out a veined hand. "Elliot, what is your answer?"

"I will not resign. I've helped pull this company out of the abyss before, back when we were facing the suit against Somnolot. I can do it again. The vaccine was sabotaged—I'm sure of it. I think I know who did it. I just need time."

A deadly silence hung in the air as the three men stared at one another. A lab tech with an unlit cigarette hanging from his lips popped his head in the door and quickly ducked back out.

Bekin took a deep breath. "I've heard about this sabotage theory of yours, Elliot. Frankly, it has everyone laughing. I'm afraid you leave us no choice."

"You have plenty of choice, Lowell. You seem to be a master at deflecting responsibility."

Bekin stood up. "You're forcing us to act in a manner that may embarrass you, Elliot. We'll have to bring in the company lawyers. It could get nasty."

"Do what you have to do, Lowell. But if you plan legal action, you had better not use company lawyers. There's an obvious conflict of interest. I am still CEO of this company."

Bekin moved to the door with a scowl. He looked back at Robbins, who sat like a statue. "Are you coming, Stan?"

Robbins waved him away. "Go ahead, Lowell. I'd like to be alone with Elliot for a few moments."

"As you wish," said Bekin as he stalked out.

Halsey stood up and moved down the table to a seat beside Robbins. He felt an inexplicable fondness for the man, despite the apparent duplicity.

"Elliot," said Robbins, "I'm sorry. Everyone on the board wants you out. There's no swaying them."

"I understand, Stan." And he did, more than Robbins could possibly imagine. Halsey looked at Robbins and saw a man who, looking to the end of the road, had surely hoped to retire in a blaze of glory. Now, the man was staring down a tunnel, and the only light was an oncoming train.

"You are the designated scapegoat," said Robbins with a grim face. "I believe you about Parsons. But something happened last night I don't think you know about, and Lowell chose not to tell you."

"What is that?"

"A reporter from the *Newark Post-Ledger* called Lowell and announced that Parsons contacted him."

Halsey's chin dropped. "I don't believe it. Where is he?"

"Parsons wouldn't say. The reporter gave us a transcript of his phone interview." Robbins dug into a pocket and pulled out a sheet of paper. "Don't tell Lowell I let you see this."

Halsey took the paper and read it quickly. "How do we know this is really Parsons, and not someone impersonating him? It's only a voice on the telephone." He held the paper up and gave Robbins a questioning look. He envisioned The Caller, closing in on him.

"An excellent question. Newspaper reporters, of course, are skeptical of phone interviews. They ask questions that can only be answered by the actual person—mother's maiden name, social security number, that sort of thing."

"And he passed?"

"Yes, according to the reporter. But he would not divulge his location. As you'll note in the transcript, he says he's afraid for his life."

Halsey handed the paper to Robbins. "He could have got all this from a man afraid for his life. You have no proof it was Parsons. Nothing that would convince any reasonable person." He made a note of the reporter's name—Ray Albinez. "You don't know," he went on, "if this guy is Parsons. I never threatened his life. And I never knew about Parsons's scheme to up the number of volunteers until it became public knowledge. As much as I complain about all the FDA hoops we have to jump through, I'd never do that. It's stupid and dangerous."

Robbins managed a smile. "I believe you, Elliot. But I'm helpless."

Halsey sat back and took a deep breath. It was becoming clear to him what he had to do. He had been floundering—a sitting target. Now with his back to the wall he had to take charge. Or go down.

He turned to Robbins, his voice friendly but firm. "Stan, tell Lowell I will not resign. I'm willing to turn routine duties over to someone else. What I need to do is get back into the lab and turn this disaster into a breakthrough on the Congo vaccine. We've been right on the edge until the commitment to go full tilt ahead with the AIDS vaccine."

Robbins held up both hands. He was plainly befuddled. "I'll do my best, Elliot. But frankly, it's all too much for me."

As Halsey left the meeting room he was startled to find Barry waiting for him. Barry was sitting on the floor, leaning against the wall, his nose in a book.

"Barry, what are you doing here? I was hoping you'd still be asleep." As he looked at his son he felt a touch of pride, a feeling he hadn't let himself experience in a long time. Barry looked much better after a night's sleep. He was a handsome young man, with dark brown hair, an olive complexion, and green eyes. He looked casual and polished at the same time. He was wearing a pair of jeans and a gray sweatshirt with the sleeves rolled up.

Barry shrugged as he stood up. "I got enough sleep." He was almost as tall as his father. He had a grave expression on his face. "I overheard what went on in there. You're in deep trouble, aren't you?"

"Come on, let's get some breakfast," Halsey said, dodging the question. As they walked toward the cafeteria he tried to remember exactly how the meeting had gone, trying to see it through Barry's eyes. He had never talked much about his work to his family. He wasn't sure why.

"Well, are you?" Barry pressed.

"Am I what?"

"In deep trouble."

Halsey stopped and looked at his son. "Yes."

Barry seemed to be digesting the simple answer as they pushed their trays through the cafeteria line and picked up their breakfast. Barry got oatmeal and juice. Halsey grabbed a yogurt and coffee. They sat down in a quiet corner.

"I'd like to hear about it," Barry said. "How does this crazy guy figure into all this?"

"It's a long story." Halsey was amazed he had never told Barry, or anyone else in his family, the story of Somnolot and Keith Heinman. They knew bits and pieces, mostly what they had gleaned from the papers. He saw now how closed off he had been from his family over the years. But he felt himself changing. Kate Crane had, just by being who she was, done that for him. She was showing him how to look inside himself and share.

He imagined what she might say to him now: "Tell him everything. Let Barry know you feel he's strong and caring enough to understand."

And so he told his son everything. When he was through, Barry was staring at him as though seeing him for the first time. "That's an incredible story," he said finally. Halsey could hear a suggestion of what he thought was admiration in his son's voice.

"Incredible but true. The man is a killer. If I'm right, he's already killed several people, just as a way of getting at me. Reports are still coming in of people dying from what may have been our vaccine. So why would he stop at my son?"

He saw a shiver go through Barry. "Jesus," was all Barry said, though his eyes, wide with horror, said far more.

As Halsey watched his son, he felt galvanized to

action. He suddenly realized how scattered—even passive—he'd been. There were so many things coming at him, from all directions. In trying to stop up all the holes Heinman kept shooting in the dike, he'd been diverted time and again from the only effective course of action—tracking down the shooter.

"Barry, I wish I knew how to nail this guy. He's so elusive." He hesitated. "Like some of the enemies you used to take on in your video games."

He saw Barry's face light up. Suddenly all the strain lines around the boy's mouth disappeared as he smiled, his memory reaching back to perhaps happier days. "I remember that one game. I never could defeat the last boss—Kronin. He'd appear, zap me, disappear, reappear in a different place, zap me, disappear. . . ."

Halsey laughed. "That's it! That's just what Heinman is like. He's around, I see signs of him all the time. I think he's even been in my office, through my desk, even into my wallet. But I have no proof. Only signs. How does he know I have a son? He even knew your name, knew you were gay."

Halsey saw Barry give him an appreciative look. He knew why. It was the first time he had referred to Barry's homosexuality in a forthright way, without skirting around the word.

"What you have to do," said Barry, getting into it, "is figure out how to make this guy mad, make him come after you, out in the open. As long as he can keep jabbing at you and retreating to his secret place, he's got control."

Halsey marveled at his son's wisdom. "Makes a lot of sense."

"Psych has always interested me." Barry smiled. "And don't forget Kronin."

Halsey frowned thoughtfully. "He wants to see the

company go down, me with it. He wants to see me suffer. His threats include murder, but what he really gets off on is my anger."

"And your pain."

Halsey felt a pang as he looked into Barry's green eyes. Yes, his pain. "I've got an idea," he said slowly. "Let me try it out on you. I call a press conference, and . . ."

He and Barry laid out a plan.

CHAPTER TWENTY-ONE

Kate's training had exposed her to a variety of maximum-containment situations. Nevertheless, BSC Four facilities still made her inordinately nervous. This particular one, on the fourth floor of Alatron's R and D building, was superbly set up. There were inner and outer change rooms, separated by a shower. Before entering the actual laboratory that harbored the Congo virus, she had to change into a one-piece vinyl "space" suit that hooked into an air source. The filters in the suit's exhaust system were so intricate even an atom would have a hard time finding its way out.

On exiting from BSC Four, decontamination involved showering, with the suit still on, under a spray of paralloic acid, an effective though flammable chemical. The shower turned on automatically, making it unavoidable for those who might be absentminded about such matters. After showering, one passed through an airlock into the outer change room.

She knew there was no real way to double-check and make sure a person hadn't been exposed to the virus after entering its domain. You just had to wait—

the incubation period being anywhere from three to ten days in the case of Congo fever. If you continued to wake up alive and well for the week or two following each exposure, you could figure you were home free. Not a way she would choose to live on a routine basis.

She marveled at the fortitude of those who did, including Elliot Halsey, who had spent much of the afternoon suited up as well, carefully going over the setup with her. She assumed people gradually acclimated to the fact that for every day you didn't die you had that much going for you.

As for the occasional visitor such as herself, it was a different story. She remembered well the time she rotated through maximum containment at CDC. She had a Yucatan vacation planned for right after her stint, but found she could never really look forward to it. She was always aware of a tiny voice in the back of her head that mercilessly tacked on a clause every time she caught herself fantasizing about snorkeling off Cozumel, or baking in the sun, or eating seafood fresh off the boat. It whispered, "... if you're still alive."

It was in this state of mind that Kate found herself after leaving the BSC Four laboratory where Alatron kept its Congo virus cultures.

She and the rest of the CDC crew had still found no evidence of technical difficulties that would allow the Congo virus to somehow escape into the room where the AIDS vaccine was made. Nor had interviews with the technicians revealed any evidence of a slipup or the evasiveness of a saboteur. Not a single technician working with the virus over the past six months had fallen ill. And only one employee, an Albert Buell, had quit suddenly without notice due to a death in the family. Kate found this to be the only slight deviation from normal and it certainly was not a big one.

Exhausted, she checked her watch. It was six-thirty. Halsey was still hard at it. She decided to grab a bite in the cafeteria. After that the thought of quitting early for the night appealed to her, but she had one more task, which, as she thought about it, made her heart and stomach flutter in perfect synchrony.

As she walked down the dim corridor to her make-shift office, Kate was impressed with its emptiness. She didn't like the thought of being in a building by herself, though she knew the floors above were crawling with Abe Feldman's crew as well as Alatron employees. Rory, having seen her a few times with Halsey, seemed to be making a production of avoiding her. Right now, there was no one on the floor, it seemed, except her. She quickened her pace down the linoleum-tiled corridor, her footsteps making a soft echoing sound.

As she turned the corner to her office, she was startled to see a lone figure silhouetted against the green glow of the exit sign. She peered intently at him and was relieved to see it was only the custodian leaning over his mop bucket. As she approached, she recognized him from their encounter the other night. A strange fellow, but familiar.

"Hello," she said quietly as she saw him lift his head to look at her.

"Hi," he said, straightening. "You look like you've had a tough day." He used that forced cheerfulness that rubbed her the wrong way.

"I have," she replied tersely, remembering what it was she didn't like about him. She turned her back to him as she inserted the key into the latch.

"Too bad about Mr. Halsey's BMW, huh?"

Her hand froze, then she forced it to turn the key. Without turning around, she said carefully, "What do you mean?"

She heard him snicker. There was a nastiness to the sound, though she couldn't quite identify what it was. She kept her back to him, fumbling at the lock longer than necessary.

"You're wondering why a small potatoes janitor like me would know about your friend Mr. Halsey and his troubles?" He laughed again, and this time there was no mistaking the nastiness. She turned her head enough to see his face out of the corner of her eye. He wore a condescending smile.

"I wondered nothing of the kind," she said, now turning to face him. "I imagine this place has quite a grapevine."

His eyes seemed to bore through her, his lips twisting into a mockery of a smile. He said nothing as he turned back to his work. He began whistling tunelessly as he leaned over and wrung out the mop.

She slipped into her office, closing the door behind her. She decided she had overreacted to the janitor's remarks, and chided herself for considering locking the door. She settled herself into her seat and stared at the phone number Halsey had tracked down. It was the home number of Dr. Rutger Kraft, who was supposed to be back after a European vacation.

She took a deep breath, stalling for time. She felt unaccountably shaken by the encounter with the custodian. She tried to shrug it off—he was just an ill-mannered creep. She knew plenty of people like that—small people who liked to impress you with how much they knew about you. It simply reflected their own insecurity.

She looked again at Kraft's number with its upstate New York area code and tiredly kneaded her temples.

She was determined to make the call—tonight. She knew Halsey had been having trouble deciding how to approach this Kraft character and elicit information about Keith Heinman that Kraft might be ethically bound not to release. She had good-naturedly snatched up the number and announced that she knew better how to talk to doctors. Which, of course, was true.

She finally picked up the receiver and tapped out the number. She could feel a disquieting churning in her stomach as the phone began to ring. Two rings. Three rings. The churning increased, joined by an unexpected feeling of relief. Maybe he wasn't home yet. She could put it off, it wasn't her decision. No, she didn't want that. She needed to talk to him.

As she went through these mental gymnastics, Dr. Kraft solved the dilemma by answering.

"Hello?" came a deep voice.

"Dr. Kraft?"

"Yes?"

"My name is Dr. Katherine Crane. I'm with the CDC. I'm sorry to bother you at home, but I'm hoping you can help me locate a former patient of yours."

There was a long silence which Kate attributed to Kraft's efforts to assess the situation.

Finally his voice interrupted the hum of the long-distance connection. "I wouldn't have such information at my fingertips, but I may be able to have someone look it up for you. Who is the patient?" He sounded cautious and a bit slow.

"The patient's name is Keith Heinman," she said. "He was discharged from Woodlawn last year."

The silence at the other end was no longer ambiguous. Kraft was stalling.

"Dr. Kraft?" she prodded. "Do you recall this man?"

"I believe so, yes. I'm afraid I can't help you."

She knew he was lying. He hadn't even asked why she was looking for Heinman. She could feel her cheeks flush with anger. She decided to take a hard line with him.

"I'm sure you can help if you choose to, Dr. Kraft. Please hear me out."

Silence punctuated with a few indignant sputters. "Go ahead," he said finally.

"When a patient is discharged from a psychiatric hospital, he is followed as an outpatient. You haven't been seeing Mr. Heinman?"

She heard a low laugh, which angered her more. "No, I'm happy to tell you I've had no contact with Mr. Heinman."

"Then he must have been assigned to another psychiatrist. May I have that name?" Kate wasn't sure of the policy, but she knew that patients were not simply turned loose on the streets. Her dislike for Kraft, and her sense that he was lying egged her on. "Dr. Kraft, it's important."

"He was assigned to no one." Suddenly Kraft burst into a gale of laughter, followed by a fit of sputtering and choking. "No one would have him."

"Dr. Kraft," she persisted, not bothering to keep the impatience out of her voice. "Please tell me where he is."

"My dear woman," said Kraft, "I would be happy to tell you if I knew. But Mr. Heinman is no longer part of my, er, gestalt, shall we say?"

It was clear that she was getting nowhere, but she wasn't giving up. She gave Kraft her number and politely thanked him for speaking with her.

As she put down the receiver, she was startled to see the janitor step into her field of vision. How long had he been in the room?

He whipped out a dust cloth. "Hey," he said, "I didn't mean to pry back there." He ran the cloth along the edge of the table.

"It's all right," she said, taking a deep breath. She wasn't going to let this strange man get to her. She tried to focus her thoughts on how to get around Kraft.

"People are kind of jumpy around here these days," he said. "I understand." He tucked the cloth in a back pocket and moved toward the corner of the room where he began stacking the dirty dishes.

She tapped her pencil on her hand, thinking, staring at the phone. She was mildly annoyed at the janitor's pushiness, but decided that was all it was. She was getting used to it.

"Oh boy," she heard him say, "looks like I need to get the vacuum in here."

She muttered a distracted noise of agreement, still lost in thought. Maybe tomorrow she would try getting somewhere with the administrator at Woodlawn. She would discuss it with Halsey. She found herself running things by him more and more. She liked being with him. There were always plenty of excuses. She sensed him doing the same thing, finding ways for them to get together to discuss matters that could as easily be conveyed by a quick phone call or memo. They had also gotten in the habit of nightly meetings to compare notes.

"You shouldn't let people like that get under your skin." The janitor had the dust cloth out again and was idly running it along the table as he moved toward her.

She felt a flash of irritation. "And you should mind your own business."

He stopped and looked at her in an odd way. "I do," he said.

*   *   *

Rutger Kraft set the phone down and studied it thoughtfully. He looked at his suitcases, which were still sitting by the front door and felt an impulse to snatch them up and drive back to the Elmira airport.

Instead he slowly rose from the overstuffed chair and poured himself two shots of bourbon. He sat back down and began to reconstruct the brief but jarring conversation that had just transpired. All that came to mind was the name Keith Heinman, over and over again, like a satanic chant.

He hadn't heard from Heinman in months, and had actually allowed himself to believe he never would again. He had been curious about what Heinman was up to, whether he was still a custodian at Alatron.

Kraft had sweated over that one, hating Heinman every step of the way, but feeling completely helpless as Heinman bossed him around in that nasty superior way of his.

Finally, pulling a few strings to get someone else to pull a few more had worked. He had worried about what Heinman might do if he hadn't come through. He had hoped, as the months passed, that Heinman had no further use for him—that the Heinman chapter of his life was over. Now this.

Now a doctor calling from the CDC, but she had left a New Jersey area code. He hadn't dared ask her where she was calling from. He didn't want to act the least bit interested in Heinman's whereabouts, or give himself away in any way. He suspected that Heinman was carrying out whatever demented plan he had concocted during his years at Woodlawn. And now came the repercussions.

He cringed. He himself had been a victim of Heinman's reprisals. Heinman's very existence continued to hang over his head. Only Heinman knew the secret of the worst skeleton in Kraft's closet: the mysterious disappearance of the nosy Dr. Goldschmidt. It had been Heinman's idea, but Kraft knew that's not how it would all come out in the wash. Heinman had made that clear enough.

As he sipped at his drink, a puzzling thought drifted into Kraft's head: the woman doctor had asked for Keith Heinman, not Ken Butler, the name Heinman had adopted. Didn't she know that Heinman must be right under her nose, if indeed she was calling from Alatron?

He put his head back and tugged at his thick beard as he considered the possibilities. She was looking for Heinman. She mentioned nothing of an alias, nothing of a man named Butler. What did that mean? It had to mean Heinman's cover was so far successful. Yet now someone was onto the scent of his true identity.

The harder Kraft thought, the more he saw a new option opening up his limited field of choices: an option that might rid him of Heinman's shadow forever. Perhaps, with Kraft's help, these people at the CDC could capture Heinman and neutralize the man. Heinman would not be in a position then to point a finger, would he? Kraft would be safe.

But of course he would have to know what it was they wanted Heinman for. It would have to be serious enough to take Heinman out of commission for a very long time. He wondered. He knew if he called this woman doctor back to find out why they wanted Heinman, he would have to be prepared to make a deal.

If only he could find out without making that call. It was then that Kraft remembered something of interest in the *New York Times*, which he had picked up after arriving at JFK from Frankfurt. Splashed all over the headlines had been a story about contamination of the AIDS vaccine. He remembered recognizing the name of the company but hadn't realized why. Now he thought he knew. He looked over at his bags and spotted his briefcase. He got up and fetched the paper and plopped back down in the chair, his eyes fastened on the story. It *was* Alatron! And there were rumblings about sabotage of the vaccine, though the CDC was pursuing other leads first. Kraft cackled gleefully.

It was all too good to be true. So good that Kraft decided he had better have matters well worked out in his mind before lifting a finger to call back the lady doctor.

"Herr Heinman," he said aloud, "your reign of terror is about to end."

CHAPTER TWENTY-TWO

Heinman stretched his legs out on the coffee table. He perused the paper as he languidly munched an apple. He smiled as he saw three stories above the fold devoted to the scandal at Alatron. At times like this he wished he had a television.

One story told how the contaminated vaccine had caused limited outbreaks of Congo Fever in and near the affected urban areas. Simple quarantine measures seemed to be keeping the virus at bay, but there was nevertheless considerable national hysteria about the disease. Man-in-the-street interviews registered mounting anger against Alatron and Elliot Halsey. Even better, there was a growing public outcry for tighter federal controls on pharmaceutical companies.

Heinman's grin changed to a snicker of pleasure as he realized yet another pressure on Halsey he hadn't anticipated—the government. Legislation would be forthcoming to control all drug companies thanks to Mr. Halsey. His competitors would regard him with nothing but contempt as they took a beating because of his greed and recklessness.

Heinman finished his apple and tossed the core in a perfect arc across the room and into the wastebasket. He could hear Parsons scuffling around again in the basement and looked at his watch. Ten P.M. Poor Dave. Rough being an insomniac when you had so much time on your hands.

His eyes went back to the lead story, having saved the best for last. He gloated over the headline, ALATRON CEO REFUSES TO RESIGN, then his breath caught as his eyes latched on the subhead, HALSEY DENIES WRONGDOING, VOWS TO PULL ALATRON OUT OF TROUBLE WITH CONGO FEVER VACCINE.

Heinman sat bolt upright, his eyes devouring the words:

"In a dramatic move this afternoon, Alatron Pharmaceutical Company CEO Elliot Halsey called a press conference and announced he had been asked to resign by the board of directors. Citing commitment to the public, Mr. Halsey refused to step down as leader of the faltering company. He further denied having any part in the recent AIDS vaccine disaster, claiming sabotage to be responsible. He would not indicate whether he had a suspect in mind.

"At the close of the conference Mr. Halsey unveiled another surprise as he announced that his organization is close to perfecting a vaccine for Congo Fever. The vaccine will be at least partially effective for a class of viruses known as the African hemorrhagic viruses. These viruses are known to have a high fatality rate. If Halsey's vaccine is successful it will represent a major breakthrough in disease prevention and may salvage the company.

"Mr. Halsey further provided a 'personal guarantee' that the vaccine, once approved, would be made available through its compassionate drug use program.

There would be no cost to those receiving it in connection with the contaminated AIDS vaccine. . . ."

Heinman crumpled the paper in a rage and flung it across the room. The scuffling in the basement seemed to get louder. He leapt to his feet and paced the barren living room, kicking the couch, then sending the wastebasket flying into the kitchen, its contents scattering.

He stalked over to the flimsy wooden basement door, threw it open, and screamed, "Shut the hell up!" He slammed the door, then kicked it, ripping it off its hinges and sending it clattering down the stairs. He stood at the head of the stairs, his fists clenched in a murderous rage. There was not a sound in the house now except his breathing.

All the while, he saw Elliot Halsey laughing at him. Daring to turn a disaster into an opportunity, and practically succeeding if one could believe the slimeballs who printed the news. He continued pacing, his mind racing. Halsey—the arrogant fool had even called a press conference, making it look as though *he* was the one calling the shots.

Heinman's thoughts flashed back ten years, and for a moment he was sitting in the courtroom again. One moment certain that he was going to get off and Alatron was going to fall; the next, looking at spending the rest of his life in an institution. All because of Elliot Halsey.

He closed his eyes. Out of the darkness behind his veiled lids appeared the image of Halsey staring at him. Always staring. The son of a bitch would never take his eyes off him.

He had not been able to stare Halsey down, watch him crack under pressure. That made him hate Halsey all the more.

But that was then, and this was now. And this time,

Keith Heinman would be the victor. Not only would Halsey take a fall, but so would the whole rotten world of perverts and scumbags he was pretending to help.

Heinman stood at the head of the stairs, staring down at the door that had splintered into a heap of useless lumber at the hands of his rage. The silence from the basement had a soothing effect on him. He envisioned Dave Parsons crouched terror-stricken in the corner. His breath came easier as his anger subsided.

He went into the bathroom and splashed his face with water, looking at himself in the mirror as he toweled off. The face staring back at him had taken on a look of cool control, which pleased him. A thin smile came to his lips as he realized what his next move must be.

Heinman got Parsons's suit out of the closet and held it up for inspection. It was in pretty good shape. He had given Parsons a pair of old painter's pants because he wanted to save the suit for just such an occasion. The time had come. He hung the suit back in the closet and picked his way down the basement steps to the room that had been Parsons home for several days.

He opened the door to Parsons's den and stared at him, his mind calculating, quickly assessing Parsons's appearance and what needed to be done.

Parsons had just finished an uncontrollable crying jag after suffering through the audible parts of Heinman's temper tantrum. He lifted his head slowly to regard his captor. His face was wet with tears, but there wasn't a thing he could do about it. What difference did it make? Heinman held all the cards. It was just that he hated to set the man off again. The rages made him fear for his physical well-being. They seemed to be happening with greater regularity now. Parsons was no psychologist, but his well-honed sales skills told him that Heinman was unstable enough to go berserk at any time.

What he saw this time made his blood run cold, an odd paradox for a man who felt like he was drowning in his own sweat. Heinman's eyes were as starkly contemptuous as he had ever seen them. The chiseled features were cold and unyielding—flesh turned to granite. The thin-lipped mouth was a cruel line. Parsons remembered the last time he had seen anything approaching this look. It was when he and Heinman had taken the plane together to administer the vaccine. The vaccine that Heinman had known would bring certain death.

Parsons's eyes met those of his captor, then shifted away as quickly as though struck by a blast of blinding light. In the face now towering over him he saw that the lips had curled ever so slightly into a mocking sneer. He knew something big was about to happen, and he could feel his heart thumping in his chest.

Heinman, without a sound, leaned over and untied the gag. Parsons took huge lungfuls of air in one big gasp. "Thank you," he found himself muttering. He remembered reading once how hostages often developed a feeling of gratitude toward their captors, and he had no difficulty understanding how that might happen. Once you realized that someone could do away with you or torture you at will, you felt grateful to them for every moment they spared you.

Heinman made no acknowledgment. A quick check of his eyes revealed a far-off look, or was it a turned-inward look? Whatever, Parsons wasn't sure, but he did conclude that Heinman was lost in thought or a maniacal fantasy, or whatever went on in the mind of a man like him.

As Parsons was making these random assessments, Heinman moved behind him and unbound his hands and legs. The sudden freedom left Parsons with a jarring sense of immobility—yet another strange paradox. He sat staring at his unshackled hands and feet with a bizarre feeling of detachment.

"Get up," said Heinman, still standing behind him.

The sound of Heinman's voice galvanized him, but his movements were weak and clumsy. He faltered and fell into a motionless heap only inches from Heinman's feet.

"Get up," said Heinman again in a cruel, measured voice. He made no move to help or prod Parsons.

Parsons tried again, more slowly this time, grasping the nearby stool. Gradually, shakily, he brought himself to his feet.

"Upstairs," said Heinman, using the same stony intonation.

Parsons's head was full of questions filtering through the ever-present fear. Every one of his brain cells seemed to be screaming at him not to verbalize any of them, but to play along with this latest plan, whatever it was.

He shuffled toward the steps, shaking his head against the dizziness closing in on him. Again, Heinman made no move to push him along, to hurry up the process. The lack of impatience on Heinman's part caused Parsons's growing dread to mushroom. He tried to swallow but his mouth was so dry his tongue stuck to his palate.

As Parsons ascended the stairs, he had to stop several times to catch his breath. Finally he reached the top and hung onto the banister for support. It was then that Heinman touched him, giving him a little shove into the living room, where he stumbled, caught his footing, then stood gasping for breath.

"Undress," said Heinman.

When he heard this last command, Parsons could feel himself fall apart. His legs felt like jelly, his arms like limp rubber bands. What was Heinman going to do to him? Odd, as he wondered whether he was about to be sodomized, he realized he had never thought of Heinman as a sexual being. Whatever it was that made Heinman tick, Parsons hadn't considered sexuality to be part of the process. Now, as he began to lift the filthy, cardboardlike shirt up over his head, he tried to imagine how Heinman would do it. Yet he sensed no energy, no movement from Heinman who was still behind him.

Parsons dropped his shirt to the floor. It was so stiff with dried sweat that it made a soft thudding noise. He stood motionless, contemplating unbuttoning the painter's pants and stepping out of them. It felt like an impossibly monumental task.

"Move," came the dispassionate monotone, now with an edge of impatience.

Parsons fumbled with the button, then the fly. His hands were shaking. He could feel goose bumps break out all over his arms and legs. He wanted to cry. His eyes stung.

When he had finished unzipping his fly, the pants dropped only a few inches, their stiffness defying gravity. The legs of the pants stayed on up to midthigh, like a suit of armor.

"Get them off," came the disembodied voice.

He leaned down and somehow managed to step out of them. He stood back up, stark naked, uncomfortably aware of Heinman's eyes probing every pore, every crease, every orifice. He stood, his eyes closed, waiting. Waiting to be violated by this monster.

Heinman now circled around him, his eyes sliding over Parsons's body as though he were assessing a horse. His lips curled with contempt. The eyes remained dispassionately cool, calculating.

Parsons's eyes involuntarily shifted to the crotch of Heinman's tight faded jeans. He felt a twinge of relief as he saw no sign of arousal. At the same time, his puzzlement grew.

Heinman didn't miss the silent assessment. "You miserable faggot," he said, his words like knives.

Finally done with his appraisal, Heinman pointed toward the bathroom. "Go shower, pig."

Heinman moved to the closet and snatched the suit, tossing it at Parsons. "Then put this on." His lips, which had been curled with contempt, turned into a genuine smile, though completely lacking in warmth. "You're going back home."

When Parsons stepped out of the shower and finished dressing, Heinman was sitting at the kitchen table, rereading the story that had enraged him earlier. Now, reading the story for the third time, he smiled, gripping the gun he had removed a day earlier from Halsey's desk. He had known about the gun for a long time. It was only now he decided he might have a use for it.

Heinman looked at Parsons with a hint of approval. "You could actually be mistaken for a human being, Dave," he said with his false cheer. "Of course, you have me to thank. You're starting to get rid of that paunch."

Parsons eyed the gun, then searched Heinman's face, desperately looking for the slightest clue. Heinman laughed. "Come on, Dave. Don't give me that pathetic 'what're you gonna do now' look."

Parsons thought he knew, but he had to hear it. He

had to make Heinman tell him. "You're going to kill me . . ." The words came out in a pitiful whisper.

Heinman threw his head back and laughed a full-bellied laugh, shaking his head. "No, Dave, I'm not going to kill you."

Parsons let himself feel a smidgen of hope, but he still had to explain the gun. And why the shower and the suit? He had struggled with the questions while in the shower, alone with his thoughts. He had managed to convince himself that Heinman was through with him, was going to turn him loose. *You're going back home.*

But that was all before Parsons saw the gun. He had to know about the gun. The grip was wrapped in what looked like a wide strip of a torn white sheet. The muzzle was long and steel-blue. It was pointing at him as it lay inertly on the table.

"Why the gun?" Parsons croaked.

Heinman gave him a shrug of mock surprise. "It's not my gun, Dave. Don't worry about it, okay?" Heinman stood up, carefully picked up the gun and jammed it into his waistband. He moved toward Parsons and took him by the elbow. "Come on, Dave. You worry too much. I'm just taking you for a little ride. Relax."

They stepped out the back door. It was late and Parsons could see the moon was full. He felt a moment of joy at the illusion of freedom as he looked at the limitless sky for the first time in days. He sniffed the warm summer air. It brought back a flood of memories, so strong that they momentarily whisked him away from the horrors of the present.

He remembered when he was a kid, maybe nine or ten. He'd been fat then, too. The kids called him Piggy Parsons. How he had hated that. He learned then what he had to do to get them off his back. He became a salesman even at that young age, offering his services by helping his classmates with their homework. For a small fee. And he became good at baseball. Good enough that there were no more demeaning nicknames. Thanks to warm summer evenings like this and his propensity for hitting homers.

He felt a shiver go through him, his mind fighting against centering on reality. He hadn't thought of his childhood nickname in years. He realized that thinking of it now had something to do with Heinman. Heinman had an uncanny ability to zero in on a person's weak points, twisting and turning the knife with morbid pleasure. Heinman had made every snide comment possible about his weight, short of calling him Piggy. Piggy Parsons.

As he felt a harsh push at his back, Parsons was brought back to the cold reality of the moment. Heinman pushed him through a door into the two-car garage, where an old blue Chevrolet sat.

"Get in the car, Dave." Heinman opened the door for him. Parsons got in.

Heinman hopped into the driver's seat and revved up the old engine, then backed out of the garage. He took to the road, heading deeper into the woods. They drove in silence much of the way. With growing distress Parsons watched the moon cast its shadow through the trees. Finally, as he saw they were going deeper and deeper into the middle of nowhere, now on a bumpy dirt road, his fear was becoming unmanageable as he felt his heart pounding. "Where are we going?"

Heinman stared ahead, eyes on the road. "You're so damn nosy, Dave," was all he said as the car bounced and rattled.

Parsons said nothing more, and finally Heinman

brought the car to a stop at the side of the dirt road. "Get out," said Heinman, his voice again cold.

Parsons did so. He stood by the car and looked up at the trees. He heard an owl hoot. He stared at the sky, at the moon, as though seeking help. He could feel the sweat dripping off his face, down his back, under his arms. Ruining his suit. He looked anywhere but at Heinman. Curiously, he could hear no sounds other than those of Nature. What had happened to Heinman? Maybe he had quietly left. Heinman moved quietly, Parsons had noticed that before. He closed his eyes, his ears straining for a hint of what Heinman was up to. Nothing. Should he even hope?

Then he heard the driver's door open and shut. Heinman had been sitting in the car. Watching him? Why? The sweat came in a steady stream now. Yet he could feel a cold chill at the base of his neck. It started when he heard the door open.

Heinman came around the front of the car and stood in front of Parsons, the gun in his right hand, which hung easily at his side. Heinman had an inscrutable look on his face, which Parsons attributed to the darkness. He squinted, trying hard to see better.

Heinman snickered. "You don't need to see me, Dave." He stepped back a few paces then stopped, raising the gun and pointing it directly at Parsons's chest. "I want you to know, Dave, that I would never do anything like this. It's not my style. You're not my enemy. I even kind of enjoy you."

Parsons felt like he was in a fog that had somehow accessed his brain. It swirled and tumbled around with his thoughts, so that he didn't even know if what he saw was real. He saw the muzzle of a gun, pointing straight at him. He saw a man holding the gun, a man he knew only as his tormentor. A man whose name he wasn't even sure of. Suddenly, crazily, he saw Piggy

Parsons, on one warm summer evening that smelled like this, saw Piggy hit a grand slam that brought all the kids to their feet. Then he heard a click, a strangely metallic noise amid all the sounds of Nature. The click, though, seemed to clear out the fog.

Then he heard the voice of Keith Heinman one last time. "I told you I wasn't going to kill you, Dave. Elliot Halsey is going to kill you. With his gun."

The last sentence was punctuated by a blast that seemed to meld with one final cold explosion of fear as Piggy Parsons felt a searing pain in his chest and felt his body being torn off the earth, thrust into the air, and out of the ballpark.

CHAPTER TWENTY-THREE

Halsey and his son were stretched out on the floor of his Alatron study with a pizza and several newspapers. They were immersed in the day's headlines.

"This one in the *Times* will really get a rise out of the guy," said Barry between bites. "They make you look like the company savior."

"Think he'll rise to the bait?"

"He's not gonna be happy reading this stuff."

Halsey frowned. "Did you see this *USA Today* story? Three more deaths in Los Angeles." He shook his head. The pizza was like a ball of dough jammed in his throat. He threw the paper down. "Sometimes I wish I could just run off somewhere."

Barry laughed. "You're no quitter. You could never do that."

Halsey pushed aside the pizza box that sat between them. "You really mean that?"

Barry gave him a quick look, then looked away, his jaw tightening. "I'm proud of you, Dad."

Halsey's vision blurred. Dad. He had waited a long

time to hear that word again. He took a deep breath. "Barry, I want you to know something."

Barry didn't look up. He appeared to be studying the pizza.

Halsey went on. "The only thing I've ever wanted for you is your happiness." He saw Barry's head come up. He held up a hand. "You've heard it before, I know. But there's more."

He felt Barry's eyes on him. Tentative. Searching. He rose and walked over to the window, looking out, collecting his thoughts. The room was quiet. He could hear Barry breathing. Barry, his son. In that instant he saw an infant standing up in his crib, smiling. A child with his eyes aglow at his first Christmas tree. A boy off to boarding school, hiding a tear. A young man, saying with a challenging smile, "If you have time I'd like to tell you something about your son. I'm gay."

He had not known what to say. Turning without a word and walking away. It had not been mentioned again. And the space between them had widened.

He sighed now and moved back to the couch and sank into it. Barry was still sitting on the floor, his legs crossed, his face not saying anything. Waiting.

Halsey reached for the boy's hand. There was no answering pressure. "I accept that you're gay," he said gently, trying to make his voice reassuring. "I had no right to judge you. It's your life to deal with. To be the man you want to be. To make the decisions that affect your life. I had my own image of what I wanted my son to be like. I was wrong. I see it now."

His voice faltered for a moment. "I know what matters most to me. You're my son. I love you. And I'm with you."

He saw the tears on his son's face. He slid down to the floor and gripped his shoulders. "Barry, I love you.

I accept everything about you. Except AIDS." His voice broke and he buried his face in his hands. "That I can never accept. And will fight it to my last breath."

Halsey could see Barry's chest heave with its quiet sobs. There were tears on his own cheeks. It was a moment of exquisite joy and pain. A moment of liberation for them both. They embraced.

Heinman stuffed Parsons's body into the trunk of his Chevy, shoving aside a crowbar and a spare tire. He took the bumpy dirt road to the highway, careful to observe the speed limit. This was no time to get flagged down by the cops. In forty minutes he was in the Alatron parking lot.

Only a skeleton crew would be on duty. And of course Halsey would be there. He was counting on that. Halsey was always there at night—Mr. Workaholic scurrying around to salvage his company. Now he had his faggot son tagging around after him. Heinman snickered. One phone call was all it took. So easy.

He parked next to Halsey's car, the infamous BMW. He smiled as he inspected the fine piece of machinery, its black finish shimmering under the light of the street lamp. His smile grew as he imagined the look on Halsey's face when the stolen car turned up in its usual parking place, right under his nose.

Heinman had developed a fondness for the German car. He liked the way it handled when he drove it back from Halsey's precious little lake. Sensitive to the most subtle manipulation. One touch and it did his bidding.

He got out the duplicate key he'd made and opened the trunk. Plenty of space. He took a look around. No one in sight, but the parking lot was well-lighted and anyone could be watching. He moved quickly, scooping Parsons's limp body into his arms, careful not to get blood on himself. He tucked Parsons into the trunk. Good old Dave was a perfect fit.

He closed the trunk, climbed into his Chevy and drove around to his usual spot behind the R and D building. He changed shirts, slipping on his uniform and identification badge. He removed the gun from the glove box and placed it, the grip still wrapped, into a duffel bag. He headed across the parking lot for the administration building, whistling cheerfully— the model employee.

He grabbed a mop and bucket in the basement and took the service elevator to the fifth floor. He walked casually to Halsey's study, keeping his eyes on the floor, as though inspecting it for spots. He put his ear to the door of Halsey's office and the adjacent study. All quiet. He decided Halsey was probably still over in R and D.

With a smile he inserted the key in the lock. He took one last look down the deserted corridor then slipped into the dark room. He pulled out a penlight and directed its beam toward the floor until he found Halsey's desk. He placed the gun back in the drawer from which he had taken it twenty-four hours earlier, removed the cloth from the grip and stuffed it into his pocket.

Moving deliberately, he returned to the maintenance office on the basement floor and placed a call to AIDS FIRST leader Gil Stryker. Then he walked back to R and D, punched the time clock, gathered up a cart full of maintenance supplies, and went to work.

Kate was alone in her Alatron office. Halsey was in the lab. She understood his need to keep pushing on the Congo vaccine, but she could see its toll. Dark circles were emerging under his eyes. His face was haggard and drawn. The pristine glow of the crusader was losing some of its luster.

As she stared at the reports before her she made a decision. It was time to act. She was more certain than ever they were dealing with sabotage. She knew she was being sucked even more into Halsey's world, Halsey's point of view. But it was all right. Abe knew it. She knew it. Still, she was after the truth. Abe knew that, too.

It was clear what she had to do. Find Keith Heinman. She had tried Rutger Kraft repeatedly. He was always unavailable, very likely using his answering machine to screen calls. She decided to pay him a visit.

She reached for the phone book and turned to the Yellow Pages, flipping to the airlines section. As her finger moved down the page, she heard a knock at the door. Probably Elliot. He usually came around about now, nine-thirty, and drove her to the hotel.

"Come in," she called, already feeling a magic warmth. They would have a drink together and chat as they did nearly every night. The one bright spot on a clouded horizon. She hadn't invited him up to her room, and he hadn't asked. Yet the connection between them was as sensual as it was anything. She knew it would happen when the time was right, if it was meant to happen at all.

She looked up with anticipation. Her face dropped. It was only the janitor. The same strange janitor, though perhaps not all that strange. There was always the occasional wacko, whose motives remained eternally elusive. At the CDC one of the custodians would hover about, plying her with questions, some personal. The fact that he wore sunglasses, even at night, didn't help. He was fired shortly after her arrival. She never learned why. She heard all sorts of stories. How he had an arsenal of weapons stashed away in his garage and kept young girls in his attic. She never knew if any of them were true. She hadn't thought of him again until now.

The janitor smiled at her in that odd way of his. She had an uneasy feeling he was reading her mind.

"How's a person supposed to clean up when you're always around? I swear, you work too hard," he chirped as he wheeled the cart into the room. "I need to restock some supplies. You're low on toilet paper and soap."

"Go ahead," she said, not looking up. She went back to the phone book and found the number for Delta Airlines. She jotted it down as Heinman puttered around in the bathroom, whistling tunelessly. As her hand touched the phone, like magic it rang. She snatched it up.

"Hello?" She hoped it was Halsey.

There was a moment when no one spoke. The static made her think it was long distance. "Dr. Katherine Crane, please."

She recognized the accent immediately. "Dr. Kraft?" She was on the edge of her seat. Only peripherally aware of the janitor at the far end of the room.

"Good evening, Dr. Crane. I'm sorry to have missed your calls. I'm prepared to give you what you want, provided you observe certain conditions."

"Yes?" She crooked her neck to hold the receiver and snatched up pen and paper. She could hear her pulse throbbing in her ear.

"Under no circumstances are you to let Keith Heinman know I gave you this information, or that you and I have spoken."

She breathed a sigh of relief. "Is that all?"

"Not quite. Should you have the misfortune of locating Herr Heinman in your midst, you must disregard any information he may offer about myself or Woodlawn."

She thought a moment. "I will do as you say, Dr. Kraft." She spoke in a low voice, increasingly aware of the janitor cleaning the windows across from her.

"Fine, I shall take you at your word." He cleared his throat. "Keith Heinman was discharged from this institution over a year ago, thanks to government cutbacks in mental health funding. A situation somewhat like New York City's Bellevue Hospital found itself in a decade ago." He gave an ugly laugh. "You may recall that particular fiasco. In the name of saving dollars our federal *Wunderkinds* turned out on the streets a new breed of homeless schizophrenics and paranoid maniacs, of which Mr. Heinman is one. Now they're packing them into our jails like sardines. But not Herr Heinman. He's too smart."

She felt strangely mesmerized by Kraft's harangue. She soaked up every word, every nuance. She could hear his heavy breathing and the doctor in her said he was not a healthy man. She guessed he was fat and a heavy smoker. She found herself inanely hoping he lived long enough to finish his story.

The janitor had moved behind her now. She could hear him scrubbing away. She felt a chilling sense of dread as she waited for Kraft to continue.

"I'm listening," she said as Kraft asked if she was still there.

"As I was saying, Heinman was released against my better judgment. He insisted I help change his identity and find him a job at Alatron. He had a mission. Normally, I would not participate in such duplicity. But as I said, Heinman was considered dangerous. He threatened me."

Kate's mind began racing, crashing through hurdles

she couldn't even see. A job at Alatron. What kind of job?

The janitor was somewhere behind her. She thought she could feel his breath on her neck. No, of course she was imagining things. She didn't dare turn her head. Didn't dare let him suspect for one moment she was thinking of him.

"Dr. Crane?" It was Kraft again, impatient, drawing her back into the phone.

She kept her voice down. "What kind of job?"

The janitor was closer, she was sure. She felt the muscles along her spine quiver. She resisted turning to look for him. Act casual, she told herself. Act dumb. But she knew the peering eyes would not miss a thing. Nothing would get by them. She kept her head down, pretending to take notes. She began writing whatever came to mind—her phone number in Atlanta, her work number, even her ex-husband's number in New York. Without smiling.

It seemed an eternity before Kraft answered her question. The janitor was now in her field of vision. Off to her left, his back to her. He was adjusting a picture on the wall. She let her eyes shift to him for a split second. She knew he was listening. She didn't know why, but she knew.

"He obtained a custodial position, Dr. Crane. A smart move on his part, yes indeed. Those fellows have keys for everything. I have no idea if he would still be there.... He could have used any number of names."

Any number of names. Ken the Janitor. Kate kept the phone to her ear, but if Kraft was still talking it wasn't registering. Her eyes were on the man who now stood in front of her, whisking a dust cloth aimlessly around the papers on her desk as he fixed her with a look of amusement. Her gaze moved to his name tag.

The tag, usually turned backward, was now positioned correctly, as though arranged for her benefit. It showed his name in larger-than-life letters with a small square picture in one corner. She didn't need her glasses. She didn't need to squint. The name popped out at her. Butler, Kenneth. Maintenance Department. *Any number of names.*

She looked up at him. She thought she saw menace in his eyes. As though he wanted her to know that Kenneth Butler was indeed one of those names.

Halsey headed through the airlock into the chemical shower. He moved slowly, limited by the cumbersome space suit. He plugged his manifold into the air hose hanging from the ceiling and let the disinfectant spray down on him. The process took about five minutes, giving him plenty of time to think. And to worry. Worry about Barry, who had insisted on returning to the city. Though Barry had a good point—Heinman would be here now, at Alatron. He would be determined to stop Halsey from moving ahead with the Congo vaccine.

Although there were barely any new cases of Congo Fever, Halsey knew public awareness and fear were never greater. At least twenty people had died of it. And no one knew if and when it would strike again.

The shower automatically shut off. Halsey stepped into the suit room, stripped, and showered again, this time with soap and water. He wrapped a towel around his waist and entered the outer change room. As he approached his locker, he saw a note pinned to it. An urgent message at the switchboard. He didn't think much of it. Everything was urgent these days.

He slipped into gray flannel slacks and a white knit shirt and approached the wall phone. He dialed the Alatron switchboard.

"Oh, Mr. Halsey," gushed the operator. "Thank goodness. The hospital has called twice now."

Halsey felt his throat constrict. His mind raced through his personal worry list. It couldn't be Barry, whom he had just put in a cab. There was his daughter and an ailing mother. And, with a moment of panic, that someone new on his list—Kate Crane. Heinman would know about their growing attachment. He seemed to know everything.

He kept his voice down. "What hospital?"

"Dr. Dougherty at Memorial Hospital in Denville has been trying to reach you. Regarding a patient, Paul Resnick. Mr. Resnick needs to see you right away."

He was baffled. "That's it?"

"Only that the doctor said it was urgent and the patient is critical."

"Thank you," he said, hanging up. Paul Resnick. He hadn't seen him since the day he dragged him out of the fountain. What could that crazy man possibly want? Some sort of trick. It would be just like him.

He looked at his watch—nine-fifteen. What he wanted to do was swing by Kate's office and take her back to the hotel. It was the high point of his day, and he wasn't about to give it up for some psycho who delighted in making people miserable.

He sat ruminating for a moment, remembering that day with Resnick. He'd had a glimpse of something else. Something to do with the look on Resnick's face when he accepted Halsey's proffered shirt. It was enough to give him pause.

He tried Kate's number—busy. He finished dressing and tried her again. Still busy. He would call her from the hospital.

Halsey stopped at the Memorial Hospital information desk. Paul Resnick was in the intensive care unit.

Dougherty had left permission for the visit. He tried reaching Kate once more. No answer. If only he didn't have to see Resnick.

With a growing uneasiness, he caught the elevator to intensive care. At the door a nurse with a worried frown approached him. "Mr. Halsey?"

"Yes."

"Paul is anxious to see you. He's ... not doing well."

He thought of the many diseases that squeezed the last bit of life out of AIDS victims. "What's wrong with him?"

"Pneumocystis pneumonia." She led him toward the room. "He may have to go on the ventilator."

She stopped. "Paul will be so pleased you came."

Halsey looked at her and felt a pang. She had clearly grown attached to her patient. Resnick couldn't be all bad. He nodded.

Resnick was propped up in bed, his lower face hidden by an oxygen mask. His chest moved under the sheet with quick shallow breaths. His eyes were closed, his face the color of dough. His long dark hair was damp, strands of it clinging to his forehead and temples. His hands were clasped tightly over his abdomen. He could have been praying.

"Paul?" The nurse approached Resnick and gently nudged his shoulder. He looked up at her with hooded lids. "Mr. Halsey is here."

Resnick's eyes opened and he shifted forward in the bed. Halsey pulled up a chair. Resnick reached out a hand, which Halsey gripped as he sat down.

"What can I do, Paul?"

Resnick glanced at the nurse and she disappeared. He pulled the oxygen mask away from his face. "I'm dying." There was none of the bitterness, none of the belligerence that Halsey remembered. Just a simple statement.

"The nurse tells me you've got pneumocystis. You can beat it." He saw a spark in Resnick's eye. "You've beat the odds before."

"Naw, I've played out all my cards."

"We'll see." Halsey let go of Resnick's hand and picked up a damp washcloth lying on the pillow. He used it to blot away the beads of sweat on the sick man's forehead.

There was a heavy silence while Halsey watched Resnick summon his strength. He felt an odd bond with the man. Maybe because Resnick, in his own crazy way, was not just fighting for his own life, but for others like him. For people like Barry. Trying to bring about change in a mixed-up world.

His mind flashed back to their previous encounter. Resnick leaping into the board room like a deranged acrobat, bristling with hatred. The antics in the fountain. Now this—bringing Halsey to his bedside, taking his hand in what could be his final moments. Life was crazy.

"You ever have an out-of-body experience?" Resnick's hoarse whisper brought Halsey back to the present.

"No." Halsey could feel himself drawn into the force of Resnick's intensity.

"I did," whispered Resnick, his eyes burning with evangelical fervor. "Last night. They almost lost me when they brought me into the emergency room." He swallowed, his Adam's apple bobbing in his thin neck. "My heart was doing wild things. They had to shock me. All I remember is looking down on these guys in green uniforms. Coming at me with metal paddles. Bolts of electricity shooting back and forth. I was terrified, and cold—freezing cold."

Resnick stopped talking. Halsey was at once relieved and disappointed. He had to know why Resnick wanted to see him. He saw with growing apprehension that Resnick's respirations had quickened.

But something was driving the sick man. Something unearthly. He started again, taking up where he had left off. His voice was faint. Halsey had to draw closer. "Then things got really strange. The paddles turned into icicles and the green guys were poking and prodding at me. I screamed. They disappeared. Then I saw you."

Resnick looked up, his dark eyes searching Halsey's face. "You were smiling at me. You handed me a warm shirt, like you did that day at the fountain."

He smiled and closed his eyes. He looked peaceful, composed.

Halsey watched the dying man—a man who had spent so much of his life hating. Now he wore a truly beatific smile. Halsey felt himself in the grip of an emotion he did not understand. He didn't know what to say. He started to put the oxygen mask back over Resnick's mouth.

"Water ..." Without opening his eyes, Resnick pointed a trembling finger toward the pitcher on his bedside table. Halsey fumbled to get it for him, glad to be doing something. Resnick leaned forward and took a sip. Halsey said nothing. He held the glass while Resnick drank. The thought of Kate flitted back and forth in his mind.

"Thanks." Resnick lay back and stared at the wall. "I knew then I was wrong. Wrong to hate ... you, all the others. People trying to help. I knew it all along ... couldn't admit it. It was myself I hated ... all those wasted years ... I had to let it go. The hatred."

He turned his head toward Halsey, his eyes red. "It was killing me."

Halsey reached for Resnick's hand. He felt his eyes sting as he watched this recent adversary fighting for his life.

Gradually, Resnick's breathing steadied. Halsey let go of his hand. "You're a brave man, Paul."

Resnick seemed to gather new energy. "Listen to me," he rasped, leaning forward.

Halsey moved closer. "Let me know when you need the mask."

Resnick shook his head. "There's something I need to tell you. About the AIDS vaccine."

Halsey's stomach flipped. "I'm listening."

"There's this guy who's got Stryker's ear. He's whipping the guys up about Alatron and you. Gil's under this guy's spell. He's wrong. Wrong about everything. Wrong about you.

"I saw it, that day we had it out in the fountain. You were ... decent. I was kicking you in the face and you offered me the shirt off your back. I didn't know then your son had AIDS. You could have thrown it at me—made me eat my words. But you didn't."

Resnick's chest began to heave. It took Halsey a moment to realize he was sobbing. "It was like a sign." He was gasping now, struggling to catch his breath.

Halsey stood up and positioned the mask over Resnick's mouth. He put a hand on Resnick's forehead. "Take it easy, Paul," he said softly. "I'm here as long as you need me."

Resnick pulled the mask off. "Sit down. I've got to tell you about this guy. He's dangerous."

Halsey could feel his heart pounding. "Do you know his name?"

Resnick nodded, closing his eyes. "I recognized him at Alatron. He was working in the research building."

Halsey winced, thinking of Kate. "Who is he?" His own voice made a hollow echo in his ears.

"Ken . . . somebody."

"What department?"

"He's a janitor."

Halsey felt an explosion inside his head. *"How did you know to find me here?" "The custodian told me." The custodian. "Hey, fella, could you get one of your buddies and clean up in there?"*

The custodian. The eyes. The smile. Of course. After ten years, only the beard was gone.

CHAPTER TWENTY-FOUR

The tires screeched as Halsey peeled out of the hospital parking lot. It was all falling into place. Ken was Heinman. Heinman was The Caller. The Caller was the custodian Kate had been uneasy about. Why hadn't he seen it? And now, this very moment, Kate could be alone with a homicidal maniac. He slammed his foot to the floor.

Within minutes he was at Alatron, flying over the speed bumps past the security kiosk and down the long driveway to the R and D lot. He brought the car to a rocking stop and leaped out.

At first he barely noticed the red-shirted AIDS FIRSTers mobbing the parking lot across the way. But as he headed to R and D they came swarming toward him. He couldn't make out what they were chanting. Not that he cared. He needed to find Kate. He started running. All at once the throng had him surrounded.

"Murderer! Murderer!" came the unified chorus as they brandished pipes, baseball bats, whatever they could get their hands on. No cardboard signs this time.

"Get the hell out of my way!" Halsey tried to elbow

his way through the ranks, but they closed in on him. He could feel his blood boil, every one of his senses sharpened, like an animal under attack. He felt the heat of their breath, the smell of their sweat. Their chanting had a rhythmic primeval thrum.

They stood regarding each other—the hunters and their prey. Gil Stryker stepped out of the crowd into the circle with Halsey and put up a hand. The chanting died down.

"Turn over your car keys," Stryker demanded.

"Go to hell."

The two men held each other's gaze for a long moment. Then Stryker suddenly turned and shot his arm toward Halsey's car. "Okay, boys, go for it."

The mob surged toward the BMW. They began whacking away at the trunk.

Halsey watched, stupefied, as though his feet were rooted in the ground. They pried open the trunk and dragged out a bulky form. At first he couldn't tell what it was. And then, stunned, he saw it was a body.

"Murderer!" The word was flung at him. And then, as the activists resumed their chant, something inside him snapped. He rushed at them, fists flying. He could hear himself screaming. He tore his way through the mob until he was close enough to see the victim's face. Even as the demonstrators lunged at him, he realized who it was. It was the last thing he remembered.

"Dr. Santos, call the ER, stat! Dr. Rose to the OR please. Dr. Rose to the OR. Maintenance, call ICU; maintenance, ICU. . . ."

Halsey's head was swimming. He was hearing voices. Where was he? He tried to open his eyes but everything was blurry. So he listened to the voices.

"Dr. Chatterjee, call the switchboard. . . . May I have your attention, please—there is a white Ford station wagon blocking the front entrance; will the owner kindly move your car ..."

Halsey tried moving his head. Fireworks went off behind his eyes. His brain rocked. There was a vise squeezing his forehead. He tried opening his eyes again. Laserlike light blasted his optic nerves. He blinked. He was aware of a shadow, a form, near him. He turned his head slightly and winced as excruciating pain shot down his arm.

A warm hand took his. "Elliot?" A soft voice. Her voice. Suddenly he remembered. He tried to sit up and gasped as pain ripped through his chest. He fell back. She was all right. That was all that mattered.

"Elliot? It's me, Kate. Do you hear me?"

He tried to nod but his head wouldn't move. Something braced his neck. He squeezed her hand.

"You're in the hospital. You took a pretty good beating, but you're going to be all right."

Of course he would be all right. She was alive. He squeezed her hand again. He could feel the warmth of his tears on his face. Thank God she was alive.

Why had he been so worried about her? He wasn't sure. He squeezed his eyes shut, searching the back corners of his mind. Memories slammed at him in torrential waves, then ebbed away. A swell of nausea sent his head reeling.

She seemed keyed in to his every need. She was there with a plastic basin. "Use this if you need to," she said, and stroked his forehead.

The nausea passed and he opened his eyes. He had to see her, had to keep verifying that she was there—with him. That she was okay. He could tell she was standing over him. She was two blurred images with two blurred smiles, four concerned eyes. Ludicrous. He felt like laughing but his chest seized up with pain.

He closed his eyes, and he remembered his visit with Resnick. Then the rest started coming back, like a sewage-strewn tidal wave. Heinman. The body planted in his car. Heinman.

He lurched forward with a sense of urgency, but doubled over with pain. He had to tell her. About Heinman. He couldn't let her go back there alone.

She seemed to rush to him, even though he knew she was already at his side. She cradled the back of his head with one hand and gripped his shoulder with the other, guiding him back against the pillow. Her touch was gentle yet firm.

"Elliot, you need to rest. You've suffered a concussion, cracked ribs, and a collapsed lung. Your neck is badly sprained. You have a tube in your chest to keep the lung expanded. Try to lie still."

The words whistled past him. He lay back, his breath coming in short quick gasps. He had to gather the air to push a word out. "Heinman," he whispered.

"I know who Heinman is," she said, magically reading his mind.

She knew?

"I'll tell you all about it later, when you've rested. He's gone. There's a lot to talk about, but it can wait. Getting better is all that matters right now."

He couldn't believe it. In the midst of a reality whose horror was unmatched by any nightmare sprang a reality as blatantly wonderful as any dream. A woman, beautiful in body and soul, was leaning over him, her very presence healing. He loved her. He was in love with Kate Crane. Oh, God, what was going to happen to her, to them? The tears came again.

Kate regarded Halsey with a frown. She blinked to fight back her own tears as she watched his stream down his bruised abraded cheeks. She surveyed the damage. One black eye, practically swollen shut. A lacerated eyebrow prickling with pointy blue stitches. A split lip. A neck brace. He was a sorry sight.

They said he had brought it on himself. Wildly striking out at the demonstrators when he saw Dave Parsons's body. She smiled bitterly. He hadn't known his own strength. Gil Stryker had a broken arm, another demonstrator lost some teeth. A few others had black eyes.

Now, as if things weren't bad enough, once out of the hospital he would face a charge of murder. All circumstantial evidence. Planted no doubt by Keith Heinman—aka Ken the Janitor. There was, of course, Parsons's body. And the gun found in Halsey's desk. Both incriminating. But suspect. The murder weapon turned up by an "anonymous" tipster.

She had faced down the uniformed policeman standing guard over the dangerous criminal. "I'm a doctor. Does it look like he's going anywhere?" she snapped as she pointed to the chest tube.

The cop was just a kid. He didn't look old enough to be carrying a gun. She blew up when she saw he'd chained one of Halsey's ankles to the bed frame. "You're cutting off his circulation," she stormed. "You could cause serious blood clots. Do you want to be responsible for a fatal pulmonary embolus?"

The cop's eyes bulged and he hastily withdrew to a position outside Halsey's door.

She plumped herself in a chair at Halsey's bedside, watching him twitch and groan in a restless twilight sleep that would have pleased Heinman.

Heinman—her spine chilled at the thought. Who else could it be? He had overheard her conversation with Kraft and it didn't faze him in the least. He clearly enjoyed standing over her, insolently swishing his dust cloth around. His eyes laughing at her.

Suddenly she felt alone. Who would believe that one demonic monster could bring down a drug company, murder one of its executives, destroy its CEO, and cause the deaths of innocent victims through drug tampering and wrecking the future of the vaccine. No one.

A flash of light and shouts outside the door caught her attention. She spotted a photographer holding a camera high above his head as the young cop shoved him back out of the room.

"No press allowed," growled the cop with an energy Kate hadn't seen earlier. She suddenly realized the cop wasn't there just to keep Halsey from escaping. He was there to protect him. So he could stand trial for murder.

The thought made her feel even more frightened and alone. Cops, reporters, demonstrators, board members reveling in a carnival-like atmosphere as they hovered outside Halsey's door. Anything affecting him would round off their day. If he died, it would make headlines. How about a nice little confession, squeezed out of him while half comatose? Or perhaps a conveniently arranged browbeating to elicit a resignation?

As if on cue she spotted two executive types wearing suits peeking into the room. Their faces seemed a mimicry of concern. The cop barricaded the door with his long arms and gave one of them a little push. She could have hugged him.

Cop or no cop, she continued to feel alone. It was up to her to find Heinman and expose him. Elliot was out of commission. The police were unsympathetic. They had a suspect, a body, a weapon. They wouldn't be expending any energy on this case.

Could she catch Heinman herself? At the prospect she felt her palms dampen, her mouth turn to parchment, her spine tingle. She knew well the primitive instincts of fight or flight, but she had never experienced them quite so viscerally.

As she watched Elliot Halsey struggling for consciousness, his face twisted into a perpetual wince, she forced herself to consider a plan. She would have to track down Heinman, outwit him, confront him—things she wasn't used to doing. Things he was a master at. She decided she had one advantage. Surely Heinman wouldn't dare show his face now that his identity was known.

Instead of feeling reassured, she sensed that now he was even more dangerous. Lurking in the shadows, ready to pounce at any moment. She looked again at Elliot, lying in the hospital bed. And she knew she had no choice. Not with him leashed to a chest tube. Not with a crew of scientists who were as skeptical of pharmaceutical companies as she had been. It was up to her.

She shuddered as she imagined Heinman's face. The personification of evil. Her fear inched its way up her throat, coalescing in a tight lump just below her larynx. She tried to push it down, tried to convince herself she could handle whatever lay ahead. She was, after all, an epidemiologist with well-honed investigatory skills. Trained in the detection of the most elusive of organisms, albeit microscopic. A great résumé, but it did not affect the lump in her throat. She shook her head, on the verge of tears as she watched Elliot writhe with pain.

Then it came to her. The lump receding ever so slightly. Harpo. Her angel from heaven. Of course.

"All right," said Harpo, "let me get this straight. This guy Heinman has not only killed innocent people with his sabotaged vaccine, but he's murdered an Alatron biggie and made it look like Halsey did it. He's also got a line to the papers and the demonstrators. That about cover it?"

"More or less."

She could hear him groan over the hum of the long-distance connection. "Jesus."

"Will you come, Harpo? We need you."

"I can't wait. Just let me double my life insurance."

She laughed. "Is that a yes?"

"I don't know, Kate ... I've got a lot of stuff going here. All due yesterday...."

She gripped the phone tighter. He was scared. Or maybe just prudent.

"Why don't you let the police handle this, Kate?" he went on. "We're only doctors. This guy is a cold-blooded killer who's had ten years to piece together a plan that would make Hitler look like a boy scout."

"The police won't help," she said, hope fading. "As far as they're concerned, they have their man. Case closed. There's a cop here, guarding Elliot every hour of the day." She gave a short laugh. "While Heinman runs free."

As the ever loquacious Harpo remained silent, she began to feel guilty. After all, he did have a wife and kids to think about.

"You're right, Harpo," she said. "The man is dangerous. People are just pawns to him. He could kill us both just for the fun of it. Or if he thinks it would finish Elliot."

She stared out the window of her makeshift Alatron office with growing despair. The image of Heinman's face seemed to peer back at her. "I wonder, sometimes, if he isn't after more than just Elliot. He seems bent on destruction." She paused. "What's really frightening is that even his one-time psychiatrist is terrified of him."

Harpo gave a nervous laugh. "You're not exactly offering me a persuasive argument to drop everything and rush over there, Kate."

"I guess not."

There was a profound silence. As though Harpo was trying to put it all together. "Hey, wait a minute," he said slowly, "I can tell by your voice what you're up to, Kate. Always could. If you think I'm gonna let you go this alone, you're crazy." He took a deep breath. "The Big Apple will just have to live without me for a few days. And Molly—hell, she's so busy studying for her master's she won't know I'm gone."

Kate's heart took a leap. For a moment her guilt and fear dissipated, pushed aside by a jolt of delight. "Harpo, I could kiss you."

He laughed. "I'll check the train schedule and let you know when I plan to collect."

She hung up with a smile. She looked at her watch. It was late. No wonder she was tired. She stretched and yawned, then reached for the phone to call a cab. She felt her heart thump as she heard a knock at the door.

"Who is it?" She jumped up and crossed the room. The door seemed to swing open on its own.

"Just me again," the janitor chirped as he backed into the room with his supply cart. "They want this place spic and span—you know how it is. Sorry."

She stood frozen as Heinman's head seemed to pivot toward her in slow motion, his eyes zeroing in like radar. How could he *dare* show up now? How could she have so misjudged him? As if in answer, he leaned one arm against the cart and slid his eyes over her, then fixed on her face.

With all the resolve she could muster, she made her eyes stay on his. Through the layers of insolence and hate she could see a deadness, the soullessness of a serpent. It chilled her to the bone.

They stood surveying each other. She moved back to the table and fumbled through a stack of papers. She tried to appear cool. But her hands were shaking.

"You didn't need to call in your pal." His voice took on an oddly metallic tone. "I'm not so hard to find." He pushed away from the cart and swaggered toward her, hands held out. "See for yourself."

He dropped his hands to his sides and moved another step toward her. "But that's okay. I can handle both of you."

Her first impulse was to run. And then there was the urge to strike out and hurt him. Even kill him. She spotted the scissors on the table, within easy reach. She could feel her hands tense, her fingers twitch, as though sensing her next move. She held her breath.

He's only standing there, she told herself. No, said another voice. He's made several steps toward you. Is he threatening you or simply toying with you? Like a cat plays with a mouse before the kill.

Heinman seemed to enjoy watching her struggle. He made another small move toward her, his hands clasped behind his back, a superior smile twisting his lips. She could feel herself back away each time he moved closer—withdrawing into herself. She knew he sensed her fear. And it amused him.

She glared at him, rage banishing her fear. "You're insane," she cried, her mouth so dry her lips clung to her teeth.

He made another step toward her. Any closer and she would have to tilt her head back to see his face.

His lips curled into a sneer. "Your friend Halsey got himself into a heap of trouble talking like that."

"You'll never win," she said.

"Win?" he echoed. "This isn't a sweepstakes." He made a sudden move with his hands and she flung her arms up. With a mocking smile he whipped out a dust cloth and began moving it idly along the grain of the table. He worked the cloth around her papers but kept his eyes on her.

She gathered up her papers, stuffing them into her briefcase.

He made a tsking sound with his tongue as he slid the cloth back and forth.

"You sabotaged the vaccine, didn't you?" She slipped her briefcase under her arm, too angry to be afraid.

He said nothing, continuing to move the cloth around, his eyes never leaving her face.

"You killed Parsons, didn't you?"

Still no answer. Just the smile. And the eyes pinned to her face.

She thought for a moment she saw a flicker of admiration in his cold gaze. Even a slight inclination of his head as he stared at her. Whatever it was, it only deepened her fear.

"I can go to the police," she challenged.

"Go ahead. They'll have a good laugh. Those jerks wouldn't know a piece of evidence if it knocked them over." He seemed to be studying her. "But you won't go. Because now it's personal, isn't it?"

She felt her face flush.

He extended a hand toward her. The hand of a killer. It looked like any other hand. Five fingers. Closely clipped nails. Blue veins in an intricate network.

"Go ahead. Take me to the police. They'll think you're just some desperate broad trying to save your boyfriend."

He was right, of course. Unless she could find something to pin on him. She said nothing and started for the door, half expecting he would stop her. She turned and glared at him. "I suggest you stay away from here. Our next conversation may not end quite so amiably."

He threw back his head and laughed. "Just what I was thinking."

CHAPTER TWENTY-FIVE

"Let's hear it, Kate," prodded Harpo as they settled into a corner booth. His train had been late and they were both famished. "You've got something up your sleeve."

Harpo looked so fit and upbeat that Kate felt her confidence returning, if only in bits and pieces. She smiled. "You must still be doing your yoga, Harpo. You look like you could take on a tank."

"Did my meditation on the train. Slowed my pulse to a snail's pace."

She laughed. "I don't think that will help us. Got anything in your bag of magic tricks?"

In response he picked up the salt and pepper shakers and an ashtray, his face the picture of seriousness. He deftly juggled the items over his head without taking his eyes off her. After retrieving them behind his back he set them down. "That's about my speed these days. Party stuff."

She leaned over the table and kissed him. "You're one of a kind, Harpo."

"Thanks," he said with a squeeze of her hand. He

looked at the menu. "We've got our work cut out for us, don't we?"

She nodded and she could feel the muscles in her face harden. "I know where he lives."

He lowered the menu and stared at her. "You mean Heinman?"

She nodded again, her lips tight.

"How'd you locate him?"

"I watched for him. Waited." Her eyes narrowed. She could hear the hatred in her voice. She could barely swallow. "When he got in his car I took down his license. A few phone calls got me his address. He has a place not far from here."

He grinned, a nervous grin. "Good work. Now what?"

"We make a house call. While he's at Alatron. He still comes to work. Can you believe it? He thinks he's untouchable."

"So far he seems to be right."

"Not much longer. We'll take a camera. I'm sure he did all his connivery there." She looked at him, a glint in her eye. "We can nail him, Harpo."

"Damn. You *do* have something up your sleeve." He sat back and gave her an appraising look. "One thing, Kate."

"Yes?" She looked at the menu halfheartedly.

"What if he shows up while we're nosing around? We're no match for this guy. Unless you went and got yourself a black belt in karate."

She looked up at him. "Taekwondo."

He blinked. "No kidding?"

"Just a few simple self-defense moves. Not enough to go against Heinman. But don't worry, Harpo. He'll be at work."

Harpo patted his duffel bag. "You remember the

old med school adage, Kate? Never assume anything. I brought a little backup. Just in case."

She took a deep breath and looked away. She didn't want to know what he brought.

The waitress came and took their orders. They sipped at their coffee in silence. Kate didn't trust herself to speak. She could feel tears welling up in her eyes. It was all too much. Even with Harpo there.

The waitress returned with oatmeal and English muffins. They picked at their food. Kate felt Harpo watching her. She felt like a fool.

He slid out of the booth and sat next to her, placing his arm around her shoulder. "Kate, it's going to be all right."

She fished a tissue out of her purse and dabbed at her eyes. "Thank you for being here, Harpo. It's been a nightmare. You're the only one I can count on. No one believes that Heinman's for real. I've given up trying to tell people. Abe and his crew are still busy trying to find a sane explanation for everything."

"He's for real all right," Harpo said, his voice like steel. "And we're gonna get the bastard, Kate. You and me."

"Elliot Halsey, please. It's important."

"I'm sorry," the nurse said. "No calls." She hated "important" calls. What people wouldn't do to rap with their friends in the hospital.

She had finished emptying the blood-tinged drainage from the plastic container connected to Halsey's chest tube. She had other chores piling up. He was a sick man. She was a busy nurse. Neither could be bothered with phone calls. "Mr. Halsey needs to rest," she continued with all the emotion of a tape recording. "You may call between eleven A.M. and . . ."

"I will talk to him now."

She was returning the receiver to its cradle when the coldly aloof tone at the other end stopped her. She looked nervously at Halsey lying on his back, eyes closed.

"Just a moment." She poked the receiver in Halsey's face. "Mr. Halsey? Do you feel up to taking a call?"

Halsey reached out and took the receiver. He was groggy from pain medication. His response was automatic. Somebody gives you something, you take it. He didn't have the slightest interest in who it was. "Hello?" He closed his eyes again. The fluorescent ceiling lights were painfully bright.

"Hey, El. You don't sound so good."

Halsey's eyes popped open. His mind for the first time since his concussion buzzed, all circuits on alert. His eyes darted around, seeking the nurse. She was gone. "Who is this?"

The laugh. "I believe you know, El. You don't mind if I call you El? It's just that I feel like I know you so well . . . El." Another laugh.

"You miserable, insane bastard . . . ." Halsey started to cough and winced with pain.

"Hey, El, re-l-a-a-ax. You really have gotten yourself into quite a pickle, haven't you?"

Halsey squeezed his eyes tight. He could feel an ugly bilelike taste in his mouth as rage and helplessness clashed inside his gut. He could think of nothing to say.

"Let's get down to business, El. I didn't call to chat. I just want to keep you updated. I know how out of touch a person can feel, just lying around like so much garbage. If you think your girlfriend is gonna bail you out, forget it."

Halsey's head was splitting. "What are you talking about?"

"That's better, El. For a minute there I thought you were losing interest. Your girlfriend and her buddy are planning something they'll regret. You see, they think they're going to get something on me. Dumb, huh? Everybody knows you're the bad guy, El. Seen the news lately?"

Halsey fell back on the pillow. "No."

"Well, you better dig out your remote control, pal. By the time the eleven o'clock headlines roll around, your friends will be history." Rolls of laughter.

Halsey heard the line go dead. His mind wasn't working as fast as it should, but he understood enough. Kate was in trouble. Kate's buddy—it must be Harpo—was in trouble. He had to stop them. Heinman was going to kill them. He had never been more certain of anything in his life.

With all the energy he could summon, he pushed himself forward and swung his feet over the edge of the bed. He forgot about the chest tube until he tried to stand. He felt a twisting motion in his side just before he was hit with a pain so intense that his knees buckled and his vision wobbled. He saw a dim figure racing toward him as he crumpled to the floor. The chest tube came whipping out and fell beside him. Blood drained out of the hole left in his chest wall. The tube hissed uselessly next to him as he moaned and gasped for air. The open chest wound sucked and gurgled like a dying animal.

He heard people shouting, felt them lifting him. He was floating. He fought for consciousness. There was so much he had to do. But his mind would not obey his commands. His vision stopped wobbling. The room went black.

Harpo drove the rental car—a white Ford Escort—while Kate sat with a Jersey road map spread across her lap. "It looks like our turn is in another mile or so." She looked up, surprised at how quickly they had come upon sparsely populated woods so near the turnpike.

"I wonder how this place escaped the strip malls and condos," said Harpo as he eyeballed the tree-marked horizon.

"Give them time. Rome wasn't built—or destroyed—in a day." She pointed ahead. "I'll bet that's our turn. I see a stop sign."

Harpo slowed down, squinting. "Do we want Route Seventeen?"

"Yes. Turn right. Then left at the next intersection, which should be Talcott Lane." Kate's stomach began to churn as they drew closer to Heinman's turf. It was dusk. Heinman was at work. They had checked before taking off. His car was parked in the same spot she had seen it the night before.

They soon found themselves bouncing along a patch of dirt road, searching out a driveway and a house number. Kate cast a nervous glance over her shoulder.

Harpo spotted the place first. "There it is! I see a mailbox—read me the number again."

"Four-five-oh-seven-nine."

He pulled off to the side of the road. "That's it all right. We'd better walk from here."

Kate gathered together her camera bag and a plastic sack full of latex gloves and other paraphernalia. She looked down the road. "Let's park beyond the house. Just in case."

Harpo nodded and pulled back onto the road. She caught the look on his face. His lips were set in a grim line, his eyes fixed on the road. He looked as tense as she felt. At the same time she felt a sense of exhilaration, a headiness, as she anticipated how they were about to turn the tables on Heinman.

They stared down the long driveway as they passed by the ramshackle clapboard house. It was a single story, partially obscured by trees and bushes. The yard was clearly unattended, overgrown with thickets of weeds and unmown grass. There was no sign of life. And no car.

Harpo pulled ahead and parked in a small clearing. Before locking the car, they double-checked to be sure they had everything. Each had a set of car keys in case something happened to the other. Harpo's idea.

Kate saw Harpo lean over and pat his baggy pant leg. "What are you doing?"

"Making sure my knife is secure."

"Your *knife*?" She laughed nervously. "At least it's not a gun."

"Hell, no. You know how many DOAs we see who get shot with their own guns?" He shrugged. "On the other hand, you can never be too prepared."

Kate imagined Heinman's hands shooting out and grabbing Harpo's knife. "I hope you know how to use that thing," was all she said. She slung the camera bag over her shoulder and they trudged back toward the house. She looked around. There appeared to be no neighbors.

Approaching the house they moved with greater caution. Kate could feel her heart rate pick up with each step. She pointed toward the front door and Harpo nodded. They crept slowly toward it, their bodies hunched forward.

Harpo led the way, keeping a tight grip on Kate's wrist as they stepped onto the wooden porch. She saw him wince as the boards creaked under their feet. He reached for the doorknob and turned it. Locked.

They moved around toward the back of the house, stopping to peer through the windows. Kate could see a simple kitchen. The usual cabinets, refrigerator, range, and sink. Through the next window she saw a bedroom with a neatly made bed, a dresser, and a few weights in one corner. She saw a door off the bedroom that she suspected was a closet. The place was so barren it was hard to believe anyone lived there.

Harpo squatted down and tugged at Kate's hand. "Basement," he whispered. There were two small windows at ground level. Kate got down on her hands and knees. The windows were so dirty it was hard to tell much about the basement except that it was squalid, in contrast to the stark cleanliness of the floor above. One window was open a crack and she got a whiff of a strong animal odor mixed with the aroma of ammonia and feces.

"Smells like an animal lab," she whispered, her excitement mounting. She scooted behind Harpo to the second window. Again, it was difficult to see, but this time she caught an unmistakable scent. "Human sweat," she whispered.

"I can't tell," he remarked, sniffing like a dog. "My olfactory nerves got pickled by formaldehyde years ago." He frowned. "What makes you think it's human?"

"It smells like a gym locker full of dirty clothes."

"I'll have to defer to you on that one." He rose to his feet. "I'm going to look around back. Maybe there's a door. Otherwise, we might have to squeeze through this window."

Kate began working at prying open the window. The rusted hinges resisted with a groan. With each tug there was a little give. By the time Harpo returned she had made some progress.

He dropped down beside her. "Good going. One more push and we can slip through." He leaned forward on his hands, got a handhold on the window frame and pushed hard. It gave another inch or two.

They got down on their bellies and gauged the distance. "Not a bad drop," said Harpo. "I'll go first then give you a hand."

"You won't fit, Harpo. Why don't I slide through, then run upstairs and let you in the front door?"

He gave her a long look, as though considering their options. Then looked back at the small opening. He nodded. "Be careful."

She dangled her legs through the opening as he held onto her arms and eased her downward. "Okay," she called. "You can let go."

She dropped onto the cement floor, flexing her knees to absorb the shock. She straightened up and the first thing that hit her was the overwhelming stench of stale urine and excrement. She thought she was going to be sick.

Heinman had parked his car a quarter mile up the road in a little glade, and approached on foot through the trees. He watched the two doctors with amusement as they stole around the house, thinking they were so smart. When they'd almost taken a wrong turn a while back, he'd imagined the looks on their faces had he pulled up beside them and said, "Wrong way."

He saw them fooling with the basement window. He watched Harpo ease Kate Crane through the narrow opening, then tracked Harpo as he moved in a crouch to the front door. Heinman smirked. Been watching too many war movies, Harp.

As Harpo moved along the side of the house, Heinman decided it was time to make his own move.

Kate allowed a moment for her eyes to adjust to the dim light. A wave of nausea came and went as she adjusted to the stench. Images began to take shape. She noticed a bare light bulb overhead. Scraps of rope, stale bread, and soiled dishes were scattered over the floor. The adrenaline surged through her. Clearly someone had been held captive here. She swung the camera bag off her shoulder, extracted the camera, and fumbled around for the flash attachment.

"Kate," Harpo called. "Are you all right?"

"I'm fine. You should see this place."

"I'm circling around to the front door. Come let me in."

"I'll be there in a sec."

She slipped the flash attachment into place and made a sweep of the room, shooting duplicates of each image. She felt uneasy each time she turned her back, unable to shake the fear of someone or something lurking, ready to pounce.

She heard a pounding noise and for a moment thought it was her own heart beat. Then she realized it was Harpo at the door upstairs. She dropped the camera into the bag and hurried out of the room. She stumbled over a pile of wood at the foot of the stairs. She cried out in pain as she felt something sink into the flesh of her lower leg. She looked down and saw a nail had torn through her jeans and embedded itself in her calf.

"Dammit," she muttered. She could hear Harpo pounding more insistently now, calling her name.

"I'll be up in a minute!" she shouted. She gritted her teeth and tore the nail out of her leg. As she felt the blood soak into her jeans she stumbled back into the basement room and snatched up one of the pieces of rope. Despite the brisk bleeding she took a moment to peer into the room's dark corners, caution guiding her eyes like beacons. Seeing nothing, she quickly turned the rope into a tourniquet, tying it just tight enough above the puncture wound to staunch the blood flow.

She went back to picking her way through the debris on the steps. The knocking upstairs had stopped. Harpo was probably furious. She tried to pick up her pace but tripped and grabbed the banister for balance.

She heard a faint rustling somewhere behind her and felt a chill at the base of her neck. She didn't know what it was but she wasn't going to hang around to find out. Limping and out of breath, she finally reached the top of the stairs. She peered into the room, which by now was almost as dim as the basement. She spotted the front entrance. "Harpo?"

No answer. With a sense of urgency she headed toward the door. "Harpo?"

"I'm here." A muffled voice, unmistakably Harpo's. With a sigh of relief she turned the lock and threw open the door.

What happened next came so rapidly she didn't have time to react. Out of nowhere, it seemed, Harpo zoomed toward her like a rocket, his head down. He hit her with such force she went over backward, the air gushing out of her. The door seemed to slam shut of its own accord. As though inanimate, a mere robot, Harpo toppled down next to her, his arm flopping across her chest.

There was something strange about the arm. She studied it in an oddly detached manner as she gasped for air. Then she saw it. The elbow was bent the wrong way. When she saw the deep gash over Harpo's eye and blood dripping down his face, her brain registered the awful truth and she could feel her throat constrict.

She struggled to sit up, still working to breathe. She looked up to see Keith Heinman standing over them, his cold eyes mocking, his arms folded across his chest. Even standing still he seemed to swagger.

"Hi," he said in the same cheerfully derisive tone he used when he came in to clean at night. "You should have told me you were coming. I'd have baked a cake."

Kate stared at him, then looked at Harpo, who was beginning to stir. She couldn't have spoken had she wanted to. Harpo's head had knocked the wind out of her. And her throat felt as though a snake was tightening around it, blocking off her air.

Heinman's cold eyes glided over them. "Did you children have enough time to look around?"

He didn't seem to mind when there was no answer. "That's all right. I'll give you the guided tour." He glanced at his watch. "If you have the time, that is."

Kate quickly assessed Harpo's condition. His face was etched with pain. He was barely conscious. She looked back at Heinman, with the gut feeling their lives—hers and Harpo's—depended on her clarity of mind. She had to throw off her fears. Fight back. Fight for time. And survival. She felt a numbness close in on her, a protective blanket. It was the kind of numbness she remembered feeling at her first autopsy as she watched the pathologist blithely slice into the brain.

Heinman leaned over and grabbed Harpo by his broken arm and pulled him up. "Come on, Harp. Time for the tour."

Harpo let out a piercing cry and Kate struggled to her feet. She started pummeling Heinman's back. "Leave him alone, you . . . animal!"

Heinman let go of Harpo who slumped to the floor. He spun around and grabbed Kate by the wrists, pushing his face within inches of hers. "Don't call me that, bitch."

She saw his lips tremble, flecks of spit spew out of his mouth. It was the first time she had seen him lose his cool. She drew away. Flinching.

Heinman seemed to regain his composure as he watched Kate shrink from him. The cold smile returned. He gave Harpo a sharp kick. Harpo groaned.

"He's useless," Heinman sneered. He grabbed Kate by the elbow and propelled her toward the basement stairs. "Guess it's just you and me, babe." He gave her a shove on the stairs and she grabbed the banister to keep from falling.

"Let's start downstairs. Where you wanted to start anyway. Just couldn't keep your hands off that camera, could you?" He snatched the camera bag. "You won't be needing it." He slung it over his shoulder.

"Stop at the first room on your right, the one you got into through the window. We'll start there."

Kate did as she was told, not missing that Heinman had followed their every move. How foolish to think they could beat the devil at his own game. Harpo had been right. They were rank novices against a beast.

Her mind was her only weapon. In what felt like a moment of reckoning, she could feel the wheels of her mind whirring into motion. She remembered Heinman's rage upstairs. Maybe she could make use of that instability. If she lasted that long.

Heinman gave her a little shove into the room. "This is where Davey Parsons spent his stay. Not exactly The Ritz, but it served its purpose. He didn't seem to like it much though, especially toward the end." He let the word *end* dangle.

She simply nodded and listened. She had no difficulty appearing interested. She saw that Heinman was in a loquacious mood. He needed someone to communicate with—someone to appreciate his cleverness.

He shook his head in mock sorrow. "Dave-boy wasn't very sharp. Just bright enough to talk his way into a position he didn't have the smarts to handle.

His unfortunate demise was his own doing, I'm afraid."

He affected a look of concern. "I know you want to see the rest of the place, so let's move on. Don't worry, we'll be back."

As they moved down a dark narrow hall, the animal odor grew stronger. They came to a closed door and Heinman pushed it open. The stench made her retch.

"Sorry," he chirped. "I have so much to do, I just don't have time to clean the cages. You know how it is—you being a busy doctor and all. Some things just don't get done." He waved a hand toward the cages. "This is the animal lab. I haven't needed them for a while. Almost a year."

She peered into the room. She saw rabbits. No chimps or rats. "Why do you hang on to them?" She didn't really care, but anything to keep him talking. Buy time.

He shrugged, his body relaxing. "Nuisance to get rid of them. I might need them again. I wasn't sure about the proportions at first."

"Proportions?" She could see that Heinman was really getting off talking to her. Then she felt a cold chill that made her heart stand still. If he was willing to be this open, give her the tour, it meant he was planning to kill her. Would *have* to kill her. She had to shut him up, buy time some other way.

She saw he was looking at her. "Yeah," he said, answering a question she wished she hadn't asked. "I wanted to be sure the proportions were right."

He had stopped in the narrow hallway and flicked on an overhead light. It cast eerie shadows that truly made him look mad. He leaned against the wall. They were standing next to a closed door. Kate knew she had to think fast. She remembered his rage upstairs. As frightening as it was, she decided her chances were better if she angered him, to the point of his losing control. Anything was better than that cold calculating scheming he seemed so comfortable with.

She eyed his muscular arms, which he seemed to enjoy displaying as he folded them across his chest and periodically flexed them. She had no hope of over-powering him.

"I lift weights," he said with a knowing smile.

The remark jolted her. She nodded. "You certainly look strong." She tried to bring a hint of admiration to her voice.

As though sensing her duplicity, he calmly reached for her wrist and with his thumb and forefinger pressed hard with a slight twisting motion. "I could snap your arm in two. Just like I did your friend up there." His eyes had lost any trace of animation. She saw the cold look that made his pupils seem three dimensional, reaching out like steel probes.

The tears brimmed in her eyes as she tried to fight the pain. He watched her face, his fingers not letting up. Whatever he saw there seemed to satisfy him. He let go and flung away her arm. The pain was so intense it was all she could do to keep from screaming.

He leaned back against the wall, his body slouched casually. He smiled, the incident forgotten. "Want to see the lab?" His voice sounded inviting, even friendly. His hand went to the doorknob.

She looked at him with dull eyes. She had to make her move. And be ready for the consequences. "I don't give a goddamn about the lab," she said.

She saw the anger flash in his eyes. He threw open the door and grabbed her shoulders, pushing her into the room. "You're going to see it," he snapped.

What she saw made her forget her pain. In the midst of all this decay and horror stood a laboratory facility with the most modern equipment. She saw a biosafety

hood, and a counter lining one wall. It held centri-
fuges, cell counters, incubators, and a small refrigerator. There were shelves above the countertops, lined
with thick texts and racks of test tubes and glass
pipettes.

"Any fool could collect this stuff," she said contemptuously, still hoping to set him off. She brushed
past him and stared into the room, her back to him.
That flicker she saw in his eyes—it had given her a
moment of hope. Maybe there was indeed a way she
could rattle him—enough for him to make a mistake.
She let out a scornful laugh.

He grabbed her by the shoulder and yanked her
back out the lab, slamming the door and moving in
front of it. He was no longer smiling, his face was
pinched with barely controlled fury. She could see he
was struggling not to show her ridicule had affected
him. It was a ray of hope.

He gave her a shove. "Time to go back to Dave's
place. No need for the camera." He swung the camera
bag in front of her, then flung it down the hall.

"What about Harpo?"

"What about him?" He leaned against the doorjamb and moved his eyes over her.

It gave her a strange feeling. His gaze held no sensuality or interest. At least there wasn't that to worry
about. Time was about all she had left. She needed to
keep the conversation going. "People will start wondering where we are. And they'll come here looking
for us."

He pulled a length of thick braided rope off a nail
on the wall and approached her with a scornful laugh.
"The only person who might even come close to
guessing where you are is half comatose. Good old El,
the white knight of Alatron. Looks like you're on your

own, babe." He cut off a length of rope with a pocket knife. "Turn around."

He wrapped the rope around her overlapped wrists and pulled it tight as he knotted it. "Sit down."

She sat, her back toward the corner. This was where Dave Parsons spent the last days of his life. And now here she was. She watched numbly as Heinman squatted down and tied her legs tight at the ankles. She said nothing. And watched.

She saw him notice the bloodstain on her jeans. "Dear me, what happened there?" He looked up at her with mock concern.

"A nail," she said.

"Too bad. That's what happens when you're careless." He rose to his feet and stepped back, surveying his work. He cut another length of rope. "Me, I'm never careless. I think we'll wrap your arms against your chest, too, for good measure." He got down on one knee and circled the rope around her upper arms and torso, pulling it tight enough to restrict her breathing.

"There," he said, springing back up.

"You're making a big mistake."

Suddenly he was in her face, his teeth clenched. "Listen, bitch, I don't make mistakes." He grabbed her wrist again and she could feel his fingers sink deep into her flesh until it felt like they were right on the bone. "Understand?" He worked his fingers deeper, between the bones. The pain was unbearable. *"Understand?"*

She bit her lip, fighting back tears. She nodded.

"Good." He let go and popped back up, turning on his heel, all in one fluid motion. "We'll get your friend down here, don't you fret."

Moments later she heard a sound that made her forget her own pain. A series of anguished cries moving ever closer. Then Harpo's bloodied body came flying through the door as Heinman tossed him around like a sack of flour. As Harpo landed in front of her on the cement floor, she could hear the air whoosh out of him like a bellows.

Heinman followed close behind and gave him a resounding kick. "Next to your girlfriend, scumbag."

He cut a few more lengths of rope and bound Harpo's arms and legs. He dragged him up beside Kate. He didn't seem to take the pleasure in tying up Harpo that he had with her. He was handling Harpo like a bundle of wood—her wonderful Harpo.

"Tour's over, kids." She saw Heinman's eyes come to life as he stood appraising them. "Too bad you won't be around to say goodbye to Elliot. I'll give him your regards."

He disappeared for a moment, then reappeared with raised eyebrows and a grin. He was holding a red gasoline can. Kate remembered Halsey telling her about Heinman's history of arson and she felt a wave of fear that made her gag. She watched as he began pouring the contents around the baseboards. She could tell by the smell that it was indeed gasoline.

The gas had an oddly nostalgic odor that made her flash to her childhood. Her first memory of the smell of gasoline had been on the family trips to the Adirondacks. Her father would pull their old Ford up to the pump. In those days the attendants would scurry attentively around the car, checking the oil, cleaning the windshield, checking the coolant. It was a comforting feeling—being taken care of like that.

Her eyes fell on Harpo and her focus was rudely jerked back to the horror of the present. There was still no sound out of him. He looked dead.

When Heinman finished he stood in the doorway and waved. "By the time your remains are found in the charred wreckage of this firetrap of a house, friend Elliot—good old El—will have paid his final dues." He shook his head. "I wish you could watch it but expediency dictates otherwise. I must say you have presented an entertaining challenge. I will miss you."

With a slight bow, he was gone, splashing gasoline as he left. Kate could hear him moving quickly down the hallway, dousing everything in his path. She heard him whistling in the odd tuneless way he did when he was performing his mundane custodial duties at Alatron. Then she heard him run up the stairs. She guessed he was doing more of the same as she heard footsteps overhead. Soon he would light a match and the whole place would go up like a tinderbox. So much for her strategy.

She could imagine what it would be like, being a human torch. There would be the pain. And the terror of watching death lick its way toward her. Then the smell of her own burning flesh.

She struggled with her bonds. She looked at Harpo. He hadn't stirred. They were both going to die. Burn to death. For a moment she envied him. At least he wouldn't know.

She turned toward him with a tremulous whisper. "Harpo?"

He didn't move. She had turned away when he slowly raised his head and opened his eyes. "He's upstairs, isn't he?"

"Harpo? Harpo! You're alive!"

He straightened up, grimacing with pain. One side of his face was caked with dried blood. "I've had better days."

"My God! I thought you were dead. I thought ..."

He managed a wan smile. "I played dead. With a maniac like that I figured it was my only chance. Stopped my breath for over a minute. And my pulse.

Like a good yogi. He put his filthy hands on my wrist. I'd have strangled him if I'd had the strength."

"Your arm . . ."

"It's shattered." He rattled his head. "And my head feels like a pit bull's been gnawing on it."

Kate felt her hope return. She wasn't in it alone. "Any ideas, Harpo?"

"Boy scouts are always prepared," he said with a cryptic smile.

She gave him a second look. Then came a loud explosion, followed by a roar of flames overhead. And through it all, gales of raucous laughter.

CHAPTER TWENTY-SIX

Kate Crane and Harpo Cosgrove realized they were going to die. Painfully. Slowly. Death by fire. You could die by asphyxiation, or die as your blood rose to a boil and your brain raged with terror.

They had no choice, and they knew it. The roar and crackle of the blaze assailed their ears as the fire doggedly sought them out. They could hear the crash of falling beams, joists, and floorboards as the very structure of the house above them succumbed to the relentless path of the conflagration.

Fire had a mind of its own, and they knew it was only a matter of time before it swept its way down the stairs to consume them. Well before they spotted the flames the stifling heat was baking their skin, the smoke stinging and blistering their nostrils and clouding their vision.

Finally the blaze roared into the room where they were held captive. They turned their heads with morbid fascination as the wall of fire raged toward them—a red-tongued agent of death. The fire seemed to breathe and pulsate with a life of its own as it puffed and whooshed each time it swirled over the pools of gasoline.

They strained at the ropes that bound them, knowing it was hopeless. Finally, they stopped struggling and ducked their heads, shrinking from death. The flames lapped at their clothes, their skin, their hair. And their souls.

In a final ironic moment, the ropes burned away and their arms broke free. They raised their hands in futile prayer.

Then they were gone, their cries swallowed up by the sound and fury of the fire.

Heinman was intoxicated by the vividness of the immolation as he imagined it over and over. He quivered deliciously to the thrill of his own power. As he drove back to Alatron his eyes were on the road, but what he saw was the house as it shot up in flames. It was electrifying. His mind drank in the pure wizardry of what he had done as he imagined again the final tortured moments of the two wretches inside the blazing tinderbox. He wished he could have stayed to watch. It would have been most satisfying. But the way he saw and heard and smelled and touched and tasted it in his mind's eye was even better.

Besides, he had to get back to Alatron. And he couldn't wait to tell Elliot. It was time, he decided, to do it face to face. No more phone calls.

He had been waiting a long time, over ten years, to squash Halsey. Missing a big part of the fun by confining himself to phone calls. Seeing the fire brought that home. He wanted to *watch* Halsey react, *watch* him squirm helplessly while Heinman told him in painstaking detail how the two meddling doctors had died.

As he approached the Alatron complex he made

his decision. He would stop in, yak it up with a couple of the janitors to establish an alibi, then head over to Memorial Hospital. He knew the place well enough, had checked it out before he ever started at Alatron.

He found himself chuckling. He had thought of everything. Then, without warning, his hands tightened on the steering wheel as he felt a cold wind of rage whistle through him. Amid the images of the two doctors turning to cinders had sprung the visage of Elliot Halsey staring him down in the courtroom. For a decade that image had both tormented and driven him.

With great effort he returned his thoughts to the fire and its victims, and he could feel his grip on the steering wheel relax. He settled himself into thinking exactly how he would spring the news on Halsey. It suddenly came to him. Of course. Flowers.

Kate grabbed Harpo's good arm as they ran for the trees. She shot a glance over her shoulder as the house blew. It was like a volcanic eruption—loud, hot, massive. Its force sent debris flying. A flaming board sailed over their heads. They ran harder. Kate thought her lungs would burst. He legs were about to give out.

When they got far enough into the woods to feel a measure of safety, they collapsed. Kate gasped for air and watched Harpo lying on his back, his eyes closed, his chest rising and falling crazily. His face was black with soot. His hair was clotted with blood. His arm was bent the wrong way. He was a mess. But alive. Suddenly she started laughing hysterically.

Harpo turned his head. "What the . . ." was all he could manage.

"The amazing . . . rubber man . . ." she squeezed out between fits of laughter. All she could think of— no, she couldn't think—all she could see was a circus show where flames and mad stunts were the main attraction. For somehow Harpo had gotten free.

She had thought they were both goners. Then she'd watched Harpo take a deep breath, as though meditating. She remembered thinking it was his way of praying. Last rites as the flames moved closer. The next she knew he had his hands out of the ropes and, one-handed, was untying her wrists.

The rest was a blur. Now she was here, in the woods, having survived an ordeal she never dreamed could happen. Not to her. Nor to the amazing rubber man beside her. "How did you do it, Harpo?"

He reached his good arm up and flexed his wrist, making his thumb touch his arm, as she had seen him do so many times before. "Simple," he said. "I used the yoga and meditation to control my pain and convince Heinman I was already done for. It worked. He was a bit careless with the ropes. Didn't notice the odd position of my thumb when he bound my wrists. Once I slipped the thumb out, the rest was easy."

"Simple," she echoed. Madness. She closed her eyes and laughed. Tears flowed down her grimy cheeks.

Harpo rolled toward her. He grabbed her shoulder and shook her. "Kate, get hold of yourself."

She turned on her side and embraced him, breaking into sobs. She buried her head in his chest. He brushed away the strands of hair clinging to her cheeks. And held her.

After a while they looked back at the demolished house. The flames were dying out, having consumed the fuel Heinman fed them.

Harpo spoke first. "God almighty, Kate," he whispered. "For a time there I thought it was the end."

She sat up and wiped at her tears with the back of her hand. "You saved my life, Harpo."

He laughed weakly. "We were lucky."

Lucky. Sure. Making a man who was never careless and who never made mistakes go against his grain. It was more than luck.

Harpo grimaced as Kate reached over and gently touched his arm. "Ow! Watch the arm."

"I'll make a splint for you."

"Okay. It's really beginning to throb." He struggled to a sitting position. "I think it's time to turn the matter of Mr. Heinman over to the police, Kate. This guy is a loose cannon. I, for one, don't care for any more tours. Christ."

She stared back at the fire. "Harpo, please. No police yet." Her eyes narrowed. "Heinman told me something about myself. He was right on."

He raised his eyebrows. "Oh, really? Maybe I should ask him to read my palm."

She ignored the barb. "He said he knew I wouldn't go to the police because it had become personal."

Harpo groaned. "Yeah, I take it personally when some lunatic tries to barbecue me."

She gave him an imploring look. "Please, be serious. I want to get him. I don't want the police. I want him to think his scheme worked—that we're dead."

Harpo seemed to be mulling the idea over as Kate inspected his arm. "And," she added, "I want you to go back to New York. I've already caused you enough trouble. I couldn't live with myself if anything more happened to you."

He frowned. "Kate, I'll make a deal with you. We'll brainstorm on this thing. If we can come up with a realistic way of nabbing him without help, I'll go along with you. In return, you have to put up with me. There's no chance on God's earth I'd let you go up against this guy alone. *Especially* now."

She looked at Harpo. She looked at the house. She thought of Elliot Halsey, helpless in a hospital bed.

She thought about the AIDS vaccine, the deaths from Congo Fever. And she thought of Akendo Maury. A bitter chill coursed through her that would make any fire quail.

"A deal," she said.

"You can't go in there, sir," said the young cop, spreading his long arms like wings as he blocked the entrance to Halsey's room. His gesture was so automatic by now, he hadn't taken the time to look at the man who was trying to pass.

The man, smartly dressed in a three-piece suit, gave him a wounded look. The eyes drew the cop's attention more than anything, though the bouquet of flowers was the most lavish he had ever seen. The eyes were stark blue and seemed to look right through him. There was something about the eyes that made him uncomfortable, but he couldn't say what. Nobody had ever looked at him like that.

The man made a concessionary step backward, at the same time peeking around the shoulder of the cop. "Is he asleep?"

The cop shot a quick glance at the patient. "He's resting. But that's not why you can't go in. No visitors allowed."

The cop dropped his arms to his sides. The visitor's manner seemed alien to what the cop thought he had seen in the eyes. He decided he must have misread them.

"Listen," said the man, frowning as he continued to peek into the room. "Elliot's my brother. We haven't spoken in years. It's my fault. I've got to make it up to him."

He sighed, bowing his head as he looked down at the flowers. "When I heard what happened, it hit me.

I realized how much he means to me. That's why I'm here."

He gave the cop a pleading look. "He's my brother." He plucked a flower from the bouquet and offered it with a smile. "Please. I won't stay long."

The cop took the flower, twirled it in his fingers for a moment, then handed it back. He glanced down the empty corridor. He shifted his weight, clearing his throat.

"All right. But make it quick and if I say go, you're out on the double. Got it?"

"Got it." The man smiled. He brushed past the cop with a nod.

As he approached the bed, he saw that Halsey was indeed resting. His eyes were closed. There was a fine patina of sweat on his forehead. Plastic tubing fed oxygen into his nose and there was another tube sticking into the side of his chest. He was in bad shape.

Heinman felt his hands tingle. It was the first time in a decade he had seen Halsey close up—in the flesh. Sure, there had been the occasional encounter in the hallway, like the time Halsey had rested his hand on Heinman's shoulder and requested he clean up the broken glass in the board room. That didn't count. It was nothing like this. Halsey hadn't known who he was then. This time he would.

Heinman realized he wasn't prepared for how it would feel, after all these years. He had been picking and gnawing at the man and soon he would be ready for the kill. But he had never thought how seeing Halsey sprawled out helplessly on a bed before him would affect him. The feeling was so violently satisfying it was almost sexual in its intensity.

He pulled up a chair close to the bed. He reached out and laid a hand on Halsey's shoulder. Halsey's eyes blinked open. It took Halsey a moment to focus and shift his gaze toward the source of the hand. He gave Heinman a blank look.

Heinman laid the flowers on Halsey's blanket. "Hi, El," he said softly. "It's your brother. Keith." He sat back and crossed his legs, smiling as he let his presence sink in.

Halsey thought he heard someone address him, but he wasn't sure. He had been drifting in and out of a twilight of wakefulness for what seemed forever, his mind suffused by fog. Sometimes the fog was thick and impenetrable, other times he could feel his thoughts reach through it, on the verge of finding a fixed point but never quite making it.

He was aware of pain all over his body, but whenever he brought his mind into focus, the pain seemed to focus, too, especially above the waist. His head felt like a melon being split open by a cleaver. When the pain was at its worst, he would break out in a cold sweat, but even in his hazy drugged state he knew this feeling was driven by something more than physical duress. It was something the fog wouldn't let him see, something he didn't want to see. Something that someone had said to him. Something about Kate Crane. Something bad.

He kept seeing Keith Heinman, kept hearing the voice on the phone, envisioning the cruel bearded face just inches from his own, seeing the look of hatred sparking across the courtroom of not so long ago. He saw Heinman laughing at him, and with each gale of laughter Heinman's visage would change. One time with a beard, then clean-shaven. Now wearing a T-shirt, next impeccably dressed in a suit. Now with a knife, next proffering a bouquet of flowers.

When the image of Heinman seemed most real, Halsey would feel his fists clench, his whole body tensing. He would hear himself cry out with anguish so deep he thought his heart would shatter. At these times a faceless nurse would approach him with a needle that loomed as large as a spear, and then he would feel the fog move in again, profound and stultifying.

Heinman, aware of the cop pacing impatiently, decided he could not afford the luxury of watching Halsey's struggle any longer. He had seen Halsey catch a glimpse of him, then draw back into himself, and he was enjoying imagining all that Halsey was suffering. He was holding back on his announcement until he was sure Halsey was alert enough to comprehend its significance.

Now he leaned forward, his mouth close to Halsey's ear. He lightly swept the bouquet across Halsey's face. "El," he whispered. "It's your pal Keith. Brought you a present, and some news."

Halsey's eyes fluttered open and moved toward the voice. This wasn't a dream. Suddenly the fog lifted as he looked at Heinman, all at once knowing beyond a doubt who this clean-shaven man in the dark suit was. Like a drunk who has just been jolted out of a stupor when his car rams a tree, Halsey felt his thoughts crystallize, transcending all the pain, the drugs, the denial. He had never felt more alert in his life.

He knew he was staring. He was seeing Keith Heinman for the first time in ten years. The beard was gone, as was the long hair. But the eyes had not changed. Nor had the cruel lips. It was the same man, even more menacing after the years of hatred eroding his soul.

Suddenly Halsey felt nothing, as though he had just stepped into a vacuum. It was an odd sensation. Just as the noncolor white is a reflection of all colors, his sense of nothingness felt like a bizarrely bland culmination of every possible feeling. Yet none of them registered. His eyes remained blankly fixed on Heinman's face.

Heinman stared back. He was fascinated to watch how the beginning of a realization filtered first from the eyes to the brain, then back to the face, giving it a telling expressiveness. He thought he could spot the exact moment when Halsey realized who his visitor was. There was an almost palpable energy that surged between the two men.

Heinman tossed the bouquet onto the bed. "Save these for the funeral. Your two friends and their so-called evidence have gone up in smoke." He snapped his fingers. "Just like that. Poof!" He sat back and laughed.

The numbness growing in Halsey's stomach now spread into his chest and down his arms. "You're lying." His voice was a hoarse whisper. He took his eyes off Heinman and stared at the ceiling.

"Have I ever lied to you, El?" Heinman extracted a flower from the bouquet and began plucking off the petals one by one. "He lies to me, he lies not, he lies to me, he lies not . . ."

Halsey felt his energy drain from him in sync with each petal that Heinman removed from the flower. He knew Heinman wasn't lying.

Bored, Heinman tossed the flower onto the bed. "El, you disappoint me. Doesn't it bother you that you're responsible for so much suffering?"

As Halsey's eyes drooped the cop tapped Heinman on the shoulder. "Five minutes." He moved back to his post by the door.

"Hear that, El? Only five minutes to tell you that your life might as well be over. But you already know that, don't you?" Heinman shook his head as he made a clucking noise. "Five minutes to fill you in on ten years. Doesn't seem fair, does it?"

He watched Halsey's respiratory rate pick up, but he was beginning to feel annoyed. Halsey wasn't reacting enough. Heinman's eyes narrowed as he studied the situation. He took in all the tubes and IVs attached to Halsey and zeroed in on the chest tube that disappeared into the flesh of Halsey's side. He reached forward and twisted the tube, at the same time giving it a slight tug. He saw Halsey's breath catch and his eyes fly open in a panicked stare.

"Ah, that's better. Now I have your attention." Heinman kept a hand on the tube. When Halsey didn't respond, he gave it another yank. Halsey bit his lip and Heinman watched the sweat trickle down the side of his face.

Finally, Halsey took a shaky breath and nodded. He looked at Heinman.

"Good boy." Heinman leaned close, his eyes gleaming. "You know what it's like, El? Rotting your life away in a hospital for psychos?" He gave the tube a sharp jerk. "I asked you a question, El."

Heinman went on, not waiting for Halsey's reaction. Halsey just lay there, marshalling his strength, watching the eyes, which now seemed almost hypnotic. "Ten years in a snake pit, El, surrounded by the dregs of humanity. Guys whose biggest thrill is picking their nose. Deranged slobs who don't know real life from the boob tube. Most of them pathetic blobs of protoplasm, about as sharp as a pithed frog."

Heinman leaned closer, his voice soft. "Ten long years. Nobody to talk to. The psychiatrists dumber than the inmates. Gives a man time to think. Know what I mean?"

Halsey turned his head away and stared at the ceiling. Heinman sawed the tube back and forth, gloating as he watched Halsey's face screw up with pain. He began to laugh, a low, nasty chuckle. Halsey didn't make a sound, other than short gasps for air.

"Well, I hate to go, but I've got to get to work. I really appreciate the job at Alatron, you know. It's opened up all kinds of doors." Heinman stood up, still laughing. "Hey, El. Look at me."

Halsey gave him a sidelong glance.

Heinman winked. "Too bad about that CDC bitch. I'll bet she was good in bed...."

What happened next was so unexpected that Heinman was momentarily paralyzed. Empowered by a frenzy of pain and fury, Halsey lunged out of the bed with an agonized cry. His shoulder caught Heinman in the neck and knocked Heinman's chair over. The two of them crashed to the floor with Halsey landing on top of Heinman. The chest tube tore out but Halsey was barely aware of the pain. As the two men sprawled on the floor, Halsey grabbed the tube and pinned it against Heinman's neck.

Heinman's arms flailed, first grasping for Halsey to pull him off. But Halsey was unmovable. Heinman then clawed at the tube but was unable to make it budge. Halsey was using all his weight to keep it there. It was biting hard into Heinman's windpipe, cutting off his air. He kicked his legs wildly.

"Hey! Break it up!" The cop came charging into the room and pulled Halsey off Heinman. He dragged Halsey back onto the bed. Heinman lay in a heap gasping and tugging at his collar.

The cop dropped to his haunches beside Heinman and slapped his face. "Hey, buddy. You okay?" The visitor's color was a grayish blue, the eyes devoid of expression.

A nurse came bustling in and attended to Halsey who lay gasping on the bed. "What's going on here?" she barked at the cop.

The cop helped Heinman to his feet, ignoring the nurse who had turned back to Halsey. "I think you'd better leave now." He took the visitor's arm.

Heinman stood up and brushed off his suit, rolled his head and squared his shoulders. He concentrated on slowing his breathing and felt his sense of control return. He managed a smile. "What can I say? Like the Bible says, 'A brother offended is harder won than a strong city.'"

Heinman took one last look at Halsey over his shoulder. He turned to the cop. "Please tell my brother I'll never forget this."

CHAPTER TWENTY-SEVEN

Heinman leaned back in the rickety chair, his feet propped up on the bed. He was snacking on a bag of potato chips as he watched the evening news. He missed nothing about the house, not even the lab. It had served its purpose. He found the motel accommodations more than acceptable, particularly the television. It provided him the luxury of watching the highlights of Alatron's demise sooner than he could find it in the paper.

The newscaster, a garrulous, pasty-faced cretin who called himself Art Weaver, reminded him of Dave Parsons. He felt an odd emptiness at the memory. He missed good old Dave. Like right now, he would have enjoyed chewing the fat with Dave about the news.

He felt the same way about the CDC bitch. He had enjoyed watching her face when she saw his lab. But she was history. And Elliot Halsey was too zoned out to appreciate what was going on, though he, Heinman, had gotten some satisfaction out of his little visit the other day. Despite, or perhaps because of, Halsey's assault on him. Even if it had left him with a sore neck.

He turned up the volume with the remote control as the ad for a local car dealership wrapped up. Art Weaver had promised a live exclusive interview with Abraham Feldman of the CDC. Should be high entertainment.

Sure enough, the white-haired Feldman came on the screen. Weaver glowed. "We're pleased to have with us tonight Dr. Abraham Feldman of the Centers for Disease Control and Prevention in Atlanta. Dr. Feldman heads the investigatory team looking into the cause of viral contamination of the AIDS vaccine at Alatron Pharmaceutical Company."

The camera closed in on Feldman smiling sagely, then panned to both men.

"Dr. Feldman," said Weaver, "we understand the CDC is expecting a major breakthrough in the case."

Heinman's hand stopped probing the chip bag. What was this? He had been tracking their moves pretty well and he knew nothing of any breakthroughs.

Feldman nodded. "That is correct," said Feldman in a deep, resonant voice. His air of confidence both intrigued and annoyed Heinman. He set the bag of chips aside.

"And what is your opinion of the problem, Doctor? There's talk of sabotage."

A slip of a smile crossed Feldman's face. "No sabotage, Mr. Weaver. We think there may be a defect in one of the filters where the Congo virus is kept."

"Meaning what?"

"Meaning the opportunity exists for the virus to escape into the area where the AIDS vaccine is manufactured. We have yet to figure out how the virus insinuated itself into the vaccine and why no employees are sick. The company's quality control is exceptional."

Heinman sat upright, dropping his feet to the floor. "You stupid idiots."

Weaver, the cretin, went merrily on. "Might the fault be in Alatron's production line?"

A solemn Feldman shook his head. "We've found no evidence of this. Alatron has an impeccable laboratory, among the best I've encountered. The company's standards are high, far and above Food and Drug Administration requirements."

Heinman was on his feet now, pacing the small room as he muttered to himself. "What the hell is this? Halsey must be paying this jerk." He felt his anger building, eating at his brain.

He stopped and looked at himself in the mirror and took a few deep breaths, spreading his arms to watch his pectoral muscles ripple under the thin T-shirt. It didn't help. He felt like blowing up the two idiots on the tube.

"Sabotage is out then?" said the first idiot, Weaver.

"We believe so," said Feldman in his ponderous way. "Our energies will be directed at determining how contamination could have sifted through the intricate surveillance system set up by the company and its able leader Elliot Halsey."

"You dumb jerks!" Heinman flung the remote control across the room where it shattered against the wall. These jokers didn't have a glimmer.

He kicked the chest of drawers, his rage rocketing. "Fools!" He looked down at his hand. It was shaking. He threw himself on the bed, torn between watching what this stuffed shirt from the CDC might say next and heaving the television through the wall.

"What about the murder of Alatron executive David Parsons, Dr. Feldman? Elliot Halsey is still the prime suspect. We understand he'll be taken into custody as soon as he's discharged from the hospital."

Feldman appeared to slide the question. "Criminal acts of this nature are not our province."

"You don't believe the murder and the contamination are related?"

"No." Feldman sat up. His face said the interview was over.

Weaver persisted. "Even though the murder victim headed up the project you're investigating? Isn't this an extraordinary coincidence?"

Feldman nodded. "Extraordinary."

Heinman watched with disgust. Any fool could see Feldman wasn't going to talk. What he needed was a good kick in the ass. Heinman got to his feet and punched the off button on the television so hard that the back of the set crashed against the wall.

He was restless, not quite knowing what to make of the interview. Was Feldman sitting on something? He paced the room like a caged animal, muttering to himself.

All at once the room seemed intolerably small and oppressive. He decided to go out for a paper.

Abe Feldman left the studio and entered the cubbyhole of a room where the station's guests waited before going on the air. He wiped his brow with a handkerchief. "Well?"

Kate, a bit worse for the wear, rose to greet him. She grabbed him by the shoulders. "You were great, Abe. I owe you one."

He sat down and poured himself a cup of coffee, refilling Kate's cup. "Kate, I still find it hard to believe. It's unreal. Like something out of *Weird Tales*."

He gave her a look of paternal concern and took her hand, inspecting a rope-burned wrist. "These marks are real enough." He gently returned her hand to her lap and studied her blistered lips and singed eyebrows. He chuckled. "I never thought I'd be saying this to you, Kate. But you look like hell."

She started to smile but winced instead. Her lips felt like a cat's claw was being dragged across them.

Feldman held up his hand. "If you're willing to risk your life to catch a killer, I suppose I can stretch the truth a bit on TV." He sipped his coffee. "You owe me nothing."

"Thank you, Abe. I'm betting our man was watching with great interest."

Feldman frowned and wiped his brow again. "Where is this Dr. Cosgrove?"

"He has an orthopedic appointment. Heinman shattered his arm."

Feldman sighed and regarded her thoughtfully. "What now, Kate? You have a diabolical look."

Her lips slowly widened into a smile. This time she didn't notice the pain. She was too embroiled in an emotional balancing act. She could almost taste the thrill of victory. But she knew all too well the meaning of defeat. If she lost to Heinman this time, she would not come out alive.

"Something for Mr. Heinman," she said, her voice quivering. "Call it a taste of his own medicine."

Heinman finished the evening paper with a degree of satisfaction. There was an interview with that moron, Roger Peck, who hovered around like a parasite, trying to grab all the headlines. Still at odds with the CDC, in particular Kate Crane. The paper referred to a competitive spirit between the CDC and Fort Thacker, but Heinman knew it was more personal than that.

There were no quotes from Abe Feldman, and no mention of any breakthroughs. Odd. He shrugged it off. The front page was predictably devoted to rumblings of war in the Middle East and rioting at a rock concert where twenty people were trampled to death. He smiled. Man against man. A theme he could relate to.

He tossed the paper onto the bed and flipped on the twenty-four-hour news station, a distraction while he worked his weights. The weights, heavier than himself, were prized possessions. He had stowed them in the trunk of his car along with the three-piece suit before torching the house.

He slipped off his T-shirt and stood before the mirror and smiled. He decided he definitely liked himself more without a beard. He looked youthful, masterful.

He began limbering up with a few arm stretches and deep breathing before launching into his workout. As he was finishing his warm-up, the jangle of the phone interrupted his trancelike state. Annoyed, he scooped up the receiver and snapped, "Who is it?"

He could have sworn he heard a laughing sound. Then, "Why, Keith, you sound upset. It's not like you." Her voice was smooth, even velvety, the mockery unmistakable.

"What?" He dropped onto the bed, the sense of invincibility he had so carefully achieved during his workout completely shattered. His thoughts darted in all directions. He felt a cold wrenching in his gut. He felt his world tilting. What he was hearing simply couldn't be.

His mind flashed back to the fire. Yes, it *had* happened. He had *seen* the house disintegrate in his rearview mirror. He had *heard* it explode through the closed windows of his car. He felt the wrenching in his gut ease slightly.

"Who is this?" he snarled.

"You already asked that question, Keith. Don't repeat yourself. You *know* who it is, don't you?"

Yes, he knew. But it was impossible. A trick. It had to be. He snatched up the shirt he had tossed onto the bed and worked himself into it. He felt a little less exposed, less naked.

"Keith? You're not afraid, are you?" Her voice was as smooth as silk. She was laughing at him. Nobody laughed at him. Nobody.

"Of *you*?" He held the receiver away and stared at it. He wished he could reach into it and grab her neck, snap it in two. He pressed the receiver back to his ear, his eyes flitting around the room. How did she know where he was? Assuming it *was* her. How *could* it be her?

"Don't you want to know how I found you, Keith?"

Yes, among other things, he wanted to know. But he wasn't about to let her think he gave a damn. "No," he snapped. "Just state your business."

"Gladly. I'd like to tell you, but it can wait."

He caught a disconcerting glimpse of himself in the mirror. His face was drawn and pinched, his eyes dull. He jerked away, feeling disjoined in some strange way. His hand began to shake.

"Keith? Are you there?"

"I'm here, bitch," he fumed, at the same time furious with himself at letting the crack in his armor show.

"Really, Keith. I thought you were above name-calling."

He lurched off the bed, out of the way of the goddamn mirror. He began deep-breathing, struggling for control. Watching with a growing muddle of anger and fear as his hand kept shaking. He shoved it into his pocket. It hadn't shaken like that since he left Woodlawn.

"Keith," came the voice, sweetly condescending. "No need to get all riled up. I just called to tell you that you're right."

He felt his grip on the receiver let up ever so slightly, just enough to ease the tremor. "About what?"

"About yourself. You see, you're *not* crazy, Keith. Just stupid."

The tremor worsened. He gripped the receiver tighter. "Explain yourself, b-bi . . ." He almost said it again, but swallowed the word this time. He heard the cold fury in his voice and reined it in. He could handle this bitch.

"Explain yourself," he repeated, this time his tone cool and steady.

"Of course," she said. "First, I'm still around, aren't I? You tie me and my partner up, set the house on fire, and presto! We're still here." A soft chortle. "Very, very stupid, Keith."

It took him a moment to respond. But he was adjusting to the fact that she was indeed alive. "Actually," he sneered, "I'm glad you're still around. Next time you won't be so lucky." He even managed a short laugh. He felt his confidence returning. That's what she was trying to destroy. Just like everybody else in this hellhole of a world. He squared his shoulders and gave himself an approving look in the mirror.

"There isn't going to be a next time, Keith. I'm going back to Atlanta. The case has been solved. There will be no more deaths. Which brings me to my next point."

"Don't think I don't know what you're trying to do," he said with a studied contempt, continuing to watch himself and preen before the mirror.

Her voice was clearly mocking now, as his so often was. "There never was any sabotage, Keith. It's all a little fantasy in your sick head. You're too stupid to pull off anything that clever."

He bit his lip. His hand shook. "You're lying."

"Am I? Watch the news, read the papers. Talk to Abe Feldman."

"You're lying."

"And you're boring. I'm through now."

He felt a tremor at the prospect of her breaking their connection when she thought she was ahead. "Maybe I'm not through with you," he shot back.

She laughed. "Give me a reason I should care."

He grinned as a thought struck him. So obvious. "You wouldn't want to be responsible for your friend Elliot dying, would you?"

He caught the pause before she replied. He had her. His grin widened at his image in the mirror.

"I didn't think you were *that* stupid, Keith. He and I are history. It was never serious."

"Now I know you're lying."

"Suit yourself. I'm leaving for Atlanta in the morning. Oh, and by the way. I figured, after burning up your own house, you would check into a motel near Alatron. It took me only two calls to find you. See what I mean? Stupid. Goodbye, Keith."

With that, the phone went dead. He held the receiver away from him again and stared at it in disbelief. The bitch hung up on him! He slammed down the phone and moved fitfully around the room, not knowing how to put it together. So many questions. How had she gotten free? She was alive all right, and flaunting it in his face. Did she really believe they had an answer or was she baiting him? He had to know.

He flopped down on the bed and laced his hands behind his head, staring at the random patterns in the ceiling. His mind raced. He sat up and looked at the paper, the germ of an idea forming.

He leaped off the bed, and, with a thrill resonating up his spine, decided with certainty that Kate Crane would not be going back to Atlanta.

*   *   *

When Kate hung up, she had to consciously relax her hand to pry her fingers from the receiver. As the tension eased she sat back and cast a glance at Harpo. Her heart was pounding so hard she could see the folds of her blouse rise and fall with her pulse.

"Harpo," she said, sweeping the hair off her forehead. "That was the toughest thing I've ever done."

"And you couldn't have done a better job," he said, a tone of pride in his voice. "You were cool and controlled."

She gave a hollow laugh. "I think I got his attention. Imagine the shock of having someone return from the dead—and mock you. He did trip me up, though. About Elliot."

"Yeah, I saw you hesitate. But don't worry, Elliot's safe as long as he's in the hospital." Harpo drummed his fingers on his knee. "With a police guard at that."

She eyed his cast and was struck again with how lucky they both were. She felt a tight knot forming in her chest and swallowed hard. "Now comes the hard part. Waiting."

"Something neither of us is very good at."

She nodded, unable to take her mind off Elliot. What if she had been wrong about Heinman? What if, instead of causing him to step into the open and expose himself, her taunting call set him off on a murderous rampage to Elliot's bedside? She knew Heinman had gotten past the cop once already. And that Heinman had told Elliot she was as good as dead. She wanted to keep it that way, for now—keep Elliot in the dark. She was afraid he would do something crazy if he believed she was still alive with Heinman at large. "You're worried about Elliot, aren't you?" Harpo said, as though reading her mind.

She looked down at her lap. "Yes."

He sighed. "I could see the writing on the wall from

the moment you two set eyes on each other. He probably knows it, but he's one lucky guy, having a woman like you in his corner."

She watched him stand up and cross to the window of her hotel room, a thoughtful frown knitting his brow. "We're gonna nail this maniac, Kate. I can feel it. Mike O'Day, my detective friend, Fed Exed two 'electronic eavesdropping' devices. If Heinman shoots his mouth off again like he started to at the house, we'll have it on tape. You'll have all the proof you need." He turned toward her. "There's one problem that keeps gnawing at me, though."

She studied Harpo's grim expression and felt the goose bumps pop out on her arms. She knew what he was thinking. "You mean Heinman's plans for me?"

He nodded gravely. "Let's face it—you're walking proof he's a failure." He sat beside her. "Let's not underestimate the man, Kate. You saw where that got us. We're dealing with a twisted sadistic mind."

"I'll be ready," she said with more conviction than she felt. She heard a calculating coldness in her voice that frightened her.

"But ready for what? He's probably already anticipating your every move, including the ones you haven't thought of yet." Harpo took a deep breath. "The guy's uncanny, Kate. If he does take your bait we should get Mike here. I've already spoken to him. He'll come at the drop of a hat. He's an ex-cop, sharp as a tack. As medical examiner, I've worked with him for years. And he owes me a favor or two."

She started to object, then realized the wisdom in what he was saying. "Your friend's retired from the police force?"

"A year ago. Now he's one of the best private eyes in the city." He put his arm around her. "It's the only way to go, Kate. Heinman's not going to make the same mistake twice."

She felt tears rush to her eyes and buried her face in the hollow of his shoulder. Harpo stroked her hair and whispered, "It'll be okay."

She sat up and looked at him with misty eyes. "Harpo, I must be crazy. I can't ask you to go through with this."

He placed a finger under her chin and tilted it up. "We have a deal. Remember?"

"Yes," she said gratefully. "I do."

CHAPTER TWENTY-EIGHT

Unable to concentrate, Kate tossed aside the paper and turned on the television. After flipping through thirty-some channels, she shut it off and glanced at her watch. Nearly two hours since she had talked to Heinman. Had she been wrong about him? She wished Harpo was still here.

She walked over to the closet and contemplated her suitcase, giving serious consideration to pulling it out and packing. Maybe she should go back to Atlanta. Let Abe finish up. But there was still Elliot.

The phone rang and she sprang for it. She stood over it and let it ring once more before picking it up. "Hello?"

"Hi, Doc."

She felt her flesh crawl. It was him. He sounded perfectly at ease, in control.

"Hello, Keith."

"You need some facts."

She managed a caustic laugh. "You're the last person I would consult."

"Cut the bullshit, babe. You're dying to know what happened to the vaccine."

She couldn't believe her ears. He was nibbling at the end of her line. All she had to do was reel him in. "And if you had anything to do with it, why would you want to tell me, Keith?"

"Let's say I don't like being called stupid."

She felt a giddy elation that she managed to keep out of her voice. "And just how do you propose to persuade me otherwise?"

"When you see, you'll know."

"I get it. You have something to show me." She paused, not wanting to ruin it. "And how do I know it's not a trap?"

"You'll have to take that chance, won't you? Bring bodyguards if you want. But what I show you is for your eyes and ears alone."

"Fair enough. Where do we meet?"

"The BSC Four lab. Bodyguards stay outside."

She sat down, her knees wobbly. He wasn't going to make it easy. The maximum-containment lab. By herself, with a madman. Now, as she felt her heart trying to catapult out of her chest, she was thankful for Harpo and his foresight.

"When?"

"Two hours."

Now her stomach churned as her heart kept thudding. Barely enough time for Harpo's friend to get here. "Make it three," she said.

A moment of silence. She held her breath.

"Two, or forget it."

Her eyes darted around the room, as though seeking an answer. She couldn't blow it now. Not after all she'd been through. "I'll be there," she said.

The phone clicked in her ear. She dialed Harpo's number, her hands shaking.

"Hello?" He sounded sleepy.

"Harpo, he took the bait. I'm to meet him in two hours. The BSC Four lab."

"Don't move. I'll be right there."

Heinman hung up, smiling. She fell for it. What's more, she thought it was her idea.

He stood up and stretched. Time to get ready. He grabbed his bag of goodies and took the elevator from the maintenance department to the fourth floor. He pulled out the security card that got him into the BSC Four lab. He quickly dressed into scrubs in the outer dressing room and went through to the inner dressing room where he climbed into the bulky space suit. By now, he was comfortable with the routine.

He passed through the airlock and on into the lab, full of its deadly viruses, the ones that had done the job. Genetic allies. He laughed to himself.

He plugged into an air source and looked around to make sure no one else was there. Not a soul. He set to work. He knelt down and removed a gallon container from a cupboard beneath one of the worktables. He gathered a half-dozen empty flasks from the shelf above. He poured the formaldehyde into the flasks, filling each one about halfway. He then removed the strips of cloth from the plastic bag he had brought. He twisted the strips tightly before jamming them down into the flasks, checking to make sure the material made contact with the liquid. When he was done, he placed the flasks, along with the gallon container, back in the floor-level cupboard.

He stood up and studied his handiwork with satisfaction, then closed the cupboard door. Before he left he took one last look around to be sure he'd left no trace.

Satisfied, he headed through the airlock and on into the chemical shower. He was ready.

*   *   *

Harpo brought the bugging devices to Kate's room. She held the two tiny metal items in her hand, inspecting them as she might shells on the beach. "These are amazing," she exclaimed. "They look like buttons."

"Smart buttons," said Harpo.

She thought of the space suits and the hissing air. "How sensitive are they?"

"Mike assures me they'll pick up your voices. He suggested sewing them into a seam of the suit. As close to the mouth as you can, of course."

She stared at the little round metal objects as they sat in the palm of her hand. They felt cold. Hard, cold reminders of what lay ahead. "Is Mike on his way?"

He nodded. "It'll be tight. But traffic out of the city shouldn't be heavy this time of night."

"Well," she said, closing her hand over the metal buttons. "Let's get going. I already have the needle and thread."

Halsey lay in bed staring at the news, though much of it didn't register. He knew his sense of time was off. There were huge gaps he couldn't account for. He looked down at himself, as if for the first time. His chest and arms were dappled with purple bruises. He no longer had a chest tube sticking into his side. There was just a thin wound with a few stitches.

That had to be good, but he didn't remember the tube coming out. He cautiously took a deep breath and felt a sharp pain. It kept him from expanding his chest fully. Like an infant, he experimented. He tried sitting forward, and when that didn't double him over, he swung his feet over the edge of the bed. He felt a stabbing pain in his neck and chest. His head felt like a top spinning. He was about to try standing up when the nurse entered the room.

"What're you doing, Mr. Halsey?" she demanded. "Your orders are for bed rest."

She put a hand on his shoulder and eased him back into the bed. He looked at her blankly, then eyed her name tag. "How long have I been here, Connie?"

She laughed. "Not as long as it seems, I'm sure." She was a heavyset woman in her forties. All business yet exuding a caring warmth.

"It seems like months. I feel like I'm finding my way out of a maze." He put a hand to his head and felt a line of stitches along his scalp. "I'm not sure what's a dream and what's real."

"You had a bad concussion. With pain meds on top of that you were really under the weather." She busied herself straightening his bedside table.

"Have I had visitors?" He vaguely remembered something about Kate. He wasn't sure what.

The nurse decided not to mention the stranger Halsey had almost strangled. "Mr. Resnick has been asking about you every day. He wants to visit when you're up to it."

He blinked in amazement, a flood of memories washing over him. "Resnick! He's okay?" For a moment he forgot about his own ills. He remembered Resnick dying, Resnick telling him things. That was when it had all started ...

"Doing well. Just a few doors down the hall. A tough fellow, that one."

Halsey lay back, his mind straining for snatches of the past. He remembered the conversation with Paul Resnick that fateful night. And rushing to Alatron to rescue Kate. Getting pummeled by a pack of demonstrators. Then nothing. Dreams, nightmares, hallucinations. Heinman. Coming here, telling him about Kate dying. Was that part real or a nightmare? He could feel the cold hand of fear clutching his insides. Some part of him remembered.

"Where's Dr. Crane?" He bolted upright and grabbed the nurse's hand.

"Dr. Crane?" echoed the nurse in a clinically noncommittal tone. She saw a wild look in his eye. He was still not himself. Not ready to hear the news. Besides, she told herself, no one had found Dr. Crane's body. She had no business saying anything that might upset her patient.

"Where's Dr. Crane?" he shouted.

The nurse drew back and began fiddling with the IV pole. "I don't know," she muttered. "What shall I tell Mr. Resnick? He wants to see you."

A feeling of doom moved over him in dark heavy waves. He knew she was keeping something from him. He took a deep breath. "I'd like very much to see Mr. Resnick."

"I'll get him. He's a patient, they'll let him in." She bustled out and he saw her stop outside the door to talk to the cop.

No one had bothered telling him why the cop was there, but he knew. The image of Dave Parsons's blood-covered body had been constant through his twilight state. And he knew it was no dream. Heinman had killed Parsons and placed the body in the trunk of Halsey's car, then tipped off the AIDS FIRSTers. Of that he was certain.

Within minutes the nurse returned with a wasted-looking but alive Paul Resnick in a wheelchair. There was a blanket folded over Resnick's lap. His gaunt face brightened at the sight of Halsey. Halsey felt an extraordinary bond with this man who popped up at the most unusual times. He felt a swell of gratitude and concern as Resnick wheeled toward him. The feverishly bright eyes seemed to reflect a spirit far too large for the frail body that held it.

Resnick dismissed the nurse, then wheeled himself up to the bedside. "Bet you didn't think you'd be seeing me around again."

"I don't know," replied Halsey with a grin that made his cracked lips burn. "The way things have been going we might have met at the pearly gates."

"Yeah." Resnick looked around and saw the nurse had left. The cop was outside the room. He leaned forward, close to Halsey's ear. "Listen, I've got some info for you."

Halsey tried to sit up and made it. "What do you have?"

"I've still got some contacts at AIDS FIRST. They don't like what's happening there." Resnick rested an arm on the bed. His breathing was coming a little harder. "There's a lot of talk among the guys. Some of them are beginning to believe this thing about sabotage. Some say you did it yourself, don't ask me why. I think it's this janitor I told you about."

Halsey nodded. "His name is Heinman. A bad apple."

Resnick's voice became a hoarse whisper. "And he's out to get your CDC friend, Dr. Crane."

Halsey shot upright. "Kate? She's all right?"

"Alive and well and so is her friend, Cosgrove."

Halsey noticed the cop peering into the room. He lay back and stared at the ceiling, his mind spinning. Kate—alive and well. The thought both filled him with joy and terror. Terror at what might become of her.

Resnick sat back in his wheelchair. The cop stepped into the room and looked around. Halsey flicked on the TV and the two patients stared at it blankly until the cop left.

"How do you know all this?" said Halsey, his eyes darting to Resnick then back to the TV.

A sly smile crept over Resnick's pallid face. "You think we don't know what goes on over there?" He paused, his smile disappearing. "There's been a lot of activity around the maximum-containment lab. More than usual. Tonight, both the janitor and your two doctor friends have been seen there, at different times. Something's up—something big. And my guess is it's going down tonight."

"Jesus." Halsey groaned through his teeth. "I've got to get out of here. But that cop practically lives here."

"You and I are thinking along the same lines," said Resnick, a hint of the sly smile returning. He patted his lap. "You'd be surprised what's under this blanket." His smile widened. "Clothes. Including the shirt you lent me. And a white coat."

He slid a plastic bag from beneath the blanket onto the bed. Halsey covered it with his sheet.

Resnick went on. "There's also a set of keys to my car. A ninety-one VW Rabbit. Red. One of my friends brought it around. It's in the back parking lot."

Resnick looked up at the TV, then at Halsey who was eyeing him with amazement. "One last thing," said Resnick. "You're pretty weak. In the pocket of the white coat is a card with the name and number of a guy who can help." He spun the wheelchair around. "Good luck."

Halsey's eyes followed the back of his improbable ally. He gripped the plastic bag tightly under the sheet. Only moments earlier he'd felt weak as a kitten. But now a sense of urgency galvanized him. He called after Resnick. "Paul."

Resnick shot a look over his shoulder. "Yeah?"

"Thanks."

Resnick continued wheeling himself toward the door. "Just getting that shirt back to you, partner."

CHAPTER TWENTY-NINE

As Heinman ascended the stairs to the fourth floor, he thought about Cosgrove, the only likely obstacle between him and Crane. Would he be too smart to show up? Or so stupid he thought he could protect her single-handed? Literally. Heinman chuckled to himself. Actually, he was hoping good old Harpo would be there. He looked forward to breaking his other arm.

At the top of the stairs, Heinman stopped and checked his pulse. Less than a hundred beats per minute, despite the fact he had taken the steps two at a time. He ran a hand over his arm. Hadn't even broken into a sweat. The muscles were firm, well defined, strong as steel. Ready for anything.

He stood in the corridor, his eyes and ears straining for any sign of Cosgrove. All was quiet. Too quiet. He stole down the hallway, staying close to the wall.

As he turned the corner onto the corridor leading to the lab, he spotted Cosgrove posted by the lab entrance, wearing what looked like a Sony Walkman and mumbling into a walkie-talkie. He stepped out into plain view and approached Cosgrove, assuming a casual gait.

When Cosgrove spotted him, Heinman saw him start jabbering frantically into the walkie-talkie. He couldn't make out the words.

He continued moving without stepping up his pace. He noted with detachment the wary eyes, the clenched fist of his quarry as he closed in. He didn't stop walking until he was practically in Cosgrove's face. He tapped the cast with an amused glint in his eye. "How's the arm, Harp?"

"Healing."

"Yeah?"

"Yeah." Harpo stuck his good hand into his pocket.

Heinman's eyes slid over him, taking in the equipment. A headset, attached to a cassette recorder clipped into his belt. A walkie-talkie, hissing static. "You look like an ad for *Electronics 'R' Us*, Harp. Recording something?"

Harpo stared at him. He held his arms up. "See for yourself. Does it look like I'm recording something?" He slipped the headset off and offered it to Heinman.

Heinman ignored it. He looked at the cassette recorder and saw a tape playing. He reached over and ejected the tape. "Beethoven's Ninth. Pretty funny, Harp. We have us a classical music buff, huh?" He flung the tape down the hall, watching it slide like a soap box on the slick floor.

Harpo glared at him. He jammed the walkie-talkie into his back pocket. "She's in there, waiting for you, Heinman. If anything happens to her . . ."

Heinman eyed Harpo's pocket. "You'll rescue her with your little Mickey Mouse knife?" He looked up and their eyes locked. Heinman held out a hand. "Turn over the knife, Harp."

Harpo shook his head. "Not on your life."

Heinman stood casually, his arms hanging loose at his sides, his head cocked to one side as he gave Harpo a crooked smile. He could have been a rag doll. Then, like lightning, his hands moved to Harpo's arm, wrenched his hand out of the pocket, and twisted his arm behind his back. The knife clattered to the floor and Heinman leaned down and snatched it up without letting go of Harpo's wrist.

Harpo managed to spin around, catching Heinman off guard enough to jam a knee in his groin. Heinman gasped and dropped the knife, but the blow served only to ignite him. He lunged for Harpo and struck a quick chop to the side of Harpo's neck with the edge of his hand. Harpo crumpled to the floor.

Heinman stood over him, breathing hard. "Sorry, Harp, but this is between me and your friend."

He leaned over and grabbed Harpo's arm, dragging him to a supply closet. He stuffed Harpo into the closet and locked the door. He took a quick look down the corridor, then headed for the outer changing room of the maximum-containment lab.

His mind and body were at a feverish pitch. He could feel an electric energy coursing through every nerve. Now it was just him and the good doctor.

Harpo couldn't see a thing. His head throbbed, his thoughts fuzzy. He tried the door. Locked. He fumbled for the blank cassette he had hidden in his sock. Despite his shaking hands and pounding head he managed to insert it into the recording device. At least he had second-guessed Heinman on that one.

He felt something pressing into his back, then remembered the walkie-talkie. He grabbed it and pressed the transmit button. "Kate, Kate, come in. Kate?" He heard static, and then, finally, her voice.

"What is it, Harpo?"

"Kate, he's got me locked up. And there's no sign of Mike. Get out of there now! Do you hear me? Now!"

All he heard was static.

Kate was getting into her scrub suit when the call came from Harpo. He sounded frantic. Everything was going wrong. She felt torn. She couldn't think. Things were happening too fast.

She heard the door open. It would be Heinman. It was now or never. She could rush out past him before he knew what was happening. Put in a stat call to security. Her common sense, hanging by a thread, told her to do just that—get the hell out of there before she had no choice. But, no, she thought, shakily tying the drawstring of her scrub pants. They would still have nothing on him. They needed his confession.

Then she thought of the knife Harpo had insisted she carry inside her suit. She wouldn't be completely helpless. What could Heinman possibly do to her in there? If he had plans to kill her, it would most likely happen after they were out of the lab. By then Harpo's detective friend would surely be here. A struggle inside the lab could prove just as risky for Heinman. He could easily cut off his air supply, damage the protective integrity of his space suit. He was too smart to take that kind of chance.

She made herself take a few deep breaths. "Relax," she told herself. It was then she saw him out of the corner of her eye. It still wasn't too late. There was room to slip past him and run.

She turned to face him. She still could have gone either way. But it was the gloating smile that decided her. A decision based on raw emotion as she felt hatred knot her insides to the point that she gagged.

She turned off her walkie-talkie and placed it in her locker. She swallowed hard. "I'm ready," she said.

Heinman gave her a peremptory nod. Her face seemed slack, unreadable, which threw him off slightly. "I see you're playing it safe. Big bad Harpo out there on guard duty."

"I hope you're not frightened, Keith." She struggled to remember how she had pulled off the phone call. Tried to recapture that bland, mocking feeling.

"Actually," he said, pulling off his shirt, "I'm flattered." He smiled as he saw her eyes regard his muscular torso. She seemed mesmerized. He deliberately dawdled with his scrub shirt, turning his back to her. He felt vividly alive as he imagined her eyes wandering over his strong lats and shoulders.

"Would you like me to change in the other room?"

She folded her arms and slumped down on the bench. "I don't care where you change."

He felt a twinge of anger at her indifferent tone. Then he smiled, his back still toward her. "I'll stay here. I have nothing to hide." He slipped his jeans off, taking his time as he stepped into a pair of scrub pants.

"I'm sure if you decide to hide something, you will manage to whether I'm watching or not."

He turned to face her as he tied the drawstring of the scrub pants. He gave her a wintry smile. "So cynical, Dr. Crane."

"Just realistic." She felt a numbness beneath which she knew was a measure of incalculable fear. She couldn't let it through. Not now. She had to remain calm, cool. Appear indifferent.

He smirked. "You're scared stiff, aren't you?"

"Why don't we stop playing games, Keith? You came to prove a point. So prove it."

He straightened. "I'm ready. Are you? Wearing a recording device, perhaps?"

She stood and raised her arms, giving a subtle skyward roll of her eyes. "You're welcome to search me. Surely you don't think I have that low an opinion of you."

He started toward her, then stopped. She saw a moment of doubt, or perhaps confusion. "What's that supposed to mean?"

She dropped her arms. Still playing on his ego. And time. "I would be insulting your intelligence if I thought I could get away with a tape recorder, now wouldn't I?"

He studied her face. She could tell he was trying to figure something out, decide how to play it. "You *have* been insulting my intelligence."

"And that's why we're here, isn't it?"

Suddenly he seemed to lose interest. His eyes veiled over. "Let's go," he snapped, giving her a little shove. "No more games."

They moved through the shower area and into the inner changing room, where they would get into the protective space suits. Kate felt a growing dread. Heinman seemed so sure of himself. Like he had it all locked up.

She moved over to the clothing rack. There were two suits hanging there, just as she had left them. Each contained a bugging device. One had a knife. She snatched that one off the hook, hoping Heinman didn't find her action odd.

She held out the suit with an air of nonchalance. "Do you care to check this before I put it on?"

He shook his head. "No more games."

She shrugged. "Whatever you say."

He stood watching as she stepped into the suit. "I've

got an idea," he said with a smile. "Why don't we switch suits?"

She froze. He knew. She looked at him, her face expressionless. She was getting good at that. "If you wish," she replied with a touch of condescension.

He took a moment to respond. Then he threw his head back and laughed, raising a hand like a stop sign. "What happened to your sense of humor, Dr. Crane?"

Without answering she climbed into the space suit. Heinman did the same. She watched him through her transparent plastic face shield after she slipped the hood on and zipped it to the suit. She wriggled into the shoulder pack.

She felt awkward in the hot cumbersome suit, as always. She could feel the sweat soaking into her scrub suit and trickling down her back. The mask began misting up. It became difficult to breathe, like a record hot day in the humid South.

She was beginning to feel faint as she moved over to the air duct hanging down from the ceiling. It was stretchable, narrow, accordionlike tubing. As she fumbled with it, she had a sinking feeling. Why had she dallied so long before going for air? How could a lifeline be only a half inch in diameter? As the tubing snapped out of her grasp, she realized her brain was sluggish from lack of oxygen. By now she was practically blind from the mist coating the inside of her mask.

How had she let herself get into such a predicament, and where was Heinman? Panic was threatening to take over.

Finally she succeeded in hooking her manifold into the tubing. As it clicked in she felt a wave of cool air whisk through the suit, and into her face, immediately clearing her mask.

She could feel herself calming down. She took a

deep breath and filled her lungs with the coolness. The hissing sound of the air wafting into the hood didn't bother her a bit. Some people found it annoying. She never had. How could you be annoyed at your link to life?

Somehow putting on one of these suits with its self-contained air supply made her feel completely isolated. And she never felt it more than now, with Heinman standing right in front of her. Even through the mask she could discern his mocking smile.

She sensed that he knew every thought going on in her head, had gained enjoyment from watching her nearly suffocate before hooking herself into the air supply. Had she wanted to fool him into thinking he could easily put one over on her, she couldn't have done a better job. She silently cursed her stupidity.

As Heinman motioned her to the airlock, she knew, had there been any doubt, that he had been to this lab before. He needed no instruction about the suit. He seemed to know what everything was used for and how to use it.

She followed him into the lab where the Congo virus grew, and where death could be hovering in the air. She felt the reassuring weight of the knife against her hip. She immediately hooked into the closest air duct. So did Heinman. The place was empty. The only sound was the soft sibilance of the hissing air. She stepped toward Heinman and motioned to him with her hands. "Show me."

He nodded. She guessed he hadn't actually heard her words, but had picked up the gist. After working in these suits for a while, she was amazed at how well one could communicate with body language. Of course, if she really had to converse with someone, she would kink off her air supply momentarily to stop the hissing long enough to hear.

He moved directly toward the biosafety hood where the Congo cultures were incubated. Kate followed. The air tubing didn't extend to the hood, so they had to stop, disconnect and reconnect deeper into the lab. She was able to move a little faster than he. Even so, they both walked like a couple of lumbering wood soldiers.

Heinman reached his gloved hands into the gloved portholes of the hood and picked up a test tube, shaking it slightly. He placed it to one side. He pulled out his arms and moved toward her, reaching for her manifold.

She watched him come at her. What was he doing? She couldn't see his face. Then the hissing stopped. He had cut off her air supply.

CHAPTER THIRTY

Halsey sat up slowly, grimacing as each bruised muscle and bone gave him a progress report. He nodded to the cop who happened to be peering into the room. The cop smiled.

He pressed his hand on the package from Resnick, well hidden under the covers. The plastic bag crackled reassuringly. He could feel the hard shape of the car keys through the blanket.

As soon as the cop went back to leaning against the doorjamb outside the room, Halsey slipped the package under his flimsy hospital gown and shuffled toward the bathroom.

He closed the door and locked it, then dumped the contents of the bag onto the floor. Resnick had thought of everything. Clothes, shoes, keys. He slipped into a pair of loose-fitting faded jeans, the knit shirt, and a pair of white socks with tennis shoes that were a little tight. He pocketed the keys and put on the white coat.

He came across the card with the name on it. He stuffed it in his pocket. No time to make contacts, plans. He had to get to Alatron. And he felt his strength coming back—erupting from a center of rage and passion inside him that had remained untouched by any drug, any injury, any amount of rest. He could feel its energy suffusing every nerve ending, every muscle, empowering him.

He glanced at himself in the mirror. He sure as hell didn't look like any hospital employee. His face was bruised and puffy. His black eye was fading into a pea soup greenish yellow. He would just have to keep his head down as he walked out of the hospital.

As he returned from the bathroom, he had his plan well in mind. He scooted under the sheets and picked up the phone, dialing nine for an outside line. Then he dialed the hospital's main number and asked for Officer Ellis. He stayed on the line while he heard the cop being paged on the overhead for an outside call.

The cop started into the room, and, seeing Halsey on the phone, turned on his heel and headed out, presumably to find another phone.

As soon as the cop was gone, Halsey hung up and hurried to the door. The hallway was empty except for a few nurses and orderlies. They seemed too engrossed in their duties to take notice of him.

He moved awkwardly down the dimly lit corridor with a sense of urgency growing in the pit of his stomach. He fell into a pace not fast enough to draw attention but enough to get him out before the cop got back. He kept his head bowed, hands in pockets.

He disappeared into the nearest stairwell, moving down the steps with surprising agility. He found himself in the back parking lot within minutes. His body was screaming at him to slow down—his head pounded, his stiff muscles felt like they were on fire. But he heard only one message: Kate.

Would he get there in time? It didn't help to wonder, he told himself. Just go. All his thoughts and impulses had to be trained on a single focus: get there.

He found Resnick's VW easily. Fortunately the parking lot was fairly empty. He felt his heart pounding when the engine wouldn't turn with the first turn of the ignition key. He glanced around the brightly lit parking area. No sign of Officer Ellis. Holding his breath, he turned the key again and coaxed the engine to life as he worked the accelerator.

"Thank God," he muttered as he pulled out of the lot and into traffic. He looked at his watch. He had looked at it so many times the time didn't register. But now he noted the hour. Ten-fifteen. With luck, he would be at Alatron within fifteen minutes.

He had no sense of physical pain as he maneuvered the little car through traffic. Only a sense of mental anguish bordering on panic. As he drove he saw clearly now Keith Heinman, visiting him that day—bouquet in hand, dressed as though for a funeral. He remembered the taunting smile, the threats. It all came back in a flash of blinding emotion. The rage at his core burned ever more fiercely, empowering him further. His knuckles turned white as he gripped the steering wheel. His foot hit the floorboard.

Kate had broken into a sweat despite the cool air circulating through her suit. The full extent of her fear hit her in that moment when Heinman cut off her air. She thought he was going to kill her. All he wanted to do was tell her something.

It was, of course, another indication that he knew all about BSC Four labs. He knew exactly how to communicate. Either signal someone to kink their air tubing so they can hear you, or kink it for them while you talk. She had done it both ways. And either way had been fine—when you trusted your companion.

She admitted to herself that he could snuff her out at will. Knife or no knife. Yet something held him. She thought she understood what it was. She was different. She was a woman. She could see he liked talking to her, bragging, showing off. As long as she gave him her full attention, there was hope.

She saw him watching her. He was saying something. She kinked her air hose.

"Don't get your hopes up," he said.

She laughed. Hopes up about what?

He gave her a questioning look, then talked. And talked. So much spewed out, and she drank it in, raising her eyebrows from time to time so he'd know she was listening.

It was as she had guessed. Only he had put much more into it than she had imagined. He had taken a strain of Congo virus home and set up cultures in his basement lab.

"When I had my cultures growing, the rest was easy," he went on. She could hear, even through the hissing air and the confining headgear, the gloating in his voice. "I simply lifted a vial of the vaccine. No problem, just the dumb old janitor cleaning up. Dropped it in my pocket. I can get wherever I want in this place. When I want it."

He stopped to leer at her. "I inoculated the vial with the virus, then injected my lab animals." He determined how long and under what conditions he could keep the virus alive. He knew there would be variables he could not control—like how long the vials might sit on the shelf before use.

What he said next explained why there were two separate outbreaks, the first involving only a few people, Akendo Maury and the Salt Lake nurse among them. "I sent out a couple contaminated vials at first." He laughed. "When the papers broke with the stories on a few mysterious deaths, I knew I had the dose of Congo just right. Thanks to your blabbermouth buddy Roger Peck. He was a big help. That's when I rounded up Dave-boy and inoculated more people." He laughed again. "Vermin. All of them."

"What was Parsons's role?"

He looked at her as though she had just asked the world's dumbest question. "Parsons had no role. Just a greedy pork chop out of his league. He made things a little more expeditious, that's all."

She stared at him. He stared back. "You killed him, didn't you?"

He gave her a crooked smile. His eyes said, "Of course." But he shrugged and said, "I only know what the papers say."

She wished the tape could pick up his eyes. She would have to settle for what she had, which was plenty.

She gave him a bland smile. She could see he was getting restless, casting his eyes about the lab as though concocting a plan. She knew it was time to end it. Every instinct for survival screamed at her that it was time to end it.

"Your story is convincing. And ingenius," she said. She turned toward the exit. She was suddenly all too aware of the bulkiness of the suit. How it impeded her movement. How it made the sweat trickle down her back. Or was that from the fear that had been gradually creeping closer and closer to the forefront of her mind?

He moved toward her, his mask within inches of hers. She could see his eyes clearly. The gleam of pride was gone. Now there was only naked hatred. His pupils were tunnels leading to unspeakable darkness.

Halsey found the nearest phone and called Kate's office in the desperate hope she was still there. After five rings he slammed the receiver down and headed for the BSC Four lab. He hobbled down the hall, not daring to stop. His chest felt like lightning bolts were sizzling through his flesh, stunning his lungs. He felt he was getting no air, yet something was keeping him alive. The thought of her.

As he careened around the corner toward the lab, he heard a thumping noise and stopped. For a moment he thought it was his own heartbeat. Then he heard it again. It was coming from a nearby closet. He ran to it and tried the door. It was locked.

He heard a muffled cry. He squatted down and spoke through the crack, trying not to raise his voice. "Harpo?"

"Help!" A few more weak thuds against the door.

Halsey stood up, his thoughts racing, his eyes searching for some way to open the door. He moved down the hall looking for something, anything, to bust the lock. He tore into a closet and found a toolbox. He fumbled through it and grabbed a heavy wrench. With all his might he swung the thing against the wood frame of the door. It was enough to break the lock. He flung open the door and Harpo tumbled out. His clothing was soaked with blood and sweat.

"Elliot," he cried, gasping for air as he sat up. "Thank God! Forget about me. Get to the lab. Heinman's in there—with Kate."

He was off. He pushed through the outer change room and shower areas and snatched his space suit out of the locker. There was no way he could tell for sure if they were still in there without looking. And he couldn't look without suiting up.

He was functioning on superhuman strength, sustained by pure will and adrenaline. And focus. Right now there was only one thing on his mind: would he get there in time?

*   *   *

Heinman had her pushed up against the wall. He twisted her air hose in one gloved hand, holding it up so she could see what he was doing. So there would be no doubt in her mind.

"Who's stupid now, bitch" He was screaming at her.

Her mask was beginning to mist over from her own stale exhaled air, but she could still see his face clearly enough. His mouth was slack and ugly as he threw words at her like spears, each one meant to erode her spirit a little more.

She felt transfixed by his eyes. They seemed to glow, fired by a fierce and terrifying energy. She felt her head swimming, her will to survive drowning, as though her own life force was being sucked out by something in him—something there in his eyes.

Odd, how analytical she felt. No hysteria. No panic. But neither was there acceptance. She felt paralyzed. Why, she wondered, didn't she struggle, just reach up and tear the air hose out of his hand?

She felt her vision darken. She reached for his hand, tugged at the hose in one last feeble struggle to hang on.

Suddenly, like a gift, he let go and stepped back.

He stood, his arms folded across his chest, watching her. Toying with her. Demonstrating his power. She knew this in the back of her mind, but all she cared about was the wonderfully cool air as it whisked through her suit and washed over her face, clearing her mask, filling her lungs. A life force.

She stumbled back away from him, thinking she should run for her life. He stood between her and the door.

She had another impulse to tear off her suit and try to dodge past him, but she knew that would be certain death. The ambient air was almost certainly loaded with Congo, looking for a place to light.

Then she saw what he was doing, and she knew death was certain anyway.

CHAPTER THIRTY-ONE

Heinman stood between Kate and the exit from the lab—from the death trap. He leaned over, and from nowhere, brought out a flask of clear liquid with a cloth wick in it. There was no question in her mind how he intended to use it. She looked toward the door. His gaze tracked her eyes, as though gauging her every thought, relishing her every fear. He jiggled the flask in front of her. And smiled.

The flasks seemed to be materializing, one right after the other. A black magic act. He was lining them up along the surface of the thick black-topped lab table in the center of the room. He seemed to have a stash somewhere on the floor.

She could see him, alone here one night, madly concocting the scenario that was now unfolding. She could see him imagining this moment—her helplessly watching his preparation. He was every bit the sadistic maniac she'd envisioned.

She tried to push through her fear, tried to think about how she might fool him, rattle the smooth facade, under which she guessed lurked uncontrollable fear and rage. She thought about what set him off: ridicule, belittlement, indifference. But she couldn't bring herself to enact any of it. Her mind was paralyzed. Her gaze fixed on the flasks.

Now he was moving toward her. She found herself backing away from him, toward a window. It all seemed by design. He was driving her there, his hand gripping the neck of a flask.

She saw his lips move but she couldn't make out the words. She reached down to kink her air hose.

"Your friend has let you down." She could even hear the gloating.

"What have you done to Harpo?" She spat the words out as though they tasted bad. She realized why. Guilt shot through her. This was all her fault.

"It doesn't really matter, does it?"

Harpo is dead, she thought. She felt the protective numbness move in. She could do nothing but stare at her captor.

He held the flask up and jiggled it again. She watched the liquid swish around the sides, looking every bit ready to blow the place up with the touch of a match. She guessed it was formaldehyde. Or some other flammable chemical. She wondered inanely why she cared. It would do the job.

Had there been any question as to Heinman's intention, it now dissipated as she watched him extract a disposable lighter from a pocket of the space suit. He tossed the pink plastic lighter into the air, putting a spin on it that caused it to somersault back into his gloved hand. Then he smiled at her.

He was putting on a performance. She was the audience. She knew what came at the final curtain. She stood by helplessly, watching. She thought about her knife. She couldn't imagine how it would help her.

She felt it against her hip, no longer reassuring. She continued to watch as he moved to the next act.

He held the lighter over the flask. There was a flash of fire as the cloth wick caught. He laughed as she gasped. He lifted the flask higher. Panic tore at her eyes, wrapped itself around her chest like a boa constrictor. He saw it. He saw everything.

He heaved the flask into a corner of the room where it exploded. He moved back toward the lab table and began lighting and heaving the fire-rigged flasks into all corners of the room. Over the hissing in her suit she could hear the glass shatter. Conflagrations burst out everywhere.

Soon, she knew, the hissing air would no longer be her life link. It would fuel the flames, become a conduit of destruction.

The sprinkler system went off and she could feel the spray splatter against her suit. She felt a smidgen of hope as she prayed it would hold the flames at bay. But as she felt the heat and watched the flames leap toward the ceiling, her hope dwindled. Once the flames got to her she knew it would be over.

Desperate, she tried to bolt past him. He seemed to be expecting her. He stood still, his legs planted wide. When she was almost by him, he threw a hand out. He struck her with such force that she went down instantly.

He backed away and flung open the door. He waved to her through the wall of fire. When it closed, it would close forever.

Halsey was at the door, suited up, finally ready to go in. He slipped his security card through the slot. He stared at the message he had stared at God knew how many times.

"Enter your code number," it said.

He drew a blank.

He took a few deep breaths, tried to relax, let his mind, knotted with fear, gain access to his memory. It had to be the concussion. . . .

Suddenly the door swung open and a suited figure collided with him. Halsey momentarily lost his balance. Even before he saw the face he knew who it was. Regaining his footing, he grabbed Heinman's suit and pushed him back into the lab.

A white rage blasted through Halsey's head as his mind registered what was happening. Fire. Heinman leaving. Kate burning up somewhere in there.

If his strength had been waning, what he saw now was all it took for that untouchable core of anger and passion to refuel him. Like a mother who discovers her child pinned under a car and summons the strength to lift it up, Halsey felt a surge of superhuman strength. And he used it.

The two men went tumbling onto the floor, neither one connected to an air hose. Halsey's mask began to mist up. He saw only wildly distorted flame, and he felt nothing but blast furnace heat.

He scrambled furiously for an air source. He had to see. Find Kate. Nail Heinman.

He forced his mind to picture the layout of the lab. He swept his hand around to find an air hose. The room was getting hotter and hotter. The flames were closing in.

His fingers grabbed onto an air hose. He fumbled with it. Finally plugged it into his manifold. Precious seconds gone. Then the cool air and its welcome noise.

His mask cleared and he saw Heinman next to him, just hooking into air himself. He gave Heinman a push as he yelled for Kate. He spotted her batting at flames along the wall.

He froze, paralyzed by a flood of relief and horror.

She was alive. But she wasn't attached to air. She was sitting against the wall, apparently having quelled the fire right around her. Her head drooped oddly, as though she had given up. Her swatting motions looked like mere reflexes, the final twitches of a dying animal.

"Kate!" He screamed. He lurched toward her, dodging a cluster of flames. He grabbed a heavy red fire extinguisher off the wall. He reached for an air hose and stretched it toward her. The hell with Heinman—let him go. Right now all he cared about was Kate.

As he leaned toward her, he felt hands on his shoulders, pulling him back. Heinman. Kate reached out and got a grip on the air hose as Halsey was forced to let go. He felt himself tumbling backward.

Kate watched as the two men struggled and fell to the floor. She was afraid to feel hope, but how could she feel anything else? Halsey had come out of nowhere. Now, with Heinman on top of him, he needed her help.

She took a moment to clear her head, then got to her feet. She moved as quickly as she could toward them as they grappled on the floor. With the fire extinguisher Halsey had dropped she began spraying the flames nearest them.

She saw Halsey jerk at Heinman's air hose and disconnect him. She felt the hope again.

He felt no pain, no weakness. The energy of his emotions fueled his muscles, as though there was a direct circuit. He felt sure of himself. He had the strength. He knew exactly what he had to do.

He managed to get to his feet. He leaned down and grabbed hold of Heinman's suit. Heinman kicked him in the gut, doubling him over.

He watched as Heinman got up. He couldn't move. The hissing noise suddenly stopped and he knew Heinman had disconnected his air. He felt Heinman's hands at his throat, and he knew before long he wouldn't be able to see. He was suffocating.

He grabbed at Heinman's arms and wrenched free. Like searchlights his eyes scanned the room, registering what he needed to know. The flames were coming under control, either burning themselves out or getting snuffed by the sprinklers and the fire extinguisher.

He spotted the one open biosafety hood, one without portholes. He knew what was in there. His mind rocked. Heinman was at his neck again, cutting off the blood to his brain.

He summoned his last ounce of energy and twisted around, kneeing Heinman as hard as he could in the groin. The cumbersome suit blunted the impact but he felt Heinman's grip on him ease.

He reached out and took Heinman by the shoulders and began forcing him toward the biosafety hood, using his own weight as momentum. Heinman grabbed his arm and tried to break free, but Halsey had a good handful of his suit. Heinman's feet were sliding around on the floor, which was made slick by the sprinklers. Halsey's shoes seemed to give him better traction, which he took advantage of.

The flames were still alive but mostly confined to the corners of the room. Halsey's vision was going dark. He needed air. But something kept him going. He kept seeing Kate, sitting there against the wall, her head drooped over. He had to keep moving. He couldn't let that happen to her. Not if there was an ounce of life left in him.

Finally, he had Heinman at the biosafety hood. Taking advantage of pure momentum, he tried to jam Heinman between himself and the hood. His arms and legs felt like lead. Everything seemed to be happening in slow motion. He sensed that Heinman was fading just as rapidly. They were all going to die.

His vision was getting darker and darker. His lungs felt compressed to the size of lemons. His heart pounded chaotically. He was about to pass out.

He heard a hissing noise. Air. A miracle. He breathed the wonderfully cool air. Life-giving air. His lungs heaved. Kate must have plugged his air hose in. He turned to find her.

A fist slammed against the side of his head. He felt himself going down. Heinman had him in a hammerlock.

He was in a nightmare. Struggling, struggling, getting nowhere. Then he saw Kate again. She hefted up the heavy red fire extinguisher, and, like a pro swinging at a high ball, she swung it at Heinman's head. He could hear the thud. He felt the weight fall off him. Heinman went reeling toward the biosafety hood.

Last chance. Halsey was fading fast, despite the air. He crawled to his feet, grabbing onto whatever he could. He stumbled toward Heinman and gripped his shoulders. Heinman seemed dazed, unresisting. The two men fell up against the hood. The shelf of the hood bore their weight as they each summoned the last of their reserves.

As Halsey fought for air he saw Heinman push away from the hood. It was now or never. He ducked and threw all his weight, head first, into Heinman's gut, throwing him off balance. He grabbed Heinman's shoulders, hefted him up, and jammed his head under the hood. Where only double-gloved hands dared go. Where man-killing viruses thrived.

Halsey leaned his weight into Heinman's body and held the stunned man's head there, under the hood.

Heinman's feet kicked and slid on the floor, unable to gain a grip.

Halsey could feel himself about to go. He wasn't going to be able to hold Heinman there. He grabbed the headgear of Heinman's suit and tore it off, taking it with him as he fell to the floor.

Kate stared, transfixed. She saw Heinman, his face exposed inside the hood, fight off the impulse to breathe. His skin was a dusky hue, coated with sweat. As Halsey fell to the floor, Heinman slipped, wedging his head inside the hood. His arms flailed like a windmill.

He struggled helplessly, unable to find the right position to pull himself out. Finally, she saw him take a huge breath, inhaling deeply of the virus and sealing his fate. The color in his face improved, but she saw the first hint of doom in his eyes.

She saw Halsey pulling himself back up and felt a flood of relief. Her eyes went back to Heinman as Halsey kneeled beside her.

Together they watched Heinman swivel his head around, his eyes widening. His face suddenly took on a look of terror, his mouth forming a perfect O, his eyes glittering pools of naked fear.

They watched as he finally gripped the edge of the hood and struggled out. His eyes held an expression Kate had never seen before. They were no longer a cold, icy blue. The pupils were so dilated that his eyes appeared black, yet unseeing. It was a strange paradox, the black representing darkness projected out rather than light let in.

Heinman gave them one last look as he saw he was free. His lips once again formed the smile that gave Kate a chill despite the furnacelike heat. He snatched up his mask and put it back over his head.

Then he ran. He slipped and fell onto one of the formaldehyde flasks. The sound of shattering glass was followed quickly by an explosion as the flammable contents spilled onto the floor and fed the dying flames.

Kate saw his sleeve catch fire, saw him helplessly bat at the flames with his hand. With the impulse of a doctor bent on saving life and placing judgment aside, she leaned down for the fire extinguisher and sprayed the flames lapping at Heinman's space suit. He jumped up and rushed past her, shoving her and Halsey toward the flames as he headed for the exit. She saw there were still a few indolent flames licking at his sleeve.

She could only think one thing. Heinman was escaping. She scrambled to her feet and lurched toward the airlock. Halsey, making a gargantuan effort, was somewhere behind her.

When she opened the door to the chemical shower room, she stopped short. She saw what was about to happen.

As Heinman passed under the shower heads, the chemical disinfectant spray turned on automatically, as always. Had he forgotten? Or had he thought it would cool him off on his way through? They would never know.

He seemed to explode in a brilliant burst of orange as the chemicals, more volatile than formaldehyde, fed the once lazy flames on his sleeve.

She heard him scream. It was a sound she would never forget.

She and Halsey stood beside each other, unmoving. They watched the flames rise toward the ceiling. Heinman had become a human torch.

She looked at Halsey. They drew close as they watched what was once Keith Heinman turn to cinders. She knew they were thinking the same thing. Heinman was no longer a man, if he ever was. He had combined with a mindless fire that didn't care who or what it destroyed.

In this way, she thought with a tiny shiver, the two were as one in a providential end.

She and Halsey embraced. She could make out his face through the mist. Or was the mist in her eyes? She wasn't sure. And it didn't matter. She knew, as she felt his arms encircle her, that Harpo had been right. It would be all right.